Terry Jackman

Dragonwell Publishing

This is a work of fiction. All of the characters, organizations, and events portrayed in this novel are either products of the author's imagination or are used fictitiously.

Copyright © 2015 by Terry Jackman

Published by Dragonwell Publishing
(www.dragonwellpublishing.com)

ISBN 978-1-940076-22-5

All rights reserved. No part of this book may be reproduced or transmitted in any printed or electronic form without permission in writing from the publisher.

Table of Contents

Chapter 1	1
Chapter 2	9
Chapter 3	14
Chapter 4	17
Chapter 5	20
Chapter 6	26
Chapter 7	29
Chapter 8	37
Chapter 9	40
Chapter 10	43
Chapter 11	47
Chapter 12	53
Chapter 13	62
Chapter 14	68
Chapter 15	75
Chapter 16	83
Chapter 17	87
Chapter 18	94
Chapter 19	101
Chapter 20	105
Chapter 21	115
Chapter 22	122
Chapter 23	126
Chapter 24	129
Chapter 25	133
Chapter 26	140
Chapter 27	145

Chapter 28	153
Chapter 29	159
Chapter 30	163
Chapter 31	168
Chapter 32	172
Chapter 33	178
Chapter 34	188
Chapter 35	193
Chapter 36	197
Chapter 37	204
Chapter 38	212
Chapter 39	221
Chapter 40	225
Chapter 41	232
Chapter 42	237
Chapter 43	242
Chapter 44	249
Chapter 45	254
Chapter 46	259
Chapter 47	266
Chapter 48	272
Chapter 49	275
Chapter 50	278
Chapter 51	283
Chapter 52	291
Chapter 53	296
Chapter 54	301
Chapter 55	304
Chapter 56	308
Acknowledgements	317
About the Author	319

Chapter 1

The king, my father, named me Ashamet. It means a copper-colored whirlwind off the desert (color of our own Kadduchi flesh). It's meant to be poetic. Huh. Apart from that, a princely life was pretty good—until my taster went into convulsions. Happily, they pinned it on some merchant's less-than-healthy crawlfish. Panic over, then; I didn't bother witnessing the execution. But I was that rarity, a single offspring, and I'd been a single step from danger, and I didn't have an heir yet.

Quite enough to make my father's mind up; I was sentenced to be married…

Now, a thread of moisture trickled down my backbone as I took my seat again for yet another day upon the royal dais, formally escorted by my Uncle Raggesh. I had picked a sleeveless tunic in my lightest silks, a minimum of jewels, my thick, black hair lay braided at one shoulder, but it didn't help. The Gate Hall, grandest audience chamber in our empire, had descended to a rowdy, yellow marble sweat-box.

Rag sat too, his longer robes spread out to swamp his sandaled, copper-colored toes. Today he'd left his close-trimmed claws their natural white, as mine were. Bet he wished he'd dressed like me as well. The tiny windows in the blue-enameled arch above our heads were meant to keep this stage-like alcove cooler. Meant to, but the Gate—the famous golden screen of star-shaped solar lamps, at present dropped between us royals and the outer chamber—turned it back into an oven. Gods, I *could* have been up on a horse. In the fresh air. With a few companions I could actually trust.

I *should* have been receiving end-of-year assessments from my generals about our southern army's readiness for action, given that my father had been taking more than normal interest in our southern borders lately.

Terry Jackman

I suspected that our empire was again expanding.

But instead I blanked my face and scanned the throng beyond the ornate, semi-private metal filigree that dangled inbetween us.

Out there, thin coils of vapor from the ordinary iron lamps obscured the vaulted, gold and turquoise ceilings. Below, my father's hairless, ochre-hided Kemik guard, exotic giants of our kingdoms, lined the path toward us, fangs retracted peaceably. The flame-reflections dancing off their breast-plates were the only movement there but outside them… Alpha Lords of every size and shade and all their twittering attendants skittered back and forth like termites, and the piled-up offerings destroyed the last pretence of taste the place had ever managed. I jerked my beard-point at the nearest jumble. "Look at it, we've swapped the Gate Hall for the Grand Bazaar."

My uncle didn't blink. "Show some grace. They're *your* wedding gifts."

I might have growled. It didn't help that he was right. With five days still to go, my marriage had progressed from bore to stinking torment. Every perfume in the world was up my nose today, but none of them could mask the ripened bodies. Worse, my sword arm itched like seven hells, and with so many watchful eyes I had to curb an uncouth urge to scratch it.

Muffled creaks, from chains and pulleys underneath our feet. The Gate began to shiver upward, to disclose… "Gods, forget bazaar. It's a cattle market!"

A pair of pure-bred white camels were being tugged forward, their plate-like pads scraping over the marble. Their willowy necks hung with ropes of pearls? Was the sheer volume of these eccentricities meant to make up for their inanity? As if it heard, one of the brutes chose to relieve itself, while the lordly fool in front attempted to pretend he neither heard, nor smelled, the "splop" of brittle yellow crap behind him. Rag's long nose pinched shut as brown-robed clerks made clucking noises. Slaves were chivvied forward. I think I sighed. "At least the color complements the marble."

Raggesh choked behind his drooping moustache. "Keep it down, Ash."

I'd have given him a sharp retort except a guard distracted me with, "Highness? There's a message from the outer gates."

I tossed the message tube back at him and unrolled the paper. "Oh joy, the bride's finally turned up… horsemen, eight baggage carts and *three* horse-drawn litters? My fingers tightened, crumpling the flimsy paper. I relaxed with conscious effort. "How many crones have they sent with her? No wonder they're so late, they couldn't use a desert route with those things."

"Uh." My uncle watched the frantic sweeping, quite ignoring my reaction. I obliged him with a beaming smile instead. At least my mouth did. She was here then, the daughter of our newest vassal-king, Farad of Sidass. The bigger picture: the last of our smaller, paler, snubber-nosed Chi cousins were finally merging into the empire; a fading dynasty was being swallowed by a newer, fiercer bloodline. From where I sat I was stuck with her, unless she proved infertile.

Small chance of that. Females were rare enough. There was *nothing* rarer than one barren. I resisted growling at the luckless messenger. "Have someone send a message to the Inner Palace, to the closter-eunuchs. Tell them to unbar their doors, their future mistress is arriving." Though they'd very likely known as soon as I had, maybe sooner. *They'd* been looking forward to it.

I read on, since cleaning up the hall had halted proceedings. Heavens forfend a lord should step in something. "Looks like the rumors about King Farad's health could be true; he's not with them."

"Uh." Rag at his chatty best. "Prince Effad?"

"Not him either. This says Prince Thersat leads her escort. That's the lesser son, right? The one who wasn't there for the surrender?"

"Uh." Rag (another lesser son, and cut accordingly, to centre our succession) raised a lordly finger. The next noble was ushered in. The Gate lowered. *More* gems. They moved him on.

"So what do we know about this Thersat?"

The Gate lifted again. One out, one in. Another gift, then Rag could answer. "At the time we assumed he'd been wounded, but now we're told he's "prone to illness"." Rag maintained his bland expression.

I drew breath. "Farad can't travel, Effad's tied to his side, so we're lumbered with a *permanent* invalid?"

"Uh," denoted end of topic as the Gate reopened.

"Great." The cursed itching made a fresh assault. It had to be insect bites. I looked about for some distraction and spied a short, bald figure, absent from the court since summer; yes, the tubby Sheshman, copper-skinned but built more Chi than Kadd, and strident in his household's blue and orange. Ah, and something loomed behind him.

My spirits rose. If anyone would bring me something more amusing, surely it was Sheshman, of the rolling gait and wicked chuckle. There was more trader there than noble, so my father said. More pirate too, he'd added, laughing.

I must have grinned. I felt my uncle's disapproval so I faced toward the lord approaching, nodding gravely, like a bigger, younger copy of my stately father. But I glanced aside again to guess what Sheshman might have brought me. Four slaves were moving up a heavy-looking, box-like… something… swathed in dull grey fabric. Hmm. A cage? An animal? The male knew better than to insult his prince—and thus his king—with something paltry.

Meanwhile, the *slightly* slimmer northern Chi in front of us, distinguished by his nose, his browner hair and pale red skin, had bent a creaky knee before us. I shouldn't have frowned, but it was difficult to see how the Chi, so often weaker than the other races, had been dominant so long, for all their boasts of direct bloodlines from the Ancestors. As for this one, kneeling made him look like a slave. Our own Kadduchi lords would never kneel, except to Father. Though of course these gifts were really *for* my father; vying for the notice of our gods-protected Voice of Heaven.

Possibly my frown grew darker; certainly my thoughts did. If I was ever crowned—I tried not to plan that far ahead—I figured their loyalty to me would be less certain. The lord before us, backing off again, looked troubled; probably convinced his present hadn't thrilled me. "What was it?" I muttered.

Rag almost shook his head. "Deeds to an orchard," he gritted. "Listen, will you!"

"What—" Now I *was* offended.

"Wine, nephew, and Sultaki brandy."

"Ah." A gift worth having.

Despite his flash of temper Rag gazed calmly outward. To those who watched, he was my father's only sibling, and his twin and his most loyal kinsman. Or to put it bluntly he was here to keep his royal nephew out of trouble. Headstrong was the least I knew they said about me; unpredictable, both in or out of battle. Rash, impetuous, a wicked sense of humour? Gods, I hoped so. Almost thirty now, and still no wiser? I ignored the carping. Sober was for years yet to come. And there was only one more presentation left before I got to see that odd-shaped box of Sheshman's.

I turned back to my duty long enough to marvel at the antique bowls a Kemik lord brought forward. They were delightful; translucent porcelain, hand-painted by a master. Not a gift one would expect from any of the rough-skinned Kemik either, who were prone to value battle gear or horses. In fact the only gift of real taste I'd seen all morning. "A rare possession. I am honored, sir." They moved him off. I signaled to the clerk that he record my personal approval. Now for Sheshman.

"My prince, I bring you every prayer for your approaching marriage." Old Sheshman bounced up, bowed outrageously, then watched me. Ah, the sight of simple, honest motives. Bribery. Ambition. Life-blood of the palace. Earlier I'd read his beaming smile with interest, now I noticed it had faded. Second thoughts? What had the scoundrel brought me?

Despite my sudden doubts I felt my back and shoulders loosen. Moments in the old rogue's company and I was feeling more myself, I almost burst out laughing. Well, Sheshman was both small and round, a difficult shape to look dignified. It was amusing to see him try though. He squared his shoulders, sucked in his paunch beneath one of those bright sashes he loved, and waved a lordly hand. The slaves, their cropped heads lowered, brought their burden up the outer steps and forward to my feet, then grounded it on recessed legs and cowered.

It seemed to float above the floor. Silently I awarded him marks for detail, and waited for more. He actually lowered his voice. "My prince, I bring you a rarity I never thought existed." The old fool waved again. Two slaves pulled free the heavy draperies. I started frowning; couldn't help it. First a puzzle, now a riddle? It was a cage right enough; rounded; big enough for a large hound. But this thing was a fantasy, its bars were curled and gilded. And there was silk now, white, stretched taut inside it. A silk-lined cage? I found I'd leaned toward it. Sheshman's eyes had sharpened, and his face gone solemn.

"Well?" I challenged, but I smiled. I couldn't help that either.

"Well enough, I hope, my prince." He drew a breath. "Perhaps." He glanced around. "Would the prince deign to open it himself?" The fellow offered a key, from around his own neck.

Rag had straightened, in surprise or in alarm, but Sheshman wouldn't leave alive if there was anything in there to hurt me. Besides, the key was silver. I rather thought I'd guessed the secret. Not so tempting as it had been but a well-presented trifle, and the cage, and lowered Gate, would block the view of those outside it more or less politely. So I stepped down and took the key (and the unspoken challenge) and turned it in the lock.

Sheshman was murmuring in my ear by then, his voice gone knowing. "Your wedding duties draw close, my prince, and your subjects know you will perform with taste and honor. But afterwards…?"

I caught the bars and pulled. Hot air rushed past me as the twin doors of this almost-cage unfurled like curving wings about me, neatly blocking the interior from anyone not right before them. The light rushed in.

There was indeed a figure; half knelt, half seated on the silken cushions. Loose white trousers were the only clothing, as I'd guessed. And silver shackles, delicate as bracelets, etched with three-point royal stars. The chain that linked them had been pegged into the cage's flooring. And the head was ritually gift-wrapped, mummy-like, in white silk wrappings.

"Such as this would stir the blood of any male, much less my prince, whose appetite is fabled." The murmur made me turn my head. The beady eyes looked up at me, expectant, earlier nerves forgotten.

I drew a breath. "I may be about to marry, my lord, but I haven't yet gone blind." I let my voice turn cold. "Nor stupid. This is no youth."

"This" was too tall, even crouched as he was. The chest, the hands and arms stretched down toward the cage's flooring all had shape, and muscle. Maybe twenty summers? Body slaves were usually at least a few years younger: newly-adult: left untouched, kept very private like a female. Hells, a body slave was often *more* exclusive. After all a contract with a female—where the cursed female wasn't royal—could be drawn up for as little as a single year. Then her family would repossess her and consider bids from other males fit to breed with.

But this one… kept apart this long, till only ten years less than I was? Virgin white and silver, on a full-grown male? What did Sheshman take me for?

Behind me Rag had risen. Sheshman's face, which should have been as yellow-eyed and copper-hued as mine was, turned a nasty shade of umber, likely both embarrassment and fear, but he stood his ground. "My prince, I swear to you, I swear he's still a virgin: more than that, a *holy* male, taken as an infant, grown behind high walls. I would not cheat you, highness." Sheshman weighed my mood and laid a final hand down. "My prince, I trust you to decide my honesty. I'll wait upon your judgment. If you judge him less than I have said, I'll… send my youngest son to grace your chambers, to expunge the insult."

Had I blinked? I'd heard that Sheshman kept a real trader's superfluity of children, but my eyes and ears said he favored that one. Give him into bondage? He'd never offer—not unless… My eyes slid back toward the cage.

I'd thought him painted. Now I saw he wasn't. Wherever Sheshman found him it wasn't in any of our kingdoms, not with skin like creamy marble that looked unreal in the lamplight. I followed the line of his neck and shoulder, the swell of his chest. His skin looked… fragile, and there was no sweat, though when I'd opened it I'd felt the metal cage was hotter than this alcove; never good. Surely he barely breathed, there was so little movement. One leg was tucked beneath him, the other raised before. Unusual, but graceful. Then I saw the triple-knotted cord about his waist. My breathing deepened. Truth, or lies, a very fine body.

Trust my fond uncle to spoil the moment. "Keep your pants on, Ash. Believe this, you'll fall for anything." Dry amusement on the surface. Mockery beneath?

I defended any outward sign of interest. "Might be fun finding out, though."

"Huh. You haven't even seen the face yet." Ever the cynic.

My own thoughts shifted. "Curious, uncle? I'll oblige you," I said outrageously. I stepped forward, right into the opening, and reached up to the wrapping. The knot, loose at the nape of the neck, slid free between my fingers. One gentle tug and the silk fell away in rippling folds.

The head revealed stayed lowered, the eyes hooded. The hair, far from cropped, was long enough it would have brushed his shoulders, lighter colored even than the Chi; not braided of course but tied back loosely. I had disarranged it somewhat. Below that a high forehead and good cheekbones framed curious brows, more delicate arches than our upswept wings. No sign of any beard, nor hair upon the chest, the face as pale as the body.

Still no movement? Perhaps the slightest swaying. As if the chains helped keep him upright? I caught the jaw and jerked it upward, gasped to feel a child-like softness, but then the eyelids lifted too, a reflex surely for he didn't seem to focus.

Ashamet, Desert Born

Wide grey eyes, like still winter pools. Rag stirred, but I'd forgotten he was there. The eyes blinked twice, all up and down—no inner storm-proof membrane?—then gazed back at me as if he was my equal. I should have felled him, or had him whipped. Instead I stared back. My mouth dried up. I felt light-headed. This creature was weak, and confused, and more? Yes, surely. How much more though?

Curse these bites, my grip had tightened in reaction so I let my fingers drop away. I didn't want my tougher skin to mark that silk-thin whiteness.

The lips parted. A tiny frown formed between the arched brows. "Are you… a vision? Or a nightmare?"

Faint, and husky. I doubted anybody else had heard him. "Call me either one too loud, they'll cut your tongue out," I said softly.

He just looked back at me with those eyes. "No," he whispered. "Real..?" His gaze lowered to the shackles at his wrists. "I saw this. I saw…" Again his voice tailed off to silence. Then the white chest heaved, one huge, shuddering gulp of air. The tethered arms began to shake.

"Call my slave master," I ordered. Someone scurried.

The world returned around me. Despite being shorter Rag was practically breathing down my neck. Indecent. I was stung to comment. "Put your tongue away, eh, uncle? If you've seen enough, I'll shut this up again."

Rag recovered with a warrior's speed of reflex. His mouth did close, but only to reopen. "Aye, best keep it hid. There'll be enough laughter as it is."

He didn't believe Sheshman, then. Not unreasonable, I conceded. To myself, not out loud. How in all the world could any male stay innocent this long past adult? But that face, those eyes. I'd never seen such innocence, even in youths whose balls weren't dropped yet. And his words… My thoughts rebounded. If it was an act, it was a damn good one. And if that was so, I'd see both Sheshman and his slave regretted their performance. I shut the cage and turned. "I'll weigh your claims," I said curtly.

Sheshman backed away as Medishel bustled forward, my half-Chi slave master, a swollen, amber echo of my own appearance in a red and yellow outer robe and broad yellow sash. When I jerked my head he pulled at one door of the cage, peered in cautiously, then backed his head out and latched the thing up again. His manners were as excellent as ever. Not a word, not a look, just a polite, "My prince?"

"Take him away, Medi. See if he's ill, or drugged. Best keep him separate, in case, until I give you other orders."

Medishel bowed, caught the key and waved to Sheshman's slaves. The cage was carted off, which caused a lot of heads to turn, and furtive whispers. I wondered sourly how long it would take for the rest of the tale to spread. Have you heard the latest? Sheshman actually claimed he'd found a twenty-year-old virgin. Gods, how many of these visiting lords would ask each other if they had a complete fool for a prince, if he was even tempted to believe such rubbish.

But in my heart I think I always believed, right from the start. Some things can't be weighed, or measured, can they?

Chapter 2

Not that I had time to dwell on Sheshman's controversial present at the moment. It must wait for later. There was still a stultifying tide of other gifts to nod at. Thanks to Sheshman, and the camels, I'd have to nod a lot quicker now too, because what was left still had to be crammed into this last day of audience.

The bride's arrival meant we were on schedule again. The wedding—gods defend me—lay a mere five days ahead now, and for three of those we Kadduchi would hold the national holiday to celebrate our "Turn of Year". That would start tomorrow evening, with an all-night vigil. To be followed by my wedding. Still, for now at least my bride would be sequestered, as she should be, so I wouldn't need to think about her and I wouldn't have to spend tomorrow cooped up in the Gate Hall either. Even princes were allowed a break to "rest" before the vigil. So I went to bed that night comparatively cheerful, promising myself a more enjoyable tomorrow. Something more relaxing…

I parried, ducked beneath Semmit's longer arm and thrust my sword-point upward, aiming just below the Kemik's ribcage. Raucous shouts, and shriller ululations from the other Kemik present, bounced off the arena walls and battered at my eardrums but my huge opponent stumbled back, his amber eyes dilated. I hadn't pulled my punch; couldn't afford to. The royal guard had height and reach on me as well as weight.

But this was a polite fight. No fangs, protective layers of padded leather and our curved swords—you try getting a Kemik to use a straight one—were wood weighted with lead. Only our shields and helmets were real. That meant one-on-one, as far as me against a Kemik counted: no outside help; no grabbing someone's balls or kicking sand into their faces. So I bowed to Semmit's gasping visage; gave him time to get his breath back.

He leaned on his sword, his long, rough fingers and their deceptively pretty lilac tips streaked with yellow dust. "Good… move… highness." Legend had it the Kemik's ancestors had traded in their race's souls for all that added stature, and of course their lizard fangs and finger-suckers. Not so bad a bargain. They were fierce warriors, hellishly good climbers, and they *never* lost their grip on weapons.

My grin said it all. Semmit, hardened captain in the Royal Guard, was massive even for a Kemik, and a cunning fighter. Besides, I didn't dare waste breath on talking. I stuck my own weapon into the sandy floor and wiped my sweaty sword hand on my thigh, ignoring catcalls. Had everybody in here stopped to watch their prince get beaten? Not if I could help it, even if the odds were stacked against me.

It was late morning now. We'd been at it some time but mine was the first killing blow landed, hence my jubilation. My arms were shaking though, for every one of Semmit's blows fell like a hammer. The sun had moved into my eyes and the walls of the practice ground trapped the heat. I dare say both of us stank like rotten meat. I must, since I'd begun the day with riding.

Truth to tell it was a relief to get dirty after all the wedding formalities, especially those with the Sidassi; so old-fashioned! Thankfully, those trials were on hold now till after Turn of Year. This time round the annual vigil heralded my thirtieth birthday. Normally my favorable birth date meant the three-day holiday was one big party, but with marriage looming close… Huh. I had resigned myself—reluctantly—to staying celibate, and (reasonably) sober. At least there was no ban on hunting, or on weapons practice.

The ride had been a light-hearted affair with a few close friends. A welcome escape, except the sun's heat had exacerbated those bites on my arm. There was still nothing visible but neither salve nor vinegar had eased the stabbing sensations. The almost-constant hot itchiness shouted fire-bug stings. I knew the discomfort would lessen once the blisters erupted but that wasn't making this bout any easier.

Semmit was still doubled over but his breathing seemed to have steadied. Better not give him too much recovery time. "Ready, Sem?"

The ingrate straightened fast, his snake-like fangs grown long in triumph, sword already swinging. Curse the male, I'd have to stand my ground long enough to grab for my own blade before I could jump aside and bring my shield up.

Or at least I meant to. As my right foot came off the ground the cursed bites made their own attack, the worst yet. I couldn't stop myself. I clutched my sword arm. Demon's luck: the shield on my other arm knocked my own sword flying. I was caught off balance, literally, and Semmit's weighted practice sword was coming at me like the wrath of Keshat, streaking down upon my helmet.

Ashamet, Desert Born

I dropped flat. It was all I could do. The blade missed my head, skidded across the shield's polished surface—and skated not toward the ground but up, toward my collarbone.

Time stuttered. I could see the weapon's path but there was nothing I could do to halt it.

Thank the gods for Kemik prowess. Semmit, shouting curses, threw himself into a spin and somehow managed to divert it. It hit my shoulder's padded outer curve, but not the crucial joint above it.

I staggered up. The yard had gone entirely quiet. I was hazily aware of gaping mouths and frozen bodies, Semmit's sword arm lowered. "Highness?"

He'd got carried away, battle phase, full weight behind the blow but with every right to expect me to defend myself. Instead I'd acted like a perfect idiot, for no apparent reason. I licked dry lips. If it had landed true I might never have borne a full-size shield again. The big male looked scared, and confused. Small wonder; I'd lowered my guard at the worst moment possible.

"Highness, are you all right?"

I shook my head to clear it. "Sorry Semmit. Stupid move, you weren't to blame. I lost my balance." I straightened. "And remind me not to wait for you in future."

Semmit's smile mixed relief with satisfaction. A kill-blow scored. I didn't argue. Tell him he had gotten through because his prince's arm was itching? Fine tale that would make in every tavern. And a poor excuse. I kept my mouth shut.

Semmit, once relieved, turned gracious. "A kill each, highness. A good time to stop, I think."

Honors even? I wasn't arguing. Besides, he'd only hold back if we continued now. So we touched sword-points to the sand, bowed and backed off. Bout over. I accepted laughing offers of help getting all the gear off. Semmit's comrades gathered round him too with jokes and ribald comments. Time to stop all right. I ached, and I needed a stiff drink. Several stiff drinks.

I left them an hour later, claiming the need to rest for vigil, sped on my way by a score of raised tankards. Medi, on the lookout, bowed me to the bath and offered food and brandy. I refused the food—I'd eaten something with my soldiers—but I took the brandy to the bath-side. Keeping celibate I had adhered to. Staying sober? It would take a great deal more than what I'd drunk to break that edict. But it looked like I'd be badly *bruised* by morning. Rotten timing. Between bruises on one side and bites on the other I wasn't going to be the most presentable of bridegrooms, not the pretty picture Father wanted.

The room was warm, and scented, robe-slaves deft and silent, startling contrast to the rowdy scene I'd come from. It should have felt relaxing, but for some reason I was on edge. Another brandy didn't cure it.

I bathed then moved into my bedroom. My head felt muzzy, my limbs heavy, but I wasn't sleepy though the heavy shutters made my spacious bedroom cool and shadowed, feigning night-time.

The aftermath of my near escape from being crippled? Hah, more like my all-too-near wedding. It was not long now until the Turn of Year and once that was over there was no escape.

Another prickling stab jerked down my arm. I cursed and twisted it to look; no blisters yet. Perhaps a patch of redness near the shoulder?

Medi noticed. "More vinegar, my prince?"

"Smart male."

A slave brought bowl and sponge. The astringent clashed with Medi's choice of incense but the sponge felt pleasant and the prickling subsided. My mind cleared too. I waved the slave away and turned toward my bed at last. Then stopped. "How's he doing?"

"My prince?"

"That slave." I took another step. "The new one." I felt hotter. I felt hungry.

"The gift, highness? Quiet. Not rebellious. He's been sleeping most of the time." He held out a hand, ready to take my robe.

"Send for him."

For once Medi's face betrayed his surprise. We were into the last days before the wedding. I wasn't supposed— "Highness." Medi issued soft-voiced orders.

The curtains in the arch behind me rattled. The hefty eunuchs who led him in kept a hold of his arms. It looked as if that was keeping him upright, at least walking straight. I found I'd grinned; maybe *his* head was more muddled than mine. But he was more aware than at our first encounter; his head was up and he recognized me at once, stopping dead, a pearl-white figure set against my deep blue curtains. The grey eyes stared across at me.

I stared back. My stomach tightened. A male could surely drown in those eyes. My hands twitched. He was so *different*. I wanted to reach out. I wanted—

He swayed; looked faintly panicked; tried to find his balance, breathing faster.

"Seven hells." The creature could hardly stand. The eunuchs had stepped in, a solid wall for him to lean on.

A burst of anger banished ardor. At myself not him. I shouldn't have had that last brandy; shouldn't have sent for him at all before the marriage. Time to stop, before I scandalized my stuffy in-laws. Sure as death the tale would leak out if I didn't. And I wasn't that much a brute, whatever other males thought of me.

Ashamet, Desert Born

I pretended to inspect him. Ignore the eerie coloring—some chance—he definitely wasn't Chi or Kemik. He was finer boned than either. But he wasn't quite Kadduchi either. Built like a Kadduchi, but unearthly pale. And too slender, I decided. "Under weight, you'd say? A while to go yet?"

"Indeed, my prince." Medi, calm restored, inspected him as well. "But there is improvement."

"Huh. No sign of anything contagious?"

"None I recognize, my prince, but I've been careful as you ordered."

"Good." When I nodded dismissal the eunuchs edged their charge back through the arch. The grey eyes never left me till the curtains came between us. I let my breath out. "Time I got some sleep."

The tiredness I had courted came at last, but not before those fire-bug bites returned to plague me. Curse the things. I squirmed. And curse the marriage and its etiquette as well. This wasn't half the birthday I'd have chosen.

Chapter 3

When I woke my first thought was relief; the fire-bug plague had left me. Then I half-recalled that something roused me.

A sound? I kept my eyes shut, visualizing my surroundings. The domed roof of my bed was supported by fat pillars, one at each corner. They were of yellow sela wood, the timber stained with interlocking triangles of blues and purples, and inlaid with bands of precious metals; a pattern mimicked by the jeweled canopy above me as I lay there, breathing evenly. Not moving. Yet.

Another muffled sound, but not too near. All right. I peered through my lashes. Near darkness. No surprise, the muslins round the bed and at the full-length windows might have dimmed the sunlight but I knew the outer shutters were what imitated night-time. Day or night, the nearer draperies blurred outlines, should I value modesty, and kept out insects, but they wouldn't foil an attacker, while the bed itself could offer only silken sheets and pillows edged with glinting gold and silver. Perfect to prepare me for a night awake in vigil. Not much use as weapons. Where—?

Then I relaxed. I recognized the furtive sounds. No threat; a slave was on the balcony outside to loose the shutters, which still left fretted inner screens and trembling draperies between us. And those pretty lattices were painted metal. Now I turned my head the shadows told me it was almost evening, when I'd given orders to be wakened for the vigil.

I took a deeper breath. The purple lossi blossom on my balcony sent in its sultry perfume and when I stretched the silk caressed my flesh. I smiled when the burly Medishel brought in more slaves to light an oil lamp or three and draw the drapes back at my bedside. My slave master since my youth, the soft-looking eunuch was as tough as armor underneath his flowing silks and city makeup. He'd got the best parts of his mixed heritage, our height and toughened skin around his Chi-size stomach, the layers of fat outweighed by bulk and muscle. In his hands my household ran like clockwork. By the time I thought to sit up he was rearranging pillows at my back, and slaves around the chamber had their foreheads on the carpets.

Medishel himself was bold enough to smile back at me. A pudgy hand, a ring on every finger, reached toward the silver tray a kneeling slave held out behind him. I could smell my usual infusion: spear leaf, with the bitter aftertaste that wakes a male faster than the coldest water.

"Thirty years tonight, my prince. A favored number. Will—?" His mouth stopped moving.

He was staring. At my sword hand? At my shoulder? I twisted, trying to see. I'd gone from bath to bed with nothing but a trace of oil on me. What had shocked the male to silence?

It was my arm, above the elbow. I stared too. The room felt colder. When I'd bathed the arm had been as glossy-brown as ever, as yet unmarred by age or battle, but I couldn't claim that any longer. There was a pale outline drawn there now, as if the brown was scraped away. A sweeping, three-point star.

I couldn't breathe. The hollow, gold-wired star, the En-Syn (or the "Child-Mark" as common mortals often called it) was the opening act for the much fancier Synia, the miraculous jeweled star my father carried. The thing had been sunk into the flesh of six of the eight previous Kadduchi Kings; the miraculous, very visible proof the gods favored our bloodline.

I'd expected to bear one too, once, even after I learned it was all a sham. It had, after all, kept us in power, and my father's full-fledged Synia, all solid gold and ruby-centered, had looked wondrous to a child.

But then, before my own initiation, I had fallen very ill. The priests daren't risk whatever they'd meant to do and, me being a rare single birth, there was no fall-back. By the time I recovered word had spread: the gods had let me live, become an adult, but they hadn't valued me enough to claim me as their Chosen.

It'd been uncomfortable for a few years, yes, but then I'd started winning battles, and that got to be a habit, so the temples bragged I was a champion; a hero. I had settled happily for that distinction. I could always rule by force if I was barred religion, though my father looked as if he really meant to live for ever, which in truth would suit me better.

But now, a Synia, or so it threatened. On me? The bed silk tore beneath my fingers.

"My prince?" breathed Medishel. His eyes were bulging.

"Send them away," I managed.

A jerk of Medishel's hand. The nearest slave dumped the tray on the carpet and ran. The rest shuffled back until they too could dart between the quilted curtains in the archways leading to my bath or to the rest of my most intimate apartments. Thank the gods Medi hadn't moved, so none of them had seen what he had. Had they?

"If any of them have seen this, silence them," I said, "permanently."

"They saw nothing, my prince, I'm sure. Nor will I, until you have informed the Voice of Heaven," he assured me, black eyes gleaming with excitement in his full moon features.

"I'm not telling my father, or anyone else, not till I know what in every hell's going on." I pushed away the single cover.

At once Medi offered me a blue and white robe, a light silk at this season. For once he kept his eyes averted as I donned it. I didn't know about him but I felt a fraction calmer once my arm was hidden. My mouth was dry as desert sand. I had to think. I couldn't. "Where's that tea?"

"Here, my prince." He stepped back to give me room to stride about the chamber as I sipped. Silence, except for the whisper of silk whenever I moved, and the muffled clicking of my slippers when I crossed bare tiles. The tart liquid cleared some of the panic out of my head. I stopped moving, took a breath then shoved the wide sleeve up my arm.

The hollow En-Syn symbol on my sword arm felt smoother than my normal flesh, and cool, beneath my fingertips. No blistering. No trace of roughness, or of smudging. Out of nowhere.

What, I should believe the gods had changed their minds? That credulous I wasn't, and this was nothing but a shadow, blatantly false. I let the sleeve fall back and went on pacing. Father had to be behind it. I stopped, cup in hand. Gods, was I meant to display it at tonight's vigil? Did he really think the court'd swallow it? In any case the ambush hadn't gone to plan, the slave had clearly interrupted. Yet there was no sign of— How then? Had the *itching* been…?

Forget how. *Why* do it? And why sneak up on me?

Because Father had seen this was one command I might not obey? He was right too. I'd lived a soldier for too long to want to trade that for becoming the next false god, under the priests' gouging thumbs the rest of my life.

I swore. It didn't make things any better. My father had just ruined a perfectly good birthday, and maybe the rest of my life. The tea splashed out across an antique carpet and the fragile bowl—another heirloom—turned into a thousand glinting fragments on the blue-veined tiles. Medi winced but wisely kept his mouth shut. I needed a plan. First step: "I've changed my mind about that short-sleeved tunic."

Chapter 4

Turn of Year. A thousand drums and torches keep us all awake, devout or heathen, citizen or pilgrim. Every district has its separate, endlessly repeated rhythm, thrumming through the avenues, the public squares, the private courtyards. Calling us to vigil. Warding demons.

But as dawn approaches all our eyes are raised toward the palace and the cage-like, pillared Tomb of Kings, its alabaster dome perched high upon the cliff-like terrace. Seen in daylight it's impressive. In the night it makes a haunting image.

Murmurs from the crowd. A slate-grey mist obscures the tomb. It boils and tumbles, rolling off the ledge above; a ghostly waterfall. The pilgrims raise their hands in fear, but we who live here know it melts before it hits us.

Suddenly the temple floating on the mist is lit by fire. The pillars turn from white to amber in the darkness, then blood-red. The flames flare higher, like a beacon. Bated breath below. The drums fall silent. Till my father's head and shoulders rise above the flames, his hands outstretched; the flames surrounding him so he appears like a blazing torch that's visible throughout the city, with his fabled "heart of fire". Then the chanting starts, like thunder.

At least that's how I've always thought it looked to those below us. Me, I'd always had a front-row terrace seat up here. I would have swapped it happily, especially this year.

I had joined my father and my Uncle Raggesh—and the three High Priests—to make this year's vigil. Arm well covered. No one, yet, had challenged me about it. As the sun set we'd descended to the cave-like crypt below and dripped our blood onto its altar. Now—except for Father, who would spend the vigil down there in seclusion—we'd reclaimed the tiny, open-sided temple right above it, to be watched by lesser kin and priests in black like us; by armored guards and slave-attendants.

From the formal terrace plots the scent of valis, heady burial herb, crept in again to fill my nostrils, cleaner than the dusty smell of death I'd come from. I had clenched my fist to stop the flow of blood out of the cut across my palm but otherwise ignored it.

Father's giant, beardless guards stood sentry just outside the open-sided temple. The Kemik's darker, textured skins could make them shadows in the night but now the firelight glinted off their cone-shaped, copper helms, their amber eyes, their plated cuffs and tunics. Fierce warriors, but no defense against my current adversaries: Father and his partners-in-religion.

The High Priests' shaven heads were hooded, faces shadowed, but I could imagine their expressions. I had had all night to stew, and I felt simmeringly angry.

When the heavy, oil-laden smoke crawled up from the entry to the crypt I ignored it. I'd guessed that secret years ago. The hermit-priests below, who lived among the dead, must have a solar box, an ancient, temple-hoarded tek, to make this "holy" vision. I had grown up with a few of those, the dwindling wonders of the Ancestors: the magic "stars" around my father's throne; the heated water in our personal apartments and the lightning messages the major temples passed across enormous distances; the constantly updated news from near and far that helped to keep our royal house in power. How they made the Synia was much more secret, not admitted.

Now, jets of flame reared silently, what looked like fiery tongues as cold as night, to lick about our king with eerie, orange light that flashed with green and crimson. I could hear the shouting from below. Despite myself my heart beat faster, he had pulled his tunic open and his full-fledged Synia, the solid three-point star, its gold and ruby permanently plated to his chest, glowed brighter than the fire.

The flames consumed him totally, then died. To those below, their Voice of Heaven must have vanished with it. Perfect timing, for the first true ray of sunlight leapt from the horizon, like a ray of hope. The distant dunes turned yellow suddenly, then golden. One by one the rooftops down below me blinked from faded rust to terracotta.

Then the sunlight washed into the temple and my royal father, mortal once again, stepped forward. Not a scorch mark on him. Fire that didn't burn; intriguing contradiction, yet another temple mystery I hadn't fathomed.

Slaves fell flat. The lesser priests touched hands and foreheads to the dirt. Guards raced along the eastern parapet to where our royal banner waited, furled since sunset.

My father led us in their wake, between the kneeling bodies. His dull black outer robe flowed back to show a knee-length tunic over trousers clasped with gold above gold-studded sandals. And of course the Synia, the star with jeweled fire at its heart that labeled him our Voice of Heaven. And bound him to the farce our ancestors had started.

Ashamet, Desert Born

I walked stiffly. Hidden by my robes, my violated arm went back to itching. Was the white-skinned slave awake to see this lovely sunrise? Curses, where had that thought come from?

Behind us, tiny birds in cages hidden in the vines against the inner walls had started piping. The dead were laid to rest. The High Priests pushed their hoods aside and everyone but me was smiling. My king and father stepped onto the platform looking out across the city as the guards, who would have dwarfed him otherwise, went on their knees to push the massive hanging forward. Cheers went up as it unfurled and flapped below the parapet, the crimson-centered three-point star against its sky blue background. The night was gone. Our holy king's communion with the gods he spoke for was successful and another year of heaven's favor beckoned.

Time to go. At last. I slotted in behind my father in procession, kept my feet and face in order till he parted from our entourage and headed for the tunneled entry to our Inner Palace. Only Rag, my father and myself could pass that way unguarded. Once inside I waited for the axe to fall. I hadn't done as he'd expected. *Now* there'd be a confrontation.

But my father walked ahead, stepped out into our inner court then right, around the shaded colonnade toward his own apartments. "That went well enough, I thought. Now all that's left is Ash's wedding."

My uncle merely grunted, heavy-footed now we were more private, turning back toward his own domain, above the sunken entrance.

Still no word about the failed ambush? Wait, had they concealed it from my uncle too? Well, two could play at that game.

My elders went their separate ways, and so did I. I didn't know what they were up to but I was considering defensive tactics.

Chapter 5

"I've sworn an oath. All right?"

The latest questioner, a younger lord, more sycophant than friend, was tactless enough to look surprised but at least it shut him up. People did make promises at this time of year. If mine required me to wear a wide silver and gold armlet, well, a lot of males wore such rather than bracelets, which could catch on weapons. It was a handsome piece, chased silver edged with bands of gold. It even—sheer bravado—had the royal star in gold right in its centre.

Two of the three holy days had passed, much of it in hunting, weapons drill or alcoholic fog; hang appearances. With one day left before the wedding the marks were still a pale outline; hadn't grown but hadn't faded. I could see no option but to face my father and to hope my arguments prevailed.

Except the cursed Sidassi blocked every chance of a private discussion. It was wedding, wedding, wedding, even though we Kadduchi were still in the middle of welcoming our new year. We—my father, Rag and I—had talked about them over breakfast, the morning before the vigil. When I still thought the subject important.

Effad, Thersat and my bride were a "sett"—their word for litter—about four years younger than me. Rumor had it there'd been quads originally. Gods knew what the discard must have been like. Still, I figured there was Kadd blood in there somewhere in the past. The royals I had seen so far had been above the average height for Chi, and hefty Effad—not the sharpest weapon—was at least a halfway decent swordsman. But this Thersat…

Not identical quads, no not alike at all, and not a sight to be forgotten with his tightly-fitted "coat"—not robe—in colors that did nothing for his pinkish-brown complexion. Or his scrawny beard, combed with scented oils like his hair, which he wore loose upon his shoulders like some lawyer. All of which accentuated narrow wrists and bony features. Gods, a Chi or not, the fellow was a beanpole. Just the sight of him was liable to damp one's spirits.

Father's view was kinder. "They say he's actually fond of his sister. Just… not a fighter, Ash. Be tactful."

Both son and brother looked at him in silence. A rare accord he must have thought it. He sighed openly. "We don't need to love the male, merely be polite to him." He picked on Rag for once. "And don't you start getting temperamental. Ash is enough, and he's at least the bridegroom. Though I don't suppose —" He swung in my direction. "You've got your lazy head around the details of the wedding."

Rag choked with quite unseemly laughter and I threw an orange at him. It hit him too, which was the only cheering thing about the conversation.

Father was right, I hadn't listened to the gory details but with one more day to go I couldn't dodge them any longer. We'd got Thersat and the Sidassi advisers coming to the pre-wedding dinner, in my father's apartments.

I'd requested a private talk beforehand. Look on the bright side, if I couldn't persuade him to let me off the hook I might not be his heir tomorrow, and the marriage could be cancelled. But I couldn't say such things in public, and he'd fobbed me off till after.

Dressing for the dinner, I chose rings at random, mind distracted, while Medishel talked housekeeping.

"Fine, yes fine. How's that slave doing now?" Despite everything else that was going on, my mind would keep returning to grey eyes, not to mention… It was devilish bad timing. I could have done with a distraction, but by tradition I was barred from such sport till after the wedding.

"The new one, highness? He still sleeps a lot." Medishel hesitated; not like him.

I had turned to leave. "What? I haven't got all night."

"Your pardon, my prince. It's not important."

"Yes it is, or you wouldn't be dithering. Spit it out, male."

"It's just that he's so… foreign." Medi saw my face and hastened. "There seems no permanent illness, most likely someone starved him."

"Not unknown in slaves," I pointed out. A shame, and not behavior I'd expect from Sheshman in the circumstances, but I'd seen no other damage.

"No, my prince, but even starved his general condition isn't what we're used to, weakened and so very pale. We thought at first he had a fever. He was agitated, even in his sleep. But then I noticed he was calmer when two of the house weren't present."

I felt my brows snap together. "Are you saying two of the house-slaves made him feverish?"

"So it appeared, my prince. Since I removed them both from those nursing him the young male rests easier, and seems a little stronger. Coincidence, probably, but…" He spread his hands to demonstrate his indecision.

I decided for him. "Keep them out. Stronger, eh?"

"He sat up unaided today, and fed himself, although his balance is not certain. He needed help to…" Medi waved a hand across his crotch.

The gesture, something in his manner, made me wonder… "He's entire?"

"Yes, my prince, uncut." Medi's face agreed it was another unexpected detail. Clearly I wasn't the only one giving our new arrival undue attention. I squashed an impulse to see for myself. I was already late, and it would only raise Medi's eyebrows again. I squared my shoulders and prepared for battle with my father.

Our Inner Palace was the crowning glory of the city, the inward-turning square of yellow stone a step uphill of the more public royal buildings, and the endless bureaucratic warrens that spread down toward the city.

My father's personal apartments spanned three floors across the west side of our central, formal garden. There was another floor below but that was partly underground, and housed such things as slaves and storerooms.

Like my own apartments—on the northern side—only the top two floors had outer windows. Even those had shutters. The only real access was via the central court. The only way to that was through the eastern portion of the building through a gated passageway beneath my Uncle Rag's apartments, which were consequently smaller. Like many before them the Sidassi had been cowed by the torch-led, underground approach then over-awed by the grandeur inside. The airy first floor salon where we dined that evening boasted marble floors and stately balconies that gave a stunning view of pale sky, just tinged with pinks and purples.

Tonight, the room reminded me my father was a Voice of Heaven. My own dining room was an unassuming place; the same cream, blue-veined tiles as my bedroom above it; dark red marble archways breaking up the whitened plaster walls, their simple filigrees of blues and golds and copper.

In contrast, Father's floors and walls were pure white marble, lavishly inscribed with arabesques of gold and silver round each white-veined, yellow archway. If that sounds plain then add a sea of silken couches, jeweled lamps and inlaid tables. And I wasn't thrilled about the choice of incense from the burners somewhere in the shadows, luring flying pests to their destruction. It was opulent, the setting for a demigod. And no, I didn't want it.

Ashamet, Desert Born

Trying to put such thoughts aside, I concentrated on the Sidassi instead. Sidass, our latest vassal kingdom, had surrendered last year to my father's "invitation". Frankly, I'd been disappointed. I'd hardly had time to build up a sweat; some minor skirmishes, one decent battle just outside their capital and suddenly they'd caved, and joined the empire.

Uncle Raggesh, further down the table, wore a pained expression. The Sidassi were on average shorter-bodied, with less stamina as well, an inbuilt disadvantage, and their generally-shorter noses sometimes verged on comic. I recalled Rag hadn't been impressed with the Sidassi fighting either, that his comments had been somewhat ribald. I had told him to be grateful; Farad seemed a better king than most, and we were still alive to *call* them fools and cowards.

Closer up, even their nobles bundled themselves into single, heavy garments rather than the layers I was used to. They maintained their "coats" were warmer. Surely nonsense. A clever male kept hot—or cold—by adding or subtracting layers, or by his choice of fabrics. Everybody knew that. And their warriors wore their dark brown hair pulled high up on their heads and somehow knotted, with a ribbon gathering the hanging ends that signified the fellows' status. They resembled horses' tails. Not impressive.

For this evening, Father's cooks had used some milder northern spices. Maybe that was why Rag looked so dismal since both scent and taste were weakened. But it didn't seem to cheer our guests; perhaps because they looked so funereal in all their dismal browns and greens and ochres. Why did northerners prefer such boring colors.

Still, at least they didn't sweat as much as they did last time in our real-desert climate, which was doubly welcome since their so-called perfumes stung my nose and made me think of cat piss. It was cooler this year anyway; it looked as if the winter rains might hit us early. Would the rain arrive before the wedding? If there was a wedding after I confronted Father....

My mind caught up. "Did you just say, "the Siddassi ceremony'?"

"Yes, highness." The eldest Siddassi seemed startled too. "As you will know—"

"Oh no I don't." I turned toward my father. Who, to do him justice, was also looking thoughtful.

"Actually he's right. He doesn't. No one's told him."

I wasn't going to be fobbed off that easily, even if the marriage was about to be called off. "I'm Kadduchi. A Kadduchi ceremony comes first. Why the hells are we talking about—"

"It was agreed that the Siddassi ceremony will be performed on the first day," my father said repressively.

But I wanted more than that. "Why?"

Thersat gaped. His courtiers looked affronted. One of Father's people ventured to lean forward. "My prince, it was considered more, er, delicate, to hold the Siddassi rites before our own."

"What's so delicate about the first day of a wedding?" I demanded. Coyness always irritates me.

"Well, erm, well, highness…" The male waved his hands in circles.

Uncle Rag took over. "Not the first day. The first night, nephew. Seems if you see a royal bride before you're wed according to Siddassi law it's treason and they'll have to cut your balls off. Legal rape," he finished, to the horror of the timid minds around him. Then he raised a mocking eyebrow.

"So I'll wear a blindfold," I said helpfully, and smiled back. There's nothing like tormenting others to make a male feel better.

The Siddassi gobbled. Father straightened his own face and shot me a look. "I'm sure Prince Ashamet was joking. Weren't you?" he asked me, oh-so-nicely.

"Of course," I said. "You surely didn't think…?" I tried to look a touch offended. That seemed to do it. "So the first day will be Siddassi," I said. "I shall look forward to it." And smiled winningly…

"*A gote?*" I'd quite forgot there might not be a wedding. "What are we, heathens?"

"What's one more dead animal compared to the flocks the cooks will slaughter," Father said, as if there was no difference.

"All right" I conceded, "so it hardly matters if we kill another. But—have I got this right?—this one's a sacrifice to some goddess of fertility? And if that isn't enough insult they're going to drain the blood and paint us with it?"

"It will wash off," Father said encouragingly.

"Oh great. Care to join us then?"

"No I don't, and stop complaining. We're building a peace. Gote's blood's a damn sight nicer way to get one than yours or mine."

That stopped me of course. Granted the marriage was advantageous, but… "I'll feel like a fool," I muttered.

Rag laughed. "No one'll notice. They won't see you past the first few rows, once they raise that hood thing over you."

"That's supposed to make it better?"

"Children!" That shut us both up. "Can we accept that there is room for other customs?"

Ashamet, Desert Born

Father was finished with the subject, was he? I thought I might at least get the last word. "Don't hesitate," I said, "to tell me if there's any other little detail I might have missed. I don't have to marry her crones as well, do I?"

"Distasteful as that would be," my father said, "I have every confidence you'd do your duty." Not a muscle quivered. Some days you just can't win. Rag was still laughing as he walked out. At which point reality rushed back. Would Father listen to my plans, or try to make me into something that I truly wasn't?

Chapter 6

"So what's so urgent?" Father raised an eyebrow, smiling. The last of his slaves had been dismissed. I figured it was now or never.

"This." I'd worn a sleeveless deep blue tunic shot with silver over cream silk trousers. And the silver on my sword arm. Now, grim-faced, I tugged the armlet free and turned the arm toward him. I didn't look. I knew exactly what the damned thing looked like.

My royal father sat up slowly. "This is… unexpected."

Playing innocent? He could at least be honest here in private. I sat, the armlet in my scabbard hand, feeling sick, and angry, and unwontedly self-conscious.

"When—? No, let me think." He pursed his lips. "You've worn that armlet since your birthday? Why wait till now… but I assume you have your reasons?" A smile threatened the patrician features. "Quite a birthday present."

"One I could have done without." I found my glass and took a hefty swallow, quite disgusted when I found my hand was shaking. Wine had dripped like blood onto my sandal. I didn't want all this. I never had done. "Plague on it, Father, why now?" I tried to curb my anger. "I can cope with pretending *you're* holy. For one thing you're a demon actor. But you've had all your life to practice the Voice of Heaven performance, and the whole world knows it didn't come when I was younger." Indignation pushed me further. "Am I such a weakling? Is that—"

I stopped, aghast. I'd stewed, the anger swelling, but I hadn't till that moment seen the real hurt, the real insult: that he'd done this as a last-ditch prop; that he had found me so much less an heir than he had wanted. Less than adequate, like dull-edged Effad? My stomach churned. I rocked to silence.

"Ash." My father frowned. "*I* didn't order this. I thought you meant *you* had."

It took a second for the words to gather meaning then I gasped for air. "But… you must have."

"Ash, believe me, I'd have talked to you about it. Don't you see that?"

Now he'd said it, it was obvious. He wasn't such a fool. But I was. I had wasted three days warding off the wrong opponent. "If it wasn't you, or me, who was it?"

Father's eyes had narrowed. "It's the temples' best-kept secret. But how could they manage it?"

Suddenly I felt more hopeful. "It appeared out of nowhere, on the evening of the vigil, while I rested. Unless, could it be linked to an itching?"

"No." Impatiently.

"Then I've no idea, but I obviously woke too early. Well, it's hardly finished, is it?" We both examined pale lines that should have gleamed with golden wire.

"In your bed? Who else was with you?"

"Give me credit for some manners. No one, not so close before the wedding. And Medishel knows nothing, that I'll swear to. He was every bit as shocked as I was. Devils take it, he believes it's real!"

"As it is," my father warned me.

"No it isn't."

"Ash, if there's an En-Syn we have no choice except to act as if we both believe it. Do we?"

"Yes we do." I pulled myself together, marshalling the arguments I'd mustered, adding new ones. "It's an obvious fake. Who'll believe it? It'd cause uproar, even if you let the priests say otherwise."

He wasn't interrupting.

"And what if it's *not* the priests, however unlikely that is? It could be a trap, for all of us. Never mind we've played the stupid game for ever, if I'm denounced the whole scam comes under scrutiny. It's not worth the risk."

"And you don't want it." Father smiled at last, if rather sadly.

"No. I don't." Saying it out loud felt surprisingly good. "But I've thought of a remedy."

Father sat up straighter. "You have?"

"It's easy. I'll stage an accident and burn the marks—"

"No, Ash, I will not see you mutilated. Wait." He paused to think. I didn't dare to interrupt him. "We need more information but, no, it has to be the priests, or one of them, though why they'd dare… Very well, I will not force you to complete the marking. Not yet anyway, till we've investigated further. As you say it's hardly convincing, and we certainly can't complete it before the wedding ceremonies." Another pause. "We won't confront the High Priests yet either, not till we're sure if all of them are involved."

"But—"

He raised a hand. "They failed to complete it. It's not credible. They're probably as upset as you are. The last thing they'll do is make it public." He sighed. "Ash, are you sure?"

"Yes, Father."

"Then put that thing back on and keep quiet, and… we'll see what happens." He found a smile. "At least I know they won't try anything worse." He saw me frown. "I made it clear years ago—when I refused their advice to replace you—what I'd do if they ever tried to kill you."

While I sat there open-mouthed his smile became a frown. "Which reminds me, I meant to talk to you anyway, about that stallion you've been gifted. Samchek said he thought you meant to train it yourself."

He'd protected me from the *priests*, all these years, because of that illness? And he dismissed the subject in a few words, to talk horseflesh?

I gathered what wits I had left and tried to match his composure. "The black? Good blood, but vicious," I confessed. "Samchek says it takes a saddle but it can't be trusted, the thing keeps trying to impale its grooms." I'd been looking forward to the challenge. Right now every risk was welcome.

"Ash, please promise me you'll leave the task to Samchek this time? Don't risk your neck unnecessarily, at least until they've curbed its temper somewhat. We still need that heir, and the brute could kill you before you give me one. Be sensible for once, eh?"

I could only nod. At that moment it was impossible to refuse him.

"Mind, if word about your arm leaks out, I'll call the priests in to finish the job, and you'll learn to like it. Understood?"

"Understood." It might not be a total victory, but it was better than I'd hoped for. I could face the world tomorrow with a clear conscience. So I spent my final night of being single somewhat wildly. Waking late, I had them pour cold water over me and braced myself to face my wedding. I'd retained my freedom from religion. I could deal with lesser problems. I would smile at the crowds, ignore the priests, accept my bride and even smile politely at her irritating brother. While—a happier thought—the white-skinned slave… He didn't eat much, Medi said, but he was definitely getting stronger.

Chapter 7

Once again the Gate Hall stank of sweat and perfume, never mind how many windows high above us were unshuttered or how many slaves were sent each night to scrub its tiles and marble flagstones. The marriage ceremonies lasted five days in all. At least only the first one was totally grotesque.

Blue and white-clad dignitaries—now of course devoted to their sacred heron only as a lesser god attendant on the greater Sarrush—presided over everything Sidassi. And I do mean everything. Between the drones and warbles of no less than three Siddassi crones behind their specially-erected gilded screening, and their males' endless, pious mouthings… well, who likes to be subjected to such nonsense?

Our own priests, clad in cloth of gold and their appointed colors, positively steeped in incense, simmered gently in the background. I figured they considered it an insult going second, even if their king himself approved it. Their mouths were smiling but their eyes were boiling. As for the gote… There I was, daubed with blood, with some faceless female lurking the other side of an embroidered curtain. I'd had the sudden thought she might still be covered with it when I had to bed her. By all the gods, I thought, maybe the poor gote had the best of this mad bargain.

So there we were. First day. First night. I'd made my mind up to be genial about it. The female was there, like me, to do her royal duty. Besides, we Kadduchi do respect potential mothers. We regard such matters as requiring due politeness. We acknowledge our indebtedness to females.

So I took her gently, and it didn't seem to scare her. I really think that she—well, that she—enjoyed it. It was different, I'll say that for it. Unlike most males I had tried it out some years before. The expense meant nothing to my father, and he always believed in planning ahead. My dour uncle had been charged with that part of my education. As I recall, my younger self had found that very funny; that he was to find me out a knowledgeable female just past breeding for a night, when I'd been sure he'd never personally had a female.

Anyway, after that Kadduchi rites took over. They won on points; four days of priests in cloth of gold, of oaths and symbols and of course their king's attendance, dressed like me in blue and gold and crimson.

Four more nights of "wedding duty" as old Sheshman called it. Four more days of food and drink and every kind of entertainment. A splendid wedding, splendid! guests all chorused; and no wonder; they had gorged themselves on all the free provisions. So had the common people down below us in the city. The palace and the lords obliged, in fact, competed. Every public square would have its spit, and tubs of rice, and casks of something potent every evening. I'd have liked to go and join them, but of course I couldn't; I was otherwise disposed of. No doubt people danced, and sang, and groped each other quite as well without my help, in every corner of the city, and the palace.

In our intimate apartments all was much more decent. Up there were only sober guards and silent slaves. Up there it was my father's quarters to the west; my uncle's opposite, a scant two floors above the double-gated, tunneled entrance. Then my own, toward the north, and finally the females' separated cloister, only slightly smaller, facing south, its only outward-facing windows on the topmost storey.

My mother being long departed and my uncle, naturally, never wed, the lady now my wife—oh, Taniset, her name was—would be free to rule the cloister unobstructed, even if some other royal female came to join her later. Zenek, master of the cloister's eunuchs, had reported everything was running smoothly and her temper was "no worse than they'd expected from a high-born female" (whatever that was). Things looked promising, Father remarked. I'd grunted.

In private then, I took my bride to her gilded bed, and pleased her enough (the eunuchs said) so that she smiled at those who courted her next morning. So it went for those five nights. "I swear the female likes it!" I told my father. I must have been in shock, to say so.

"They tell me some Sidassi favor females that way, those who can afford it. It's supposed to be an old tradition. Not a widespread custom, but accepted, quietly, in the north." Father looked sideways at me.

"Ye gods, you mean they *choose to bed with females? For amusement?*" His smile widened.

In fact it looked as if everyone was satisfied. Except me. I took a soft, round body in my hands and went about the task of getting an heir, but I'd begun to *dream* of wide, white shoulders, slender hips. And haunting grey eyes.

I did penance by honoring the marriage period in full before I slept again in my apartments. Politics aside, I would not choose to slight the lady. She was probably a worthy choice; good-looking for a female, far more than her siblings. My heir might even turn out handsome. She deserved respect, assuming she proved fertile.

And I was not a cruel master, or I didn't think so. A few days more, I told myself, would leave him stronger.

Ashamet, Desert Born

A few days more, I thought, a few days after, and my blood might boil! My lady Taniset seemed gratified she'd got a sex mad monster. In honor, you see, she was the only one I *could* have while the wedding ceremonies lasted. In fact until the next full moon. And have her I did, in full accordance with my duty, probably a deal more than expected by her eunuchs. *They* of course reacted with delight at every visit. *She* appeared willing. Trouble was that didn't cool my fever. All it seemed to do was stoke the fire and make me feel hotter.

Twenty days after the wedding we bowed politely to each other. I told her I was happy with our contract. I'd visit, I said, when it was convenient to both of us. Then I left her to arrange her new existence as the foremost female of an empire.

Back in male territory I drew breath, and gave new orders. The next night when I walked from the bath, in a loose robe and slippers, Sheshman's gift was at my bedroom fireside, lit by shaded lamps and modest firelight. An "ashamet", the sudden desert storm I got my name from, had been threatening the city walls all day. Result: the night had turned unseasonably chilly, prompting Medi to command a modest fire for my added comfort. I could hardly tell him I was hot enough already.

As was the custom on the first occasion he was tethered, to a ring set in the marble of the hearthstones. He was half in shadow, and that pale flesh, where lit, was warmed by fire. Unless I was mistaken he was near as tall as me, and my height was remarked on. No chest hair, that was more like Kemik, but his flesh was surely smooth as any cub's, as if it hadn't toughened since he was a babe in arms. All that pale color, and the single lids and fragile flesh, so many contradictions wholly foreign to our empire. Hardly bred to deal with the deserts either.

Still too thin, that was my next thought, then I noticed that his eyes were clearer, full-awake now as he turned to watch me enter.

Still that odd, half-sitting posture. He'd been leaning back against the hearth but now he straightened. Still no fear, or cringing. Nor a thought of kneeling to me? It seemed not. My doing, I supposed. I had told Medi not to teach him new ways, not yet.

Medishel, who'd followed me in, bowed and awaited my decisions. When I held my hand out he placed the silver key in my palm, then waved the rest of the slaves off their knees. Those wretches scuttled out, cropped heads properly lowered. The sound of slapping feet receded as the curtains settled.

Logs shifted furtively, but otherwise the room was very quiet. When the wind rattled a creeper against the lattice I think we both jumped. And when his head swung back he spoke, not waiting for permission. "You… They said I was to call you "my lord"." The huskiness was gone, he had a clear tenor with a trace of foreign accent I found equally attractive.

Had that been a statement or a question? Feeling his way, I diagnosed. Very well… "Then they said truth."

He studied me for all the world as if he was the lord, and I was the outsider. "They said I am your… property."

"You have been since you came here," I said bluntly.

"A body slave, they said." There might have been, at last, a hint of frowning.

"Indeed." He seemed proficient in our tongue but it was, after all, a relatively new term, and not one used every day. "And do you know what that is?" I waited.

"No."

No. Was he waiting for an explanation? I needed a drink. I crossed to a table, poured wine into a cup, and spoke with my back toward him. "No, my lord," I said pointedly.

A slight pause. "No, my lord."

When I turned back, cup in hand, he was still watching me, head tilted. I was looking straight into those liquid eyes.

I'd waited for this night; lost sleep over it; come back this evening, stripped and bathed and hardly tasted what I'd eaten, knowing he would be here waiting. Now I could do as I liked.

I didn't know what to do. It's those eyes, I thought desperately. Too clear, too open. Waiting. "Do you have a name?"

"No, my lord, not really."

Had the words come easier that time? Make him talk? Make him relax? And me. I raised an eyebrow.

"I only—I'd forgot. I had a newborn name once. It was Keril." He looked at me as if to win approval.

"Keril," I repeated, and felt the sound shape my mouth. My feet took me toward him.

"Yes, my lord?"

I tossed the key at him. "Here, loose that chain." He caught it, awkward in his shackles, then bent to look what he was doing.

The token fire felt even hotter. When the chain ran free I said, "Come on," and turned toward the bed; heard his bare feet on the tiles and swore at myself for feeling relief that he'd obeyed me. Dammit, I was master here. Anger made me swing around to snap at him. Surprised, he stumbled on the tasseled border of a carpet and I caught him by the shoulders.

Fascinated by the feel of him I stroked my hand along one shoulder, very slowly; sighed with pleasure. The wait was over.

The grey eyes stared straight into mine but there was no awareness, only maybe he was puzzled. Had he no idea, no concept…

"Keril. You are mine now." I could feel my muscles tighten.

"Yes, my lord?" No resistance, nothing.

I drew him closer; slid my hand up the long neck; stroked the angle of the cheekbone. Medi had chosen well as usual, the slightest touch of perfume in the hollow of the throat, so faint I hadn't caught it till that moment; something delicate, elusive.

The eyes had widened, bewildered first, then worried. Suddenly his breathing faltered. "My lord, I am not… meant to be touched. It's forbidden."

"Nothing is forbidden, to your master." So Sheshman's tale was true, I thought in passing. He was reared in seclusion. I touched his pale hair, so fine, and turned him toward the bed.

"You do not understand." He was so earnest. "No one is supposed to touch me."

Startled, I raised my eyes from the silver cord at his waist. "No one… touches you? At all?"

"No, my lor—" At last the features showed the birth of understanding. The words stopped dead then trailed his stumbling thoughts. "My lord, why would you… But… They told me you had married." He had the dignity of innocence about him. Very solemn. "Males and females marry. People here spoke of that," he said slowly. "Do you—are you—touching me—as if in marriage?" Such amazement. "But they said you have a wife."

"A —? What kind of heathen country do you come from? Females are for babies," I told him plainly, my hands dropping, skating over his ribs, reaching again for the cord. "Males for pleasure."

"No!"

There was no "my lord" this time. He tried to back away but the massive pillar of the bed brought him up sharp. He had nowhere left to go, not without fighting. I'd have dealt with that, of course. But he didn't fight. (Little good that would have done.) Instead he stayed put. He shook, and his gaze was pinned on me as if I was a monster, but for some reason he didn't move at all. Had Medishel done that good a job instructing his behavior? I figured not. Something was going on in that strange mind, but what I'd find out later. Right now…

I pressed against him. His eyes *glazed*, and he began to mutter to himself in some outlandish dialect. I'd undone the first knot in that cord before it dawned on me that he was chanting. Very soft, but right against my ear. Chanting? Or reciting. *Praying?* And every inch of him (except of course the part I wanted so) had now gone stiff and wooden.

It was, can you believe, as if someone had dowsed me in cold water. Mind—and body, alas—shriveled and numbed. I found I'd stepped away. Oh, he was still desirable, but I couldn't *touch* him. Those damn prayers rang in my head. I couldn't concentrate. It felt like sacrilege, to think of —

"Get that chain back on," I growled. I couldn't think what else to do. I was fighting to re-light what I'd been feeling, and it wouldn't return. I had the urge to strike him, but I found I couldn't. A priest? And obviously a devout one. And he wasn't resisting me, was he? Just sort of… comforting himself? Wrapping faith about him, to endure what I was doing? "Damn it, get yourself chained up, now!"

He backed away. I didn't fool myself he'd learned some manners. No, he wanted to keep me in sight, didn't he? Back at the hearth, he crouched, chained up, made helpless by his own hands, and watched me down the rest of my wine. What was it, I wondered, some rule that said he mustn't fight? Priests could be like that.

He was still watching me. I felt it. In the end, I left. I strode about the inner courts half the rest of the night, trying to clear my head. All right, so he was a priest. Had been a priest. I'd known that, or at least suspected. Not our religion though, some weaker deity, if any gods were real. And if his god was going to strike someone then Sheshman would have been in line before me, so he hadn't so far, had he? Right then. A feeble god, if real. No god at all, I thought, if he couldn't keep a prize like this one. So there; no reason why my plans should falter.

He was still awake when I went back and threw myself onto the bed. Much later, when I turned over, I saw his eyes gleaming in the firelight. And when I woke, late that morning, his head lifted almost at once. Neither of us spoke.

I called for Medishel. "Let him eat then put him back beside the fire," I ordered. Gods knew why I was so restrained. By then I was plain mad. I couldn't believe I'd dithered like a coward over such a trifle. Priest or slave, it didn't matter. Right, I thought, this morning, now, as soon as I've bathed and eaten, we'll have this settled. Prayers or not, I'll have you as I meant to.

I was at breakfast when a robe-slave prostrated himself at my feet.

"Well?" The fool was shaking and I wasn't in the mood for trouble.

"My prince, the body slave…" The male trailed off and tried to burrow through the tiled flooring.

"What?" I sat up and glared down at the fool.

"Lord, Master Medishel sent me. I'm to tell you—tell you." A low wail, then the rest. "He tried to jump out of a window."

I threw the dish aside and strode toward the doorway. "Medishel!"

The damned place was a warren. The slave master came running just as I'd begun to plan his execution. "My prince. I come. I was giving orders."

"What orders?"

"Only to watch him closely, highness. There was no injury except perhaps a bruise or two from where they held him. Would you see him?"

"Yes." I drew a breath, and followed. "What exactly happened?"

"They left him to wash, which he did, highness. A most particular young male. I have no need to teach this one to be clean. Then they gave him bread, and meat." Medishel was looking sideways at me.

"Meat, eh?"

"He *was* ill, highness. He still needs strengthening so I've been sending him a little meat." A sigh. "They say he never eats it. Today, I watched him for a while. He pushed away the meat as if it crawled with maggots, lifted the cup of water then put it down again. Upset, I thought, but then, if it was truly his first time…" Medishel trailed off discreetly. "I had other things to do. He seemed to be behaving well enough. At least I thought so." Medi looked upset about it.

Interesting. So Medi had believed the white and silver too. He'd thought it was the first, that Keril was adjusting to being bedded. All right, to being raped. I supposed to Medi it was a commonplace assumption. Probably, I thought, the only reason he had thought to keep a watch on him at all was that it was so weird to have a child-like, full-grown male to deal with. "So where is he?"

"This way, highness. Two of your robe slaves caught him. Very fast they must have been." The eunuch nodded real approval. "But if they hadn't…"

He left the rest unsaid as we arrived at last; a small, bare cell beside the rear stairway, normally a hiding place for slaves to wait, or work unnoticed. The only thing it had worth noting was a narrow window, built that way against attack, I wasn't sure that even Keril could have fit through. But if he had there'd be a sheer drop outside, as I recalled: three storeys, almost four, and onto stone not soil. Likely he'd have split his skull wide open.

Right now the space was far too crowded. Two hefty eunuchs stood before the window and another two outside the doorway. Medishel was definitely worried.

Keril sat on the stone floor in the centre of the room. No marble here, and little comfort. The few bits and pieces—a stool, a wooden table, a small tray with its meager contents tumbled altogether—had been moved aside and there was water dripping off the table edge; no one had thought to clear it up yet. Had he hoped for a knife, and settled for the window, or would that too have been against some rule he tried to live by?

"Keril!"

The head lifted. The eyes, duller now, looked straight into mine again. Someone breathed in sharply. The rest waited for me to name his punishment.

"Do your gods demand you try this?"

Medishel blinked but Keril's head dropped. Shame? Yes, shame. At trying, or at failing? That was important. "Would they approve it?"

The head sank lower. He shook his head slightly.

"Will you try again?"

Another shake of the head. Slower this time.

"Look at me, and tell me!"

The head came up. So obedient. I could cheerfully have knocked him across the room. With one hand, even; the place wasn't that big, was it?

"No." The word was bleak. "No, my lord, I will not try again. I must control my fears. I am not, not allowed…" He lost the words, or the will.

Damned if I'd let him see I was relieved. All the same. "From now on you'll eat, and drink, whatever Master Medishel bids you."

"Yes, my lord." The head was down again but he had answered, and I found I had believed him. So that ruled out starvation. Medi looked amazed, and pleased, as if the problem had been settled.

"No windows," I said curtly.

Medi's smile disappeared. "No, highness. Should I… I'll change those shackles now, of course."

Sheshman's finely crafted silver. Of course, they thought I'd had the fool last night, and *that* was why—"No. Leave them."

"My prince?"

"Leave them, for now. I'll tell you when I want them off him."

"As my prince wishes," Medi said in clear bemusement.

"See he eats," I said, "and then return him to my hearth." I don't think Keril heard, or even noticed when I left them.

Chapter 8

A battle, that's what it was. A challenge. It eclipsed everything else. My marriage? That was mere politics and duty. The would-be Synia? I told myself that was an inconvenience it looked as if the gods were kindly overlooking; a challenge to my liberty that I could surely cover up and cope with. But Keril…

This was war. My blood was up. A crazy kind of war: no weapons; carried on in near silence. Oh, it was polite. I didn't shout; he didn't struggle. But he stared down at my knees now, not into my face, and if I got too close dull shutters came across his eyes and that warm marble turned to wood beneath my fingers. If he slept I never saw it, even when I took to going in and out at all hours. Whenever I was there his eyes stayed open.

Close friends asked if I was well. Slaves ducked their heads and kept their distance. Medi's customary serenity began to leave him. He couldn't, of course, understand what was going on. A slave kept chained at my hearth, day and night? He'd gone so far as to take him out mornings and evenings, presumably to wash and feed him. I almost told him not to, but it wasn't worth it. The lull before the storm, you're saying? I think we were both waiting for the first flash of lightning.

It'd got to me that Keril wasn't fighting, in however odd a manner, over which of us was master. For him that didn't seem to matter. For him I figured it was a war between me and his beliefs; between good and evil. I knew which side I was on, of course. Probably I should have thrown him on the bed that first night, or the morning after, and taught him he had no right to argue. It was those prayers that were the trouble. I knew if he started on that again I'd back off like a total coward. Right or wrong it wasn't pleasant, feeling like a heathen. And it didn't do a thing for my libido.

All that praying also meant I couldn't *not* keep thinking of the failed En-Syn once again, of its mysterious appearance, out of nowhere. Was it possible, conceivable, the gods I'd grown to doubt were watching me more closely these days? Was I being *tested*?

I'd even got to wondering, after three days of it, if those weird sounds he'd made could be a spell, or curse. Stupid notion, but why else could I not bring myself to take hold of him? Luckily for him he showed me they weren't aimed at me at all.

I'd walked into my upper chambers late that morning, so quietly even the slaves guarding the first landing never heard me coming. By the time they woke up to my arrival I was waving them off and heading for the second stairway, better guarded, through my top-floor rooms and then the double arch, each thickly curtained, that led to my most private places.

As a slave reached for the drapes I heard the muffled, unintelligible sound of Keril, praying in that heathen version of our language. For himself, alone. When I stepped through he stopped at once and stared at the floor. So his prayers were for his comfort. I, in person, didn't matter, it was his gods who were important.

I felt frustrated, and don't say it! Give in? Acknowledge that his gods had had him first? Return him to whatever distant temple he had come from?

Damned if I'd do that either, even if I ever found it. I'd thought, at times, my father and I had not that much in common, but one thing we did: we neither of us ever turned our backs on what we wanted. It was a revelation, to see that I wanted Keril the way my father coveted another kingdom added to the empire. There would be no peace till this was settled. Hang the gods, he was in *my* possession.

Anger I'd held in check for days erupted. "Do you know what I can *do* with you?"

"I think so, my lord. I was told I could be punished, if you were angered." There was a heaviness about him, lack of sleep was showing.

My anger didn't leave but it retreated. "By who?"

"The gentleman called Medishel. He told me."

I'd bet he had. Give the old gote points for trying, even when he didn't see the reason. "Did you understand the things he told you?"

"Yes, my lord." I thought his shoulders sagged.

"Good. Then you'll drop this silliness, and do as I command you?"

"My lord, I can't."

"Because of your teachers, or these gods of yours? You still think they protect you?"

The pale head came up again. "I must," he whispered. "My masters said I'm meant. I was intended… I was…"

"Am, or was?" I threw his own words back at him. I'd seen the first crack in the wall he'd built around himself. And then, when maybe I could have made a telling blow, Medishel had to stroll in.

The whole tense moment slithered into limbo. How could I be seen talking religion with a half-crazy slave? I was getting enough strange looks as it was.

Ashamet, Desert Born

So it dragged on after that for two more days. By then I'd made up my mind I'd gag the fool, and take him that way. It might have worked. Well, something had to. But I thought of that very late, when I was almost asleep myself, and come the morning Keril lay, his back to me, his head down on my hearthstone, arms bent up to where that chain was tethered. Fast asleep? Yes, sleeping, and so tired after all the times he'd stayed awake he hadn't woken when I moved this time. He hadn't moved a muscle.

Chapter 2

The small evening fire was long cold, the day's heat no more than a promise. I edged across the bed and reached for a robe. I could hear faint noises rising through the air from more distant portions of the palace as the day began for those below us, but the room around me seemed to hold its breath.

I was holding mine by then, but he still didn't stir. He even looked quite peaceful. I think I frowned. He lay on his side, head and shoulders on the hearth, breathing evenly. Somehow, flat cushions had found their way beneath his head, cream silk that blended with the pale marble underneath them. Keril? No, I thought at once, he wouldn't look for comfort, much less steal it from my couches. But who else would dare to pamper him when he was being punished?

Medishel, decide to give a slave a bit of luxury? I almost chuckled then remembered not to. Instead I crept across the floor, as silent as a slave on my bare feet, marble cool and slick beneath them in between the carpets.

He doesn't pray while he sleeps, a demon in me whispered. I took the key down from the ledge, too far above for him to reach it, then I knelt. Bent forward. Still no movement from him. I released his shackles, hardly breathing as I eased the chain free link by link and laid it on a stretch of carpet so it wouldn't clink against the tiles.

Still no reaction. I eased the curtain of his hair aside, let my fingers trace the shape of head and neck, hesitated at the broad curve of a shoulder. Keril sighed, then slept on.

I was a practiced lover. Other males have praised me. I used all I knew to good effect that morning. My hands were slow and gentle and each time he stirred I stopped, to let him settle. I was breathing deeper. Was it possible, to rouse a male, yet not to wake him? It was, in fact, a challenge. I kept tight control. Even so it pleased me. I was breathing in that perfume. Touching him, arms, shoulders, back, stroking the warm flesh was like drinking good wine; it heated the body, made the blood run freer. I bent and kissed his neck.

Ashamet, Desert Born

He moved. I held my breath. His side fetched up against my knee. One hand swung outward, clutching air, his ribcage shifting underneath my fingers. Then he moaned, so quietly I almost missed it. My own body was responding too by then, making more urgent demands. That silver cord so near my hand was once again a magnet. I brushed across the flat stomach, heard him moan once more and felt the muscles ripple as he shifted underneath my hands. And then I reached, so delicate, to untie that triple knot.

This time I made it past them all. My hand, inside those silks, found more than I'd expected. More, and growing! Elated now, I traced the outline of him with my fingertips, then, driven by need myself, I found his balls and cupped them, stroked them. Harder. I had him now. He couldn't think to argue this time.

A gasp, the grey eyes wide and startled. Shock, then fear? I held on, eye to eye. My body arched above him and my other hand was ready if I needed to subdue him. Oh, I'd have stopped his mouth this time all right.

Raw breathing. Sudden, total waking. Shaking. Then he jerked helplessly under my hands, and I felt the throbbing pulse that meant he'd come to peak before I'd wanted.

"What?" His body shook all over and his face… There was a kind of horror. Despair too maybe? No, more like shock. A shock so deep… I stared down at him. Not touched, he'd said. I'd understood. Or thought I had. But his expression was revealing more, much more. This wasn't just about what I'd done, was it? Unbelievably, it was about what his own flesh was doing, without his knowledge. Without his… understanding? How in seven hells could he have lived this far without some notion?

Logic wasn't helping. I decided to revert to instinct. "Easy, Keril, easy now. This is all normal. You're a male, that's all. It's part of being a male."

His eyes were haunted. Gods knew what he could be thinking. All of a sudden he twisted in my grasp. I thought to get free of me, but then he was as sick as any drunkard, spewed up all over both my sleeve and a very costly carpet. I grabbed his shoulders, hard, and let him run his course before I shouted.

By the time the first slave bolted in, and out again for reinforcements, I was on my feet and clear of the mess. And Keril was a mess, no doubt about it. He was still shaking too. Badly. And still no sign of Medi. Anxious now, I grabbed a cup and forced a dose of spirit down him. He gagged, and shivered, and tried to bring all that back up as well.

Imagine it, what Medishel saw when he finally stumbled in: his prince, soiled, scowling like thunder, crouched over a wretched body slave.

Wretched indeed. Sprawled at his master's feet, half-raised on trembling elbows, his head hung in complete exhaustion. Apart from all that the room stank like the city sewers. The sour smell of vomit overlay the rest of it; sweat and sex and brandy. Keril was wet through, in every way one could imagine.

Drained, and gasping, and still shuddering violently.

Small wonder Medishel stopped in his tracks. He looked appalled. I had a crazy urge to burst out laughing. Gods knew what kind of orgy they were picturing, and in all this I still hadn't actually— I choked back the mirth, and tried—gods, tried—to put some dignity back into events. "Clean him up," I said. "Then, bring him back." One battle didn't win a war, now did it? Let him count himself lucky for the breather. I'd finally had a taste of him, and I wanted the rest; now more than ever. I went off to bathe—I needed it too— and left them to deal with the state I'd caused them.

Bathing brought a very welcome ray of sunshine into the proceedings for it seemed to me the outline of the En-Syn on my upper arm had weakened. Very slightly, it was true; the merest hint of fading, but enough to make me notice. Cheered, I left the bath with energy, and appetite, renewed. I knew exactly how I'd use them.

But they were still removing carpets, washing tiles. There was no sign of Keril but the atmosphere was brittle and the room was flooded with the scent of all the lemons they were using, fighting with the blossom from the opened shutters. It felt undignified, to wait about till they were done. He'd be returned when I came back that evening. Even have a chance to think, while he was left alone, and in the place he had discovered what his body was designed for.

Chapter 10

In the end my return was a lot later than I'd intended, half the night lost dealing with urgent dispatches. Naturally Keril had remained awake as well, resisting his exhaustion.

The silver chain was back in place, as ordered. He was looking at the flames again when I walked in. Behind me, slaves pulled at the curtains then their footsteps dwindled quickly. Within the darkened room I caught a whiff of incense from the shadows; something soothing.

"Calmed down, have you?"

A slight frown. The shoulders were slumped. He didn't face me. It *looked* like defeat, but I'd learned not to assume.

"Still think your gods protect you?" I taunted him. Well, why should I think of being kind? It wasn't me had found release that morning. "Still think they have any say about what happens to you?" Yes, I pushed him.

"They. I. Yes. My lord," he added. Far too well mannered, even now? Me, I'd have sworn, but *he* remembered to address his lord correctly?

"Oh? They could have stopped you being captured?"

"If I wasn't meant to be." He'd said that with new confidence, a return of some conviction. *Not* what I'd wanted.

"Stopped your being given to me? Stopped me touching you, as you so delicately phrased it?"

The "yes" this time was just a whisper. I sensed an opening and pushed the knife in deeper. "Then, if you're right, that means they didn't want to stop me. Does it not?"

His head came up and he started to tremble, though I didn't think he knew it.

I tossed him the key again. I still don't know what made me do that. "Here, and get up. You make my neck ache, craning it to look at you down there." I sat by the fire, made myself comfortable in a chair. When he rose I waved across at the tray. "Be useful for once and fetch me wine, instead of causing me unnecessary trouble."

He obviously didn't know one drink from another. When I didn't think to speak he poured out brandy.

Well, why not, I thought; except he hadn't picked the glass up yet. "What is it this time? Can't do anything without your gods to guide you?"

All right, it wasn't kind, or tactful. Since when have either been due a slave? Besides, I was tense, and not as certain as I sounded. So of course I pushed; it's in my nature. Wasn't I entitled?

His hand went out over the tray. Ah, at last, I thought. Brandy wasn't so bad a choice, at that. Then he poured a second one, and drank it!

I think—of course I couldn't see—my mouth fell open. Give him my brandy once, he thought he could help himself? He choked on it again, but it stayed down this time. To my astonishment another, following straight after, went down even faster. Then he drew a shaky breath—it must have felt like fire—and leaned his hands against the table. I could hear him breathing faster. Working up to something?

"I sent you for a drink," I said, pretty sharp.

I doubt he even noticed the tone. Four measures, was it? And he was certainly no drinker. In fact I was impressed how straight he walked when he carried my glass over; didn't spill a drop either. He stood beside me, not quite looking at me.

"Feeling better?" I took a sip. Gods, it was the Sultaki as well, the most potent thing on the table.

"No, my lord." If there was a slurring you'd have had to listen hard to spot it.

"No? What is it this time?"

"I… am changed," he said, rather carefully.

I laughed out loud at that one. "You are, aren't you? You were free, I'd reckon, not so long ago, and now you're mine to order. You were a babe in arms, for all your years, and now you're growing up too fast for comfort. You believed—" I broke off there. Even in this mood I wasn't that cruel.

"I believed, and I have come… to this." His head swung round, examining the lofty room, and all its luxuries, as if he'd never noticed them till now. The sudden move disturbed what I'd already judged was a deteriorating sense of balance. Drink I understood. Fatigue as well; it would have left him weaker. This time he swayed, caught the back of my chair, stared at it—then seemed to think another drink might cure the ones he'd had already. I chose not to comment, took a second sip and watched him tread a gently-curving path across the room with real interest.

This one didn't go straight down, at least. The first swallow was enough to free his tongue. "I thought." He frowned into the glass. "I thought I was meant to come here. I trusted." There was pain in those words.

"Betrayal?" I said slowly. "Is that what's eating at you?"

He turned toward me. Lost. Worse, deserted. "I obeyed. I let my instinct draw me, as I should. I trusted." He almost sobbed. "I didn't know I'd be asked… asked." Another swallow.

"What's done is done." I shrugged. It had never worked with me but it was worth a try.

"What's done… I fear I am defiled. Ruined. My mind… my body."

So that was it. "Since both belong to me now, you will be whatever I command you."

"Then." He waved the glass. "That means…?" He shuddered suddenly and took another hefty gulp. "Your hands, or my forbidden thoughts, what does it matter which destroys me?"

"Say that again." I rose and crossed the room. "Do you know what you just said?"

"Did I say something?"

"You said." I took the glass away and set it on the table then I raised a hand and stroked his cheek. "That being touched, like this, aroused you." What was that scent Medi had picked out? I could hardly smell it for the brandy but it made me think of pine cones mixed with roses. It suited him but I still didn't recognize it.

He hadn't moved. "Did I?" he said doubtfully.

"Is that where your mind has been since morning?" I looked in vain for a reaction. "Reliving what you woke to? Realizing that you… wanted? Did you want this?" I caught my hand under his chin, raised it slightly, and kissed him.

The grey eyes blinked. The lips had parted.

"Never waste an opportunity," I said, "or so my uncle told me." I kissed him again, and pushed those lips wide open.

Sweet. As I'd imagined. Slow, and lingering, my other hand behind his neck, our bodies still not touching.

"Oh."

It could have meant anything, but I chose my own translation. I took his arm and tugged. He almost toppled that time. If he hadn't had me to lean on he'd never have made it as far as the bed. Hells, when he fell back against my pillows he was as relaxed as half a flask of Sultaki brandy can make a male. He just lay there blinking at me.

"You don't need those." I gestured at his white silk trousers.

"Don't I?"

I laughed, and shook my head. He looked surprised when I freed the silver cord, and when the silk pulled away, so smooth, he actually looked puzzled. "Now, I'm going to shed this robe." I paused deliberately. Did he understand? At all?

Without the robe the only thing that left me less than naked was that cursed armlet. It was a weight. I didn't want to scratch that skin. I hesitated then remembered Keril wouldn't understand the scrawny shape behind it, let alone be free to talk about it, so I tossed the thing aside for once. It startled him. The grey eyes widened. Gods, but he was beautiful.

The bed was wide enough for twice as many. Six could manage, actually. I knew that for a fact. We barely needed half of it. His head descended on my shoulder. I ran my hands over him lightly, enjoying the amazing skin, the hollows, muscles, and smooth warmth. Savoring the triumph when he shivered. "Not so bad this time?" I asked, my mouth against his earlobe.

"No-o." A sigh. The blinking was getting worse. "I'm tired," he said suddenly, as if the fact surprised him.

"You're drunk as well." But I was smiling.

"Drunk?"

"Too little sleep and too much brandy. You'll be out of it in seconds. Shall I play the host, and let you sleep a little?"

No reply.

"Keril? Hey." I laid my hand on his thigh, and slid it higher.

"Yes, my lord?" Drowsily.

"This is what you wanted. Admit it."

"This is…" His voice faded, his eyelids lowered. I grinned and settled back into my pillows, wondering how long to leave him.

Chapter 11

Dawn crept through the lattices and woke me. Somebody had tiptoed in to douse the lamps and draw the bed-curtains around us. Had I slept that soundly? Not like me to do so with a stranger. Still, no harm done.

There were distant sounds but all was quiet here. Scents invaded as the flowers outside unfurled their petals, threatening the subtler scent of Keril still asleep beside me. I wondered belatedly how hard a Sultaki hangover would hit someone so unused to drink, then couldn't resist reaching to push a lock of the long hair aside. Had I pulled it loose, or had it loosened itself?

Kadduchi hair was black, and very straight. His tried to curl around my fingers. There was still no sign of stubble; he was genuinely beardless, like the Kemik. No chest hair either. So *smooth*. I propped myself with pillows as the light increased, and studied him in careful, self-indulgent detail.

Tall like me, but skin and hair astonishingly lighter. On impulse I laid my hand beside one of his on the sheet. The sheet was a pale blue. My copper coloring looked good against it; better than his. It turned him blue-ish where the sunlight made him shadowed. Black sheets, I thought. Black silk, or maybe chocolate, or royal crimson. The image was like fever and I wanted him awake. My hand went out, and then drew back. He looked so… peaceful.

So I looked a while longer. His hair was the color of one of my favorite mares, a soft brown with the feel of grey about it. I'd never seen the color, ever, on a male. Nothing like it. Where in all the heavens had he come from? Sheshman must have travelled far beyond our kingdoms. Which suggested that the old rogue was a deeper puzzle than I'd guessed at. Worth seeing more of? Why not, I thought lazily, he'd always been amusing. And it takes brains, quite often, to amuse me. That, or courage.

"Uh?" Half groan, half sigh. The head rolled on the pillows. Grey eyes opened, blinked then stared up into mine. A long hand pushed the fine hair back again. I noted idly that the hand looked strong, the wrist as well.

It didn't seem important at that moment.

"Sleep well?"

"Yes… I think so."

Confused? Probably couldn't remember how he'd got from hearth to mattress. Would he recall the rest, or was that gone as well?

"So how's the head?"

"My head? It's fine, my lord. I think." No trace of understanding. Nor of wincing.

"Nothing wrong at all?" I didn't believe it.

"I do feel thirsty," he decided, after he'd watched me doubtfully and given the question due attention. "At least, my mouth is dry."

Only thirsty? After all that brandy? Maybe his gods were watching over him, at that. "There's water over on the table."

"Yes, my lord." But he didn't move. Just lay there looking up at me. Still didn't move when I pushed the single sheet aside, and left his stomach naked. The hair down there curled slightly too. When I looked up again his eyes were clear, no sign of panic. Or of horror. Just… uncertainty.

"You *are* mine." I said evenly. "You understand that now."

"Yes, my lord." His breathing was a little faster.

"Mine, to do with as I please?" I leaned in closer.

"My… lord." The words were jerky this time.

"And if I take pleasure of you, that will please you too now, won't it?"

He licked dry lips, then raised his hand until it brushed my shoulder. Eyes fixed on mine, he tried to smile. "I… hope so."

I couldn't hold back any longer. I pulled him closer, ran my hands along the narrow hips and down the spine to cup—He froze. "Relax, I'll show you what to do." When he began to gasp the sound enflamed me. "Keril," I said urgently, "I'm in a hurry. *Do* you understand me?"

A moan for answer.

"Keril, it may hurt a little. If it does, that's normal. Don't be frightened this time."

"I'm… not afraid."

A bare-faced lie, I thought, and wholly unconvincing, but I didn't say so. He was trembling but he seemed determined. "I have oil. That helps." I stretched a hand out for the bottle waiting by the bedside, tipped a little on his stomach, set the thing aside and smiled as I recognized its perfume. Keril's eyes had widened, more so when I pushed the liquid lower. "Makes it easier," I said. I turned him on his side and swiped the oil past his balls then up behind. He jerked. "That's where it needs to go. All right?" If any gods *were* listening they had to give me points for patience.

His mouth half-opened, then he nodded.

Ashamet, Desert Born

I took patience as my watchword but eventually... He cried out when I entered him. Males boast of conquests, of the rush of blood, the crashing of the senses. I had had a host of males, but none like Keril. This was different; hot and cold at once, a shivering inside me that exploded in both head and stomach. Both of us were gasping, but I pulled him close, his back against my chest, and held him till he quietened, savoring my triumph, feeling... "Gently now," I said. "It's done. It's over."

"I'm... all right." He sounded so surprised.

I chuckled. "Yes, you are. Now sleep a little."

When his breathing steadied I pulled the sheet over him and slid from the bed. While he fell into sleep as suddenly as a child, I felt wide awake, and ready for my breakfast. Ready for anything the world threw at me!

For histrionics? Me? I was too old for such foolishness. I threw on the cursed armlet then a robe and strode out. But I couldn't wholly wipe the smile away, even when Medi's eyes widened.

"Breakfast." I'd tried to sound stern. It clearly hadn't worked.

"Breakfast, yes, my prince, at once." His eyes darted to the curtains behind me.

"Let him sleep. Make sure he eats later." Laughter welled. "He's earned it."

Medi beamed. "My prince is pleased?"

"Your prince is starving." Medi's signal sent slaves running. "And there are matters needing his attention."

Right, get a grip, I thought, starting to eat. Stalking Keril had been a distraction, a momentary madness, but add in the whole marriage period and I'd spent far too long half out of the loop. Well, that was over. I was back, as sane as ever, ready to take charge again. By now, with any luck, Father would have found out who was behind the feeble lines I was hiding under this armlet. I could deal with the culprits and my life would once again be normal.

Unfortunately palace life was never that simple. I returned to the world, fired up for action, only to learn my father was in the Gate Hall, presiding over the first of this year's public audiences. Worse, Medi said apologetically, *I* was required to yawn through them as well and—no one being brave enough to wake me earlier—I was likely to be late. A pointed message from my father threatened; better hurry.

Under the circumstances I expected snatching a private word with my father to be difficult, and it was. I couldn't get a word in all that day, or evening. So I had a watch kept on his doors next morning.

By the time I ran downstairs and out, Father had opted for strolling the garden paths rather than the colonnade around the sides. This early, most of the plants were still wet with dew, the birds caroling the coming of daylight; it offered him a brief tranquility before the mayhem. Shame to spoil it, but…

A quick bow. "Father." And straight to the point. "Any news about..?" I twitched my arm.

"And a pleasant morning to you too, Ash." Father smiled at my impatience but he waved his own attendants off to a discreet distance. "I thought you wouldn't wait much longer. In a word, nothing."

"Nothing at all?"

My father shrugged, a gesture he would never make in public. "I'm assured there are only two priests entrusted with the secret of melding gold and gems to flesh, and if they'd been ordered they couldn't have done it that day; they were definitely seen attending ceremonies in the temple." We reached the gated entry and descended to the tunnels beneath Rag's chambers. Once inside our footsteps echoed and we lowered our voices as we had a hundred times before, so that the louder echoes of our feet would hide our words from others.

Father filled me in. During my enforced absence his eyes and ears had scoured the palace, and the city, for a hint of intrigue: a lordly plot not yet reported; lesser things like subtle craftsmen new in town, experiments among the jewelers, or a suddenly ambitious section of the priesthood.

"Nothing," Father sighed, "except." A gesture of apology. "It looks as if my interest might have alerted the High Priests. I'm told *their* spies are sniffing round the palace more than usual."

"A thousand—" I muted my reaction as the curse rebounded off the tiles. Priests getting "interested" was all I needed.

"Quite." Another shrug. He was really letting his hair down. "But it is a curious detail. If they knew, why would they bother?"

The second gate swung at our approach. Past these guards, we had a short walk across open ground then we climbed the shaded outer stairs that led to the entrance of the hidden gallery that took us to the Gate Hall's dais. After that our privacy was over. I considered his reaction. He'd begun to doubt the priests' guilt? I hadn't, but if Father was now treating the matter as more annoyance than threat I *was* inclined to join him that far. With Father on my side my dithering subsided. Hiding the En-Syn scratches had been easy enough. I was becoming more angry than scared.

It had to be the priests though, surely. They were just covering up. The only real question left was how they'd reached me undetected, and that I *had* to have an answer to. I hadn't reached thirty by being universally loved, whatever people said in public. If nobody had ever got to me in my home before, it was because I'd made damned sure they couldn't. "I'll question Medi again,"

Ashamet, Desert Born

I said quickly. And the war-trained eunuchs at my doors and stairways, and the robe-slaves in my uppermost apartments. Someone must know something.

Father merely nodded; we had reached the dais. Clerks flocked round us as we took our seats. The Gate was opened on the day's agenda.

Anyone could ask my father's judgment at such times, they turned up in their hundreds. Anyone he called for was obliged to sit here in the Gate Hall to "advise". Since Rag had returned north, where he governed, as soon as the wedding was over, it inevitably fell to me this time to be the high class decoration, like the lesser gods were in the temples, though I swear the clerks were far more use than I was. The wonder was I didn't fall asleep from sheer boredom.

There was a dispute over water rights. Surprise. My mind returned to my own problems. I figured the priests knew as well as I did that their pathetic attempt wasn't remotely credible. So what next? I could see a few possibilities.

One: they'd try to persuade or even bribe me into letting them complete it. But they surely knew that bird wouldn't fly.

Two: a threat to make the subject public after all? Embarrassing for me, but surely not a strong position for the temples when the thing was incomplete and unconvincing?

Three: another sneak attack in an attempt to finish it. I'd like to see them try.

I realized the male currently arguing his case had swallowed visibly, and mended my expression. The High Priests were the enemy, not him. Killing *them*, now that would settle the matter. Except I wasn't sure all three were guilty.

Even unsure, I was tempted. It was such a neat solution. But my father wouldn't wear it, so looked like I was stuck with acting innocent, and doing nothing.

Glancing at the next in line I saw five males in threadbare clothes. No lords or merchants these, perhaps a village deputation? Kadd, and Southerners as well. I was diverted. It was my job to keep the south in order but a village normally petitioned to its region's overlord for justice. Ah. That left me only one conclusion.

They shuffled forward when the clerks directed them but then they stuck, their faces frightened rather than expectant, looking round them at the walls, the vaulted ceiling way above, the Kemik guards, whose looks alone must daunt them never mind their weapons. Four looked anxiously toward the fifth, their spokesman, who bowed until his nose was level with his knees then straightened up and stared, transfixed. The setting and the company had made him speechless.

I put a hand before my face. It was amusing but there was no need to show it. Every male who dared to face his king should be respected, not made mock of. Not unless they earned it. So for once I found myself in sympathy. I mean, a homespun village headman in the fabled Gate Hall, faced with giants and lords and most of all his Voice of Heaven on the starry throne? How could he not be scared? And what was serious enough to bring him?

The fellow found his voice at last and spoke the magic words. "My king, we suffer from a desert lion."

A lion? They were rare these days. I straightened up. There'd always been a royal bounty, but the desert was an endless hiding place and it was years since anyone had claimed it. I'd been lucky; I had faced one in my teens—I hadn't been allowed close in, alas—but most males only knew them from the illustrations in a hunting manual, or from the famous hanging in the entrance to the outer palace where the creature's bony mane and iridescent scales had been stitched in silks and sequins, and its poisoned tongue lashed out above an armored, gold-crowned hunter with heroic muscles.

The headman stumbled through his tale. His king was patient with him; more than I was. I had energy to spare, I had to stop my fingers tapping and restrain myself from interrupting. These villagers had begged their overlord for aid but he had left them to it? I swear I felt my father stiffen there above me. And now they'd lost a child and desperate, at least they said, had travelled to the palace. How could this be true, and yet if not, how could they dare to say it? At the least my father would be asking pointed questions. At the worst…

I glanced toward the throne. The south was my responsibility. This was one problem I *could* settle. Above, my father caught my eye and nodded in agreement. We would split this task between us. He would scrutinize their lord, while I, the lucky one, would hunt the lion!

Chapter 12

It was mid-morning when we heard the story. That day was lost in preparation but it wasn't wasted. I decided on a demi-troop of Kemik for some muscle and a team of royal hunters headed by a tough old hound called Sota, who had been my father's choice to guard me on my early hunts and teach me how to stalk a quarry. "A desert lion," I said. "A killer seemingly." The male's eyes brightened, it would be a prize to boast of.

By the time everything was organized it was after dark. My original plans for that night had included Keril, but if I didn't get some sleep I'd be useless tomorrow. Ah well, work before play, especially when the work was so attractive. Besides, he was a dish to savor, not to gobble, I consoled myself. The wait would make it all the sweeter. So I left him in whatever corner he was housed in now and slept alone, eventually.

Rising early, I rode downhill from the royal stables to the Kemik barrack yard to find my fifteen Kemik gathering, and Sota and his huntsmen lounging in a quiet corner. Well apart from both I saw the village headman and his strapping son were waiting too, as ordered. I was bringing them to guide our final steps. Apparently their village didn't have a proper name, at least not one my clerks could find on any of my map-scrolls.

The headman swore the two could ride. I hoped so. Using local guides would get us there to deal with the threat much faster. Their companions I had left to travel at the pace their cart could manage sticking to the roads behind us.

That would be well behind. Each male with us would lead a second mount; by trading off between the two they'd travel faster. Myself, I'd brought two extra mounts, and a groom. It might be self-indulgent but my horses needed workouts, and besides it would be such a shame if someone closer got that lion before me. So we'd ride hard, which meant our guides' ability to ride remained in question. Well, if all else failed we'd have to tie them to their saddles!

It looked like Sota and his team were ready, lounging to one side, their horses saddled. The Kemik troopers had their mounts in order. Peaceful at the moment, they had left the dainty-looking fluted horns between the horses' ears uncovered, though I knew they would have packed the metal caps that made the horns an even greater weapon, just as I had. They had packed their polished copper elbow-greaves away as well, and had their burnished, cone-shaped helmets slung behind their necks. The dust-scarves tied to every helmet showed a slew of tribal colors, personal additions to their uniforms their law demanded. I had seen these fly like banners when they galloped into battle, stirring sight, but now the scarves were lifeless, hanging off their brawny shoulders or behind them in the space between, where scabbards crossed and held a pair of curving broadswords. Their crimson capes and plated tunics had been stowed behind their saddles too. That left them in their crimson under-tunics, padded at the shoulders, over loose black trousers. Polished boots, and leather gauntlets stuffed in padded sashes, opposite their heavy daggers, finished off a pleasing picture. As always they looked practical, and disciplined, but then the Kemik had no need to make a show. Their reputation did that for them.

Their captain, Semmit, easily distinguished by the jagged scar across his forehead, stood across the yard where grooms were bringing out four extra horses for the two villagers. He hadn't seen me yet so I reined in and watched unnoticed, signaling my groom to wait behind me. If they weren't up to this...

The horses being led were decent stock, a world above a village carthorse. Kemik-trained as well, no easy option. The village males had turned to watch. I sidled closer. Both were staring and the father had gone still. "You're putting us on these, sir?"

"If you can handle them." Semmit, understandably, was looking doubtful.

But the headman found a twisted smile. "We'll manage, Captain. It'll be a pleasure, though I doubt you'll think it's pretty. It's been years since I rode a decent animal, while for my son, it's what he's dreamed about but I could never give him."

My ears had pricked. The captain asked it for me. "So when did you ride anything like these?"

"I did my five," the headman told him proudly. Ahah, I thought, ex-army. Older, yes, but he'd have ridden hard back then, it wasn't easily forgotten. I relaxed a notch. He'd manage. What about the son though?

The cub was edging forward. He'd forgotten we were here; all he saw was horses. They'd given him the gentlest they could find, but Kemik mounts were big. They had to be. I wasn't sure the cub would have the strength they needed even if he had the courage.

Tall enough, I thought. Long-legged. Clear-skinned. A yellow tinge suggested some of his forebears had come from further south. Or maybe just a tiny dash of Kemik in there somewhere? Sixteen summers, maybe; legally an adult, old enough to make the journey here but probably his first real city? He was slighter than his thickset father but with farmers' muscles in the arms and shoulders. And, it dawned on me, it wasn't only me who'd noticed. Kemik too were looking.

Old Sota chose that point to saunter up and bow, then stand at ease beside my stirrup. "My prince." He glanced across at the lad. "A pretty morsel."

I shrugged. "Not bad, but I was thinking more that Kemik usually turn their noses up at foreign food."

"Looks like their diet's getting more adventurous," said Sota dryly. "Maybe it's the way he's staring at their horses."

"Hm." The cub had reached a hand to take the reins of one horse from its handler. Now he rubbed the gelding's nose. It didn't try to gore him. So far so good, but Kemik mounts could be a handful.

Beside me Sota stiffened. "Careful, lad," he muttered.

The horse played dumb until the cub had one foot in the stirrup and the other in the air, then it started turning, fast. By that time every rider in the yard had stopped what they were doing. What happened next was going to be very public. The father stood there with a closed expression. Yes, I thought, the cub has no idea, but the father knows he's being measured.

But the cub was quick. His leg swung over and he kicked the brute, just lightly, telling him to behave and for a miracle the horse decided to oblige. The cub reined in and turned toward his father, flashing him a brilliant smile. That finished it. The males around me practically sighed with pleasure. He was a novice really—willing but ungainly—but his heart was in the saddle. No, he wasn't all that big, or noticeably handsome, but put him on a horse and he was gloriously happy, and it seemed that made him irresistible to Kemik.

The father saw. His smile of approval faltered as it might well do; his son had just been tossed into a pack of wolves that could decide he was the lamb they'd have for dinner. Time to take a hand? I nudged my mount toward them.

If they'd stared at all the livestock here they gaped at mine, but then I don't suppose they'd seen such horseflesh even from the lord they bowed to. The way they acted, neither one remembered who *I* was. The cub was lost in wonder but his father made a clumsy bow while raking over every detail of my dress, my horses and the single groom behind me. Not that I was all that splendid; light blue robe, a plain brown sash, a blue and yellow headdress, simple boiled-leather scabbards for my sword and dagger. Practical, not ostentatious.

I could almost see him thinking it: the finest horses but no slaves, no company of any status? He'd almost frowned. A noble, he'd decided. Royally related, otherwise the Kemik wouldn't be here, but perhaps a lesser line, a rough and ready sort but competent enough to run a royal errand. Oh yes, his face showed due respect but in his heart he had dismissed me. Much too easily.

"Ready, Captain?" I enquired sweetly.

Semmit bowed. "When you are, highness."

The headman's mouth fell open. That'll teach you, I was thinking, thank the Ancestors I'm in a pleasant mood this morning. "Let's move then."

The captain called his demitroop to order. Four took point and rode toward the gate to lead us through the city. The others circled, waiting for the rest to fall in line ahead of them. The rearguard had a sergeant with them, a younger, better-favoured fellow than his captain; glossy skin and flashing smile; but the males obeyed him quickly.

Sota brought his team behind me as the captain came to join us. My groom, Jaffid, fell in behind the hunters, handling the three spare mounts, all highly bred and fresh, with all the ease that only comes from growing up with horses. It was a pleasure just to watch him work. I nodded briefly in approval, to which he bowed impassively across the saddle.

Impassive was a good word for Jaff. So was deceptive. Quiet, well-mannered, from a line of royal stablemen, he was well into his twenties now, still slightly built, still almost delicate-looking, with big brown eyes and a warmth in his smile—if you ever saw it—that more than compensated for the plainness of his features. He'd be my eyes and ears on this trip, and take my findings back to Father.

Meanwhile the village headman swung up onto one of his allocated horses, stiffer than I'd like but still a rider. "Ammet," he said sharply. His son looked round. "This way." He jerked his head.

"This way" was firmly sandwiched in between the hunters and my extra horses. I suppressed a smile. Away from all the Kemik? And from me as well? Relax, he's safe, from me at least, I thought. I wasn't mightily attracted now I thought about it. But the Kemik…

When Semmit waved us off, the lower gates swung open noisily, hooves clattered on the line of stones that lay between them. I had the massive Semmit on my left, the scrawny Sota on my right, so under cover of the noise I smiled and spoke into the air between them. "Let's treat our villagers with due politeness, shall we, gentlemen? I doubt they're used to such attention."

Sota snorted. Semmit found a bland expression. "Certainly, my prince." The warning was delivered, and acknowledged.

By midday we had left the city for the open road. Despite the awning-palms routinely planted by the wayside it was hot and dusty; pausing at a reasonable inn to take a well-earned break was very welcome. By then my words had gotten round and I was hiding my amusement. What might have been a stalking contest—Kemik having somewhat rougher customs than Kadduchi—had become a courtship dance, a test of pretty manners.

Lounging, glass in hand, beneath the tarnished fringes of the canopy outside the inn, I figured half the guards had given up the minute they discovered I had deigned to notice but the other half were being circumspect; no threats of force or blunt demands, not even blatant invitations. Nothing I could possibly object to. But there were a lot of glances. First one warrior and then another had encouraged the young Ammet on the road, or offered him advice, experienced rider to a novice.

Ammet was a little flushed, but that could be the ride, and seemed to like the regular attention. Ammet's father watched in silence, looking thoughtful. He saw the game all right but hey, the cub was old enough and it was plain by then they were behaving nicely. In fact I thought the father was probably more concerned about whether my friendly instructions to play nice might mean the scruffy prince commanding them had formed an interest in his offspring. A common lad did not refuse a lord's attentions, even less a prince's, not without a solid reason.

That was when I realized I really wasn't tempted, not at all. He was too young, I thought, too… coarse. I thought of saying so to put the father's mind at rest, but then he might regard that as an insult so I left him to it. Besides, it was an unforeseen amusement; a seduction scene to while away the journey till more interesting action beckoned. How long before the cub became aware he'd set so many giant hearts aflutter?

According to the map their village occupied a valley south and east of us, a fertile little pocket only separated from the desert proper by an ironstone ridge that sheltered it enough to keep the desert storms from ruining their crops and smothering their soil. But not enough to keep them from a hungry lion at the height of summer. Odds were the thing had burrowed through into some hidden cavern that had led it deeper. Coming out again it must have been surprised to find its world so altered, barren sand exchanged for fields and netted orchards.

According to the headman—Micah, he was called—it was eleven days since they had left their village. It took us four to get him back there, lightly laden, trading mounts and using inns along the way for food and shelter. Each time we stopped the captain used his badge to commandeer us service. Every red-doored inn and every private house was bound to take us, but they'd be repaid. I tossed a coin or two besides so we were doubly welcome; males and horses royally fed and watered. Fare our villagers weren't used to, I suspected. I was having thoughts about that village.

Meanwhile Micah couldn't work me out at all. His jaw had dropped a second time the first night out when I had joined the other males to tend my horses. He was uncomfortable with a prince beside him in the stable. But Jaffid had five horses in his charge as well as riding, and my mounts were bred to be an even bigger handful than the Kemiks'. They could cause a deal of trouble, even injury, if left to amateurs. Much safer if I took a hand. Besides, it loosened stiffened muscles and ensured I slept, however poor the mattress. And it kept me up to date with Ammet's doings once his father wasn't there to watch him.

On the second night our handsome sergeant—"Fychet? Gentle with a horse but reckless in a battle," Semmit had described him—helped a tired young Ammet bring his mounts inside and lent a generous hand to groom them, tethering his own beside them in the dimmer reaches of the stable. From near the door, I watched with interest as I rubbed my second horse down, Jaffid working there beside me. People often said the Kemik were a surly lot but Fychet positively chattered now he was near Ammet.

He seemed to be explaining something. Ammet listened carefully. The cub was moving carefully as well. His body wasn't used to this sort of punishment, but he wasn't moaning. He might have made a decent rider if he'd kept it up but in a farming village, no, it wasn't likely. It would be a waste, I mused, to keep him stuck behind a plough when clearly what he loved was riding horses. I'd already noticed Jaffid looking at him with approval, and he was as good at judging males as livestock.

Ah, but Jaffid wasn't going to get a look in. The cub had dropped his brush. He bent, then winced. The gallant sergeant stopped him with a touch, knelt down and found it for him. Ammet, suddenly the taller, thanked him earnestly. The sergeant laughed and rose in front of him. The laugh was deep and rich and Ammet's eyes had widened. Fychet saw it. A casual look around the barn invited us to notice too. Keep off, the look was saying. A pair in front of me exchanged a rueful glance and shrugged. I hid behind my horse until I got my face straight. Beside me Jaffid sighed.

"You were outnumbered," I consoled him.

He blinked then grinned, his eyes upon his horse. He seldom looked at people. "Good legs, some muscle in the shoulders and his teeth are sound as well. If they'd scared him off I wouldn't have said no."

I laughed. It was entirely typical of Jaff to talk about a male as if he was a horse. As typical as thinking of a subtle ambush.

Other males were heading in for supper. One thick-set Kemik bowed extravagantly to the sergeant, openly conceding him the field of battle. In Kemik minds there didn't seem to be a doubt about the outcome now. The place grew quieter and the atmosphere relaxed, and maybe only Ammet didn't understand how things had shifted round him. Soon there were a pocket of us left toward the doors but otherwise the place was clear, except for Ammet and the sergeant in between their horses, working on the last together. Me? I worked on quietly, my movements masked by slapping tails and equine munching. It was peaceful. It was definitely entertaining; worth delaying supper.

Ashamet, Desert Born

Eventually Ammet straightened up and eased his back, and somehow knocked into the bigger male, who promptly grabbed him by the shoulder to maintain his balance. Ammet smiled and apologized. That smile…

My hand had stilled. An accident or not? Was Ammet not as blind as he appeared? Either way the Kemik's hand had tightened. Fychet murmured something, shifting round behind the cub so he could knead his shoulders, very slow and gentle. Ammet stiffened then relaxed and leaned his arms across his horse's back to keep him steady. Neither spoke. I saw the sergeant slide a hand inside the youngster's shirt. I thought the cub had shivered but he didn't stop him. The few of us still here kept quiet and left them to it. Ammet arched his neck. A darker hand caressed it and the sergeant bent to whisper in his ear.

My breathing quickened. For a moment the warm hide under my hand became pale flesh. I could even smell… The horse shifted and reality rushed back. I was a witness here, not a player. I could see the youth in profile, eyes shut tight, lips parted. Yes, I thought, and very nicely handled too. As if my thoughts were audible the sergeant jerked his head in my direction, met my eyes and seemed to see I wasn't angry. I watched as he relaxed enough to make a tiny bow in my direction then he led the youth away to supper, a proprietary hand upon his shoulder.

I was left to shake my head. A masterly seduction but I had to wonder who had been seduced. I chuckled. Was I being fanciful? I thought about the courtship as I walked across the yard toward the smell of herbs and something roasting. I was hungry. Thirsty too. It had been fun to watch such play, of course; the trouble was… But Jaffid was to hand, and might be feeling disappointed? Maybe I could cheer him up. He wasn't bad, as I remembered.

"Highness." He'd brought the brandy bottle as I'd asked. I'd downed the first half over supper. Closing the door, he poured another measure for me then, when I took it, hesitated, waiting further orders.

"Young Ammet settled for the night?" I asked. The brandy warmed my blood.

"He joined his father at the table but when the old male headed for the dormitory he stayed downstairs. A little after he and Fychet wandered off into the moonlight."

"Oh? Where to?" Everyone but me was in the common dormitory but I knew there were a few more private cubicles for hire.

Jaff's lips twitched. "My guess would be the stables."

"Not a bed? The sergeant could afford it."

"The way they were behaving earlier I'd say the horses were a bigger turn-on, highness," Jaff suggested. "All that heat as well?" His voice was smiling.

I could see his point. A stable full of horses gave off heat to beat a furnace. Warm and dark; a fair environment to take your clothes off, right enough. "It's settled then? Both sides are willing?"

"It looked it, highness." Jaff's quick smile. "Some are richer by it too."

So there had been a wager going too. I might have known. "So did you win or lose?"

"I lost, both ways." He shrugged.

"Or not," I said, and waited.

He was always quick. "My prince is always kind." He bowed and smiled, his eyes discreetly lowered, then began to take his clothes off.

Shortly after, he sat up and reached for his clothes. It hadn't needed long. For either of us. There's nothing like the sight of others getting hot to bring a male to speedy climax, and Jaff had known my need was simple. Aside from that it went unsaid that he would join the rest before they missed him. "Any orders, highness?" he said briskly in his back-to-business voice, another thing I liked about him. He wouldn't call me "my prince" again either, to betray a personal allegiance.

"Have you picked up anything about this lord of theirs refusing them protection?"

"The headman isn't talking but I got a little from the son as we were riding, in return for talk about the royal stables. According to the lad their lord's the Chief of Nusil, though I doubt the cub has ever seen him."

"Nusil. Hmm." No warrior; no courtier either though; a male about my father's age whose girth was almost equal to his height, as I remembered. With such a load he seldom travelled far from home; too fond of creature comforts. Not the brightest light we had but there was nothing worse about him, not that I had heard of. "Did he talk about the *lion*?"

"He *said*," said Jaff, "they found some tracks but weren't too certain, then a gote went missing from the fields and they found the bones a few days later. You'd know how clean a lion leaves them. So his father sent for help. It took a while because they use the old way, village passing word to village."

"And?" I raised myself against a lumpy pillow while he put his boots on.

"Says they lost another gote while they were waiting but that Nusil's guard turned up eventually. Then he stiffens up and looks away."

"To lie?"

"Not so much lie as dodge. As far as I can tell the guards arrived all right, and stayed a while too. He said they went out looking, didn't find the lion and left again. That's plain enough. It's what he doesn't say." Jaff frowned. His face looked fiercer by lamplight.

"Go on."

"I'm guessing, highness."

"Guess away."

"He doesn't talk about these guards. He doesn't *want* to. But he did let one thing slip. He said they left because "the meat was gone" but then he dropped the subject like a stone. I did ask if his father hadn't sent for help a second time before they brought it to the king. He just said no. As if —" Jaff paused to search for words. "As if it was unthinkable, which doesn't make much sense. That's all I have though, highness."

"It's enough for now. Talk to anyone you can when we arrive tomorrow. Once we have a clearer picture you can double back. The king will want to hear about it."

"Yes, highness." Jaff was buckling his sword belt, his wiry, muscled body camouflaged by clothing. Unassuming, quiet as ever. He was one of the best ears I'd ever had. It was amazing how much people told him; half the time he didn't need to ask, an inborn talent no one had uncovered yet. Until they did he was a real asset both to me and indirectly to my father.

"Go get some sleep," I said.

"Goodnight, highness." He bowed and left. I lay there in the dark and listened, but as usual I couldn't hear his footsteps. I was more relaxed but oh, I missed my pillared bed, with Keril in it.

Which was nonsense. Keril wasn't in it anyway while I was absent. I shifted slightly, readying myself for sleep. Another day would do it at the pace we'd managed so far.

Chapter 13

The light was fading as we came upon the village; early evening, not too dark to see yet but it would be in another hour, even for Kadduchi eyesight. Daylight vanished quickly this far south. No one was working in the fields outside its woven fence, nor irrigating now the heat was fading. Riding on toward the flattened hillock isolated villages traditionally built on for defense, I saw the fence above us was already closed, as if full night *had* fallen.

I almost shook my head. That fence was a modern replacement. For all its fringe of sharpened branches it was barely halfway up the mound. They must have shifted it to make the compound larger as their population increased. No doubt it was fine these days, in normal circumstances, but the present palisade was neither high enough nor strong enough to stop a lion if it made its mind up. They hadn't bothered with a watch tower any longer either, far inside our borders. It looked as if I'd have to put the captain to a quiet talk about defenses.

I could see the tops of low-roofed huts behind the fencing, their tiles sometimes brownish-grey not red. Wood tiles instead of clay? They wouldn't last, I'd spotted cracks, and gaps in places where the summer rains had rotted some. Yet still not mended? Farmers in a spot like this should have sufficient coin to pay for decent roofing.

And they'd cleared out their stocks of meat while housing Nusil's guardsmen? What was going on? My father would be very curious about such clear poverty, here in the centre of our empire. Was Micah totally incompetent or were there other, darker reasons?

Micah, unaware of my suspicions, trotted down the beaten track toward the fencing. "Ho there, who's on watch?" A head popped up then ducked. "Hey, Lek. It's me, you fool, with help. Undo the fence."

More heads poked up, peered down, then vanished. There was scuffling then several males unbarred a section, dragging it aside to leave a space a cart could enter. These were dressed no better than the headman, yet the cloth was good.

They'd had fair quality not long ago, suggesting their decline was sudden. They spoke, heads down, low-voiced, to Micah, looking nervous, shuffling behind their woven panel as they moved aside to let us through, for all the world as if they used it as a shield.

They had the higher ground. No tower should have meant a peaceful place, but suddenly it didn't feel it. Semmit took one look and sent six males in front. His face had hardened; Sota's too. Without an order Sota's males and the remaining Kemik spread around me, seasoned fighters all. They had it right but their suspicion chilled me. When had I ever had to watch my back this carefully in a *Kadduchi* village?

I said nothing yet. We rode up and in. There was the usual double ring of huts, but it was much too quiet. On watch, we headed for the centre. Being mounted gave us the advantage now we'd topped the rise but still… I scanned the nearest rooftops.

As we passed, the village males began to sidle out from hiding. No females, obviously, but no cubs either? The females' hut was visible within the inner ring, it looked to be the usual sort of structure with an open courtyard in the centre. But the outer doors, which should have been pushed back till darkness fell, were closed up tight; unspoken insult. Were the cubs hidden in there too? I counted over forty huts, but fewer folk than that suggested, and the ones that were here kept their distance.

I'd tensed. My horse reacted, shying nervously. Where were the smiles, the cheers, the bows and open-mouthed, admiring glances? Where were all the younger males and the cubs? Where were the cooking smells? The only things my nose was picking up were dust and gote and urine.

The open space inside the rings contained their well and its attendant, brick-built troughs, the life blood of a rural village. There was no fountain to the well and less than half of it had awnings, but there was a pump, its iron mouth above the highest of the water courses, as you would expect; a civilized arrangement. The higher basin was for drinking. From there the water forked into a sloping pond for washing and the narrow channel for the animals, the nearest as we entered. Our horses tossed their heads, they'd smelled the water. But their wary riders curbed them.

What else? Not much. The village had a shrine, beside the females' quarters, but it wasn't big enough to have a temple. Or a priest? I hoped not, I was happier without religion at the moment. They had a village guest-hall, longer than the houses, but the molded decoration round its door was patched and faded. Once, they'd made it bright and welcoming; they'd used it for their ceremonies, taken pride in its appearance; but they hadn't touched the molding in at least a year. The pride had died some time before they lost that child.

Past the hall there was a single, sorry-looking gote tied up in shade behind one hut. An old male had untied the animal and clearly been about to lead it off. And hide it? Caught, he stood there looking dully at me.

"Captain."

"Highness?" He was swift to answer, by his face prepared for any order I might give him.

"You'd better get them organized. I want," I looked about. "A cook fire, pots and water and some volunteer cooks." I smiled. "Let's have a party."

"Highness." Semmit grinned, a startling change, and started giving orders. I was left to wonder what he had expected me to tell him.

There's something about the smell of meat cooking over an open fire. It makes a male's mouth water and it works wonders when you need to make friends and influence people. Once the villagers believed they too would get a share of what we'd brought they came alive and foraged. Tubers came, were washed and wrapped in leaves and thrust into the embers of the spit-fire I had ordered built in the usual shallow pit, outside the hall where it would light the village square come sunset. The sleeping village woke, or say we roused it; brought out makeshift rugs to line the open space, and motley bowls and platters. Things began to look quite festive; faces brightened. Micah organized them now. I stood and watched until that old male shuffled up and offered me a stool, a luxury round here. And yes, I could have called for such, but I had waited. I suspected there'd been too much taking. So now I sat here like a lord and let events unfold around me.

It looked as if the fire would be our only light by sunset, which would not be long now. Why no lamps? I hadn't commented, nor sent anyone to search the buildings, figuring that Jaff would do that for me. He'd already gathered extra hands to help him with my horses, first among them Ammet and the sergeant, who appeared to like to work together. Those two at least might know the value of my stock. The other villagers he'd put to cleaning tack and fetching things. I thought they watched their friend with envy.

Whatever Micah told his people must have reassured them but the real shift was down to Ammet, I decided. He had made a conquest he was proud of and he naturally wanted everyone to know it. By the time the fire was crackling villagers who'd edged around our fierce troopers weren't so careful any longer and the youths the villagers had hidden had emerged as well, although a few of them looked anxious even with their elders round them.

"Will you eat now, highness?"

"Gladly, captain. Do we have enough?"

"There's ample, highness. You were right to bring so much, though how you knew… Their second harvest won't be long but as it stands right now they're near to starving." The day before he'd eyed the sudden rash of panniers and sacks with disapproval, though he'd had the sense to keep his mouth shut. Not that his expression changed much. Silent honesty was what I liked about him.

"Tell Sota and the headman they're invited over, will you?" I got up and let him walk me over to a threadbare rug that put me in the centre, with my back toward our new-swept "barracks" in the guest-hall. Jaff had fashioned me a semi-private corner by the inmost wall with rope and tent-cloth. It would do, I'd told him when he came to tell me. By now our gear was inside, unguarded, but there were twenty four of us, all armed, and offering to feed them.

So we sat outside as night came down. There was a moon to make the fire-light softer, and there was drink, for those allowed it. I had made it clear to Micah I assumed his folk would do the serving as our hosts despite the fact we'd given them the meal. My males arranged themselves accordingly around the square on empty sacks and carpets. I noted portions being taken to the females' quarters first, which argued they were capable of better manners. Ammet, called to order by his father, joined the servers, walking round their guests with confidence and thereby giving it to others. By the time we'd eaten things were getting friendly. Villagers were sitting down between these strangers. Talk had started.

Well it might, since I had given orders to be pleasant and to use the time to teach these people what was wanted come the morning. "And tonight we sleep," I'd added, looking sideways at my sergeant. He had bowed, no doubt to hide a smile, and sauntered off to break the news to all the other males, not least to Ammet. I was getting quite the gentleman, I thought, but yes, I'd give these wide-eyed village youths the time to feel safe around us. And of course I also wanted everyone well-rested.

As the evening passed I watched as Sota's males slid in among the villagers and started telling stories. Each male gathered an attentive audience and there were bursts of startled laughter. I noticed Kemik drawn as well. All well and good; the villagers were growing comfortable with the bigger males while learning something of the rules of hunting. Ammet, having pouted earlier, had joined a knot of youths a little separate. He'd been the focus of attention there. I figured by tomorrow evening any Kemik who approached such rustic fare would find a willing partner. There was nothing there I wanted though. The rest were less than Ammet. No, I didn't feel the need of further entertainment. Something in the scene was making me more thoughtful than romantic. Maybe it was all the contrasts playing out before me.

The fire was dying now, they'd bank it soon. Some villagers, less disciplined with drink, were weaving off into the darkness. Jaff appeared behind me, quiet but attentive. "Time for bed," I said, and rose. "I'll see you in the morning, gentlemen." Sota and the captain rose and bowed and so belatedly did Micah.

Smiling still, I headed for the trench against the outer fence the village dug for their latrine, with Jaff still in attendance. Naturally I was granted lordly privacy. "What have we got?" I asked him softly. It was a cloudy night, so dark back here I almost found the trench the hard way—or should that be the soft way?—but the smell forewarned me, and the sudden upward slope where earth was piled before it, waiting to be shoveled back when it was time to move it. Rustling leaves a little to my left would be the vines they'd planted in the last one.

Jaff spoke fast and low, on guard behind me, words no louder than the sounds that I was making. "These huts have nothing left of any value, highness. Not a scrap of metal anywhere I looked." So that explained the lack of lamps. "Once harvest comes again they'll manage but I doubt there's coin to buy in anything before that. As Ammet said, no meat worth mentioning. That gote's their only milker. They have only rice and vegetables and not enough of either."

"Their saviors ate them out?"

"Or took it with them. There are marks on several huts that no one wants to talk about. The younger ones." He paused. "They're scared of strangers."

"And their elders hid them from us," I completed. I rearranged myself and stepped away. "Makes sense. So Nusil's guardsmen helped themselves to food, and cubs, then left the village to its own devices once the fun was over."

Jaff said nothing.

"How far it goes will be the king's concern. You'd better leave tomorrow."

"What about the horses, highness?"

"Take your own, of course. I'll get the Kemik to attend to mine if I'm engaged. Or wait, would Ammet manage?"

Jaff thought that over as we walked toward our rustic billet. There was light enough again to see him grinning. "He'd be keen enough. Besides I doubt he'd do it single-handed."

"True." I laughed. "That's settled then. You'll tell his father?"

"Highness. I'll see he's there to saddle for you in the morning."

"Goodnight then."

"Highness." Jaffid bowed and went to look for Micah and I got myself to bed, a simple task; no bath, no curtained bed and certainly no Keril. Nothing like. Compared to him these villagers… forget it. I sighed. Bad timing, that was all. I'd only had him once before I came out here so my mind was still obsessed with conquest of the taller, whiter male and with the passion he'd engendered. Little wonder nothing here attracted when my current interest was so novel, so exotic. Till the novelty wore off I would be bound to make unfair comparisons. There was no point in trying others. For tonight at least my best recourse would be a shot of brandy for a sleeping partner.

Ashamet, Desert Born

And I feared the local fleas would think me better fare than tough-skinned Kemik. Damn. Sota would have packed an oil for that. If I had thought… but too late now. I wouldn't wake him, not at his age. He would need his rest for what was coming.

There was porridge for breakfast with bits of dried fruit for sweetening and solid enough to stick to my ribs. Ah well, I had been pampered in the palace. It would do me good to suffer.

Ammet had my horses saddled as instructed but he wasn't going to ride. I wasn't going to risk a horse. His father stayed afoot as well; his choice. He'd said it made it easier for him to lead the villagers who'd act as beaters. Last night I'd seen him nose to nose with Sota, going over what we would be doing. Nusil's males had ventured out without the villagers as backup. Amateurs, or just not trying?

With Micah's help we'd made a map. It showed the curving ridge a few miles east that kept the desert out. Its inner slopes were vines and open orchards; cover for our males but also for the lion. Micah had discovered burrows in it to the south of us before he'd left. The trouble was there might be more by now. He'd told the village to avoid the slopes and work the fields instead where it was easier to watch, and easier to run for cover. Sensible—it meant that no one else was dead when we arrived—but we were short of current information. We would have to kick our heels till Sota knew which way to aim us.

Sota and his team had left before the sun was up. His signal came midmorning, earlier than I expected, and from due south. An arrow tied with scarlet ribbons rose into the sky. The ribbons fluttered gaily in the wind as it arced toward the village. Younger children laughed and pointed. Kemik eyes grew brighter too, their teeth flashed white. That blocky fellow laughed. I liked the rare occasions when there weren't a pack of lords between us. Kemik were a fierce race but they'd retained a talent for enjoyment. "Time to move," I said and went to mount.

Chapter 14

We rendezvoused with Sota three miles out beside a decent stream that cut across the fields; probably the one that ran beneath the village. Both males and horses drank and saved their water skins for later. Sota's speech was hampered by the chewing leaf he always used in private; he was trying to finish it without me knowing. Fool, I thought, as if by now I didn't know. His teeth were stained with green, sufficient reason on its own for someone to avoid the habit, let alone the way it made his breath smell.

"There're recent tracks a mile further on whuh hill meets field, highness," Sota mumbled, "and a hole that wasn't on the map, too big f'vermin. Nearer tuh the village." He abandoned subterfuge and spat the wad of leaf aside. "The beast is getting bolder."

He meant the lion was digging in. It could have slithered back into the desert; we'd have lost it then. But it had got a taste for gote, or people.

Well, it wasn't getting us, but gote was on the menu. We had brought the last the village had. I had to wonder how they'd kept it safe before. They must have cursed when we turned up and saw it. They were cheerful now. I'd paid in coin to feed the creature to our lion; enough, if Micah used it carefully, to tide them over while they waited for my father's justice. If our plan worked perfectly they'd even get the gote back. If we could be fast enough to beat the lion to it. Otherwise they'd have to manage till they bought another. It was that or use a person to entrap the lion and that, I wasn't doing.

"One gote." I waved grandly toward the creature in the pack of villagers behind me. We had ridden slow to keep them all together. "Where would you like it?"

"Thank you, highness." Sota's voice was carefully polite in front of witnesses but he was grinning. "We'll stake it out a little further east, with your permission?"

I raised my head. The breeze was coming at me from ahead; south-easterly. The gote would be upwind of the latest burrow. "Fine."

Sota took his gote. I moved the rest a little west. Our scent would blow that way and hopefully conceal our presence. Then we sat and waited.

And we waited. Every time we heard a distant bleat our heads came up, and every time the stupid animal complained for nothing.

Still nothing when the sun was past its highest, but I'd hardly thought we'd lure the beast that easily. Such quick solutions are for children's stories, not reality. It might be days before the beast got hungry and resurfaced. I loosed my heavy leather tunic and advised myself to practice patience like my hunters. I was stuck here till we had a target, or until the night when lower temperatures would slow the lion's colder blood and put it out of action, and release us till the morning. In the meantime…

Good thing we had some shade. The open fields were baking but I'd used a stand of trees to hide us. The trees had flourished here because the villagers had dug out irrigation channels from their stream to feed the fields and a tongue of wilder orchard had crept downward from the tended woods above us. There was a mix of scents, from black-edged sooty-palms and pale green bushy-willows interspersed with spear grass. No doubt the villagers took nuts, and bark for fires, and would twist and plait the tougher leaves, for cords and mats and baskets; useful things as well as aromatic.

Every male had been rationed bread and a handful of dried fruit, and most had eaten. I had chosen solitude against a citrus tree that had escaped its fellows. There was fruit above my head—the smell was there, the usual southern graft of oranges and lemons—but nothing near ripe enough to eat yet. Everything around me said that this had been a very comfortable place, according to its lowly standards, till its peace was shattered.

I tried to settle, feeling irritated. Sota's males were gods-knew where, except that they'd be north, toward that burrow. Here, the two distinctive groups had formed two separate camps in tiny clearings, fifty paces in-between; the Kemik quiet and orderly to the north of me and Micah's lot more easterly, in an uneasy huddle. I was roughly in the middle, wondering how else to meld them all together given I had ordered quiet. There were lookouts posted but the rest of us were idle, waiting for the action. Happily, the insect life was mainly interested in the horses. Their unbound tails swished from time to time but mostly males and animals were dozing.

The hours crawled as slowly as the sweat that trickled down my back. Midafternoon I tugged a sprig or two of early watercress their foraging had missed and nibbled at it, savoring its mustardy aroma. I'd got to thinking that we might as well have waited in the village; that the lion could be resting too, holed up until the heat eased off again. I found a new position. It was peaceful though, attended by the sounds of horses, humming insects and the faintest whisper from the water. A tiny breeze was lurking somewhere—not that I could feel it, sad to say—

but I could hear it rustling the leaves not far from my position.

I sighed again. I was a spoiled brat, whatever others said. When I was in the palace I was hungry for adventure but I had to own that there were times I missed its creature comforts. Right now I could be on my balcony, a glass of wine in hand, a bowl of fruit beside me, and the rustling would be the perfumed lossi vines, or maybe Keril walking out toward me in his white silk trousers. The breeze would waft his perfume—

My eyes jerked open. That smell… wasn't perfume! My brain caught up and yanked me to my knees. There. Past the villagers. A hint of movement in the trees that wasn't breeze at all; a flash of grayish-yellow hide; a snake-like movement.

"Lion!" I ran toward the villagers. "Wake up, you fools!" Gods curse the lazy sods on watch down there, they must have nodded off. They'd left our flank wide open and the lion—

The lion had been cunning, circled round the tethered gote and looked for trouble.

By now the area before me looked as if I'd stirred a giant ants' nest. Rudely-wakened bodies stumbled every which way. Behind me I could hear Semmit bawling orders but in front the villagers were sleepy and confused.

"Fall back," I yelled. "Toward the Kemik!" Some stopped and stared at me instead! I'd lost the lion but I spotted Micah. "Micah, shift your people to the Kemik. It's behind you!"

Micah started to obey then swung toward the lion. "Ammet, no!" The idiot cub had run right past him. What the—? There. Another youth, a younger one, was going to be a hero. If I didn't shift myself he'd be a very dead one; all he had to fight with was a wooden cudgel. Ammet was beside him, tugging at his arm and shouting.

"Keep quiet," I said, or thought I did, but naturally Ammet didn't hear, or understand. I'd *wanted* noise but not so close to where I'd seen the lion. With so much movement everywhere the odds were high—I'd thought—the lion would take fright. But Ammet and his fool companion, shouting out like that, were way too close, outside the herd and all. Too tempting.

My fears were realized. The rustling increased. A second later something yellow loomed among the leaves. The youngster dropped his weapon. Ammet gasped then bent to grab the cudgel. By then I'd reached them, holding back my curses. "Back away." I shoved at Ammet, nearest.

"But," said Ammet, looking anxious. Angry as I was, I had to own the lad showed courage.

"Do it!"

The snake-like snout pushed past the nearest tree trunks. Gods, I thought—I'd had to raise my head—it had to be a big one, didn't it.

How many of these males would panic? Lions' burrows always gave a false impression. People thought the beast that made them would be smaller, but the lizard body that could eel through those passages could raise itself above my head once in the open.

The three-pronged lizard tongue extended, snuffing up our scent. It was a male judging by its size. Yes, male. First came its snout and then the mane; the fan-like ruff of bone and leathery skin that male lions spread in warning. Once the mane went up the head looked three times bigger and more fearsome than it was to start with. Then the heavy-looking legs appeared, all scales and triple bulbous toes, and sunlight lit the greenish yellow hide, its streaks of brown like earth or shadow. Colors that could blend in desert were too bright against the forest, probably the only reason I had noticed.

Someone near me, Ammet or his pal, had pissed themselves. I didn't blame them but it wasn't only me whose nose reacted. Barely twenty steps away the lion's tongue flicked out again, its head snaked forward, stretching out toward us; greed had made it blind to other dangers. On the plus side that meant we might take it down despite our lack or readiness but on the minus, standing where I was, my tunic hanging open, would I live to see it?

I stood. The acid smell behind me stayed as well; they hadn't run. If I could keep the creature off them for a little longer... If the Kemik got their act together. Semmit couldn't be so far behind me. Could he?

Jumbled sounds; the horses panicking and people shouting, thudding feet, the clash of weapons, but I couldn't risk a look. How long before they came? I backed a step and almost flattened Ammet, pleading with his friend. The fool had stuck and Ammet wasn't going without him.

Swearing at them both I gripped my sword and drew my dagger; puny weapons. All I had to do, I told myself, was wave my sword and make the creature hesitate until the Kemik got here; keep it off the weaker target. Surely once it was outnumbered...

All I had to do? The lion was in the open now. The beast must be a good twelve steps from nose to tail. It had lowered its head, not good, its strangely flattened teeth were showing. Crazy as it sounds I found myself recalling one of Sota's lectures. "See the teeth, my prince? They're made for grinding rather than for cutting. Lions pull their prey apart to eat it."

"Not me," I told the brute. It paused, for all the world as if it understood me and had stopped to weigh up its opponent. So close now that I could smell its musty breath. I shifted to the side. Cold, lizard eyes tracked the movement so I moved again, a little further from the cubs.

But Ammet moved to back me up. The lion swung his way instead; a scaly leg pushed out. "Oh no you don't!" I was in front of them again, my sword extended, threatening a stinking haystack with a needle.

The lion hissed and jolted forward. Knowing this was it, I rammed my dagger back into its sheath and grasped the sword two-handed. I had barely got my feet in place, with one behind to brace against the impact, when the broad teeth snapped at me.

I ducked. The head went over me, the poisoned tongue so close I felt its wind against my ear. Rising fast, I swung my blade—no time to aim—and felt it bite. The lion gave a rattling scream and jerked away so fast I almost lost the sword. My fingers tightened on the hilt; I kept the blade but lost the lion. It freed itself and left me stumbling forward. Not good enough, I thought; a neck wound, not the chest as I'd been hoping. And those amber eyes had fixed on me as its attacker. Ah well, that gave the cubs—

A grubby hand swung past my shoulder and a cloud of dirt flew upward at the lion, while from the creature's right a rain of iron arrows whistled; bolts with star-shaped heads that Sota's males were armed with.

The lion, stung and blinded, screamed again and swung to find its new attackers. Sota, looking frantic, was reloading as he ran toward me. "Down, my prince!" He raised his crossbow.

I never got the chance. The massive tail arrived before he'd finished shouting, flying at me like a falling tree. There was a rush of air. I got a twisted view of running Kemik bodies then the ground came up at me and flattened what the lion hadn't.

"Highness?"

I blinked and swore. It felt as if a dozen hands were helping me sit up, and every one had found a sore spot. "Lesser gods, let go." I shook my head to clear it. "Did you get it?"

"Yes, my prince." Was Sota sounding shaky or was that my hearing?

"Thank the gods for that much. Anybody hurt?"

"A cut or two." There was a buzz of talk not far away, and slapping noises, and the heavy smell of blood; they must be butchering the carcass. Good, I thought, a thread of sense returning. There was a tree behind me once again, I realized. My back hurt. "How long have I been out?"

"Not long. I thought—" He sounded normal this time but he'd quite forgotten I'd grown up now. When I focused properly it was to find him frowning blackly. "By all the—A sword, against a lion? Have you forgotten everything I taught you? You want an arrow, or a steel-tipped spear at closer quarters, or—"

I wasn't in the mood for lectures, "Arrows, yeah, I know. So what went wrong?"

He stopped and drew a breath, then shrugged. "Who knows, with lions. When we realized we tracked it back but—" He threw his arms out.

"Where were your lookouts, highness? How in heavens did they let you—"

I waved him off. "It was the villagers. The damn fools fell asleep. So lecture them instead." I started getting up and found a host of other tender places. Still, no blood, I'd settle happily for scrapes and bruises. I was well aware that I'd been very lucky. Which reminded me. I scanned the busy scene. The ants' nest I'd disturbed before was moving now with organized precision, cutting lion meat and packing it to carry to the village, supervised by Sota's males and Kemik. After this they'd boast the finest larder in the district, I thought hazily, then saw my targets. I pointed. "Those two." Kemik pushed at them and scowled.

The younger cub had tear tracks down his cheeks and still looked frightened, swallowing a lot. But then, he'd almost killed a royal, and I don't suppose I looked that reassuring.

Ammet looked the calmer, till one saw the way his fists were clenched, held tight against his body, and of course his eyes were wider than they—

Ah. I turned a sigh into a scowl. The idiot. I had, as Sota said, behaved as if I knew no more than they did, like the total fool he'd nearly called me. Definitely not a hero. I did my best to alter his opinion. "Next time you're given orders you obey them, understand me?"

"Yes, my prince." A fervent nod, the younger lad a silent echo.

My prince? It only needed that, a claim to personal allegiance. The words were ignorance, no more, I told myself, and waved them off; they'd either learned their lesson or they hadn't. An older male stepped up to drag the second cub away and Micah tugged at Ammet, talking softly. Ammet's back was eloquent of his dejection. Past his lowered head I saw a now-familiar Kemik face. My sergeant stood there watching.

Around me everything was movement; horses being led away upwind to calm them; hunters working on the giant carcass. Villagers were helping, more subdued than might have been expected. Others had no doubt explained, and pungently, how they had almost killed us. I refrained from cursing them as well. It hurt my head. It would have been a truly stupid way to die though, when I'd weathered so much worse before this.

But Fychet stood there, like a rock, and stared from me to Ammet? Then he strode to intercept the youngster, brushing past his father, took the youth by both his shoulders, gripped them tight enough to bring a wince to Ammet's face then shook him. Hard. His face was angry but a second after he had hugged the cub instead. I shook my head and turned away. I ached and I was filthy and the hunt was over. And I rather thought I'd netted more than lion.

I considered as I walked toward the horses. The cub was old enough to choose; his father couldn't stop him. Might not want to, I supposed. Ex-army after all; he'd seen the world beyond his village. Maybe he would want the cub to.

Of course I could refuse to take him on but then I guessed he'd follow anyway, if only for the sergeant. So either way…

Oh what the hells, I thought. The cub was hot for Fychet, not for me, and hero worship was a child's ailment, soon grown out of. And my horses were in sight, a moot reminder that they needed grooming and I hurt enough already. I sighed. The males between were moving from my path, and bowing at me more respectfully than I had any right to at the moment, and here came Ammet, abandoning his new-found love and running past me, reaching for a bridle. Claiming it his task to serve me; no doubt summoning the nerve to ask me for his heart's desire. I scowled at him to hide my laughter. Which did he desire more though, caring for my riding stock, or Fychet?

Chapter 15

We'd take our time getting home, I'd thought. My bruises had agreed, but they were fading by the time we neared the city. Ammet, very keen—at least at present—was attending as my groom, no doubt with help from Fychet, which left *me* free to heal in comfort. But it was a boring, dusty journey. By the time we saw the city walls again, a trembling grey and yellow vision floating in the early morning heat-haze with the palace ghostly-white above, my thoughts were more on what my father had uncovered in my absence, both about our interfering priests and Nusil's dealings. And with other, more confusing matters.

As my mood improved so Keril had returned to plague my dreams, like hunger, till I had to fight an urge to gallop. Plague on it, I'd won that war. Then been on an adventure, then gone back to an obsession with a mere plaything. Was I sickening for something? Seven hells, my first excitement for the male should have faded, even if I hadn't had enough yet. But apparently it hadn't. Which was puzzling. I mulled it over as I rode. The males beside me must have caught my mood because they left me to it.

The first sighting of Kadd always looked so deceptively close but the sun was set before we even reached the outskirts. The city gates were barred by then but watchmen rushed to pull them open at the sight of the Kemik. There was a sliver of a moon, and cloud, so males about the darkened streets were flickering shadows in the light from inns and houses as they called out welcomes, ducking heads respectfully when I was sighted.

The whiter walls holding the gates to the Outer Palace looked almost insubstantial at night, but the welcome here was more formal, never mind the hour. I dismissed my followers and headed for my own apartments. A good outing, but it was good to be back too.

Someone must have run ahead. Medi was awake, he'd even dressed. He looked alert where I was feeling heavy. I would bathe, I told him, eat a bite or two then sleep till morning.

I bathed and ate, but the rest— A curtain rattled. When I glanced across my "mere plaything" hesitated in the bedroom's archway. His chest rose and fell. I clean forgot about being so tired.

"My lord is back."

It was the most unlikely seduction line I'd ever heard, but it was instantly effective. I abandoned supper.

He met me in the centre of the room, moving when I did, jerking to a halt when we were almost touching; drawn, but hesitating.

"So I'm back." I reached out. "What are you going to do about it?"

I'd read him right, this time he was as eager as I was. When I pulled him closer his lips fastened on mine, soft at first then more demanding, his hands either side of my head. That kiss stilled time, and made me feel drunk. Surfacing at last I laughed out loud and pushed him on ahead of me. "Bed."

I was tired though. It went faster than I'd have liked. Maybe because of that I became more the aggressor this time round. Well, he was willing, and he knew what to expect now, and despite his frailties I couldn't any longer see him as a weakling.

Nor a coward either, when I pushed him on the bed and up against the corner pillar, so the climax was a burst of fire in the darkness. For a moment there was nothing but our bodies. Then the lamplight showed me Keril's fingers clutching at the wood, his head arched back. I grinned, well pleased, and fell against the pillows.

"Keshat's balls!" I rolled away and clutched my sword arm.

"My lord?" He'd slumped against the pillar.

Fine. I didn't want him alert, not now. I forced my hand off the cramping pain in my arm and pressed it lower. "Stomach," I said quickly. Thank the gods I'd always been a decent liar. "Something I ate. Go to sleep." I found my feet.

"But. Shall I—" Sounded like he hadn't got his breath, or brain, back yet.

"Stay put." I headed for the bath; as good a hiding place as any and it matched the story.

Thankfully the place was now deserted. I stood still and told myself to stop panicking. So there'd been a twinge. Maybe I'd strained a muscle; Keril was stronger than he looked and I hadn't held back, not this time. Yes, a massage was the answer. Only first I'd take a look.

The single lamp by the entrance was more than enough for me to examine the spidery lines on my arm more closely. Only they weren't spidery any more. They weren't just thicker but a clearer, pale yellow.

I closed my mouth, my eyes too a moment. Surely this was beyond any trick the priests could muster? Gods, what—

Gods? What if it wasn't a trick after all? What if—?

Father took one look at me and waved me to be seated. "Ash, welcome back. Have you eaten yet?"

"I. Yes. No, not yet." It was almost midday, but food had been the last thing on my mind that morning. I'd returned to the bedroom and sent Keril away bleary-eyed. That'd roused the household so I'd had to order Medi out as well, with terse instructions no one should disturb me till I called them. But I hadn't slept, however much I needed to, and that was showing if my father's face was anything to go by.

"Then you'll eat a little?" He was smiling but it was an order, and a warning. Everything we did was noticed.

"Yes, of course." I pulled myself together. Food arrived. I didn't taste it but I ate it.

Father sat and sipped a while, then broke the silence. "I gather you got the lion."

"Yes."

"Nine days. That was quick. You look as if it was a worthy battle."

A remark that would explain my rough appearance. I swallowed, woke up and followed the script. "It was. The lookouts fell asleep, the damn thing nearly got me." I gave a brief description. "What's Nusil say?"

Slaves hovered. Father waved at them to clear the dishes. "Nusil's failing was his sloth, as ever. He had abdicated almost all his duties to his chosen heir. He called it training." Father had relaxed enough to look disgusted. "The son informed me he'd decided it was time to "tighten up resources", that their revenues took precedence; that he had "delegated such a trifling rural problem" to inferiors, considering it was beneath his notice.

I'd started taking notice. "And you said?"

"That I would tighten things myself—around their lazy necks—if there was word again about his males marauding and their lords too fond of luxury to curb them. That a selfish lord would not *stay* lord of Nusil." Father settled, calmer. "Nusil has the reins again, at my insistence. I have told him when he next considers stepping down my southern governor will help him pick out his successor."

That of course meant me. I drank, and tried to dredge up breeding records. There was a lesser son. Yes, and a couple of other kin the age for competition. There'd be a rash of hopefuls thinking about polishing their acts. "That should do the trick," I said. "If not—"

"If not, I'll pass them onto you to deal with, since it's in the south, and call *that* training." Father grinned, his temper easing. All the slaves were gone at last. My tension had resurfaced though, however well I thought I'd hid it.

"Ash, what *is* it?"

I stopped. Repeating the tale didn't make it any easier to deal with, even though I knew my father had believed my words the first time. This time round the High Priests sat like statues, staring fixedly at my bared arm.

"A portent," Fire-Lord Sil suddenly suggested, in his creaking voice.

I fought a scowl. Sil was priest to Keshat, god of fire; the warrior's god; which meant I'd suffered Sil's "advice" too often. Less in recent years, but he could always raise my hackles, even when I didn't have a damned good reason. At his side our solid Earth-Lord, Gantamin, had started smiling through his beard, while Hainil, Water-Lord, half-Chi, the nearest to me and the youngest, didn't comment, blue eyes flicking to the others. Looking for a lead, or a reaction?

Funny thing but Sarrush's high priests always managed to have blue eyes. Even if they didn't before. Apparently it was a gift from their god. When I'd pulled the armlet off all three had frozen then they'd listened avidly. For once, their differences were forgotten. They were gathered in my father's sitting room like brothers and all three, no matter if they chose to smile or frown, were struggling in their different ways to hide a dog-with-bone expression.

Gantamin was staring at me still, as if he hoped the yellow lines might turn to gold while he was watching. But fierce old Sil had made his mind up. "Surely there's nothing to investigate, my king. A sign from heaven, on the prince's birthday? Most appropriate." As if he believed every word, when he of all males knew the En-Syn *didn't* just "appear".

Only this one had—whether they believed it or not. And as Father said, we couldn't take the chance. However little I *wanted* to believe, it was beginning to look like I might not have much choice.

Believer or not, Sil was in full flow. "We must announce the joyous news."

"Oh no we mustn't." I looked to my father. Sil was champing at the bit and only he could jerk this bridle.

"Nothing will be said." He watched them. "Till I order."

"But." Sil actually dared to protest.

Father's eyes flashed. Sil went quiet. "Nothing. I have given Prince Ashamet my word on this."

They hadn't realized till then. They'd assumed he was delighted, maybe even—if they'd told the truth—that it was him, not me, behind it?

Now they were thinking fast. They'd shut their mouths and blanked their faces, bowing their submission. High Priests or not—hells, *gods* involved or not—they knew my father's subtle mind. They knew they could ascend to heaven much earlier, along an unexpected, much more painful path than they'd envisaged, if my father found they'd disobeyed him.

Ashamet, Desert Born

I breathed a little easier—they hadn't talked him round—I could ignore their pious vows and try to work out which of them, if not all three, had been behind it. If there was a way, they knew it, and between their subterfuge and heavenly intervention, I'd be a lot happier dealing with the subterfuge.

Sil then? Narrow-beaked and narrow-eyed, who seemed determined to assert blind faith? So old he'd been around when Father's Synia had "manifested". I had always pegged him for the greatest cynic of the three. No, Sil was surely no more innocent than Gantamin or Hainil, nor more senile. He was just declaring the official line, and telling all the rest of us we'd have to walk it.

But it could be any of them. None of them were simple-minded or they wouldn't be here.

Gantamin? He'd been anointed in my fourteenth year. I recalled I'd been attracted by his gentle smile, which had seemed to contradict his somber mass and muscle. Certainly the way he looked at me right now, I had to wonder. Unlike me he really looked as if he *wanted* to believe in this. Or was he just a demon actor?

Hainil then? The pale blue borders on his robes always made him look softer than the others. He was the youngest, wittiest, and most approachable. His followers adored him. But I'd seen him twist the truth a time or two to trap unwary victims; sometimes I'd suspected simply for the quiet amusement such maneuvers brought him. Could his agile brain and subtle humour instigate a move as strange, as magical, as this one?

Logic pointed me to Sil or Hainil but all three had means and motive. Somebody was lying. Had to be. I watched. A wasted effort. I couldn't tell if it was one or all of them, but now all three were in on it, regardless, which meant my future hung upon their faith, or fear of my father. If even one dared to speak out…

I suppressed a shudder. If the thing was a fake, and shown to be, the scandal could uproot the empire.

But if it was real?

Me, the Voice of Heaven? I knew better. Truth was I'd be ruled by everybody, servant to the gods, the priests, the whole damn empire. I wasn't naturally cunning like my father, who'd had years of experience and who could use the role to play one side against another, to protect the empire and remain a real power. I was just a simple warrior. I'd end up nothing but a figurehead. A gilded puppet.

Fuck the empire, *and* the power. What about my *life*? No more real battles, no more flitting through an enemy's defenses in disguise, not even down into the city for a night of anonymity and ribald entertainment. If I fought for practice, even, who'd make any real effort to defeat a Voice of Heaven? If I won I'd never know that I'd deserved it.

Every freedom I had grown to love would vanish; every challenge; and pretence would be my prison. Father never had a choice but I'd become so thankful

I was spared the lie, that I could face the males that I commanded as an honest soldier, one I hoped they could respect, not one who falsely claimed their worship.

Now I dithered. I had told myself to doubt the gods for longer than I'd known I *wouldn't* be a Voice, the day that fever stopped the priests from marking me at the appointed moment. Only neither fact felt solid any longer. And the priests weren't helping. They assured me that the yellow lines were real, but were they? I assured the priests that I believed it too. But did I? I barely heard what they were saying. I wanted it to be a fake. And yet the thing had altered, while I was awake, and only Keril, half asleep and in my sight, was near me. I surfaced as they all agreed the strange event would stay a secret.

"Till it is complete," said Hainil cheerfully, and Gantamin agreed at once, while Sil just nodded, more impatient than reluctant. He'd "believe" whatever gave him power.

Father and I said the right things and got rid of them.

"Ash?"

"I don't know, and I'm not sure they do either." I'd replaced the armlet. Now I found myself tracing the gold star decoration on it with my fingertips. Annoyed, I jerked my hand away.

Father spread his hands, a gesture of helplessness from the most powerful male in the empire. Somehow that said it all.

I rose. "I need some air."

Surprisingly, he smiled. "Of course. I wish I could join you." But he'd carved a gaping hole in his appointments and there'd be a horde of lesser mortals penned up somewhere waiting.

I bowed, respectfully for once. "I wish you could too. I'll see you later?" I was almost at the door when he spoke.

"Ash, if it is true, it's a great thing; you know that? Perhaps the greatest miracle in our history."

"Oh yes." I didn't turn to face him.

I'd intended to ride but by then I'd been awake for two days. I was dead on my feet, and forced to acknowledge the fact when I tripped going up my own outer steps. If I took a horse out I'd probably break my neck. Huh; one way to prove all this was a fraud.

Exasperated, I plodded up to my top floor, hoping a long bath would be some sort of substitute. One thing for sure, I wasn't about to resort to a sleeping draught. It'd make me a sitting duck. Medi met me at the topmost landing, looking at me with concern.

"I need a bath, and a drink."

He issued rapid orders. As usual, having something to do calmed him. If only. I made for the bath, pulling my dagger out of my sash. Medi, scampering to match my longer stride, took it and handed it on to be cleaned. Reaching the bath I tugged at the sash as robe slaves gathered. Medi stood aside, but hesitated. "What?" I dropped onto a bench and stuck a foot out. There was comfort in such everyday activities.

"About the body slave, highness. What punishment did you wish?"

"What?" The robe slave at my feet froze. When I looked up, Medi's face had gone solemn. "Body slave" today. Not "Keril".

"Punishment?" I felt my eyes widen. "Oh, blood and— Has he slept since I sent him off?"

"No, highness."

"Highness" as well. The formality made sense now. I recalled Keril stumbling off. Not awake. Confused. And me snapping at people.

"Get him in here." I took the wine being offered and tossed it down in one, waving slaves off. "I don't suppose he's eaten either?"

"No, highness, of course not."

I suppressed another curse, just as Keril came through the curtains, so suddenly I figured someone out there pushed him forward. Once inside he stopped dead.

I snorted. "You look as rough as I feel."

He lowered his head. Almost the first time he'd meant it. "My lord."

"Last night, you were forward enough to come to me, without being called." I paused, searching for words. "You pleased me too, but after, there were other matters waiting my attention. Matters more important than you." That ought to do it, surely; both rebuke, and reassurance.

His head came up fast. "I thought." He actually licked his lips. "I thought you were angered. I didn't know what…"

Didn't know anything. That was the root of it all. I'd made a male of him one night then left. One taste then nothing. Then come back and taken him again, and roughly, then dismissed him. And with Keril everything was more black and white, wasn't it?

"You are not due an explanation of your master's actions," I said, fixing him with a look.

"No, my lord." The fool was almost smiling. "And I am very ignorant."

"So it appears, and now, if I was so inclined, you are not *fit* to please me." The smile died. "I'm sorry, my lord."

"Huh." When I glanced round Medi was smiling instead. "He eats, sleeps, and comes to me at dawn." I waved impatiently. Medi signaled. Keril was hustled out. "Gods, Medi, I know he's a fool, but couldn't you have reassured him?"

"My prince." Ah, my prince now. "You looked so enraged. I asked him what he had done to displease you, but he claimed not to know, so I kept him apart and awaited your wishes."

Without food, thus confirming in Keril's odd mind that he was out of favor. I'd brought him to orgasm then thrown him out, and like the child he was he couldn't understand it.

I had to laugh. I wasn't used to dealing with such delicate flowers.

The atmosphere round me relaxed. Slaves moved again, removing my sandals. I pulled off my shirt. Keril had panicked about nothing, maybe I had too? I was dog-tired, after all, not the best state to make judgments. I would wait and see how the world looked by morning.

The morning looked like Keril. It looked shy, but hopeful. I began the new day laughing. Later, when Keril heaved a sigh I took as a compliment, I decided my life didn't feel so bad any more either. Sated, that was the word. I rolled aside and grinned.

Keril smiled back. His third time in my bed. Definitely auspicious. If there *were* gods getting interested in my life they'd been kind enough to send me the most responsive lay I'd ever had. It was almost worth all the uncertainty of the En-Syn.

As if it heard, my blasted arm twitched. Maybe I grunted. Keril's head turned on the pillow. "My lord?" A serious expression. "Should I…?" He started to sit up.

"Stay. No, fetch me some tea, then stay."

Judging by the smile, being sent on an errand wasn't at all the same as being sent away. He slid into his trousers—trained by Medi never to go nude except when I required it—and left me with a loping stride that declared him both refreshed and relieved. Me, I lay back and wondered was there, anywhere else, another creature whose world could be so easily upset as Keril's? For whom a word, a touch, could put all to rights again? Gods, the fool was too sensitive to live.

But I wasn't, and he was a timely lesson not to jump to conclusions.

The slap of bare feet heralded my tea. I smiled and took it from him. I'd made his world better, maybe he'd done the same for me. I was no longer so scared of what I didn't know. Priests, I could deal with if I had to. Gods… hells, if they were real, nothing I did would make much difference.

Chapter 16

Two weeks later Medi, flushed with satisfaction, introduced a candle-burner to my bedroom. Keril had persuaded him to teach a mere body slave to brew my favorite infusion. Just the way I liked it too, so sometimes now I woke to hear the bubbling of the tiny can of water in its distant corner, followed by the smell of spearleaf. I would turn my head to see him carrying the cup toward me.

Oh, I sent him off some nights, to make the point, but I'd begun to understand that pleasing me, in any way, gave Keril pleasure. Such a simple attitude to life. I found it calming.

As for my arm, it hadn't faded but at least it wasn't any bolder, and it wasn't itching, and the priests were being careful not to crowd me.

Better still, my bride sent private word that she was pregnant. I complimented her discretion, then I informed my father, who grinned and punched me in the stomach. No one else would mention it, of course, but word had surely leaked for those I saw were most respectful and the priests wore smug expressions.

An heir, already? And the priests supportive? Me, I felt like laughing. Someone's gods must love me.

Mine, or Keril's?

Still, the pregnancy *was* something to give thanks for. Taniset seemed satisfied as well, but then she should be. Her fertility ensured respect, a safer future, and she could please herself now, pretty much, until the litter was delivered. She had smiled, and paid me compliments. And seemed to feel it made her more attractive. Strange ideas Sidassi females harbored. Still, I felt the tide had turned, I thought we both felt things were going as we wanted.

Her mawkish brother proclaimed himself delighted and left, praise be, to take the word back personally to his father and his greater brother, so the alliance seemed to be successful too; another triumph. I'd even let the fellow see his sister, with her crones around her and with closter eunuchs in attendance. It was, apparently, what they were used to.

Outlandish custom, letting males inside our females' quarters, even brothers. Still, I'd wanted to reward the female, and show due attention to our new alliance. I discussed it with my father then with his approval I escorted Thersat through the iron gates into the closter. Frankly if I hadn't gone I doubt the closter-eunuchs would have granted him admission, never mind my order. Every face I saw in there was tight and frozen, barely hiding their revulsion.

Except for Taniset's. She obviously hadn't been informed; her face lit up. She almost ran across the chamber then recalled her manners, stumbled to a halt and bowed. "My royal husband."

"Lady Taniset." I bowed as well. "You have a guest, if it would please you?"

"Oh, yes!" Her smile was dazzling, a brighter thing than I was used to, no mistaking her delight was aimed at Thersat.

"Tani!" Thersat's smile was even wider.

"Then I'll leave you." I gestured Thersat forward, trying to be casual about it. I had granted him an hour, and the eunuchs would remain throughout. I'd no desire to join them so I bowed and left them, knowing every word would be reported to me later, by the closter-master, Zenec…

"They held hands," the gleaming-headed Zenec told me stiffly.

"Huh." I wasn't pleased, but didn't show it. "Nothing more, I trust?"

"Just talk. I have the transcripts here, my prince." He laid the pages on the table. "Nothing that your highness will object to." Other than the blatant scandal of the meeting, Zenec's pinched expression added.

"Good." I sent the male away and told myself I would forget it. Except both parties took the time to thank me; Taniset with words (and touches).

"Still feels indecent," I remarked to Father. I meant the meeting. Not the touching, naturally I hadn't mentioned that part.

"Foreign manners." He scribbled his initials on some document a clerk held out to him. "As you said, no harm done. It may seem bizarre to us, offensive even, but one must stomach other customs. Kadduchan is such a diverse kingdom these days."

It seemed a fair assessment. "As long as it isn't going to be a habit," I said, and left it. I would make a point to pay her visits every now and then, and ask if there was anything she wanted. We might need to make more children, of course, but I thought our motives matched, as they were meant to, even if the female had these odd ideas of being attractive.

I thanked my father for his wisdom. He grinned. My uncle, also present, merely grunted, the eternal skeptic.

He'd always frowned at mention of my mother too. I'd never worked out why. She'd been a quiet lady, not unmannerly, or selfish, with a temperament that would have suited my more thoughtful parent. I'd always been encouraged to visit her, more than enough to know that much about her. In any case, my uncle never met her, so…

Ashamet, Desert Born

I found myself looking from Rag to my father. Rag: devoted twin and loyal supporter, who had been allowed to live, even past my own survival. Rag, who seldom truly smiled, unless my father seemed to want it. He was smiling at him now.

Uncle Rag had feelings, for my father? Rubbish, I'd have seen it years ago. Or would I? I stared into my glass and thought about it.

He'd have had to keep it quiet. Even from my father? Well, affairs of equals weren't uncommon but between close kin, that was a vastly different matter, practically our sole taboo regarding sexual encounters. (Probably because it made it much more difficult to kill the sibling, to ensure succession, if you'd slept with them beforehand?) Yes, he'd definitely have to hide it and accept that it was hopeless.

So did *Father* know the way Rag felt about him? Was that why he'd trusted him enough he'd only cut him, when he came to power? Crazy notion, but if I was right… it could so easily have started ugly rumors. And that could have cost Rag his life, not to mention threatened my father's succession. Mine too? Maybe I should think kinder thoughts about my uncle. Maybe he deserved them. Maybe he wasn't as cold-blooded as I'd always thought him?

Or maybe I was just a fool, and seeing love and romance all around me? I laughed, and let a slave refill my glass. Dismissed, he shuffled off. My father raised an eyebrow. "What, is he so ugly?"

"What? I glanced to where he knelt against the wall. Dark, half Kemik maybe, which was less than common; slender, and the young body slightly oiled. "No, good-looking. New?" I added, since he seemed keen to have me take an interest.

"Not like you not to notice. You always liked the darker ones, although I'd heard your taste had gone the other way just lately. *Was* that male a virgin? Rumor says you almost split him."

Too much to hope the tale had stayed in my apartments, though whatever had spread would bear little resemblance to the truth. Well, it could hardly be less likely, or more twisted. And my father was still waiting. "Yes," I said.

"He was?" My father sat and thought. And then he wanted to continue. "He'd never been with male *or* female, this new toy? In some lands, as I said to you…"

"No," I said. "Neither."

"Amazing. You are quite sure..?"

"Yes." I really had to give him proper answers. "Quite sure."

"Well, you should know. Rag says he caught a glimpse and thought he was good-looking, if outlandish. Healthy?"

"That too, Father." They'd talked about it? I cast about me for a change of subject.

Rag grinned and got his blow in while he could. "He must be fit, I'd think. The word is Ash has kept him active." Father laughed, and switched the talk to horses then the clouds now gathering upon our east horizons, so the inquisition ended.

Two days after that the Summer rains arrived at last, a crashing blast that turned into the usual sweating, enervating torrent. Keril seemed to find it novel. I found him out of bed and staring at it through the lattices one morning. "What's wrong?" I raised up on one elbow.

"I heard about rain, but I didn't know that it could be so… fierce." His eyes were wide with wonder. Irresistible. I never thought to question his reaction.

I crossed to stand behind him as his gaze returned to all that falling water. "Yes, the rains can do a lot of damage. They can ruin crops and trigger mudslides. They can kill." I wrapped my arms around him, pulled him back against me, breathing in his perfume. "But you're safe enough in here."

Not so all the world outside. The poorer folk had cause to worry, even in the city. All across the land there would be fervent offerings to Sarrush, anything in blue especially valued. I made the gift that was expected of me; an appearance at the greatest of the city's temples…

Chapter 17

It should have been an easy ride along the wider streets around the outer palace, but I'd obviously been expected. Lordly households emptied out to ogle and the twisting streets around the temple square were even more congested.

It took my mounted escort plus the temple guards to clear a passage through the swirl of citizens and pilgrims. Males shouted their approval of my mission. Hainil's lookouts were awake and probably forewarned; he came to welcome me in person at the outer doors, in sky blue robes today, his cheeks and nails painted blue and silver.

I'd chosen silver cloth and deep blue trousers, silver in my braid and on my fingers. Even for the gods I wasn't wearing face paint but my ears held loops of silver hung with sapphires, tiny stones like water droplets. Between the pair of us we must have made a decent show and we were carefully polite to one another, playing to the gaping audience all round us.

"Prince Ashamet, may Sarrush favor you this day." He bowed then led the way beneath the triple arches to the vaulted court within.

More crowds, though quieter now. The place was always crammed with worshippers. It hosted shrines to every deity the empire worshipped; altars to the lesser gods providing window dressing for the greater. Pilgrims rested in this courtyard, holy males as well, and novices attended them. The yawning chamber never emptied but a clear avenue appeared in seconds for the Water-Lord and his august companion.

From this court I had three choices. Naturally. Every choice would lead me lower, swallowing me if you like. First, left: the carved wood screens. They masked the tiled ramp that took one to the cave-like Earth Hall and its yellow marble effigy of Keltis, male and female both, reclining, with his lesser gods the effigies of stone and plants and animals and such—ensconced in niches in the stone-built walls around him. Everything in there was dark and hushed and smelled of earth and vegetation, and no one spoke. The silence made your heart beat louder.

My second option was the Fire Hall behind its sculpted metal shutters, darkened tunnels sacrosanct to Keshat and his order. Keshat's face, a golden sun, was mounted on an armored iron body bathed in roaring, leaping flames, and yet it never melted. If you dared to touch the shelf in front of it your flesh would fry and scar. Some did it, as a token of devotion. Once a year it was my father's "privilege" to lay both hands on all that red-hot iron, and come away undamaged. Ouch. I'd often wondered how our wily Fire-lord worked it but I hadn't so far pushed my luck and asked him. The thought that I might have to…

Third and last—although of course no precedence applied—my current destination beckoned. At least it was the most appealing.

"Sarrush welcomes you." Hainil bowed and waved in that direction. With the priest in front, my guards behind, I crossed the court. Heads bowed everywhere. I nodded royally and Hainil made a waving sign of blessing. Very stately. Very public.

Entering this inner temple, weaving through these maze-like screens of precious, blue-green glass and down an undulating, blue-tiled floor—no doors as such—reminded me of following a stream bed. As a child I had loved it. I had had to be restrained from running.

The noise outside cut off. The glassy panels reared higher. So did the glass-tiled roof, it felt like walking underwater. Even here my guard stayed close, and moved to flank me once we cleared the twisting baffles.

Inside the Water Hall the music of a hundred little rills and fountains greeted us. Glass prisms hidden in the ceiling bent the light and caused them all to sparkle. I relaxed a fraction. The Earth Hall always made me more aware that life was growth, the Fire Hall that its end could come at any moment, but the Water Hall was where I felt that life itself was joyful.

Hainil gestured me toward the furthest end. There was no need to clear a way in here; the water took my name and echoed it all round me. Other worshippers, and Hainil's priests on duty in here, hurriedly retreated.

I passed the laughing pools before each lesser altar. There'd be multi-colored fish in some, light-hearted things which I had always lingered over as a child, but not today. I gazed ahead and looked devout, responsible, and all the rest. I knew my escort would be fanning out to form a cordon. No one else would be allowed to join me at the altar though they'd all bear witness.

The sacred waterfall ahead of me grew ever taller as I walked, until its tumult towered over me and I was almost deafened; the water's play become raw power. Such a simple thing, and wholly natural, but I admit it dwarfed a male and stilled his heart a second when he stood before it.

The noise and fury weren't the only reasons. They said the Water Hall disdained a graven image. But sometimes there would be a hint of something in the fall: a reaching hand, a half-seen face; one tantalizing glimpse. It tugged the eye;

an awe-inspiring vision to the child. Alas, my older self admired its beauty but had come to think it merely clever. Growing up provides us with so many disillusions, does it not? I sometimes envy those who keep their faith and *know* their gods are with them. Me, I know the priests, too well. The gods? I'd thought I knew, I wasn't certain any longer.

It was impossible to reach across to the fall itself, the waters plunged and dashed on blue-veined ledges, each one higher than a male. White foam spilled down and danced across an azure pool until the wavelets calmed and flowed away on either side, down darker, deeper channels where the waters fell below the ground and vanished.

In front of me a wall of dark blue steps rose shoulder high to dam the water, each step broad enough to lie on. That day's offerings already filled the steps to either side of me, but I preferred to give my tribute more directly to the waters. What's the point of being royal if one can't be different?

Officially the priests approved my antics as a gesture of devotion. Unofficially? It meant that Hainil's solemn priests would have to strip like fishermen and dive in to retrieve it once the hall was empty. Hey, it made *me* laugh. What better reason? And Sarrush hadn't struck me down, so maybe he too had a sense of humour.

I bowed before the lowest step then held my hand out. My captain offered me an opened silver casket. Show time. Climbing high above their heads, I raised the double fist of tiny sapphires I had taken, held them forth the time it took to breathe the proper prayers—I said them too this time, "in case"—then tossed the polished baubles up and out across the water, like the spray that rose around them.

Exclamations from the crowd behind. The gems reflected light and turned the spray itself to glittering magic. The sight was almost worth the cost, but then the sparkling fragments drowned, and it was over. I bowed again then waited, knowing everyone was watching. One was meant to meditate, in case the god should deign to send the giver some religious message.

My thoughts were always apt to drift at this point, often straying onto subjects gods would surely not approve of. Today the sight of all those jewels, and the gasps behind me, easily diverted me. I wondered: which hall here might most resemble Keril's distant temple? Would he smile at this rush of water, he who I had found was sensitive to beauty? Or would he denounce it? All that pale flesh, I thought—I almost laughed out loud—would make a decent job of representing Sarrush, should they ever want a statue to replace those moving fragments. Keril, water running down his body. For a while my thoughts were frankly irreligious but there was still no sign that Sarrush was offended. Perhaps he took it as a compliment.

The roar increased, as if the water heard my thoughts and bellowed laughter, cutting off all sound of those behind me. I supposed *their* prayers were more devout and yet if anyone in here was blessed then surely I was?

And my father, in whose hands our empire flourished?

"Are you real after all?" I murmured. "Do you bless us, even if we don't deserve it? *Did* you send this mark? And if so, why?"

The nearest wavelets chuckled and a cloud of spray reached out to touch me. "How can I be certain?"

The pool below me calmed; unusual. I saw myself reflected. Most of me was indistinct, but suddenly my arm flashed gold and silver, very clear, before the water boiled again and ripples swept away the picture.

My arm? I shook my head, forgetting witnesses. The Syniad were false; they always had been. Why should I be any different? Defiantly I dared the waterfall to prove me wrong. No, nothing but a wall of water. "I think you'll have to settle for the jewels, Sarrush—if you're really there." I dared to grin. "I'm past salvation, don't you think? I mean, how many hours will it take the priests to fish for all your sapphires in these blue-tiled ledges?"

God or not, it was a thought to send me back into the city with a smile.

There was another thing about those gems; they bore no lesser price than I had given in the past, nor any greater. I was sure that Hainil understood; there wouldn't be the slightest hint of bribery, or begging favor.

I turned away. He stood below me, waiting; looked me in the eye then glanced across the pond and smiled slightly. Yes, I thought, you understand the message, and the joke. And take it lightly? Should I assume you innocent? Perhaps. Or maybe you were part of the attempt but now, frustrated by my vigilance, would rather let the whole affair blow over. Or do you actually think your god will finish off the Synia, the way—

The way it changed again, all by itself, the night before I told you?

I froze, one foot about to quit the highest step. Then sense returned. I saw the watching faces, took a hasty breath and smiled. As if, I mocked myself. So every Synia's created by the gods themselves and not the priests? Oh yeah, or I'm the only one whose Synia was ever made with real magic? Hells, maybe Sarrush will appear from his waterfall and kiss me, here in front of everyone, to prove it!

Enough. I smiled innocently back at Hainil, ignored the steps and leapt. My feet were on the ground again, my sudden panic over. "Water Lord." I bowed and gave him both my hands, the child to the father.

He pressed them close between his own in blessing, stepping closer. "Never doubt, highness," he murmured.

I stiffened, but we were protected by the downpour.

"Our duty is to serve our gods however they demand. We carry out their wishes. Think of that, my prince." He stepped away as if his quiet words were nothing but the normal blessing.

I headed past him. My guards would be between us now. My pace was steady but my mind was racing. Had that been an actual confession: that he'd "served" by trying to put a Chosen mark on me? Or that he thought all Synia, however they arrived, *were* sacred? Or that it was irrelevant what I believed, once I was chosen?

A double turn, at speed. The clamor of the restless flood retreated till the water was a melody again. He hadn't followed, he had left me to negotiate the rippling baffles to the outer temple. Left me to my thoughts?

Up and out. The light grew yellower again. The hum of talk outside replaced the sound of water and I stepped into the waiting crowd, relying on the guards to clear a passage. I knew my face would be serene, one did not frown on such occasions. The mind behind it was another matter.

Was that what Hainil truly thought; that all those times the priests had faked the Synia, then told the world that they were sacred, they'd believed they followed holy orders?

Hells, the only surety I had was that I'd earned a drink. I'd done my duty, and had made it entertaining. That was all I could be sure of.

Offerings or not, the rains continued. Daily life became a steam bath. Rivers flowed in barren desert. In the city, streams rose past their banks and poorer lowland streets were flooded. Palace gutters gurgled day and night, the cisterns overflowed, my clothes felt clammy and the gardeners built walls of plaited straw round tender plants then suddenly—the god presumably appeased—the weather eased, the steam evaporated. We were back to normal.

Bit by bit the year waned, the days grew milder. Evening fires became the norm. I could have made believe the markings on my arm had never happened if I hadn't given clear orders no one, *no one* save for Medi and his safest minions was to interrupt my bathing, when it was uncovered. Or my slumber, if I was with Keril. Or if I couldn't feel, on those occasions, how my arm had roughened where the armlet's edges rubbed the skin beneath it. Hells, I might as well wear Keril's silver slave-bracelets. But the thing stayed shrouded, and at least it *hadn't* altered any further. Its existence stayed a secret.

No one had set eyes on Keril either, except the eunuchs in the topmost storey of my quarters. I hadn't encouraged visitors up there much recently, though it was remarkable, when I thought about it, the number of lords, young and old, who'd lately hinted at an ardent interlude. I figured their noses were longer than their pricks.

According to Medishel, who'd smiled slyly as he told it, the virgin (he said they even called him that now, out of my hearing) was said to be a magical silver color, skin softer than a cub, with silken hair, and luminous eyes, and a lot of other, *very* detailed attractions I couldn't wait to find. I'd laughed, but I still hadn't decided if I was really that amused.

I thought Keril quite unaware anyone but me had any kind of interest in him, let alone there might be males who'd bribe or whore their way to glimpse him. Interesting, that, because it meant for once my eunuchs had been censoring their gossip when he was in earshot. All the same it was indecent, when I thought about it. A body slave was *private*. That was the attraction, wasn't it? So it was downright rude, this prying. They'd be poking into my cupboards next.

Still, it did clear up one minor matter. I'd long ago sent a flask of brandy to old Sheshman, with his prince's compliments. Sultaki had seemed appropriate. And I hadn't sent for his son, which told him I was satisfied his claim was honest. Both responses meant he'd beamed his way about the courts for some weeks after but I'd figured that smile was the sum of it. He wouldn't have needed to be so gross as to say anything, the smile and the palace grapevine would have done that for him. Hence the fact the gossips talked about "the virgin."

But the fact these rumors were so very detailed…

"So much gossip might be thought, my lord, to lead in your direction. But then the details, some of them quite graphic—"

Sheshman looked a trifle apprehensive.

"—made it clear to me at least you weren't the donor. I doubt you'd have thought to call him 'sultry'."

I'd had to grin at that one. I'd asked Keril, the evening before, what words he'd choose, that best described him. I'd offered him some beauties. "No, my lord. I'm sure I'm really very… common." From anyone but Keril it might have sounded disapproving. I think I taught him, later, that some of my offerings were more appropriate.

Sheshman relaxed again, and eyed me sideways. I'd come upon him in the palace corridors, a public spot. There was a knot of scribes and lawyers, dark robes noticeable in a nearby patch of sunlight where the passage led into a courtyard. There were mailed soldiers stationed at an intersection, tucked into the shade and stiff as pokers. But there was no one near enough to overhear us once my escort waved the nearest off.

Despite the privacy he kept his voice discreetly lowered. "My prince honors me with his confidence. In honor then, I should admit I might be just a trifle guilty." His small round eyes were brighter. "Dreadful thing, my prince, but as a male grows older so his tongue grows longer. I do believe I may have let slip a point or two about your virgin. But only to those dear friends who were most grateful."

I choked. "You old rogue. Exactly which of these outrageous stories did you foster?"

"Not all, I swear, but a male must keep an eye for any benefit that comes along, my prince," the male said shamelessly. "I swear I gave them only fiction, and it does my prince no hardship to be envied."

He shook with laughter when I clapped him on the back, because of course that sign of favor was more valuable in court than any bribe. Although he left the court soon after.

Mind you, he'd been half a year with us, longer than he usually hung around. I had to wonder about Sheshman. For instance I had noticed, in that empty corridor, he wore no perfume. Never mind he didn't smell as rank as some, it wasn't fitting and it didn't square with his ornate appearance. Unless he found it useful not to leave a scent behind that might identify him? If, for instance, he was used to being somewhere that he shouldn't? I wondered where his travels took him this time. And what he'd really gone for. Not for long though.

Chapter 18

All right, so I'd been both annoyed and amused by all those offers to share my bed. More significantly, I'd turned them down.

I'd taken others for a night. Of course I had. A friend I'd shared a bed with off and on for years; a Kemik youth another friend, had offered after dinner at his house, who'd looked both wicked and exotic. And I hadn't wanted to offend him. Jaffid, when my blood was quickened and I'd tried to cool it down with brandy.

Friendships, curiosity and drink? It took me some time to add those facts together. For years I'd picked from those about me freely, as if I was at market. Slaves or almost-equals, both were for my pleasure, just a different set of manners. It appeared my tastes were changing.

Was I getting old, I wondered? Had the Synia I still kept hidden made me less a male, less potent? Curse it, I had seed enough to make a female pregnant! Only Lords seemed jaded, youths too callow, slaves too feeble.

Maybe I was just acquiring gentlemanly taste at last? Discrimination, as my father would have phrased it? Gods knew he'd shaken his head often enough when he saw those I'd chosen in the past.

My father inspected Keril with far more attention than most of them had ever earned…

A normal enough day: riding out at dawn and weapons practice later, in the drill court for once, beside my troops. Then the afternoon spoiled by a rash of reports that created a string of petty orders winging or galloping south, only one I cared about enough to have it channeled through the temples. The sun was dipping fast as I arrived inside our inner courtyard and began the walk around it, the only sounds the splashing from the central fountain and the swishing sound of running water through the narrow radiating channels.

Around me everything was deep in shadow, every flower was closing and the air felt cooler. I was alone at last and thinking that a bath—

"Ash?"

No warning, curse him. I took my hand off my dagger and made a sweeping bow. "My revered father."

He was alone for once, upon a bench beneath a tree, his face in shadow. Dressed in burgundy and black, with garnets, I had missed him for a moment in the growing darkness. Now he stood and came to join me on the colonnaded walk around the building. Attacks, or mockery, his manner said, he'd deal with either, if he had to.

As he fell into step beside me our footsteps echoed softly on the painted tiles. Two different notes; my father's sandals made a higher sound than boots, reminding me that I was scruffy.

"I saw you at practice earlier. Impressive." He smiled. "Even your detractors don't complain about the way you keep in shape."

"Don't they? Do they think that's why I do it?"

"Who knows, or cares. It keeps them happy. And keeps you sharp for when you're needed."

"You have a mission for me?" I was half hopeful. The thought of some action... I might be pretending calm but I'd never liked waiting.

"No. Suddenly the world's gone very peaceful." Father sounded just a touch regretful.

"Bored, Father?"

"Say thoughtful, Ash. When it goes quiet one wonders where the mischief's building."

"Spies not saying?"

"They seem uncertain. So we wait, and guard our backs, and keep in readiness with sparring." Father's smile was knowing.

We reached the half a dozen steps and studded northern doors that barred my own apartments. I didn't knock or call. I'd heard the grating as the watchman at his spy hole gave the word to raise the heavy bar inside and give me access.

My father paused before he carried on toward his gilded, just-as-guarded eastern entrance. "Finished for the day?"

"Gods, yes." I yawned, my foot already on the lowest step. "A bath, and supper, in that order, if I stay awake to eat it."

"I'll join you, if I may."

"Feel free. Will you bathe as well? I have an oil old Sheshman sent me recently. You might admire it."

"Really? That sounds pleasant."

I was thinking only that we seldom met in private these days. I had no qualms about it as I bowed my father in, and called for slaves to serve him.

We were royally escorted through my lower chambers, up the inner stairway to my middle floor and then up higher. As we neared the bath my robe slaves scampered round. There was the usual fuss.

One curtain parted in the furthest archway. Keril, come to greet me, smiled welcome then stopped in his tracks. He'd heard my voice, but hadn't thought of strangers. He knew so little of the palace. He didn't need to, I'd told Medi. In fact the less he knew the more I'd like it. But he had been warned that he was something private, and that "privacy" meant kept secluded.

His gaze flashed to mine, aware he'd failed me. Next moment he was gone, as if he'd never been there. But my father's head was turned in that direction. "So," he said softly. Curious, was he? Come to think of it, he would be. Still if I ignored the lapse, good manners should require he did too.

We settled in the perfumed water, chatting inconsequences. By the time we climbed out the admirable Medishel had my father's own robes and attendants fetched in. The Voice of Heaven smiled at him. The nearest slaves stared fixedly at carpets. Everybody tiptoed.

Father's people had provided him a long-sleeved, milk-white tunic, heavily embroidered in gold thread, with crimson sash and trousers. They had brought him jewels to choose from, in a gold-edged casket.

Medi, not to be outdone, had brought me darkest green with yellow panels at the shoulders over matching yellow trousers, and a slew of rings and bracelets. Robe slaves threaded fine gold chain into my hair as they re-braided it. For a quiet supper in my own apartment? I was laughing inside, but I made no comment.

Back in my most private sitting room beyond the curtains, wine and steaming dishes waited. From somewhere out of sight came music; plaintive strings played softly. Everything was glowing from the lamps and firelight.

On the table there was scented rice and tiny, battered fish, a dish of skewered, seeded lamb, diced gote in sour sauce and dainty packages of duckling wrapped in vine leaves. There were candied fruits and frothy gotes' milk sorbets, followed by a creamy cheese confection served with sugared lemon slices and a sweet dessert wine. Nose and stomach could rejoice but otherwise…

The place felt like a temple. Supper had become an act of worship in my household? I could deal with that. I grabbed a skewer, took a hefty bite then raised my glass. "My royal father," came out none too clearly.

Father chuckled. "Hungry, Ash?"

Suddenly I thought of wide, white shoulders and regretted Father's presence, but I had been raised a royal liar. I waved the skewer. "I'm entitled."

The tension round me eased at last. Irreverence had always been our way, in private. Eager slaves cleared empty dishes. Wine and fruits were offered then the slaves departed for wherever Medi sent them.

More idle talk; a current scandal. Father was inclined to be indulgent. "A fool's a fool," he said. "You'll never change that. Don't tell them privacies, or lend them money."

I laughed, and toasted him, "To wisdom."

He smiled, sipped his wine and savored its aroma, swirling it within the goblet. "Was he still wearing silver?"

Ouch. Tactless of him. "I liked it that way," I said lightly.

"Hmm. You still enjoy him?"

Tactless was hardly the word, I thought, startled into stillness. "Why not."

"Why not indeed. I confess to being piqued by all those rumors. Will you humour me for once?"

"Father?" I said blankly.

"May I see him?"

Tell my father, and my king, this was unseemly? That it wasn't quite polite, what he was asking? I think I frowned. I know I kept my mouth shut as I rang the bell.

A slave ran through the nearest curtains, dropped to his knees and touched his forehead to the carpet. "Send Keril to me," I said curtly. The head bobbed and the rest made speed to follow orders. It wasn't long, I don't suppose, although it felt it.

The heavier outer curtains to my bedroom swung aside and Keril hesitated by the entry, bare-foot, bare-chested, tall and straight and somewhat anxious. "My lord?"

No doubt he thought he was in trouble. And thought I was alone again, because I'd called for him. The curtain closed before he realized I wasn't. He stopped right there, and waited. After that first, startled glance he wasn't looking at my father. Hadn't knelt either; hadn't been taught to, at my orders. Didn't, possibly, even know who it was he was so carefully ignoring?

My lips twitched. I wondered how my much-feared parent would stomach being treated like a nobody—and by a bed slave—after all the fervor he'd been treated to since his arrival.

My reading of him answered; he looked too bland for anger. I figured some amusement had been added to this sudden thirst for risqué knowledge. "Serve my guest some wine," I said then smiled a little.

Encouraged, he stepped forward, flicked a look—he knew the difference nowadays—and brought the proper flagon. "Wine, sir?" Quiet. Respectful. Not fearful. Not the proper fawning titles, or the kneeling shuffle. Nor the eyes averted. His eyes were as I'd liked, direct and open. Right now more curious than nervous.

I had a sudden stab of panic. If Father decided to be offended… It had seemed just an amusing gamble, but it was Keril's head—and mine—laid on the table. And it was too late now to change it. He'd have to play the cards I'd wagered.

Keril, unknowing, bent to pour, with concentration. Wasn't used to strangers. Thought, perhaps, he might disgrace me? His hair, which I had kept, was caught behind with silver cord. It slithered forward when he bent. I saw my father eye it. Task completed, Keril glanced my way again. I held my glass out so he crossed the room, and dared a silent question. *"Why am I here?"* his eyes were asking me. *"What are you up to?"*

Risking your neck, I could have answered, because I never trained you. It didn't feel so simple any longer. I touched his hand as he served. Without a word he put the flagon back then folded down beside me in that foreign way that always seemed to suit him. Sitting there I breathed his perfume. It was a distraction, one that made my pulse beat faster.

Father didn't slow it down again. "That name…" he queried.

"Keril," I repeated. No title, not even "father". He must have known by then what I was doing, he ignored the rudeness of my answer. Instead he focused on the white-clad slave who'd settled in below me on the carpet.

"Keril. Are you, as it seems, as tall as your master?"

"Almost, sir." The grey eyes fixed on him, attentive. Hells. Keril wasn't deaf or blind, as slaves should be; he had a mind, however different. I'd let it stay that way. Right now I hoped he'd use it.

"And your age?"

"I was told I'm counted twenty, sir."

"Your country?"

Keril's brows furrowed. "I'm… not sure, sir."

My father was raising his glass. His hand paused halfway. "Not sure," he repeated.

"I know it must be far from here, because my lord says so, but I never saw anything that—" He broke off, then said, "There was a village, before I was… brought here. It was called Lusbenan, or something like that."

"You came from there?"

"No, but a child was sick. I nursed him." Keril spoke quite freely, I thought. I wondered why I'd never asked such pointed questions. I watched his face, and then my father's.

"You have some skill at healing, then?"

"I thought, a little, sir." He hesitated, seemed to think my father's interest was genuine, confessed, "At least I had, but now I fear it's fading."

"For lack of practice?"

"Lack of—" Keril glanced up at me. "Of what I was, sir."

Defiled. That was what he'd said that evening, what he was thinking now, perhaps. Did he believe his purity had given him the power of healing? By all the gods, this was a crazy conversation. Slave and king debate the slave's religion? Which should be only as his master thought, but all-too-obviously wasn't.

How would Father take it?

"Does your master forbid you your prayers?" Father asked him, far too kindly. Was I in for a lecture too? At least that made it partly my fault.

"My master has not done that." Oh very tactful, he knew I didn't like religion mentioned. Then he straightened. "But then I am no longer the same person anyway, and it would be stupid to dwell on the past, would it not, sir?"

I almost gasped. A question of his own? He was putting his neck in a noose, and no mistake.

"Hmm." My father nodded! "So, have you found a new religion here in Kadduchan?"

Did the grey eyes widen slightly? "Sir, I do not know your gods. Does that offend you?"

There was a silence. Me, I sat like stone, and prayed my father kept his sense of humour.

My fervent prayers were answered. The Voice of Heaven Keril didn't know he spoke to raised his eyes to mine, without expression. "Your master's told you nothing of his own religion?"

Keril almost frowned before he answered, "No, sir. Perhaps he does not wish to."

I almost interrupted that time.

"Ah." My holy father turned his head to Keril. "Then it is entirely proper. A slave should know no more than what his master chooses."

Keril stared at Father for a moment. "I will remember that, sir. Thank you."

"You will, but why?"

"Your words have made things clearer, sir. They tell me... who I am now."

"And who would that be?" Father asked him.

The questions were growing stranger than the answers. Where were we heading? If they knew it was more than I did.

Keril seemed undaunted. "I am a slave, that's all. It's very simple. I have a name again, my master uses. I am to be... whatever is required of me." As if that was too obvious to mention. I saw my father even nod approval.

But suddenly I saw a male who'd answered all of this with calm and reason; whose face showed nothing but serene acceptance, despite his youth, his strength, his whole, impressive presence. My stomach tightened. It was the *priest* I had here at my feet, a glimpse into a past I never looked at. It was disturbing, and I didn't want it. I knew, then, why I'd never asked such questions. Why I hadn't followed up my earlier request for information.

"Whatever he requires," Father echoed softly, then looked at me as if I was a book he'd never opened. I shifted on my couch. Enough was enough. As if I'd spoken, Father nodded graciously and took his eyes off Keril; signal that the interview was over.

Dismissed, Keril set his palms together, bowed, and turned away. The weighted curtains swung behind him. My father eyed them. "Curious," he said abruptly. "I can see…" He looked at me.

"Don't ask it."

One raised eyebrow. "Ah. Then I won't." He looked amused, I guessed he'd meant to bait me, and succeeded. "Has it occurred to you that you have taken his religion from him? His vocation? For many priests that's ten times worse than losing freedom."

"Slaves have no purpose but to serve their owners," I said harshly. "You trying to say I'm in the wrong?"

"No, not at all. You're in the right, he said so too. But I wondered, Ash." He hesitated for a moment. "Perhaps *you* are his new religion."

I burst out laughing. I really couldn't help it. "Father, how can you even think that? You've told me time enough I'm halfway to a devil!"

He didn't smile. "Ash, be careful, will you? When a priest gives up his life, he's content with his lot, because he's sure of his choice. But a freeman taken as a slave, he serves, however well, against his will, and maybe still remembering his freedom. Which of these fits your virgin, Ash? He wasn't cowed, in fact it seemed to me the male's obedience is *his* decision more than yours."

"Oh, come on—"

But Father raised a hand to stop me. "A slave is no one, but do you forget this one, when he's out of sight? I've only seen him once, but I think I'll find myself wondering, in a day or so, what he's doing, even what he's thinking. Ash, I spend my life measuring males, but I don't know what you have here, and what we don't know can harm us."

I wasn't entirely loath to bid him goodnight, affable as he was after. He'd left behind unsettling questions.

Chapter 19

Not that I was one to shoot at shadows. The weird exchange was mostly nonsense, I decided, and as long as Keril was obedient—and shivered at my touch—why should I care about his motives? I put the whole thing out of my mind. Or I thought I did. A few days later, one bright morning, I heard myself asking, "What d'you do, in daylight?"

Keril's lips twitched, then his head turned on the pillows. He did look heavy-eyed that morning. Probably I was the same. But then he smiled. "Sometimes I sleep, my lord."

There was a look my father certainly hadn't seen. Medi had been teaching him the arts of gentle massage. I had tried him out when I retired the previous evening. He had good strong hands; so good I'd taught him a couple of other tricks, which needed demonstration. Not surprising we were late next morning.

"Meaning you miss too much at night?" I challenged.

"Some nights are... very wakeful." He was, of course, trying not to laugh. He did laugh now, till he recalled himself to Medi's "suitable behavior".

I grinned. "You'll sleep today then."

"W-with my lord's permission."

"Where?"

"My lord?"

"Where do you sleep?" I sat up, abruptly. "Not with the other slaves?"

"No, Master Medishel sends me to a room."

"A room, eh? Where he put you when you first arrived?"

"No, one he says is more private, and more convenient for you, my lord."

"So he favors you," I said, relaxing.

"Yes." He nodded seriously. "But it is a very small room, and I am forbidden to sleep with the others anyway, so he does not really treat me any better."

"His words?"

A startled glance. "Why yes, my lord."

Now *I* was curbing laughter. "Medishel is correct in all things," I said. And found I was still curious. I pushed the cover back and swung onto my feet. At once he left the bed as well to offer me my robe and slippers. "Show me this room, then."

Did he look surprised? Of course he didn't argue, only holding back the time it took to find his trousers, fastening the cord as he moved past me. Slaves appeared as the curtains parted, alerted by our exodus—only Medi entered uninvited these days—but I waved dismissal.

It *was* small. More like a cupboard, barely enough for the pallet and the bucket it held. A hint of Keril's perfume battled with a trace of disinfectant.

I'd never considered that before either. No, of course, he wouldn't be allowed to reach the lower drains as other slaves did, nor reveal himself to any but my eunuchs. I supposed the bucket was the best solution. There was, of course, my own accommodation, only steps away, but Keril *was* a slave, and Medi would have palpitations.

There really was nothing else. Plain and bare, and the window higher than most. A dog couldn't have squeezed through it, let along Keril, which I supposed was why Medi had picked such a place. I wasn't sure what to say. Except when I turned round to leave there was a battered copper lamp, a meager thing but still an unexpected trifle for a slave to have, beside the doorway. "Why the lamp?"

Did Keril look embarrassed? That was new. "For when it's dark, my lord. When I can't see."

"You can't see in the dark," I echoed slowly.

He hung his head. "Not when it's wholly dark, but Master Medishel still hopes I will improve, now I am fitter."

"Hmm." Except he *was* fit now. *And* still lacked an inner eyelid. Born with weaker eyes then? Still, that was a minor defect, certainly for someone closed up here in the palace.

"If my lord has seen enough? It's only a place for sleeping," Keril said, as if afraid he bored me.

"When you're awake, where d'you go then?" I turned to leave, and he fell in a step behind me.

"If you aren't here, my lord, I go to Master Medishel. Or exercise. I am not idle."

Was that what he thought, that I suspected he was lazy when I couldn't see him? In my upper sitting room I chose a couch by the long open windows and settled down in comfort. "What sort of exercise?"

"As I always have, my lord, to keep me healthy."

"Show me."

Very strange. A stately sort of dance; no hurry, no exertion. Waste of time, I thought, then wondered. Keril didn't eat much but he had no freedom to... "Again." I stood and moved behind him.

Stately, yes, but not as easy as he made it seem, and I could feel the exertion by the time I stopped him. That explained the muscles on him. Interesting, but I wasn't going to try it anywhere in public. People would... "Enough." I threw myself into a chair and waved him to be seated on the carpet. Keril offered grapes. I took them. "So what orders do you receive from Master Medishel? Are they amusing?"

"They are useful. At least, I hope so."

"What? Cleaning?" I had to smile. He was always spotless. The mere thought of him scrubbing a floor... besides, I thought, I wouldn't like it.

"I've cleaned your boots, my lord," Keril offered.

"My boots. From hunting?" But he wouldn't know that, maybe.

"When you speak of hunting, I've noticed that you often come back dirty. I thought it was on horseback."

Clearly, these words said, riding should have kept me clean. Did he assume I kept falling off? "Did you now? What do you know about hunting? Or horses?"

"About hunting, nothing, my lord, but I did sit on a horse once. It was a very nice animal."

"You did?" Sometimes one could treat Keril like a male—in bed, increasingly so—but this, I felt, was one of the other times.

He smiled. "But not as you do, my lord. You don't *sit*, you..." Words failed him.

I was startled. "When did you see me riding?"

Grey eyes, suddenly uncertain. "From the windows. Is that too not permitted?"

"No more than what his master chooses." A plague on fathers. He had no idea how literally Keril took things. "Show me."

To my surprise he'd picked the eastern corner near to Rag's apartments, a boring length where our adjacent top-floor outside balconies were walled apart; where narrow, deep-set windows marked the corner, iron shutters set inside the flimsy wooden lattices, that could be swung across to protect my flank.

But now, the shutters flat against the openings, each deep stone niche was plenty wide enough to sit on. I suddenly recalled I'd sat here hours one summer, as a cub, till shooed away for safety by my eunuchs. I hid a smile. A tiny window when Medishel was looking, but perched behind a flimsy screen above an open drop when he wasn't? Did Keril realize that Medishel would have forbidden him to go there?

Well, he'd said he wouldn't jump again, and he hadn't; small point now losing sleep over it. I leaned across and examined the tiny segment of the world outside he'd found to look at.

The city was nothing but distant sounds, hidden by the thick white inner walls. From here I couldn't even see the yellow ones beyond them, let alone the jumbled rooftops. There wasn't much to see inside them either. A walled-in garden lay below me, to the left. A few slaves tended plants and swept its tracery of tiled paths but no one was in sight beyond; no courtiers, not even soldiers though I knew there'd be some circling the building. As I recalled my father seldom used that garden, both of us preferred our inner courtyard.

Below and to my right, the nearest portion of the Outer Palace reared, as tall but on a lower level. The nearer walls were decorated with a giant, somewhat faded mural of the desert, seldom seen by others. As I watched, a troop of real live soldiers marched across its lower border.

Was that what Keril had been watching? Soldiers on routine patrol and pictures of a world he'd never lived in? He wouldn't know it but behind that single guarded stair there lay our private passage to the Gate Hall's dais or the formal audience chambers, which was why these murals took the place of doors and windows. Our forebears had learnt to guard their backs with fervor; a single exit over there and access here only round the corner to the east, the maze-like walkway under Rag's apartment, while down below us double-thickness walls and padlocked storerooms lay between our subjects and our safety.

He'd picked an unused garden, ancient, painted walls and empty sky to stare at? Not the best of entertainment, when my wider sunlit balconies lay round the corner offering him distant glimpses of both plains and desert, and entrancing sunsets. Why not loiter there in comfort?

Because below and to the right, before the Gate Hall's murals rose and hid the rest, there was a glimpse into the royal stables. I'd clean forgotten, but now I recalled the final stages of my slow recovery from desert fever, those uncertain weeks and months that robbed me of the priest-created En-Syn. Sitting half the day with eyes bent to those stables, because I couldn't get down to my horses, and because there was always something going on, and other people.

A prisoner, I'd felt like. Very lonely.

"My lord?" a startled voice enquired.

"Nothing." Then words came out before I thought them. "Keril, *can* you ride?"

Chapter 20

Stupid. Unheard-of. It'd cause a scandal. Plague on it, I thought, so what's one more. A speck, compared to what I'm hiding nowadays. And I'm my father's son. The rest, apart from him, can walk around me. With that in mind I cornered Father; at a banquet where I figured he would have to smother his reactions. Conversation eddied round us, almost drowning out my words. "You're leading me astray, you know that?"

Father only smiled. "As I recall, you've never needed leading." He was examining a dish of brandied apricots.

"Ah, but this time it's your doing. You said I should find out more." I drank my wine.

His hand retreated, waved the kneeling slave to leave us. "Do we talk about your new possession?" Face impressively impassive. Not a hint the razor-mind I so admired was active.

"He says he's sat a horse." I turned my head enough to watch.

This time his brows shot up before he stopped them but he didn't look at me. He waved another slave away, the gesture more impatient this time. It was noted. He controlled the world without a murmur. We became a small oasis in the clamor all around us. I watched him as his agile brain selected and discarded. He struck, but at an angle. "You would let the world inspect him?"

Inwardly I gave him points for tactics. "Less than you did," I retorted.

"But—" He had the grace to hesitate.

"But you're my father? Does that make it different?" Attack, then part-retreat. "Don't panic, he won't step out half naked *this* time." I smiled, and drank again, as if our talk was nothing.

Father frowned, aware I'd weakened his position, and covered it by drinking too. "Do as you please with what you own. I have to say I find the thought surprisingly distasteful in this case. Does it not bother you at all?"

At the time I'd shrugged and hadn't answered but it had. It did. It had almost ended the mad impulse there and then. But I'd woke next day, left Keril to his tasks for Medi, and his exercise, and all the empty hours he never mentioned, returned that night and issued orders. Medi had blinked twice before they sank in. Now he was wracking his brains, trying to give me what I wanted.

It was two evenings later before I got to see what he'd come up with. It was a good thing I was sitting down. My mouth, I fear, fell open. I know I choked. "Keril, is that you in there?"

"I think so, my lord." He sounded muffled. And rueful. Probably because of my expression. But really… The fool looked like a walking anthill. He was swathed from head to foot in pale grey cloaks. It was a wonder he could see where he was going. And as for the shape of him… Chop his legs off at the calves, I thought, it could be Sheshman in there.

I began to shake with laughter, leaning back among my cushions. "Gods, Medi," I got out between gasps. "I said he had to be covered, not smothered. Keril, get out of there before you melt."

Medishel looked lost. "My prince," he said forlornly.

Keril was still fighting his way out of all the mass. Yes, an inner cloak as well, and then a voluminous white robe. It looked as if Medi had lent one of his. The cloth wrapped itself around Keril's neck as he tugged at it and reminded me…

"Desert gear. I should have thought. I must have shelves of it around here somewhere."

"Your own, highness?" Medishel stepped back in shock. It'd been much more fun baiting Medishel since Keril arrived. I hadn't done so well for years.

"Why not? The size'll be all right." My eyes fell on bare white feet as the final layers came off. "Even my boots might do. His feet are no longer than mine. Might be a bit loose, though. They're narrower, wouldn't you say?"

"*Boots*, highness?" Now Medi really was shocked, but if I was going to do this…

"Boots. And gloves, I'd think. Some decent trousers, a shirt, a light robe, and a full-length desert head-dress. And take care about the trousers." I grinned at the older male. "They'll need to protect some parts of him I'm rather fond of, and he isn't used to saddles."

"My—prince." Medi said faintly.

Keril coughed and turned his head away to hide his laughter. Then jerked back to face me. No, I hadn't told him.

"Horses?" he ventured, grey eyes wide and startled.

"Horses," I said firmly. I think he forgot to breathe, till Medi hustled him away, presumably to raid my wardrobe.

White desert robes, a modest mix of silks and cottons. Loose trousers tucked into soft boots. A wide cloth sash. The laced shirt would be soft as well, collarless, the sleeves long and gathered. Not airy muslin; too revealing, even hidden by the flowing outer robe and tailed head-dress.

The last bit solved the final problem of his staying private. The band around his head that held the veil in place secured a flip-down visor. Flipped halfway the visor gave protection from the sun—or put his upper face in discreet shadow. (Dropped right down it would, if he had ever needed it, have been an extra barrier against a sandstorm too bad for *our* inner lids—the ones *he* didn't have—to cope with. But he didn't need to know that.) When the veil beneath was open, its two ends would reach below his waist. But wrapped around his neck, as they were now, they hid his face so well that nothing but his eyes were showing.

And his hands below these flowing sleeves. I'd never really thought how elegant those were, before that day. Now I found I was studying them. They twitched. Nervously, I realized. I hadn't spoken.

"That'll do." I rose, and signaled Medi out. His slaves left with him. Keril stood still and let me walk all round him. Gods, those eyes above the veil. "I tell Medishel, cover you, and now he's managed it I find I want to tear the clothes right off you." I grinned. I thought the grey eyes glinted. "Maybe not tear them off," I said, continuing behind him. "Maybe I'll just remove them, piece by piece." By then I'd found the pin behind his neck that held the veil secure, and freed the lips inside it. When I came around in front of him again I saw that they were smiling. It was another day before the robes were used as I'd intended.

Yes, Keril in clothes was a new experience. Not for him, though. I supposed he'd worn stuff not dissimilar much longer than the year he'd been without them. Boots as well, perhaps; he moved as if he owned them.

He was very careful over the veil though. That had Medishel all over it. I watched him check the head-dress, tug the silver pin behind his neck then pull the pale leather gloves on. Only the eyes were visible, and even those were shadowed this time, by the narrow, flip-down visor that extended from the upper border of the padded headband. Then he stood and waited.

"Calm down."

A gulp, behind the veil. "Yes, my lord."

"Stay by me, and follow orders," I repeated.

"Yes." He'd have walked on his hands if I'd ordered it, he was so het up. I hadn't seen him this unsettled—out of bed—for ages.

"And when you fall off," I added nastily.

"My lord?"

I had to laugh. "Just make sure you stay covered up. We don't want Medishel having a heart attack, do we?"

"No, my lord." That sounded better.

"Right. The stables."

A brisk walk to the upper stairs—even that would be new territory for him—down and across the middle floor. My pulse was up. We were about to leave my private quarters, where he was a body slave. Exclusive. Past these doors a slave was normally fair game, but I'd concealed both face and body, publicly defying custom, and my presence was a silent warning.

Down the final stairs, past portraits of my long-dead forebears. A sour-looking lot. I half-expected they'd start scowling, but everything stayed obstinately peaceful.

Through my outer doors and down the steps into the open air. I paused upon the marble walkway as the doors swung to behind me. Keril didn't seem to notice, gazing round. Of course, he'd never had an open view of all that lay below him.

When I stepped down again and took the nearest garden path he followed me at once, our feet a muted shushing on the tiles.

Across the inner courtyard, cutting through the fragrant gardens. Honeybells assailed my nostrils and the mustard fronds of water grasses brushed against my trousers where they fringed the narrow sunken channels. I chose a course that kept us in the shade of lemon trees and awning-palms until we had to cross the open, sunlit octagon around the central fountain. The turquoise tiles, set with specks of mica, glittered brighter than the giggling waters. This place was a balm to all the senses, only not today. My nerves were twitching.

We passed no more than garden-slaves to start with, but as we approached the inner gates I saw I'd dodged a pair of Father's generals with their mandatory Kemik escort, skirting round beneath my northern colonnade to reach his western quarters. One glanced across, the other didn't seem to notice.

Rag was back as well. More trouble in the north? I spared a passing thought to what my father might be planning—nothing south or he'd have called for me as well—but didn't dawdle, since the inner gates would likely still be open. Which meant the outer ones were closed. That was the way it worked. And if its guardians didn't hear the proper signals nasty things would start to happen in the maze between them.

Up two stairs onto the colonnade again, straight past the inner guards and down the ramp into the passage. It was always colder under here, and dimmer, and our footsteps echoed. Keril matched my steps until we left the light of day behind but then he wavered, reaching out to touch the wall beside him. I remembered then his sight would be defective in this almost-total darkness. Damn, I should have called for torches. But when I slowed and took his arm his breathing steadied and he murmured, "Thank you, lord." So I went on as I had started.

Considering, he made it through the middle of the maze without much trouble, nothing bar a stumble at a corner sometimes. More aware for once of my surroundings, I spared a glance toward the iron hatchways in the ceiling he was blind to, and the "studded" walls that were in fact iron rods, each long enough, released, to chop this narrow passage into caged compartments. (And heavens help the male too slow to dodge them.) The ignorant were always startled by the torchlit, "bare" stone walls, the switchback corners and the sudden slopes, but then they didn't know, as I did, how the inner gates could close in moments, or what deadly tek survived to make this building tighter than a fortress.

Meanwhile Keril's footsteps matched my own again, entirely trusting. Did he recall being brought through here? He wouldn't have seen much anyway, of course, but mightn't he have felt the drop in temperature, and noticed how the sounds had hollowed? And the curses Medi must have uttered, maneuvering that cage around these corners? What would his face have revealed if I'd been here to see it? I had seen some scared expressions under here. Had Keril realized, this second time, how strong the prison was around him?

We threaded through the zigs and zags and reached the final upward slope. A single ray of daylight beckoned. I released him and he fell behind again. Below the beam of light the iron outer doors rose grimly, twice my height and still in shadow. Today they seemed to loom in disapproval and my heart beat faster at the challenge.

The guards sprang into line. Their captain bowed and signaled. Slaves, shackled to the gates, began to turn the wheels on the crossbars. Metal groaned in protest. Keril's footsteps faltered.

I drew a breath and snapped, "All right?" I felt... the way I did before a battle. The doors began to swing aside upon their massive hinges, light intruded, arrowing toward him. Heat came with it.

"Maybe you shouldn't do this." He sounded strained. "I am a fool, I do not know your world. I will disgrace you."

"You'd better not."

The band of light was growing. In its spotlight Keril's eyes stared out into the world he feared, as if its warmth might burn him. Which it could, I thought—all that pale flesh—if he'd come out uncovered. But it wasn't that he was afraid of.

"I'm not meant to do this, am I? Slaves, especially those like me, are *meant* to stay untaught. That's why they bar me from your lower quarters; why I must not touch your books." He'd had to drag his head around to face me.

"My books?" The doors were open and the guards were waiting but... He could read? It wasn't that surprising, now I thought about it. "Do you want them?"

"No." He shook his head.

"Keril, did you ask, about the books?" I said more patiently.

A sigh. "Yes, my lord. I'm sorry. I asked Master Medishel, once. He told me slaves don't read, or write, so I know it's not permitted. I do understand that," he said seriously.

Curse you, Father, I thought, if there was a way to *forget* how to read, he'd find it, wouldn't he? I shook my head. "You think I'm angry? I'm not. I should have wondered if you could read. Most slaves can't, that's what Medishel meant." And if he hadn't, he would do once I'd had a word about it. Keril hankered after my books? It might be interesting to see what he made of some of them.

Keril's face might be out of sight, but his doubt was painted head to toe. I dropped the subject. Right now he was spooked anyway, perhaps the dark had sapped his courage. "Ready now?" I took a step. The guards stood round us, deaf as trees. Or so they were pretending.

"My lord?" I turned. His head was down. Unusual. His eyes were hidden by the tilted visor but I heard him swallow. "Are there… many people, out there?"

Finally it hit me. Untouched. He'd even exercised indoors. I kept my voice even. "You've never been in a crowd, have you?"

"No, my lord. Except." A gulp. "The day you came."

The Gate Hall. "You could see them?"

"No, I heard. I…felt." His breathing wasn't even.

Stepping close, I told him, "There won't be crowds today, I promise. Less than usual, in fact, it's late for riding." Too right it was. Past noon. The keener riders would have set out earlier, and I'd had Medi find out who was due to ride that day, and have a watch kept to report their leaving. It was as quiet as I could make it, though I hadn't realized… "You turning coward on me?"

"No, my lord." Half insulted, half resigned. I kept a straight face, but when I stepped outside he was behind me.

Past midday, I've said, and hotter than a furnace. One breath and I decided the best route to the stable yards would be if we cut across the Gate Hall. Fewer lurked in that direction; only slaves at first, who ducked their heads, but past the Gate Hall we encountered people who stayed upright. Then it really started.

Whispers. Heads turned then averted fast. Then turned again, of course, as soon as I was past them. I'd worn the veil too, for riding out, but mine hung open and my outer robe, though white like Keril's, sported blue and amber braids, atop an amber shirt and trousers and a blue and white striped sash adorned with gold and amber fringes. And of course I wore a dagger at my belt, a second tucked into my boot, and went barehanded, merely carrying my gauntlets.

While behind me Keril's garments were unnaturally plain; no color anywhere, no weapon either. Medishel had removed every touch of decoration, every royal emblem. Still, once someone glimpsed the glint of silver on his headdress—I knew they'd guess what I had brought into the open.

Blank faces. Careful bows. I smiled affably and dared them to say, or do, anything they'd regret. It stayed peaceful all the way to the yard. I figured word would just about have reached my father and reminded myself I'd warned him. He could have voiced a veto, but he hadn't. I still wondered about that; was he curious too, or did he think he'd said enough to stop me.

The gate beneath the stable arch swung open so I knew the guard above had signaled my arrival; a step or two of shade and then the inner yard. By now the quadrangles within the white-walled stable blocks were wells of blazing sunlight. Buildings shimmered. I was dazzled when I stepped from cover. I blinked to clear my sight, then strode forward.

This section was the nearest to our private quarters, any mount that made it this far had a royal owner. The buildings round the sides were whitewashed brick, a generous square, and squat, round towers rose like giant bee-hives at the corners. There were covered walks inside the edges, and the stalls and storerooms had flat roofs so guards could move above, all round the yard and its approaches. But the yard itself was open to the sky, the yellow ochre earth that floored it baked as hard as tiles.

It was mildly busy: slaves at sedentary tasks, tucked into shade, and horses being led away; familiar sights and smells and noise. My spirits lightened. "Come on."

The head groom, Samchek, was a Kemik; wrinkled now around the temples, but still a barrel of a male in yellow cotton trousers and a sleeveless leather tunic. The Kemik race were famous for their skill with animals, and fighting. I'd have preferred his absence. Ah well, I ought to ask about young Ammet.

Samchek came to meet me, bowing. The copper key chain round his darkskinned neck, his badge of office, glittered in the sun like jewels, the contrast startling as ever. They jangled as he straightened up. He flicked a glance behind me, almost bowed again then stiffened, nostrils flaring. Ammet vanished from my mind.

"My prince?" he rumbled. Grooms went quiet, slaves' heads ducked into their shoulders. Free or slave, they all feared Samchek's temper.

I, of course, ignored it. "I'm not going far, don't worry. It's too hot now. Give me the grey. We'll see if she's recovered." Samchek didn't speak. "And whatever else needs exercising."

The nod was decidedly forced, but the male backed off quick enough. Which was as well. I wasn't going to take his outbursts, especially today. My father had indulged him, they'd been young together, but I found myself increasingly less patient with his prejudices and resentments. I watched him giving orders; every gesture spoke his outrage. Felt insulted, did he? One of these days, I thought, he'd go too far, even for my father. Maybe he knew that, or had worked out where to set his limit. At least he knew when he should keep his mouth shut.

I wondered what his underlings would go for. The grey, and what? Judging from Samchek's mood it certainly wouldn't be anything too valuable, which I supposed was only fitting. And I'd be wise to use this wait for something useful. "Keril?"

"My lord?" He came around to face me. The veiled eyes were solemn.

"Do you know how to mount?"

"To get on? Yes, I think so."

Why did I not feel reassured? "Are you sure, or shall I teach you?"

"My lord, I do think I can do that." A certain confidence? It sounded like it.

"Very well. They're bringing out two horses. Mine will be a grey. As pale as you." I smiled to reassure him.

"Very well, my lord. Am I—am I to get on the other horse, when it comes?"

"Mount, we say mount, and yes, if you feel happy about it go and mount up when you're ready. Don't wait for me to tell you, but don't try to rush things, all right?"

"Yes, my lord."

Now we were here he did seem calmer. I figured the best thing was to look confident, and let him get on with it. And hope he did all right, because the towers and several doorways had acquired bystanders, all carefully *not* watching.

Keril's eyes had shifted past me. "Two horses, my lord; one white and one black."

"Fine. Don't—" I stopped myself mid-warning. He'd said he thought he could do it. It seemed to me I had to let him find out. "Go on then." He walked past me while I spared another, oh-so-casual look at all those doorways. Easy, Keril, don't let me down now, I was thinking. A lot of eyes found targets elsewhere for the moment. I turned back.

The grey was right before me, in my way. I caught the reins and mounted in one swift movement, wanting to see how Keril managed, but the grey, too long unridden, jerked her head and twisted. By the time I got her in hand again, and turned, Keril was head to horn with the other horse.

He'd said black, but I'd never dreamed— They'd brought the half-tamed stallion. It was dancing on its toes and pulling forward.

Jump off? Shout a warning? Which was faster? The panic (and the burning anger) took a single, thumping heartbeat, but the chance to act was over. Keril had approached the brute as if it was a pony. Now it towered over him. He had his hand raised too—ye gods—to pet the creature, was it? If it dropped its head the brute could spear him in the face and if not, at best he'd have no fingers any second; Samchek *knew* the black had had one set already.

The groom who'd brought it out had backed away. The reprobate had loosed the reins as well. And no one else was near enough to grab them. My heart lurched. "Keril!"

The white-clad figure turned. "My lord?" Behind his undefended back the horse moved *closer*, nostrils flaring, and the dainty-looking fluted horn set high between its ears tipped forward, angling to attack him!

"Get away from there. Now!"

He wasn't moving fast enough, I thought desperately, kicking the grey forward. Then I realized the black was coming after him, its head still lowering. "By all that's holy, Keril, shift yourself! The damned thing's—"

The damned thing was following him. Not chasing, not attacking. Like a dog at heel. When Keril stopped so did the horse. I choked down words Keril would think aimed at him, and told myself not to make a public display. Then my wits caught up with me, and I began to smolder.

"Did I do something wrong, my lord?"

"No." I drew a slower breath. "No, you didn't. Keril, what did you do back there?" I picked on past experience. "You didn't... pray, did you?"

I saw him blink. "No, my lord. I don't," he said carefully.

"Then what the— What did you do, with that horse?"

When Keril turned his head the black nudged him in the back, with its soft nose. I swear Keril was smiling at the brute. Don't ask me how I knew.

"I introduced myself, my lord. It seemed polite, to do that?" He looked up at the horse, and stroked its head. Behind the ears. The black, I'd been warned, was touchy about its ears. The ears in question twitched. The head came over Keril's shoulder.

"You said hello. Right. Likes you, does he?"

"I think so. Is that not good?" Keril had begun to sound puzzled.

Not half as much as I was. "No, that's fine. Do they always do that?"

"I haven't met many horses, my lor—" He'd spotted all our watchers.

Somewhere deep inside of me a storm was rising. Samchek. No other male would lose control so suddenly. No other male would dare. His dignity was wounded, was it? Thrown one of his famous tantrums, given word to bring a rogue for a beginner? What had been his purpose? Make my slave look stupid? Break his neck?

Insult his prince?

I smiled at Keril, outwardly serene. "Get on, d'you think then?"

"If you wish, my lord."

Still quiet. No longer taking anything I'd said before for granted. Curse these vultures all around us. I nodded my permission.

He wasn't used to stirrups; took a hold of mane and saddle, bounced on his toes and leapt; pure muscle. The landing wasn't perfect, but the black stood like a rock and let him, and few of the idlers watching could have done it better. He understood the reins, though, gathered them together in one hand, and only then looked down at what had been in his way.

"Stirrups." I rode in alongside. He studied my near foot, all but the heel of my boot now hidden in the toughened leather sling, and fitted himself into his own, more clumsy about that than what he'd done before. "If you want to turn?" I watched his hands. The sun lit the leather-clad fingers, and glinted off an edge of dainty silver shackle where one sleeve had lifted. The hands didn't move, I'd need to—

But the black moved, slowly, carefully. His knees? I'd missed the game entirely. "Other way?" I asked him. This time I looked lower. The knee moved, no more than a touch, but that was all it took. The horse responded.

This horse obeyed him? I must be drunk, or crazy, but if I was it looked like half the stable had joined me. Some of the bolder ones had even ventured from their doorways for a better view. They looked astounded.

I'd meant to stay here, but this was both too crowded, and too public.

"More?"

The veiled head turned. He wanted it so much he couldn't say it. Why? Because the horse and he had found an instant mutual attraction?

When the stallion shied away I mended my expression. Had I scared the horse, or its rider? Did he sense my anger? Think he'd caused it? That I'd changed my mind?

"Stay close." I started forward. This yard led down slope to others, to horses, hounds and hunting birds, and thence into the greater palace and eventually the city. None of which was private. But a smaller gate across the way was wide enough to let a horse through, and would let me skirt the formal gardens, curve around within the outer walls and use a less frequented outside gate, due east toward the desert.

Seeing what I wanted, slaves who'd turned toward the larger exit changed their minds. I walked the horses as they passed us, giving Keril time to settle and the slaves a start to run ahead and warn the sentries at the other gates we'd pass through. I noted Keril's hands and feet were still; no fidgeting. No trouble. The black was still behaving when the final gate appeared before us. I wondered how far I should take him.

Chapter 21

The sun was dipping lower when I brought him back and he was tired, and winded. I was feeling, if I must admit it, somewhat guilty. After that amazing start... I should have known; he'd never lied to me. He really hadn't more than "sat" a horse, he must have worked out how to turn from watching others. After that he had no notion. But the black cooperated. I had seen it. I was trying to believe it.

Maybe whatever fascinated me had drawn that thoroughbred. It *liked* unseating people, but I swear it was upset when Keril fell. It didn't even need to be recaptured; the damn thing skidded to a halt, stood over him and nudged him till he rose again. I tell you, I'd had trouble keeping quiet.

I'd opted for the edges of the desert, a few miles east of the palace. It was downhill and it'd taken us a while to get there, starting at a careful walk and ending at a canter as he grew more confident and I was sure that he could turn between the rows of stunted trees without a problem. They were fruit trees, most the grafted mix of oranges and lemons. Not too close together; not enough to hide our presence from the walls above and weaken our defenses if attackers tried to storm them. But enough. A branch weighed down with unpicked, over-ripened fruit could wake the senses.

I breathed in deep then pulled a face. The smell of dung was not so pleasant. Gotes and pigs were herded here too. There was a flock ahead, their youthful herder, looking scared to death, endeavoring to hide behind a tree trunk. But there were no other people and of course no houses. The town had never been allowed to spread in this direction, partly so that Father could encamp an army out here when he wanted to. The gate we'd used was meant for that, we seldom used it if the army wasn't mustered.

Out here there was a welcome hint of breeze, but once beyond the trees the change of scene was sudden, and dramatic; from tidy, irrigated orchards offering partial shade to dusty scrubland; spiny, moisture-hoarding plants and tracks from last year's troop deployments. We were high enough at first to gaze across the undulating waste that heralded the desert, right to the horizon. Nothing out there but a sea of swelling ochre hillocks sliding into eerie purple shadows.

Keril stopped. And stared?

"Desert. Do you understand?" I waited several heartbeats.

"Sand. And barren?" He hadn't turned. He sounded breathless.

"Good enough."

"Is everywhere out here...?"

"Desert? A lot is. There are fertile stretches, some are lusher than the palace, but they're mainly scattered to the north and south. We don't need to go down any lower here though, it's not too friendly." Better anyway to use the scrubland lower down this slope beside a dried up river; good a place as any for a lesson.

He was a willing pupil (though I noticed now he didn't look again into the distance) but the plant life had gone grayish-green, and brittle, dormant now until the rainy season, and the yellow ground was iron-hard with unexpected cracks and furrows. There was nothing soft to land on. The third time he came off he took a while to raise himself. The horse went frantic, swinging round protectively to keep me from him, butting at him with its nose—but not its horn—until he got his head up.

"Time to stop," I said. He'd made it to his feet but he was swaying.

"Yes, my lord. Of course." He sounded downcast and was very dusty now, a mix of earthy streaks and desert ochre and, when he came toward me, limping. "I didn't mean to scare him."

"Never mind that brute. Are you hurt?"

"It's nothing, my lord. I'm sorry. You told me not to do that."

I'd had him making ever-sharper turns. He'd raised his head at something and the black had twisted like a top and thrown him. Then stood over him to guard him? Someone had meant that horse for battle before they'd realized their error. The thing could pivot on a button; not a trick for a beginner.

"These things take time," I said. "We'd better get you back." A quick, submissive nod. He used the stirrups this time. Beneath the trees again I found a need for conversation. It might take his mind off his discomfort. And mine off the resurgence of that cursed itching. Every time it waited till I'd stopped expecting it. Hells knew what it was doing to me this time but I couldn't face that here in the open. "Did you read about the desert somewhere in the past? You obviously hadn't seen it."

"No, my lord." He was behind me once again.

"Then how...?" I waved him to ride forward.

"I've heard it spoken of in your apartments."

Reasonable answer. No it wasn't. Even if he'd come from far away... Tread gently? "So tell me, how does this compare with what you came from?

"Cold. Flat, metal walls. And always quiet." He had stiffened in the saddle and the words were too abrupt. The black had shied as well. So much for going carefully.

I gave it up. "Where were you from, male? Hells, you must know something."

A pause. "I only know it feels… very far away, my lord. I think I travelled to the mountain in my sleep, from somewhere else. When I awoke… It was the same to look at, in my cell, but… suddenly the smell was different. I had no other way to know at first, I never saw the world outside, until one day they came and took me out. I saw the mountains, and the sky…"

The way he said it… "That was *recent*? But when you were a child you must…?"

Another tiny pause. "I think my masters *always* kept me separate, my lord."

I gaped. "No family at all? No friends?" Keshat's fires, no *sky*? Indoors, and isolated, even as a child?

The veiled head swung my way at last. "Not then, my lord."

I couldn't think of anything to say. He answered for me. "I didn't know there were such things. I'd never seen them but…" How could one *hear* a smile? "Down here is warmer."

The black began to prance. He murmured something soothing, dropping back to give it room, the conversation tacitly concluded.

The yard was quiet again, the shadows lengthened. Most of the beasts were in their stalls, some with their long heads over the split doors, the strange affairs of humans for their entertainment. Two-legged onlookers might have given up waiting but my four-legged friends all turned, acknowledging our entry with a host of bobbing heads and stamping, warning anybody there of our arrival.

With luck we'd be away before the word spread further. Keril's robes were anything but white in places. Oh, he wasn't obviously hurting, they wouldn't see much else worth crowing over. But I found I didn't want them spoiling his achievement.

The narrow gate swung closed behind me. Grooms ran forward. I reached the centre of the yard, reined in and turned my head to look for Keril.

Samchek stood with one hand on the stallion's bridle. Where had he appeared from? The black backed off a pace and snorted, tossed its head then steadied at a quiet word from Keril. Stiff-backed, the stable master held his other hand out. Keril gave up the reins then shook his feet out of the stirrups. What did he think he was going to do now?

Feet free, reins gone. He touched the black on the neck and murmured something. The horse ducked his head. It was as if Keril expected it. He swung one leg over the beast's neck, turned on the saddle and dropped two-footed.

As smooth as anything I've seen but then he spoiled it all by lurching sideways as a stiffened leg gave way beneath him.

Samchek caught him; reflex action. Touching Keril.

My mount shied. The yard stopped moving. Slowly I unclenched my fists.

After a pause we might have counted, Keril got his balance. "Thank you, sir." He made that bow of his and Samchek let him go. I found my breathing was quite even.

Samchek turned and tried to walk the black back to its stable, waving grooms aside to do it. A public gesture, I decided. Probably the only one who didn't realize was Keril. The stallion tugged against the reins, one wild eye rolling. Keril muttered something calming. Samchek looked from horse to rider. He'd abandoned looking scared in favor of astonished. A second after that his face went grim; his gaze had swung in my direction. Without a word he passed the reins to someone else then stood his ground and waited for my verdict.

"I'll see you later," I said curtly.

"Highness." A face like stone. Until he caught another glimpse of Keril. Then he looked bewildered. I knew that feeling. After all, I'd been the same route, hadn't I?

"My lord? Have I been… trouble?" So much for that obviously not hurting part. Keril had arrived below me, at my stirrup, moving very carefully. And waiting to be blamed for being, as he'd feared, ignorant or stupid?

"No. Let's get inside." I swung down, threw the reins to the nearest slave and headed for the stairway to the Gate Hall. Half way up I slowed. I'd realized Keril was limping. "Can you make it?"

"I can walk, my lord." Oh very dignified. He put a spurt on and we reached the top. The shade was welcome. Happily the cool interior was short of noses but he was slowing again by the time we'd crossed the Gate Hall, to the hidden door that let us cross the open ground before my private quarters.

"How bad is it?"

"It… hurts, my lord." He sounded nearer laughter this time. "I'm sorry I'm so clumsy. You said I'd fall."

"Three times," I pointed out. The guards outside the tunnel spotted me and called inside.

"Yes, my lord." He sighed at that.

The iron doors clanged shut again behind us. Downward, into night compared with what we'd come from. I heard him stumble once, and grunt. I didn't comment, but I caught his sleeve and helped him steady. Past the inner gate, back in the light, I led him down the single marble step to cut across the flowered court again then up my stairs in silence. I was imagining him wincing behind the veil. "Medishel, I'll need." I thought. "The bath, good hands, and probably some ointment." I had to grin at that one.

Medi looked complacent. "All waiting, my prince."

"You're a treasure," I told him, and to Keril, "Come on, you. Let's get those filthy clothes off."

A couple of robe slaves waiting by the bath made haste to help him when I gestured. He was having trouble with his balance and his movements weren't as smooth as normal. I sat down and let another slave tug my boots off, pulling off my headdress then my shirt and dropping them onto the tiles, accepting watered wine from Medi.

The slaves who handled Keril murmured words of comfort when he winced as they undressed him. He breathed in sharply when the pungent, herb-strewn water hit his lower body. I'd spotted a nasty graze along one thigh, but I figured his real ills were stiffened muscles, and his backside.

"A soaking first, then we'll sort the rest out." I handed back the cup, stripped off, except my armband of course while there were so many others present, and went to join him, but across the circle of the little pool. Medi and his hordes were all around us, and for Keril the bath was a new experience. Another time, now… why not, I thought. I'd have him in here, and a whole lot closer. I had to look away before I started things I figured Keril couldn't finish at the moment.

The water in this pool would stay warm, the pool and nearby sweat-room heated by pipes concealed beneath the floor tiles. The room fell quiet as the robe slaves left us or retreated to the shadows. I breathed in warm, damp air—they'd added an astringent to the water—then lay back. They offered Keril drinking water, which he took once I had nodded, then encouraged him to do as I had, sinking lower in the soothing waters.

I stayed put as long as seemed useful. Keril looked sleepy by then. "Time for you to move."

Grey eyes blinked at me. "Yes, my lord, of course. What should…?"

"They'll guide you." I waved at two big eunuchs, stripped to the waist and waiting by the tables. Keril looked at them quite calmly. Either no nerves, or no sense, I thought, for about the hundredth time.

He stiffened when they touched him at first, but gradually I saw his muscles start to slacken. When I lay down on the other table that seemed to make him think that he was safe. At least he closed his eyes, and left them to it.

"Massage will ease your muscles," I told him. "Otherwise I doubt you'll move tomorrow."

The "Yes, my lord," was muffled in the towel. I let them work. The room was almost silent, just the slap of hands on flesh, the whisper of their feet upon the tiles. The towels were soft, the air was perfumed and there was a muffled burst of laughter from another chamber. It was "warmer" here, he'd said. I shivered, but the moment passed. I almost fell asleep, and Keril did. He never felt them spread the ointment. "Leave him there," I told them as I left them, "but have someone keep an eye on him, for safety."

"My prince." Medishel escorted me outside before he said, "The king has sent a message." No business in the bath, those were his orders, not unless we were invaded.

I laughed. "I'll bet he has. What was it?"

"He invites you to a private supper."

"Of course." I had expected something like it but one played the game of being royal from the day one woke and yelled for everyone's attention. I smiled my way from my apartments to my father's table.

Uncle Rag was wearing shades of blue to match my father. Royal colors, though the proper "formal" shades were paler blue with yellow-gold and crimson. I'd chosen reds. A gesture of defiance or of celebration? You tell me. They'd obviously been talking but there was no sign of food yet so I hadn't kept them waiting. "My father. Uncle." Might have known he'd muscle in. A shame he hadn't stayed up north a few days longer.

"Ash." My father watched me cross the room. I settled, took the glass a slave was offering, and waited for it.

"Good day?" my father queried.

Rag's mouth stretched a little. He had a nasty sense of humour; always thought so.

"Very, Father. Quite productive."

Rag started huffing. "Hah. You set the palace on its ears."

"All I did was go out riding."

"It wasn't *you* that caused the uproar." He sounded more than usually grouchy. I looked across at Father.

"It did cause talk," my royal parent finally informed me.

"Doesn't everything? As you said, I thought I'd dig out some more facts. Keril's a rider. He told me he'd only ridden once before, but—"

My pleasant-mannered uncle snorted. "Nonsense. They're saying—"

I curbed my temper. "I *could* waste my breath telling you the male doesn't lie to me. Since I know you won't accept that I'll tell you I've spent half the day teaching him, and he's a total novice. But he has a real way with horses."

"So we heard. The black," said Father.

"Exactly." There was a moment's silence while we thought about that. "He— The brute *likes* him."

"Likes him. So, what next?" That from my loving father. I wondered how indulgent he was feeling; might as well find out.

"Who knows? If he rides as well as I think he might, and he can handle other horses..." I paused, then said what had been stewing in my mind since I'd regained the palace. "Samchek's going to teach him."

"Ah. Samchek." Never wasted words, my father.

Despite myself I started scowling. "Samchek's latest tantrum could have crippled him. Or killed him. And Samchek knows it, so he's going to earn forgiveness."

My father raised an eyebrow. "With riding lessons?"

"Yes," I looked him in the eye and waited; saw the wily brain consider.

"But... the insubordination?" Rag protested.

"Oh, he'll suffer," I assured him. "He's going to teach a slave, himself, until the slave is perfect. Which he will be," I said with conviction, feeling better. "He's going to see him ride as well as *he* can, maybe better, *and* he's going to look as if he likes it. If he can do all that then maybe I'll forgive him."

"A good decision." Father smiled.

Rag grinned. Never the prettiest sight. "Who knows, we might make a king out of you yet. Now tell us how in all the hells your virgin tamed that stallion."

I had to laugh. "He said "hello" to it."

Their faces were a picture. "I beg your pardon?" Father said with great forbearance.

"Well, he didn't have time to do much else. By the time I realized what he was facing it was all over. The cursed horse looked like a pet."

I had to tell them every detail of the lesson I remembered and still they couldn't take it. And that was just about his riding. I omitted any mention of his fear of crowds. Or open spaces. Or the fact I couldn't ditch the feeling that the horse had made him feel safer. Or about that total isolation he had come from.

He had lived in metal walls? I had begun to ask myself, belatedly, what weird kind of temple Keril had been raised in. Why, despite his innocence, was he afraid of people, when he didn't any longer seem at all afraid of me, or of my household? Why, despite the fact that he could read, he *knew* so little?

I'd ignored the subject; now I couldn't. Keril wasn't half the fool I sometimes called him, yet he couldn't name his homeland; didn't seem to understand his own religion? No, I didn't like it. Right, then. If I couldn't solve the mystery of my religion, or the bloody En-Syn, maybe I could fathom Keril's?

Jaffid. I would see what Jaffid could uncover. Keril said he'd nursed a child. It would surely be remembered? Find that village then track back from there? I'd better start with Sheshman.

Chapter 22

Sheshman's tale, told by lamplight, was both comic, and dramatic.

"I was wondering when you would ask, my prince. It was a touch of fate; a chance encounter." Sheshman took a dainty sip of wine and then continued. "I was chasing rumors far into the north, beneath the fabled Walls of Ice. I'd hoped to find a little profit but the weather…" Sheshman actually shuddered. "Fogs, and fierce snowstorms, dreadful place. I'd a map but it was useless, passes that it promised blocked by snowfall. Well, I'd got that far. I hired a local but the storms put him off course as well. We fetched up in a so-called village in some valley I never did know the name of, and never want to. Huts made out of tree bark! I swear, I wasn't warm one day I spent there," Sheshman told me earnestly. "And I almost failed to get back here for your wedding."

"But the slave?" I interrupted. "You found him up there?"

"Yes, my prince, I did, and it was the only good thing I got out of the whole trip. Not a mine or a slave market in sight and most of the people too poor to think of shipping goods to. Yes, a single purchase. But a singular tale." Sheshman paused, expectant.

Had his story ready, did he? One he thought would win me? "Get on with it," I told him. But he smiled, he knew he'd captured my attention. He even took another sip to keep me waiting.

"We were at an inn. A poor place, oh dear yes. Your highness would have burned it down rather than risk sleeping in it. But I am old and need a roof to keep the cold out. Well, I was at dinner—mostly of my own provisions—still held back by awful weather when a shifty ruffian begs my guards for entry." Sheshman settled, starting to enjoy himself. "He'd told them he had "merchandise", and I was bored. My prince will understand that."

He paused, as if he saw a scene I couldn't. "The male spoke in circles, but traders do. I knew, of course, he was no honest merchant. One knows," the old male said modestly.

Ashamet, Desert Born

I believed him. Takes one to know one, as Rag would have said.

Sheshman continued. "His goods, he said, were worth my trouble.

"Fair enough, I said, off hand, he could present them and I would consider.

"He couldn't bring it here, he said at once. It was a confidential matter. Between gentlemen, he said." Sheshman looked scornful. "And there we stuck, and all the time he's looking round as if afraid of being overheard.

"My prince, I'd probably have turned him down except I hadn't made a penny from my foray. And I scented something. So I had my males disarm him then had him lead us to his camp-site."

"You didn't fear an ambush?" I was genuinely curious. He'd never before struck me as a hero.

"One always fears the worst, does one not, my prince? That way one is always prepared."

This was a Sheshman I hadn't measured in his years of brief appearances around the palace. One who backed his instincts when he took a gamble? He'd had the guts to bring me... "So?" I urged him.

"So we braved the bitter weather, left the village behind and followed the frozen ruts they called a roadway. We could see where the fellow had joined it; footprints straggled down the hillside. I sent two males ahead. They found a cave and signs of horses. Six, they thought. Five males left to deal with then, I thought. Not bad. So I went to look."

Sheshman looked complacent then saw my frown and stopped wasting time. "Not five males after all. Only three. Some loot, but nothing precious bar a single slave, and he was gagged and bound and almost frozen.

"I thought at first it wasn't worth the journey. My moustaches were turning solid. I was fearful I'd lose toes, or fingers. But they fell over themselves to sell him, it was all they wanted." Sheshman's turn to frown. "He was no purchase, he'd surely been waylaid, or even kidnapped. They couldn't keep their mouths shut either. One can read faces, and bodies too, as I'm sure my prince knows, and these were terrified of what they'd gotten into. Maybe of the local people's anger, or whatever gods they worshipped. It takes brave males, or fools, to defy their own gods, and these weren't brave, not by the time I met them. They babbled like children.

"He was young and strong, they said. So what? I said."

Sheshman, unconsciously, began to mimic that exchange, shifting his head and altering the tone of his voice. I had to hide amusement.

"Good to look at, they said. Too thin, too pale, I said. Well, one must bargain, highness, and I thought at first his color was from freezing. A *holy* male, they said, but lately from some shrine. Of course I scoffed, as you would too. They tugged him closer to the firelight. Look, they said, there are religious symbols on his clothing, there's the proof. He might have all kinds of virtues.

"What, I said, an honest priest? I laughed and turned to leave. They panicked. Great lord, they said, be gracious. We cannot free him, but to kill a holy male… they shook their heads, and fingered barbarian amulets. Meant to keep them safe, I suppose.

"Hm, I said. How holy? But they were ignorant of details. I doubt they could read anything, much less those arcane symbols. They only knew they were in trouble. They could hardly let him go and that meant kill or sell him, and they couldn't risk the locals passing on the story. They must have thought the gods had sent me there to save them.

"They'd painted me a picture, highness. Claimed by priests, taught only to be virtuous and faithful. Knowing nothing, as we judge it…

"And I wondered, and I wondered, till I had to cross and grab him by the shoulder. When I shook him his eyes opened for a moment." Sheshman licked his lips. "My prince, I saw your face change, in the Gate Hall. I think you saw the truth at once, as I did? A miracle, and they were blind as bats and never guessed it.

"I paid them nowhere near his worth." Sheshman's face showed fleeting satisfaction. "Forced them down and down until they tired of the struggle. But I knew what I was buying; something so rare… I swear I never touched him again." Sheshman avoided my eye, for the first time since he'd started. "I gave him over to my eunuchs and I brought him south, to you, my prince. I dreamt of you that night, you see, a dream so strong… Your eyes were silver stars. It seemed an omen."

Regret hung in the air between us. For the pleasure he'd denied himself, or for the loss of so much profit? It seemed his loyalty was deeper than I'd ever guessed. Although…

"Cheap, was he?"

"True value can't be weighed in gold," Sheshman said haughtily, then ruined it by adding, "though with the cage to be acquired, and the silver shackles, from a *master* craftsman…"

He'd made his point. "Those clothes?"

He sighed, and gestured. The slave who'd knelt behind him was a eunuch, rouged and powdered city fashion and as rounded as his owner. He drew a flat parcel from within his robes and laid it gently on the table. Sheshman watched me unwrap the cloth, his face somber. "They're clean now but they'd starved him. He was thin, near frozen, soiled and draggled. But even then… see for yourself, they're no common cloth, nor common garments. And there are the three symbols, as I told you."

Narrow trousers. More like Thersat's. Flimsy sleeveless shirt. A sort of hooded robe that would be less than knee length on him, with a matching narrow sash. The outer garments were a dull grey, felted wool or something, thick and only slightly padded; made to fasten close at wrists and ankles, yes, but surely still too insubstantial for those mountains.

Hmm. Neither fine enough for a noble, nor coarse enough for a pauper. Nor meant for warmer climates. The symbols on the robe were done in lighter colored thread like melted wire, in a column from the shoulder to the heart. Fine work, the calligraphy more elegant than the cloth it graced, but I couldn't read them either. I'd never seen their like, in all my travels. Though of course the north was really uncle's province.

Sheshman broke into my thoughts. "There were boots once, I'd think. And my eunuchs think an indentation, gone now, says he must have worn a ring as well before the robbers took it. Very presentable he must have been; quiet, but impressive. Rather like my prince himself," he ended shamelessly.

I grinned. Accusing me of subtlety now, was he? But Sheshman had a map and knew a guide. I had a place to start from. And more questions.

Waylaid, so casually? I shook my head. A heathen land he must have come from, if it desecrated its own temples. A worthless god, to let them do it, one I surely needn't put much faith in. All the same, I hadn't heard of crimes against a priest for years, in or out of our kingdoms. Was there a war somewhere so far away I didn't even know it? Definitely time I knew more. Jaff could leave tomorrow.

Chapter 23

Meanwhile Father offered me a garden for the riding lessons, the one below our north-west windows. Probably to lessen talk. That was a bonus, though I doubt the gardeners saw it that way when they got the word to root up everything except the trees and vines around the walls, and pack the earth down hard and even.

Rag had left again so I was spared his comments and in any case his balconies were too far round to overlook the garden even if they'd been unshuttered. To the world at large the spectacle was lessened, even if the gossip fattened. And it meant that I could leave them to it.

Not entirely, of course. I guard my possessions, as does any male of sense. I might put faith in Keril's conduct but in others'? Samchek was escorted from the stables. Royal guards made sure he only went where he was meant to and remained on guard outside the garden walls until he finished. And Medishel, with several attendants—not to mention parasols, and cushioned benches—oversaw each session and escorted Keril to and from them.

And sometimes, when I could, or would, I watched him too, from high above them.

Keril had real promise. Though to do him justice, Samchek made an effort. And effort it was, as I'd intended. Rules were set: there'd be no contact; he would call his pupil Keril, *nothing* else; he would retreat, if ever Keril's veil was loosened or his pupil asked it. Rules received in blank-faced silence. And he was to follow Medishel's instructions.

That last was almost where it ended. Indulge a slave and now obey a eunuch? Kemik didn't hold with eunuchs; their cubs ran wild; their crones secured such bodies as were private.

When I considered, some of their customs were as strange as the Sidassi's. The older females taught the girls to use a knife. A Kemik male who went to bed a female knew she'd have a dagger handy, even when his presence was approved of. It was a weird point of honor. The male won points if he could overcome the girl yet leave no marks upon her but the female was more valued if the male who quit her bed was bloody, proving she would give him offspring fit for battle. A wild measure that could only come from such a warlike people. Any Kemik seeking heirs must take his prick in one hand and his courage in the other!

But the lessons prospered, even though an anxious Medi sought to end them. "But, my prince, there is increasing danger!"

"Risky maybe. Learning is." I tried for patience. I'd sent Keril off to wash and change. "He's got to try things."

"Yes, my prince," a downcast Medi answered. But I'd seen him stop the lesson twice. And Samchek's face grow darker. By the time I oh-so-casually joined them only Keril didn't look relieved the lesson ended early, and for all I knew he could have been as well, behind that veil.

"Samchek is being careful," I repeated. "He knows what'll happen if he isn't. And Keril wants this, Medi."

"Yes, my prince."

"All right. Trust Keril's nerve, and Samchek's knowledge. Tell him he can carry on while I'm away as long as you're available to watch them." An order the returning rider must have overheard but it took him four days to pluck up the courage. I'd almost given up on him by then. It was always interesting to see which way he'd jump.

He chose his moment. Not in bed—not Keril's style—but when Medi started fussing over what I would be taking with me. Keril marked off riding gear laid out, and talk of weapons.

"My lord is riding a long way?"

I vetoed half what Medi had selected. "A few weeks, maybe." As if I wasn't paying much attention.

Thus encouraged, Keril eyed the small amount left out for packing as the slaves returned the rest to closets. "Hard riding?" No, not stupid.

"Too hard for you."

Silence.

"No."

A sigh emerged, but nothing more defiant.

There was no comment when I told him I'd be off next morning. No comment either when I rose from breakfast, informed by Medi that my escort was already at the stables. No comment then because he was nowhere in sight, although I'd had him in my arms as dawn crept through my windows. I hesitated, cursed, and went to find him.

He was downstairs in my library. A hefty robe-slave bowed and stepped aside for me to enter. Keril knew he was allowed this far but Medi always saw that he was properly escorted.

Racks of maps and scrolls and regimented shelves of leather-covered volumes made it almost soundproof. Overlapping carpets deadened footfalls. Keril had his back to me, across the room between a rank of bookshelves and a heavy wooden table, fingering a row of books. He heard me though, turned round and gave that funny bow of his. A pair of solemn-looking tomes lay on the table and another on a leather-covered chair beside it. Keril, I surmised, was taking care of empty evenings with a vengeance. I coughed. "Don't read them all at once. Too many words can blind you."

"No, my lord." But he wasn't looking at me, even though I'd spoken.

Exasperation made me sudden. I strode across the carpets, shoved him up against the oldest, oiled-leather books, endangering their fragile covers, and kissed him. Hard. "And do as Medi orders."

A gasp, but when I stepped away he'd started smiling. "Stay safe, my lord?"

That sounded too much like another heathen prayer for anybody's comfort. It got me out of my apartments, through the tunnels, right out to the stables. And no, I didn't look back, or up, as I rode out the gates. Damned if I would.

Chapter 24

The "few weeks" lasted seven, or was it eight? I wasn't really counting at the time although I was impatient by the time it ended. I was feeling restless, and the Synia was itching. Probably related. But at least the winter was upon us and the weather cool enough for serious travel. Plus a journey north had been exactly what I wanted. Kill two birds…

Sheshman had sent me yet another son—it seemed he had no cares at all about succession—with a note from Jaffid. I had told Jaff not to use the army network, or the temples', didn't want them thinking this was a religious matter, did we? And code or not I didn't like the possibility that someone else might learn what Jaffid found, before his master.

Jaffid's messages were always terse and this was no exception.

"North, then east, with maps your contact has provided and an introduction to the guide he hired. Guide agreed to lead me to the village where the contact met our quarry."

Short and sweet and tactful. Even in a coded message he'd omitted names. So Sheshman was behaving like an ally but such messages would be sporadic, via Sheshman's limited connection. Jaffid would be better off with reinforcements but I had no business sending males up north where Rag had jurisdiction. There'd be tantrums. Questions. Hells, I couldn't.

Only, Sheshman's son brought other information: news that offered a solution, even some additional excitement. Law and order in the north was Rag's affair but he'd complained for years his biggest problem was corruption. This time, evidently, Sheshman had outbid the opposition. His informants swore the bandits in the harsher regions north and east of Sidass, who'd become a real menace, had a stronghold in a chain of barren hills called Devil's Anvil.

Once I passed that morsel on to Father the exact location had become my uncle's next assignment. He hadn't liked us interfering in his territory so he'd left at once, with Father's promise he would send a force to aid him that we *knew* was loyal.

So I quietly tagged myself onto the mission. Neither Rag nor Father realized in time to stop me. Tullman—Tull for short, the troop's Vanguard and a long-time ally—thought I'd joined him with my father's blessing. Well, he hadn't said I couldn't.

Truth to tell, the Synia-mess—the secrecy, the priests' attention, the uncertain future and the constant *waiting*—grated on my nerves. I needed action. This way I could maybe get a bit of fighting in without a slew of royal bodyguards to spoil it. And once the mission ended it should be a simple task to divert one or two of Tullman's force to back up Jaff and run his errands. Who would notice?

So I escaped the palace, and the priests. As if it sympathized, the itching on my arm subsided. Perfect. Though it took us the best part of two weeks to get as far north as my dearest uncle thought convenient, and then he kept us waiting five more days inside the disused hilltop fort he'd chosen for our meeting. The view up there was pleasant and the breezes not too irksome but every day we wasted meant Jaff's trail got colder. By the night Rag turned up, his nephew wasn't in the best of tempers…

"Gods, uncle. I thought you were supposed to meet us," was my idea of a greeting as his mount was led away to water.

Rag swung round. "You. I might have known. Cool down, I couldn't get here any faster, I've been chasing information ever since I left you. What that Sheshman sent us hardly scratched the surface."

"So what've you got?" I curbed my tongue and led him to the fire, waving Tull to join us.

"Enough."

"*What*, exactly?" Tull kept quiet and listened.

"Give me a drink, I'll tell you." He collapsed onto the rug I'd risen from, leaned back against a broken bit of wall and held his hands out to the flames. "I swear these hills are drier than the desert." Mug in hand, Rag shouted for a map. The firelight showed he had exchanged his usual finery for plainer garments. The choice of muddy reds suggested he was meant to be mistaken for a travelling scholar but his rings would feed the scholar, and his family, a year. He had always been too fond of jewels. I considered saying something but he'd only throw another tantrum, and he did look tired…

"You're sure, my lord?" Tull looked as dubious as I was. A hidden valley, accessed only through a narrow canyon, where they met to share their spoils and drink together. Not a permanent arrangement; left unguarded in between-times. Practically perfect.

"Yes, I tell you." Rag turned to Tull. "Rest up another day or so then get your males in first and you can lie in wait to take them."

Tull received it as an order, nodding. I still wanted answers. "Where'd you get the information?"

"A regular patrol picked up a go-between. They didn't realize at first, of course, or probably I'd not have seen him," Rag said bitterly.

I saved my sympathy. "Where is he now?"

"He's six steps under. Do you think I'd run the risk he'd get away to warn 'em?" He stared into the crackling fire shouting for a refill, gulping at the watered wine before returning to his favorite grievance. "I've been after this bunch for four years. I'd've had 'em by now as well, if the march on Sidass hadn't taken half my forces for a year. And if I wasn't riddled with informers."

Rag spat. The north was his particular employment, as the south was mine. His failure clearly rankled and this lot, by the sound of it, had gotten far too strong while we were occupied with Sidass. Which was why his king had sent a small but hand-picked force (and me, unknowing) up to help him. Not that Rag was thankful, more like took it as an insult.

Since he'd said he couldn't trust his local troops we'd dressed as roving mercenaries, not as royal soldiers. And my father had selected Vanguard Tullman as our leader. Tull wasn't pinkish but he was a paler color than the norm, enough he could have northern blood, and he could still spit out a stream of gutter language if he wanted, though he didn't like to be reminded of what depths he'd had to sink to in the days before I met him.

We all looked low enough right now, myself included, in a ragtag mix of clothes and weapons. Me, I'd stripped off all my jewels, found some gods-awful striped trousers and patched boots and added a full brownish robe with a ripped hem. Then I'd twisted up my hair in red and brown rags in the fashion of these northern hill males, and finally I'd wrapped a grimy orange scarf around my sword-arm, so it hid the solid silver armlet that I couldn't easily abandon. Just because I'd almost grown inured to having half a Synia didn't mean I planned to advertise it.

Tull had failed to hide a smile. The scarf was weighted down with tarnished silver tassels. It was the sort of thing a common male might brandish as a lover's token. Still, it hid the far-too-valuable armlet, that was all that mattered.

Tull on the other hand was decked out as befit our leader, with a headscarf trimmed with coins across his forehead, another northern style. He had a reasonably good, now grubby, blue and yellow cotton robe with silk embroidery he'd borrowed from his trooper-servant, a much-washed yellow linen shirt, an orange sash and dull brown trousers. And a wealth of beaten copper bangles halfway to his elbows. When I'd laughed and eyed him up and down I swear his gold complexion darkened.

Vanguard Tullman, as I'd often pointed out to him, was too good-looking for an honest soldier anyway, and even in such tawdry gear it was already plain the northern youths we'd passed all thought so. Lips parted when they saw our dashing leader. I, in rougher clothes, got quite passed over. When I complained he said they had good instincts! "They're afraid you'll rob them." He had no idea how to flatter.

Odd really. Tull *is* good-looking, and I trust him, absolutely, yet I've never had him, no, not once in all the seven years I've known him. It's never been the moment, or perhaps it's just we never had that sort of friendship. For friends we are, as well as comrades. Even if Tull, forever conscious of his rank—and worse, disowned—is always careful not to seem too forward. And yes, perhaps a bed would sour things. He might find it patronizing and I wouldn't want that.

As for this foray…

"Relax, Uncle," I said kindly, "Tull and I will soon clear out your rats' nest. It'll give him some employment. He's been getting fat and lazy stuck in barracks."

Rag scowled then grunted, definitely short on manners. Tull hid a grin behind a tankard but it wasn't Tull he had a go at. "*You're* not going. Ash, it's far too risky. Your father—"

"Doesn't like me lazy either. Nor do I. Why else would I be here?"

"Ash!" He didn't like it but he knew he couldn't stop me.

Not a flicker of suspicion that I might have any other motive? "Gods, it's only bandits, not an army." If I bristled was it so surprising, treating me… "Stop arguing. That goes for you as well," I added, seeing Tull's expression. "And we'll leave tomorrow," I decided. "Better now than later."

Rag objected to the rush but Tull put down his wine and called for water; a professional's reaction. He was brave, but careful, and he hadn't even thought of arguing with my decision. Yes, we could have sat around a day or so but leaving right away would put us in this secret valley well before the bandits were expected, give us ample time to reconnoiter, let the dust we'd raise subside and any wildlife settle back to normal. "Yes. Tomorrow," I repeated. I had wasted too much time already.

Chapter 25

"Seven hells," Tull muttered from behind me two days later.

I didn't answer, but it was an apt description. We had crossed the last few miles in pre-dawn dark. The grassland had deteriorated into scrub and with the dawn the hulking presence looming up before us had become…

Tull's males had halted in our wake and sat their horses, muttering together. Rag's male, ahead of us, began to pick his way between the scattered boulders in our path then realized we hadn't followed.

It wasn't so much a canyon as an angled fissure in the cliff face, hung above us, leaving us in purple shadow. As if a giant long ago had cleft the mottled, slate-grey stone with one clean axe-blow, with a blade so sharp the rock face either side of us looked glassy.

Here at the entrance it was wide enough for four abreast; we set off briskly. But a hundred paces in it went to half that. A shallow rift, you would have said, that wouldn't go much further. It struck me as a perfect trap. I didn't like it.

Not much light in here till the sun was higher. Vegetation dwindled. Gradually the bare grey rock closed in around us till we rode in single file. At times it grew too dark to see the colors on our clothing, even with our boasted night-sight. The air was still, and colder. Hoof beats echoed and disturbed a flock of birds from nests above. We heard them more than saw them. Closer, tiny, pale green creeping things I couldn't name would scuttle into crannies as we neared. They caught the corner of my eye yet were invisible whenever I would turn to face them.

I sought the open sky instead, but peering upward only made me dizzy. There was a thread of pale blue sky. I had the crazy feeling I was looking *down*, into a deep ravine, as if some nameless god had turned the world right over; that the blue was actually a narrow river and the darting shapes above were really fishes. After one disturbing look I kept my head down, sweating, cursing my imagination when a rain of pebbles clattered down somewhere behind us.

Up or down, the place gave me the shivers; the horses' hooves were slipping on the loosened rocks and eerie, muffled noises made us hesitate at every unexpected twist and turn and finally, when we were two hours in, we met the rock fall I'd imagined.

We were passing round a bend into a wider section, elbow room at last. Was I the only one who breathed a little better? Other males kept glancing up and Tull had dropped behind, encouraging the laggard. One minute, silence; nothing natural except a very little muttered conversation and the sound of hoof and leather, sounds made hollow by the barren rock all round us.

Next thing, a shushing sound. As one, we raised our heads then someone pointed upward. Someone shouted. Then the hush was swept away by rattlings, then a roar like thunder drowned our curses as the cliff came racing down to crush us.

"Back!" yelled Tull. The rearguard fled, but I was too far forward. One of Tull's males literally dragged me off my horse and threw himself on top of me behind a slab of rock he thought would give us cover. It did, too, more than I expected.

Eventually the roar subsided to a mutter—or I'd lost my hearing—and we dared to lift our heads. He came up coughing from the choking dust, with double vision and a broken bone or two, compared to which I suffered next to nothing: even more disreputable clothing—practically rags by then— my smothered hearing and a headache, cuts and bruises and a blazing temper.

The cries from injured, panicked horses echoed in the dust-filled air around us and ahead one rider bent, with tears on his face, to cut his horse's throat. He didn't seem to realize his trouser leg was ripped to ribbons, his own blood mingling with his horse's in the dirt around them. I could see a body sprawled behind him.

Smaller rocks were still in motion, tinny sounds that hit my woolly ears louder somehow than the roar before them, but no one shouted threats. I stayed behind my rock. No spears descended. I could see no movement up above us either so I straightened, wincing. If it was an ambush then the enemy was rock, not people. Pure bad luck then? But at least we were alive to ask the question. Most were anyway.

I shook my head. It seemed to work, my hearing cleared a little, so I coughed, spat dust then turned to deal with the situation.

I found my current mount—he had a cut along one haunch, a score of lesser nicks, but nothing to prevent him being ridden—then I rooted out my only other outer robe to cover up the damage. It took till past midday to clear a path and get our wounded, and the brace of bodies, back outside the canyon entrance, always conscious bandits might arrive ahead of schedule and spot our movement. If they'd been above us, waiting… but they hadn't, so it all became logistics.

Barely half our force was fully fit to meet them so it was a real relief to find some cover, not to mention running water, in a tiny gulley to the south where cliff turned into rocky hillside, stunted trees about it. Only one way in and out but we could tend the wounded out of sight and send a rider back for reinforcements and a wagon.

Tull, not too fit himself—a wrenched left knee made walking difficult—was all for heading back at once. I vetoed the suggestion. "Some aren't fit to ride. Besides, I thought I'd take a couple of your males and check that landslide, see if we can climb there."

"Climb? Ash!" He changed his tone. "My prince."

"Stop and think. The fall was accidental but if rocks can fall so easily on honest males, why can't I help them fall on bandits?"

His mouth opened, then surprise turned to enjoyment. "Not without protection. I'll come with you."

I grinned. I had suspected his desire to run away was for his prince's safety. "You'd be going *for* me if I thought you'd make it. But you wouldn't, so you'll stay here with the wounded."

In the end I got away an hour later, with six of his males, the fittest we had left. The light was fading by the time we reached the canyon and we needed torches once we got in deeper. It was cave-like. At the slide we piled rocks to hide dead horses—nasty job—and picked up any other evidence we'd been there. It was cold by then as well.

One soldier took our horses back, and all the salvaged gear. The rest of us took shelter where we could and rested. Well, we tried to. Bedrolls failed to keep the icy draughts at bay and boulders next to bruises don't add up to comfort. But at least the dust had settled.

At dawn, once there was light enough to let us see which rock was which, we rolled our gear, including our unwieldy crossbows, in our blankets, slung them on our backs and started climbing. It was quite sensible. I'd reasoned since most of the loose rock was at the bottom what was left above was likely to be relatively solid. And so it was, until the rock I put my foot on came away beneath me.

For a heartbeat—I could swear I heard it—I was hanging by my fingertips. My boots were scrabbling for purchase; not succeeding, and the world was tilting; sky and rock, and living nightmare. One hand was secure, the other slipping helplessly. The load upon my back was pulling me away. I couldn't get a grip. If ever it was time to test the gods' intentions—

"Hold on, highness!" Calloused fingers grabbed my wrist. The world about me steadied. I suppressed a cry. "A toehold, to your right." The male was breathless.

So was I. I nodded, squinting. Gods, I hated looking down. "I see it, thanks." I dug my foot into the crevice. "You can let me go now."

Slowly, carefully, the male released me, rashly holding back so I would have to climb above him. If I slipped again, I'd take him with him.

So I'd better not. I slowed my heart, refused to shake, and toiled upward. Not much further.

It was still pretty nerve-wracking, even with the end so near. The sky was in my sight above the cliff at last, a glimpse of heaven, but my hand kept getting slippery. With blood. The sudden lurch had torn my fingers on the rocks, the reason it had failed me. I had to wipe it on my robe at intervals or it was useless. And I couldn't climb too slowly, conscious that the bandits might already be approaching. We'd be sitting ducks for arrows if they saw us and although I'd given Tull strict orders I was worried, if they did appear too soon… He didn't have the males to mount a rescue.

So yes, I was entitled to relief when I could haul myself onto the final ledge, my rescuer beside me, suck in air and look around at what we'd got to.

It was everything I'd hoped for, if I didn't look behind me. We could see beyond the cliff, across the plain we'd had to travel. And there it was, still faint, a cloud of dust. It couldn't be our reinforcements, it was coming from the wrong direction.

"Bandits, highness?" My protector pointed.

"Right." I grinned. "Let's build a landslide." He grinned back. They all did.

We found the perfect spot just past the first one; rock and shale with boulders loosened by the slide that nearly killed us. Rocks below suggested there'd already been some movement, and in any case they'd have to lead their horses to negotiate the mess before it. With luck—which surely we deserved—they'd be on foot. We set to work. Each male in turn lay flat and kept a watch, and got a break from piling rock and bending double.

The birds had settled by the time we were done, so when the bandits came they rode in unsuspecting, as I'd reasoned. Curses floated upward when they reached the site of our disaster and they saw the rubble in their way.

I lay above them, veiled to disguise my shape, and waited. I figured I was practically invisible in any case, another dusty rock against the skyline. Down below a force of maybe forty males with extra horses, heavy-laden, had gone quieter as they picked their way among the debris. I raised a hand behind me. "Nearly. Now!"

The males behind me pulled the ropes that dragged the keystones from beneath our piled rocks, but nothing happened. I was scared we'd failed. Then the lowest stones began to slither, oh-so-slowly.

Such a little thing; a sliding rock or two; a grating sound. The birds rose up again but their alarm was quickly swallowed. Pebbles clattered, rocks began to bounce then suddenly the entire slope was moving downward.

Screams, and frantic leaps. Was that what we'd escaped? The dust roiled up toward me and the ground below my feet vibrated, so much so I scuttled back in haste, afraid the solid rock beneath my feet would fail me. So I didn't see the rock fall reach its target, only heard it.

When the ground grew still again and I heard shouting down below I edged up with the others, peering over, all our crossbows primed, their cases fully-loaded.

I almost leaned too far. The cliff held firm but something whistled past my head from down below. "Watch out!" The rest ducked too but no one followed up. It must have been a lucky shot, no more, I told myself as breath returned. With all the dust down there the bandit must be firing blind, from panic.

"Careful, lads." I poked my head out once again and caught a movement in the stinging fog, below and left of us. "Pick your shots." I shoved aside a stone that dug into my hip and sighted, choosing to ignore another arrow bouncing off the rock beside me. It had given me my enemy's position. Right then, watch that clump of boulders. Easy, now…

The murky outline altered as a head and arm detached themselves from cover. As the bandit loosed another shot I fired too. His missed me by a mile but mine flew straight into his throat. "Hah." I pulled the toggle to reload the oiled feeder chute beneath my crossbow, tucked the stock securely in against my shoulder, waiting for another target, barely conscious of the muffled "thut" as other bolts were loosed by those beside me. Dragging all that metal up here wasn't fun but it was worth it now. The crossbow's range offset our lack of numbers.

Suddenly it was all over. Dust was settling and bodies sprawled, unmoving. I had done for four myself. Not bad; the crossbow wasn't normally my choice of weapon.

We hadn't got all of them, of course, that was too much to hope for. But anyone alive was cowering among the boulders. Nothing stirred except a last few rocks that clattered to the bottom.

No point us lowering ourselves down there, I thought, where any bandit still alive could see us. "Come on, lads, we're finished here for now." I creaked onto my feet. I ached all over but I'd done it. "We'll stay up here until we're back above the entrance. Bring the ropes. We'll need them to get down again."

Tull was limping round in circles by the time we reached him; trying not to look relieved as well. He'd likely spent the time composing letters of condolence to my father.

"Relax. See, not a scratch."

"Oh yes? Then where's the blood from?"

"Cut my fingers," I said shortly.

"And you wiped them on your back?"

Hells, it must have soaked right through the extra layer of fabric.

"My prince!" Oh-oh, he'd gone all formal. "You told me you weren't hurt. You said so. Look at you."

"It's only scratches." I tried to ward him off. "There's nothing broken." But he wouldn't rest until he checked me over while we sat and waited for our reinforcements.

I'd kept quiet about the headache, they'd have thought their prince a proper baby. And about the swollen ankle, which was worse from climbing. They stayed hidden but my back, it turned out, was another matter.

"You look as if you've been flogged," Tull said, before he thought of being tactful. "I can't do more than clean the worst of it, not here."

"It didn't stop me climbing. Ow!" I jerked as fabric came unstuck and blood-stained linen fell around me. "Do you mind? You're ruining that shirt." It was the only decent garment I was wearing.

"It's had it anyway," was Tull's attempt at comforting his betters. "D'you want my spare?"

"Since mine is only fit for kindling I suppose I'll have to make do with cheap substitutes."

He laughed, and started picking bits of rock out of my gashes. Some were lower down, which definitely put an end to flippant conversation. And to careless sitting.

The fresh shirt stuck to me too but there wasn't much I could do about it. It was a dreary ride back to the fort with all the wounded loaded on the wagon but I kept my grouching to myself. The wounded males had far more to put up with.

We took it slowly—Tull become a proper mother hen—and left our fittest males to go with Rag's replacements, to clear up behind us. They would count the bodies and collect some heads for Rag to set on poles at crossroads.

Rag had lookouts posted at the ruins. Males came fast to shift the wounded under cover. It was eight nights since we'd left him in camp, fourteen since we'd arrived. I'd given up all hope of finding Jaffid.

"Ash?" Rag watched me limp toward him. "Your messenger said you weren't touched!" He sounded more annoyed than anxious. "Here, sit down. I'll call for the physician."

"No, leave the male to deal with those that need it. All I need's a wash and supper, and a good night's sleep. But first a drink; a stiff one." Then my tongue betrayed me. "Lesser gods, I never did like climbing."

"Climbing?" Rag's eyebrows almost disappeared. He was one of the very few who knew I hated heights. He'd known it from my childhood. Heights with boundaries, like balconies or ramparts, those I'd grown accustomed to but open ledges I avoided like a plague. Rag knew it. Thankfully, Tull didn't.

Well, naturally I'd kept it quiet; it was a weakness, one I wasn't proud of. And if I'd sweated on the climb, well, so had all the rest; there'd been no difference to notice. But a slower, simpler way back down, with ropes to cling to, had been very welcome.

What with the mopping up and such the moon had cycled twice before I headed home again. There was no chance of sending males up north unnoticed now. We'd had to leave five males behind, not fit to travel, and another three had earned their place among the blessed. But I was fighting fit once more the day I strolled back into my apartments.

Chapter 26

Apparently not. Medi did one of his swooning acts before I'd even got my shirt off. I growled something appropriate to shut him up before he had hysterics. Gods, I ached once I'd stopped moving. All I wanted was the bath and peace and quiet.

Stripped, I waved the slaves away. I figured I could do without an audience till I was in the water. I was easing downward, careful not to lean back, when footsteps on the tiles broke my concentration.

"My lord has not stayed safe after all." Very neutral, his tone was. Not a comment, certainly not disrespect. Oh no, just observation.

"Don't you start." I sat. And winced, and hoped he hadn't noticed.

"Some cuts have opened," Keril's voice said coolly. "I could bathe them, if my lord permits me?"

"Go ahead." Inside I cursed. I'd thought the cuts were healing. "Too much riding," I began then stopped myself. A slave is hardly due an explanation.

The footsteps went away, came back. A white-clad knee slid into sight against my shoulder. He had knelt behind me. "Did you fall off?" His voice was shaking. Was he hiding laughter? Enough was enough. I was about to deal with such cheek when my back exploded.

That's genuinely what I thought at first. I was in flames, it felt like. "Ye gods, Keril. What—?"

"The Sultaki… seemed appropriate, my lord." Another tremor.

"*Brandy?*" I was speechless. Damn it, I was gasping. He'd poured brandy down my back?

"Alcohol, to kill infection," Keril added calmly. Too damned calmly. No apology for laughing, not a trace of sympathy for his afflicted owner?

"You— aa-ahh." Strong fingers soothed away the fire; deft, and careful. It seemed no time at all before my tired muscles stop protesting and the pain across my back was almost routed. He began to wash me, leaning down into the water.

I closed my eyes and let him, breathing herbs, and heated bath, and Keril. I was so relaxed I didn't realize what he was up to till he tugged the armlet free. I hadn't looked beneath it since I'd quit the palace—safer that way—so it was a jolting shock to see the Synia was stronger yet again; those yellow lines had deepened, almost golden, worse again and once again by magic. Horrified, I sat there staring at it, trying to assure myself that needn't alter anything significant. As long as no one ever saw it. As long as Father kept the High Priests off, and I kept quiet.

Keril noticed too. "Is that a mark from birth? I've read of such."

I figured he was curious, but not suspicious. He had seen it, dimly, in my bed but had no notion what the symbol stood for. "No." I looked away. "It's just a decoration."

Thus dismissed, he dropped the subject and resumed the gentle massage to my back, his fingers sliding over me like music to the senses. Whatever medication he was using was impressively effective. I felt my pulse rate settle down again.

"My lord? If you are feeling better, Master Medishel has supper waiting."

That was more polite, and the thought of food was most attractive. Yes, a decent meal, some more Sultaki, where it ought to go, and bed. And Keril, properly compliant?

But when I recalled him later he hung back until I actually shouted. And when he settled in beside me he was, it dawned on me, afraid to touch me.

"Plague on it, I'm not glass."

"I know, my lord, but you *are*… cracked, in places." His lips twitched, curse him. Still found it funny, did he? Hells, I thought suddenly, he wasn't serious, that remark about me falling off? Or was he? I shifted on my stomach, propped up on my elbows, searching for an explanation. Told myself, again, I didn't have to. Then I felt long fingers kneading gently.

At first he knelt above me, concentrating on my neck and shoulders. Everything went quiet. Then his hands slid forward. As they travelled down my chest his head came forward too, his perfumed breath against my ear. I don't know if I sighed or groaned. Old Sheshman had no notion what he'd given me. Those hands could change from iron to velvet, and that mouth…

"My lord should rest." The aches, and then the room, receded.

Gods, but it was wonderful what a decent night's sleep did. I felt a new male next morning, and this time Keril was far more willing when I pulled him over. By the time I got to breakfast I could have eaten one of uncle's bandits! All that fuss about my travel-worn appearance; there was nothing wrong with me a few nights' more such "treatment" wouldn't deal with. I grinned at Medishel, who beamed with pleasure, and I smiled at my father when I joined him later to report on our adventures.

While lecturing me for interfering in Rag's affairs my fond parent was inclined to be philosophical about almost losing his heir under a cliff. Ironic really; if the bandits had been responsible he'd have had an army out to slaughter every last offender, but a fall of rock he just shrugged off. He scanned the list of dead and wounded, then the note that Rag had sent, and seemed to think the matter ended. I had learned from him to weigh the past, but focus more attention on the future.

And the future added one small detail. Within a week my back showed only minor damage where I had resigned myself to some degree of scarring. I twisted round before the mirror but as Medi said, the marks were fading. "What did you use?" I asked, intrigued.

"My prince?"

"What medicine did you give Keril?"

"My prince, I gave him nothing." Medishel looked puzzled. "All he did was wash you, to my knowledge. But." He hesitated, glancing at my armlet then away. "The cure was surely sent you from on high, my prince?" He shut up after that, presumably put off by my expression.

I passed it off. And studied Keril's hands with new attention. He'd told my father that he feared his healing skills were failing, I recalled. I had to wonder. And no, I didn't mention it again. It wasn't just my back I didn't want discussed too freely now, the cursed Synia had altered even more. Deny it as I might, and yes I tried, the lines were thicker.

I was getting paranoid. I even asked myself if it was Keril, but of course it started half a day before I ever saw him, and he didn't *know* about our family deception. Hells, he didn't even know we had our own religion. Or he hadn't, till I beetled off and left him.

It sounded as if he'd read his way through half my library while I'd been absent. He had even sweet-talked Medi into letting someone in my household coach him in our dialects as well, so he could try the more foreign volumes. I'd acquired a scholar. Casual discussion of an evening went in all directions these days; some of it, I noted, things he might perhaps have known already but conveniently "forgotten". "I am what my master requires". Now I'd let him read he thought it was acceptable to understand? The creature's mad, I thought, defeated.

Except eventually, with a deal of hesitation which I only saw with hindsight, out it came; he feared he'd stumbled on forbidden knowledge.

Ashamet, Desert Born

That about described it once I dragged the details from him. He hadn't known our legends, had he? How they'd grown to form the faith that was the cornerstone of the Kadduchi empire. No, of course he hadn't since I hadn't favored him with a religious education. But the blood-cursed books had.

In the end he chose a full confession; came into my upper sitting room one evening, solemn-faced, and laid a heavy volume on my nearest table.

I'd been reading too, reports from southern border surveys, so my mind was more on troop deployments than religion, but I glanced across and knew it straight away. It took a second, though, to make the leap from subject to expression.

"Ah." I laid aside my sheets, picked up the tome and flipped the glossy pages, seeing once again the close-set printing and the lavish, hand-inked illustrations. Keril didn't speak, just waited. "So you've stumbled on a new religion."

"I didn't realize at first." He paused. "I think I should have put it back, my lord." Another pause. "I didn't."

"Read the lot, did you?"

A nod. He did look guilty.

"More than I ever did." I found I felt ill-done-by. "I suppose you had to find out some time. Better tell me what you learned."

"My lord, Master Medishel says your gods have terrible powers and this book, it says… the king your father… is a demigod?"

The hesitation told me he was doubtful; not surprising. Me, I felt embarrassed—it was bad enough with people who believed it—but I hid my feelings well enough he didn't notice. Trouble was I couldn't leave it there; it was too risky. Doubt, or even questions, would be heresy to those around him. So I gave him the official version. Hating every moment.

"Had trouble following the writing, did you? The thing's two centuries old at least, and flowery at that." I waved him down onto the carpet. "It's a simple story really." (So simple I continually wondered how the world could be so dumb as to believe it. Once perhaps, but surely we knew better these days.)

"Right. An ancestor of ours, a desert chieftain, was his father's heir. Back then we didn't have an empire, more a tribal region, but when Eskel's father died another male usurped him in his absence. When the heir came home he found himself outnumbered and eventually cornered.

"Surrounded by his enemies, Eskel's only options were surrender or to go down fighting, so he prayed, they say, to make his peace with life, and asked the gods to help him; not to save his own life but the lives of those whose loyalty had kept them at his side, a faith that now condemned them."

I took a breath then soldiered on. I had to give him all of it; the myth that formed the basis of Kadduchi faith and built our empire.

"But the gods chose to favor him. When they advanced his enemies were ringed by fire. They were all consumed yet Eskel and his followers were left unscathed. They never even drew their weapons."

My mouth felt dry. Would Keril, no one's fool in many ways, see through the legend, or believe it? His very ignorance had been a shield. Now he'd have to be a convert.

"So that was how it all began." I persevered. "The survivors started out to build an empire dedicated to the gods who'd helped them. Later kings became a channel for the gods' intentions. When our line produces such we name them Chosen. They become a Voice of Heaven. Like my father. Living proof the gods support us; demigods, as you described him."

Keril swallowed. "The male who came here, who asked me…?" He sounded breathless.

"Bit of a shock, is it? Yes, the male who was so gracious to you."

"I didn't know."

"Of course not, and you were forgiven." Keril almost spoke again then hesitated. "What?" I said.

"My lord…" His eyes were even wider. "Will… you become so?"

"Hells, no. It doesn't happen every generation," I said firmly.

"But… how can you be sure?"

I found myself averse to both the truth, and lying. "The gods would send a sign," I said. The hidden Synia—as real as my father's, if I thought about it—tried to burn its message through the armlet. "I am your prince and master but the king my father is a near-god, as you've discovered. So now you know. He walks between the gods and the Kadduchi, and ensures our power," I said, more baldly than I ever had before. "But it isn't something we gossip over," I concluded, hoping that would end the matter.

It did. The book was taken back to the library and the entire subject left strictly alone from that day on. Positively ignored. Absolutely avoided. Just the way I'd wanted. It gave me a headache, ignoring it so much.

Chapter 27

On a lighter note, Sheshman reappeared. I suspected he had been to Sidass. Since he had been summoned to my father straight away I'd have to wait to hear if he had anything from Jaffid.

Apparently the Sidassi king hadn't left his northern city since he had returned from giving oaths of loyalty to Father. More than that, said Sheshman at a quiet supper with my father, Rag and me—yes, Rag was back—King Farad's people hadn't seen him out in public lately either.

"Hm." My father frowned. "Our priests in Sidass haven't seen him either, even when they've tried." With the surrender, our Kadduchi holy star—and its assorted priests—had taken charge of the Sidassi temples, practically the only outward sign of occupation.

Father looked surprisingly concerned. "I always liked old Farad, both as male and ally. When he asked for my help—"

"Your help?" I'd interrupted but I couldn't help it. Rag was looking startled too. But Sheshman wasn't.

Father gazed into his wine. "Farad faced the fact that Effad doesn't have the brains to rule alone. We both knew there was ultimately only one solution so I sent you into Sidass. Farad chose surrender and the treaty, to protect his people."

"Seven hells." Rag scowled. He hadn't known either then. "Does Effad know?"

"The heir knows nothing. Farad didn't care to hurt his feelings." Father sniffed. "The male has no idea, but he'll get his chance to rule for us. I promised Farad that much."

My own thoughts had taken a different direction. "So that's why the war was so short; why we only made an alliance with Sidass? I did wonder."

Father smiled approval. "Yes, I was content to have Farad as an ally rather than a subject." A knowing smile. "And it showed the world we don't always conquer. But if Farad's failing, we may need to tighten up in Sidass."

Sheshman tried to look portentous. "The market traders hear he's fading fast, my king. They don't look forward to the heir as ruler either, even as a region of our empire."

"Hardly matters much to us." Rag shrugged. "As long as Effad follows orders. Still, perhaps I ought to take some reinforcements north with me and keep them handy at their border?"

Father nodded his agreement, looking thoughtful. I said nothing. I was feeling doubly foolish. Father had invited Sheshman here and talked of secrets Sheshman hadn't blinked at. Father was accustomed, then, to trusting Sheshman's observations? I'd been far too slow to spot that Sheshman used his roguish reputation as a cover. He was one of Father's ears, and of some importance.

When he was dismissed I followed. "Come and have a drink." I waved the guards aside and led him round the courtyard, ending in the middle floor of my apartments. There, I settled him with wine and raised an eyebrow.

Sheshman smiled into his glass. "I brought a message for you too, highness."

It was coded, naturally, but I was used to that. I read it on the spot.

"Highness, our initial quarry headed south at speed once the transaction was completed. Questions in the few villages along the way revealed another party asking their direction. It is possible the other males you spoke of also tracked our quarry."

Keril's priests had chased the robbers? If the thieves had realized, it certainly explained their rush to sell him. I read on.

"One village found two bodies by the road, and buried them. They match descriptions of our quarry. By the look of them they didn't die too quickly. No sign of the others. Possible we've lost that source of information.

"Heading back to the transaction village to attempt to backtrack, though I doubt I'll be successful. Since I'm so far south I'll take the opportunity to send this with our contact."

He'd been moving south while I was up there in the north? If I had only known.

But Sheshman's beady eyes were on me. "Your male, would he be looking for the virgin's origins?" So casual, but in his eyes was calculation.

Did he think I wanted a replacement? I decided to be honest. Mainly. "No, a rumor of some strange religion."

"Ah." His face smoothed out. A different subject; politics, not baser profit. But politics, in Sheshman's mind, meant information so I wasn't much surprised to hear him offer, "There's a town along the north-east border where the trade routes intersect. I have a house there, where your male found my contact. I could leave my eldest son up there if that would please you, highness? It would make the flow of information smoother." Sheshman sipped, and waited.

He was offering me a higher level go-between, perhaps his best. And dealing himself in on royal secrets and on any future action. I smiled. "Stay to supper?"

Nothing more was said about my search but he did offer other words of wisdom. "With respect, my prince, with King Farad ill, and Prince Effad likely to be king quite soon, it seems to me *your* role in this is strengthening the *next* alliance. You already have the sister. Effad is a shadow of his father, but bind him to you now, before he reigns, and you'll ensure the peace their common folk devoutly wish for. Give them peace, and justice, and they'll bow to you as willingly as to any Voice of Heaven."

Good advice. I didn't take offence.

The rains came round again to plague us. And Prince Thersat. He camped out on our doorstep like a cross between a vulture and the herons we'd displaced above his temples. Well, that was what it felt like, with his narrow trousers, hollow chest and rounded shoulders. When I enquired after Farad's health he dodged the question, talking of a gift he carried from his father to congratulate me on the Lady Taniset's "condition". Then he sent for it; a pretty goblet, solid gold and set all round with cameos, an art for which their land was justly famous; this time images of birds and flowers and insects. Ostentatious, maybe, but I must admit attractive, and he had presented it in private.

Unfortunately after that the fellow lurked about the palace hinting that he'd like to see his sister yet again. I drew the line at more than once, and told him so.

He looked offended. "I had expected—"

"Not here, you shouldn't." I'd had enough by then of being tactful. In fact, I was doing them both a favor, if he'd only see it. "She was your sister. She is now my wife. Our ways are different."

So different the details had rather shocked my father. They'd filtered through his spies that winter while I flattened bandits so I'd only heard it all much later. It seemed that males and females lived more… mingled… in Sidassi houses. Oh, well-born females were still guarded, but it seemed that sometimes only meant by crones or mothers, like the Kemik but without the daggers. Had Father known before, I might not have been married off to the Sidassi.

The last thing we needed right now was Thersat shoving the matter under his nose. Her pregnancy, although not publicly acknowledged, had so far saved the lady from rejection. I wondered if she realized how insecure her tenure had become. There were always other females, if I had to, but we'd wanted that alliance.

My uncle wasn't helping matters, sniping at the subject. As he had, I vaguely recollected, at my mother. And really, was it worth it? After all, an heir was what we wanted. "Fair's fair," I told them both. "You took their offer. If I can stand them being weird." My uncle snorted. "It seems to me you ought to. It's a bit late now to jib at details."

I was as blunt with Thersat. "To let you in the cloister, even once, was not our custom. Be grateful I allowed you there the first time."

Thersat did pause at that, give the male his due. "I beg your pardon," he said stiffly. "I confess I may not have tried hard enough to see this through your eyes. A Sidassi, especially one who cherishes his sister… Certainly my father—" He broke off. "But as you say, she is Kadduchi now. I'm sure," he ended faintly, "I can make my father understand that." His face betrayed his panic.

His father. A king, and, so they whispered, failing. Fool that I was, I ended up relenting.

"I am *much* beholden, Prince Ashamet." His speech was a lot more flamboyant than his clothes. "My sister speaks of you with great respect. My heart is lighter, for I have missed her sorely."

I took refuge in my wine. The fellow had been used to meeting all his female relatives, as if— I thrust the image from me, and did him the signal courtesy of being pleasant. "The lady does me honor."

"Ah yes, the child of course." He beamed.

I couldn't find an answer fast enough. I think my mouth was open.

"Yes, the future all males wish for," he went on. "Your royal father too, must feel…" He trailed off at last. He must have seen me stiffen.

"My royal father would undoubtedly be pleased, should I present him with an heir." I tried to drop the subject. Had the male no manners?

"Our prayers will match your own, to bring about a happy issue."

He stopped there, thank the gods. I'd been about to end the interview abruptly. But the fellow was sincere, I thought in fairness. And if he was any measure, Sidass was as keen on peace between us as my father.

Don't get me wrong, I'll never be my father but I know there's more than wars to handling a kingdom. And Sidass as an ally, honestly content to serve us, was a prize worth working hard for. So what we needed was to ignore these alien ideas, cross our fingers, and be patient. Providing Thersat could be gagged, or kept well clear of Father.

The day came. Word came from the closter eunuchs that the lady was in labor. I cancelled hunting, holed up in my library and tried to read reports. I read a dozen, and remembered nothing. Picked at dinner. Told myself to get to bed but didn't feel at liberty to send for Keril. Well, we might be interrupted.

In the early hours there was a stir below. I hurried down. The cloister eunuchs had already been admitted, with a tiny bundle wrapped in undyed silk.

Their painted lips were wreathed in smiles, even Zenec's. "Highness, the gods have blessed us with another single cub."

My throat constricted. I allowed myself one look. So small, so wrinkled. I nodded, since to talk about it was improper, and they left again, with closter guards all round them.

Next day I made offerings to all three altars. Never mind that I mistrusted priests; if there were truly gods I wanted their protection for that baby. And perhaps they heard, and interceded? Thersat took "the news" back personally to his ailing father. "Thank all the gods for that," I said, and meant it too for once. My father raised his head. I scowled. "He talks about it."

"Ah."

"It's damned embarrassing. He doesn't seem to care who hears him. I had to send for their ambassador, to corner him and explain how crass he was behaving."

"Ah," Father repeated, looking more amused than angered, "and did that work?"

"Did it? He stopped discussing privacies, but started apologizing. He was still at it when he left," I said bitterly. "You know, you've really dropped me in it this time."

Out of sight, and talk, my son (as I privately thought of him) grew and thrived, or so they told me. Happily, the En-Syn didn't, though by now it was so bad that was small comfort. It felt as if the gods were all too real *and* playing with me. Trying to ignore my helplessness I found relief in action, making two more forays out of Kadduchan; one west, one south, the latter very quiet. Governing a region isn't always done through show of power, or through official channels.

Keril had read all my books twice over now, I reckoned, but I bought him new ones and he drank them down like water. His conclusions sometimes made me re-examine things I hadn't previously questioned, even made me late to bed, but not too often.

Medi had enquiries made from time to time. The child, Zenec said, was fat and healthy, walking now, and learning simple phrases. Soon the winter was upon us. Soon it would be time to name him. There would be a slew of celebrations and I'd have to make that long-expected trip to Sidass to cement the joining of our bloodlines. Everything was going smoothly, I thought sourly, just when I was in the mood for trouble.

As Spring brought rain again, so Keril finally enquired about our customs over children. He'd heard (from the eunuchs, probably) I'd sired an infant, and it clearly puzzled him why no one would discuss it. He stuck it out though, less from fear than politeness, knowing him, until the year was almost up and Medi, grown impatient, let a wooden horse into my chambers. Carved and painted, it had leather reins with tiny golden bells that made me smile in recollection when I found it on the landing on return from watching Keril riding.

Grey eyes studied it, then my expression. "A toy, my lord?" He prodded gently. It rocked, back and forth.

"Indeed." I practically heard him thinking.

"For… your son?"

Oh, very cautious. I indulged him as we took the stairs. "For when he becomes my son. Not long now, although we shouldn't talk about it till that happens."

He seemed to think he had been gagged and followed me in guilty silence. Perverse, I chose to chatter. "We name a child when he reaches his first year, not before."

He stripped off his robe then shirt as we approached the bath. "Name? As if he isn't born yet? But… why, my lord? Is there a reason?"

"A very old one," I said frankly as I tossed my clothes aside as well. Belatedly I wondered if I should have talked about our history to Thersat, only somehow it was so much easier explaining things to Keril. "I told you we weren't always a royal house, nor city dwellers. Once we were desert lords."

A nod of understanding.

"A lot of babies don't survive out in the desert. If times are bad, the youngest suffer." I didn't give him details; how if starvation circled it was the oldest, and the youngest, tribes must sacrifice to save the able-bodied. He had the wit to see how harsh realities could turn to custom. "So we name a child a year later. After all." I shrugged. "Who wants to own a child who's turned out weak, or crippled?"

"And… is this child… well?" He joined me in the water, sponging down my shoulders.

I grinned. "Why d'you think Medi looks so cheerful?"

Keril looked suitably enlightened. "So the horse is a birthday gift?"

"No, merely one of Medi's fittings for the child's apartments, come the summer. If he gets there." (I don't take anything for granted.)

"He will leave his mother?"

"A year-old should have learned to walk and talk, but now it's time for him to run, then think. Such things are for males to teach him, not for females."

"But… will he see his mother?"

"Of course, whenever he wants to." I was surprised he asked. Surprised that Keril found our ways so strange still.

Keril thought about it. "Did *you* want to?"

Another unexpected question. I took my time, while Keril combed my hair out. In the end I answered his question with one of my own. "You're concerned about the mother?"

"I wondered... might she miss her child? Even if the child forgot her," Keril ended, sounding... guilty?

Ah. I turned my head. "Is that what happened to you?"

His head was turned toward the tiles, not me. "I have recalled a memory of someone but it's very garbled; more a dream than something I remember. My masters told me to forget. I thought I had. They said my place was in the present."

That sounded like the sort of crap religions spouted. Though... "It's often better that way for a slave as well," I said. "But Medishel will see the child visits her, until he's old enough to make his own decisions."

"Master Medishel will leave u— you?" Keril, surprised, almost forgot his manners.

"No, but he'll oversee the running of the child's apartments, and train the overseer I've appointed. You can have every faith in Medi's supervision, when the time comes."

"Indeed, my lord, I didn't mean..." He trailed off, embarrassed.

"If Medishel allows you, you could see him."

"Me? Is that allowed?"

I raised a mocking eyebrow.

Keril finally relaxed. "Yes, since you are master here, and no one dares to argue. I would like to see your son, my lord," he added.

"Teach him gentler manners, when you visit," I suggested. "There'll be enough who'll teach him worse ones. Especially while I'm away."

Silence held its breath, and wouldn't question.

"Once the cub's acknowledged as my son I'll need to visit Sidass; oil the wheels of power a little."

Still silence; it appeared every time I went away now.

"No. I won't take you along, not this time either."

A sigh. "They wouldn't approve."

"You know that, do you?"

"I... added it together."

"Two and two made four?"

"They often do. I would offend them, and that wouldn't help you, would it?"

"Not much."

Another pause.

"I could be gone several months this time. Mind your ways, as usual, and do as Medi tells you."

"Yes, my lord."

"You'll have to stay inside as well this time; no riding, even in the garden." I'd get that said as well, before he wondered. "It would be awkward for Medi."

"No, my lord, of course, not in your absence. That would shock people too." He seemed resigned. I scowled for him. He disarmed me. "How, so— when will you go, my lord?"

"When? When all the fuss is over," I shook my head. "Gods know why they have to have such celebrations. It's not as if the cub will notice."

Chapter 28

Summer rushed toward us. Time for a name, perhaps, I graciously acknowledged. The entire palace fidgeted. No one would dare tempt fate by talking openly of what was coming. Not till Thersat, plague upon the male, returned, offensively discreet about the gifts he carried for the child.

Sheshman turned up too, with knowing smiles. This time I invited him to supper, where he packed away enough for two behind his garish sashes.

"My second son has talked with traders from Ossaresh, highness. The Sidassi capital's agog; it's common knowledge our temples there plan a ceremony to announce the child. Prince Effad has been hiring extra entertainers, much as we have, so it looks as if there's going to be a public celebration." Sheshman beamed as slaves removed the meats and offered fruit and almond pastries with a sweet dessert wine.

So the Sidassi were celebrating and Effad leading them? "Good," I said. Father's foresight seemed to have paid off; the new alliance had been strengthened. "Good," I said again, and made a mental note to be polite to Thersat. Curse it, I might even let him see his sister.

The day before his birthday, my infant son was presented to me. It was very private. Medi brought the cub, with Zenec, up into my intimate apartments, leaving all the rest to kick their silken heels below us. Zenec followed Medi through the curtains, bowed to me and set the child on his feet and only then became aware of Keril, sitting quietly on a carpet by the windows.

Keril, used to eunuchs after all, looked back at him quite calmly. Zenec didn't change expression, but he looked his fill before he turned in my direction once again and nudged the infant.

The child made a stab at bowing to me. I bowed back. We looked at one another. Solemn little cub, and stockier than I'd expected but at least he looked Kadduchi, not a bit like Thersat, or that square-jawed Effad. Eyes like saucers at the moment, but he wasn't trying to hide in Zenec's robes or anything like that. Indeed he stared at me with every sign of hopeful interest.

I squatted down, and tried a smile. No reaction, so I held my hands, palms up, toward him. "Come."

He moved when Zenec prodded gently, made it almost close enough to touch then stopped and glanced behind at safety.

"Watch." I waved my hands across each other once, then back. A sweet appeared—yes, like magic—then it vanished and my hands were empty. Sleight of hand had always been a useful skill when I was in disguise. I'd never tried it on a child before, it seemed to work though. Eyes that might have been my own were frowning at me; clearly this was unexpected. But he took another step toward me.

When the sweet appeared the third time round he snatched it from my hand before it disappeared, and beamed his triumph.

"Very good." I smiled back. "Now make your bow to Master Medishel." I turned to Medi. "Here you are, another prince for you to teach some manners." I watched indulgently as Medi bent and gestured, offering a toy to play with.

He had hand-picked all the cub's attendants. My son (my son!) would be as royally looked after as he should be, once he quit the females' sanctum for the almost-separate apartment at our southwest corner, in between my father and the closter.

And I watched as Keril ventured closer. Unopposed, he touched the child's head lightly and the cub smiled up at him, as if he knew him. I pretended not to notice.

"He'll be Prian," I told Keril as the child and Zenec left us. "That means "first" in old Kadduchi."

"First in your heart. Of course."

What could I answer? I laughed at myself. Was this how every father felt, I wondered? Had my father? Keril saw too much good in people. Still, at least he thought I had a heart. How many slaves would say that of their masters? I told him so, that night.

The grey eyes glinted. He was bolder these days, his hand slid upward past my ribs to find the topic of our conversation. "I know you have, my lord, for I can feel it beating." Then his fingers reached my neck. Discussion ended. Life, right then, had only good to offer. Maybe the gods' favor wasn't so bad after all. They'd surely sent me Keril, and they hadn't made me throw away the all-concealing armlet.

One day after his birthday Prian entered his new home. It might not be as spacious as the closter but it was entirely his and crammed with every childish comfort Medi could envisage. He tottered through the guarded entrance, his Sidassi nurse a nervous shadow just behind him, saw the puppy Medi had imported and settled in, so Medi said, as if he'd always lived there.

The nurse, who'd tend him for another year, shuffling between the closter and the cub's new quarters, was a doting, tidy-looking female past the age of bearing, but it would be our own Kiddush customs Prian would grow up with. It occurred to me that wasn't totally unlike what Keril had recalled of *his* beginnings. Maybe Prian too might one day barely recollect this nursemaid. But I'd see to it he knew his mother's face. He wouldn't leap from infancy into a prison-priesthood.

All that remained, here at least, was the formal presentation to my father in the Gate Hall. The three High Priests were there in all their glory, full of self-importance, with an army of attendants and a lot of fuss and flurry. On this auspicious day my father wore an open tunic that revealed the three point star that lay above his breastbone. I thanked the gods—increasingly afraid I should—that mine stayed hidden and the priests stayed silenced. I could all-too-well imagine what they'd tell the world about its being on my sword arm, rather than my heart, if we were ever forced to make it public. I'd begun to wonder, was it possible the gods as well as me preferred to keep it secret? Well, they hadn't forced the issue. Everything was peaceful, no more itching even. I'd forget about the marks for days on end at times, until I took the armlet off to bathe beneath it.

Today, I played my part. So did the priests, despite our latest disagreements. They'd been keen to plan ahead to faking the En-Syn on Prian. I had vetoed any such discussion. Not until my arm was understood, I said. If ever. Outwardly content, in front of witnesses including Thersat and a bundle of Sidassi envoys, I named my child Prian and the Voice of Heaven dealt with his anointing. The heir my father wanted from me—an auspicious single heir as well—had been delivered, and acknowledged, and our royal lie perpetuated. Even so, I had a son! I told myself I shouldn't grin so much, and managed better manners here than when the wedding gifts were offered.

Rag, to my surprise, gave Prian Kemik triplets, only five days younger than their future master. Generous, since pure-bred Kemik slaves were rare outside their kingdom. Gods knew where he'd found them. I waxed eloquent for once. The old rogue looked complacent. Obviously my heir had his approval. Thersat said a lot as well (what else?). I even smiled at that. He can't help being what he is, I thought. His brother's gobbled all the muscles. Then I had a novel thought; he might have been a sneakier opponent, being more a lawyer than a fighter. And he did have taste; that pretty goblet…

Plague on it, where had I put it. Curse it if I hadn't gone and lost political advantage.

"The Sidassi goblet, highness?" Medi looked surprised. "It's with the wedding gifts, you gave no other orders. Should I not have?"

"No, that's fine." I turned to go. "I only wondered. No, have someone fetch it. Send it to the table. Better late than never, eh? I'll share a toast with Thersat at this evening's revels; show him that I value both the present and my kin-by-marriage."

I felt quite clever. Even Rag would class this as a courtly gesture. It would be remarked on, and remembered; another thread to weave into the ties that bound Sidassi to us.

Night had fallen and wine had flowed by the time we neared the end of the formal dinner. According to our custom, my father, clad that night in gold-embroidered crimson with a scattering of rubies, held the centre of our knee-high royal table, with the only really decent seat. It had a back on. This evening it was one he often favored, polished wood inlaid with radiating gold and silver bands, so rays of light appeared to spread behind him like a sunrise, glowing in the lamplight.

I'd sworn a private oath I'd never use the thing. I couldn't see myself in something so pretentious, even if— Forget it. Concentrate on dinner.

Since it was a state occasion I had dressed to complement my father's choice of colors in a crimson tunic trimmed with gold and amber stitches, gold and amber also prominent among my jewels.

The higher of the lords who filled this banquet hall got curving, short-legged stools with arms on while the lesser did without the arms, so we were clearly ranked, and just in case some idiot should care, the greatest lords, like princes, had their stools supplied with silken cushions; crimson ones that evening. Such a load of nonsense.

I was on my father's right, of course. As Prian's nearest alter-kin, Prince Thersat's cushioned stool was next to mine. I noticed he wore crimson, brown and gold. It looked like he was picking up our customs. My uncle, clad in white and crimson over purple, flanked my father. He'd said he meant to stick around until the Turn of Year, and the vigil. Maybe longer, knowing him. He much preferred the capital to anywhere the north could offer.

Quite the family group, and Medishel had set the goblet in among my other cups and glasses, though if Thersat saw it he politely failed to notice.

I too was minding my manners, though in my case it was harder. Thersat had experimented with his mode of dress as well. He had eschewed his heavy cotton coat for silks. There was an outer robe, the color of a muddy puddle, open to reveal a crimson tunic and some pale yellow, gathered trousers, the ensemble finished off with gold and tortoiseshell as decoration. It should have been at least presentable. Instead it served to show him as a stick-thin puppet, every ring a burden on his fingers.

Mind you, despite his bony frame he put away more bread and meat and rice than I did. You'd have thought the male had starved himself beforehand. He pointed out Sidassi delicacies added to the feast before us at my father's orders, urging me to try them, but I noticed he himself chose stout Kadduchi portions. He was still stuffing his mouth when my father gave up waiting.

They cleared around the goblet. I hadn't used it yet. By then he must have wondered, but he hadn't asked. In fact his manners, gluttony aside, were perfect. In peace-time, sexual laxity omitted, Thersat gave no grounds for any of our other vassal lords to claim Sidassi blood might sour our blood lines. And it must be clear to all he was no mental weakling. Take his dinner conversation, it'd made a pleasant change from hunting, war, or horses.

Our discussion veered from food to different customs.

"…our laws apply as much to peasants as to nobles," he was saying. "The protection of our children, for example. Even a laborer's child will have its second father. I was deeply honored to be Prian's. Please don't be offended if I say my family was much relieved your house accepts the custom. It is yet another sign your house is not a mere dictatorship but tries to rule with wisdom. Historically," Thersat smiled, "We must both be aware the two things seldom go together, but such enlightened gestures explain the peace and the prosperity across your lands, and give my nation reassurance in our future."

Whew. Quite a speech. "You are most observant," I told him solemnly. Well, I kept a straight face over it. "And you echo my intention that this child will bind our dynasties together." One never spoke about succession, not until one's king himself announced it.

"One's king" was listening, I thought, and smiling, very slightly. I pretended not to notice. Slaves arrived and offered tiny jeweled cups for desert coffee, peach liqueur or brandy. "To mark that, let us drink a toast." I reached across. "But with your own Sidassi token."

Thersat gulped. He practically gabbled. "You honor our kingdom, and myself, Prince Ashamet." He drew a breath. "Here, let me make the pledge as we in Sidass do, and speak the words we wish our children."

That cup was out of my hands before I knew it. Thersat beckoned to a slave, who filled the goblet, then he raised it.

Thersat held the goblet up, the curving metal gleaming softly in the lamplight. "May this child be strong, and well-protected. May he grow in wisdom, and be wisely guided. May he live long, and deal with honor." He could drink as well as eat. He downed considerably more than half before he lowered it. By then a host of eyes were watching. Older heads were nodding their approval. He sipped again then lowered the cup, offering it to me with both hands.

Oh, very stately. I took it, promising myself to match his eloquence, aware our words would be repeated. "Your words describe the future every male desires for his children. My son could have no better prayers than these from his Sidassi second father." Though I'd better check that second father nonsense, later. "On his behalf, I echo you." The cup was practically empty but I downed the rest in one as he had.

It had been Sultaki, I could just about pick out its flavor. Damned waste, I thought, to bring it out so late; like drowning it in muddy water. After all the different wines, and those Sidassi spices, you could hardly taste its subtler texture.

Chapter 29

To tell you the truth, I forget a lot of that night. There was some gambling. I remember that part. Games sprang up as usual at one end of the hall. The table I sat in on escalated from a rowdy game of Hound and Chicken to a fierce, full-blown game of Conquest, every hazard tile included. It engendered heavy betting, both from players and the circle of spectators.

I was doing well till someone talked me into going off to watch the jugglers. Sidassi, someone said, and very skilful. I remember tossing silver and applauding. Then Kadduchi fire-eaters ran onto the floor, their dance accompanied by war drums and the clash of cymbals. Stirring stuff, except they turned the hall into an oven. By the time I got back to the table I'd had a fair bit more to drink, I supposed. At any rate I realized my ability to weigh the odds had shortened. I pushed up from the table. Most of the guests were gone anyway. Come to think, a lot of them had come to bid me goodnight. I'd forgotten. I was only fit for bed, I thought, then thought of bed and found I'd *giggled*.

"Ye gods!" I said out loud, or something like it. My balance was off too, and worsening by the minute. I lurched into someone, who cursed until they realized who'd hit them.

"My prince? Are you all right?" The question echoed, but I recognized the speaker. Sheshman's fruity tones were getting quite familiar.

"Fine," I said, "I'm fine." I laughed and left him.

Sounds grew muffled after that. I walked through blinding lights, then darkened passages. The centre of the palace, left in darkness? Shadows lengthened till it grew so dark I couldn't see where I was going and the way grew narrow. I was in a maze of tunnels. There were booming noises. Fortunately someone, not sure who, was helping me along them. Pretty useful having someone there to lean on. Tried to say so but the words got mangled. Sounds were tangling up as well; the dark was full of flashing colors then a voice raised, giving booming orders. "Medi?" I said doubtfully. It looked like Medi but he rippled, and he didn't sound right.

"Indeed, my prince. All's well. The stairs are this way."

Was it well though? I tripped. His face expanded. Some while after that my bed appeared. It spun, and tilted. Black silk. Perfumed but with something sour and horrid, musty green and purple. Being horizontal made my head swim too. Now where…

"My lord?" The grey eyes anxious.

"Keril." Something moved between us. "Keril?" I said urgently. He reappeared. For a second there I'd had the strangest notion… "Did you leave me?"

"No, my lord, I'm here, always. Are—are you ill?" I had relaxed by then but he seemed bothered.

"No, course not, 'm just—" I concentrated on not slurring. "Drunk. That's all." I managed that quite clearly.

"My lord, are you sure? Lord Sheshman sent us word. He says—"

"Too much to drink. Not clever, but regreb— regrettably normal. Seven hells!" A wave of dizziness attacked me, followed by a fit of coughing. I hoped Medi was ready for that; I wasn't. Afterwards I lay back feebly while they stripped my clothes off. I was vaguely grateful. And, vaguely, displeased with myself. It was years since I'd got as bad as this. All right, I had a son. That didn't make me too old to hold my drink. Did it?

A white hand laid a cool, wet cloth against my aching forehead. He still looked worried but at least the room had quietened. Gods be praised, someone had cast muslins across the lamps and dimmed them to a gentle glitter in the furthest corners. Firelight flickered too. I could have done without the fire, this room was every bit as stifling as the banquet. I was panting.

"Need to sleep it off, that's all," I reassured him. "I'll be fine again by morning." That was when I started shuddering. I couldn't stop. I felt him leave me though, and heard him shouting. That was when I realized— "Keril," I got out, or thought I did. "S'thing's. Wrong."

He swam toward me, leaning forward. "Yes, my lord, I know. I have to do this."

Do what? I opened my mouth to ask. A sea of water filled it; noxious stuff, more salt than liquid. I gagged, and turned my head to spit it out.

Or would have. Long white fingers clamped like iron bars along my jaw. I couldn't move my head, or close my mouth. An ocean of the filthy stuff flowed in, till I was forced to swallow, and my ears were popping. I struggled, but it made no difference, then I puked until my throat burned, till I was too weak to notice. Someone yelled, or was it Keril, chanting in his heathen language? Hated that. I didn't want a priest. I wanted Keril.

Ashamet, Desert Born

He wasn't there when I next surfaced either, but at least the geometric patterns in the canopy above my bed had ceased to twist and topple. I felt as if someone had turned me inside out. My jaw ached too. I wondered if I had some bruises. So much for the gods' protection.

Last time everything was shaking, me included. This time my hand, above the sheet, looked fairly steady, though my head felt smothered. Still, the room had cooled to something less a furnace. Since it looked like I was going to live I decided to try sitting up.

Not so good. Granted, as soon as I stirred the slaves against the walls fetched Medi, and I did, eventually, sit higher on my pillows, but it wasn't easy. Keril hadn't rushed in with them. "Keril?" I muttered, once I'd got my breath back.

"Highness?" Medi leaned in close.

I hadn't realized I'd been that quiet. I made an effort. "Where... is he?"

"Who, highness?"

"Keril," I said irritably, in a throaty whisper.

"About, my prince. He's probably asleep."

That wasn't good enough. I tried to say so, but the words got jumbled.

"Sleep, my prince. Grow stronger." Medi's voice threw echoes and his face grew darker. Sounded far too sensible. As bad as...

The next time my eyes opened was distinctly better. You know those mornings you go from sleep to waking in a breath, so that your mind seems bathed in light? All right, so maybe not that good, but it felt it. Medi didn't stoop this time to hear me either. I took that as an indication I'd recovered. I was awake, alert, and with a lot of questions. First among them...

"How'd it happen?"

"It was after your return, my prince. You were... exhausted." Medi hesitated.

"Drunk, you mean. I'm sure I looked it. Anybody else fall victim? Is my father well?"

"Of course, my prince."

"Fine, so—" Then I stopped, examining his woebegone expression. Medi and assorted slaves but still no Keril? "Keril sleeping this time too?" I couldn't believe it. It wasn't... Keril. "Gods, not him as well? But no, he wasn't even there. Where is he?"

Medi shuffled slippered feet, then faced me. "Keril's... gone. I didn't dare tell you before."

"Gone?"

"Taken, by your royal father. Highness, you aren't strong enough to—"

"Lesser gods." I wanted up. I couldn't make it. "Where's my father?" I hadn't known I had so much control, but I could feel it slipping off already. "Find my cursed father," I repeated, panting.

"I've already sent him word, my prince. He'll come at once, I'm sure. We've—" Medi hesitated. "All been… very anxious."

I saved my breath and thought that over. "How long?"

"Three days, highness," Medi told me gently. "There've been prayers in all the city's temples and the priests made special offerings to ward off demons."

Praying for me? Were there priests here now? And was my arm still hidden? I raised my head. There weren't—at least not here in my bedroom—and it was. All right. I got my wits together, far too slowly. So much for thinking I'd recovered. "When? When did he take Keril?"

A sigh escaped the male I'd trusted. "Toward evening of the first day, highness."

Three days. And nights. Probably sleeping. I felt much stronger now. I felt like battle. "You ever lie to me again, I'll cut your head off, understand me?"

Medi went as white as Keril. "You were too ill, my prince. I did my best for you, at least I thought so. If you lived I knew you'd find a way to bring him back to us. And if you died, what would it matter?" Medi said forlornly. "Keril wouldn't care, not if he'd killed you, though I tried, I really did, to tell them all he'd never *mean* to harm you."

"Harm me? What in—? *Where in all the hells is Keril?*"

Chapter 30

The most secure of all our cells were carved into the bedrock underneath our private gardens, wholly separate from the more official dungeons further down the hillside. Convenient, my father called the place. And secret.

It felt an uphill struggle, trudging down from my apartments, round the colonnade and through the bushy camouflage that hid the double iron grating in one corner. Guards came running from below to open up. The hinges needed oiling. Males fell back to clear my path on stairs that twisted at uneven angles. Few males saw what lay beyond these turns, and less came out to tell it.

I hadn't been there for a while. It seemed steeper than I had remembered. I motioned Medi down ahead of me and kept my hand upon his shoulder for the brief descent. It kept my balance and reminded Medi he was on probation. By the time we reached the single passage down below—the solid wooden doors, their shuttered spy-holes—he was shaking.

I had to stop a moment there, my head was spinning. We were entirely underground; no windows and the lamps were fitful here; a draught disturbed them. Had I shivered?

It was a very small cell furthest from the stairway, not the better-ventilated ones they gave to nobles. It would be practically pitch in there until the door groaned open, a worse ordeal for somebody who had no night sight.

It must be near the drains as well; the rough-hewn rock inside was cold as ice, and damp, as if the stones were sweating. The pale huddle by the farthest wall looked ghostly set against the grimy backdrop, and what had always been so straight was doubled over, didn't seem to notice my arrival. Maybe he'd been dozing.

Then he raised his head, and spotted me, and croaked, "My lord?" The smile was brilliant. Painful.

My throat constricted. When I swore his smile faded and his head dropped. When I grabbed at him he winced.

"Gods, male, you're filthy," I said stupidly. The fine engraving on those shackles was engrained with dirt, or was it blood that marred them?

"Yes… my lord."

I felt him trembling in my hands. Or maybe I was shaking. "Who did this?" I demanded. On such white flesh the bruises were obscenely livid.

I wasn't strong enough to lift him up, I had to stop and lean a hand against the clammy wall. I swore again, and snapped at Medishel to help him.

Keril made it to his feet, but couldn't straighten, not completely, and his breathing sounded shallow. I'd assumed he'd wrapped his arms around himself for warmth, or comfort. Now, I worried that his ribs were broken. "They beat you," I said foolishly. I couldn't seem to get my mind around it.

He was leaning back beside me, skin against the clammy wall. "Yes, my lord." A tired murmur. Then his head came round, with care, as if that hurt, expression suddenly uncertain. "They said… it was your order."

"My prince!" I must have tripped, Medi had hold of me again, was calling for a stretcher.

"Damn it, Medi, send for a physician too."

"I'll have him at your bedside straight away, my prince."

"Not me, you fool, for Keril. Look at the state of him!" My rage exploded. "I'll cut the balls off whoever did this. I'll—" The cell began to spin. I caught my breath, and called myself to order. Hysterics weren't productive. "Cover him and get him to my quarters. Gently!"

There was no question of putting Keril in that cramped den of his. We needed space to tend him. Medi organized a proper bed in one of the surplus warming rooms beyond the bath; a private spot convenient for water. When they got to cutting off the ruined trousers Keril didn't seem to notice. He was probably exhausted.

A court physician watched my eunuchs start to wash his patient, nostrils pinching. "Starved a bit, and beaten. Dehydrated. He'll survive." I'd twitched. The blockhead flinched and made a real examination, conscious I was watching every movement.

Told Keril it was my doing, had they? That item smoldered through these tedious ministrations. Anger made me feel fitter.

"Hey. You." The fuss was over and the room gone quiet.

The grey eyes fluttered open, dulled, and hazy. Drugged. They'd put it in the water. Three days in he'd been so thirsty he'd ignored the pain it cost him. Sinking fast. I hoped he'd last a little longer. "Feeling any better?"

"Yes, my lord." He didn't look it.

"So. You believed them." It was a statement, not a question. I'd known the answer since he'd said it.

A pause. He looked straight at me for a moment, then let his gaze fall, all submissive. "You're saying that I'm stupid?" Barely audible and yet, astoundingly, he tried to smile.

"I thought you had more sense." How could I possibly stay mad, when he was glad to be berated?

That seemed to rouse him for a moment. "Why did…?"

"Don't know." (Yet, I thought.) "But clever questioners know words can hit as hard as hammers. Always remember, truth gets lost when males are angry." Had I said that? Me? Philosophizing at a sick-bed?

Keril thought that over. "Males do lie. I've read of it. I should have known that."

Blamed himself now, did he?

"I *was* stupid," he concluded, "but this." A hand fluttered. "Will remind me, won't it? Your… pardon, my lord?" The voice was fading.

"Forgiven." I said it soft so no one else would hear, and touched the hand. The fingers moved, then settled when I held them. His shallow breathing slowed then deepened. Gods, he did look ill. I wasn't sure which I was more angry at: the poison, or my father.

It must have been many years since anyone had sworn at my father in front of witnesses. Except before their execution. Predictably he hadn't liked it. Now, we both stood looking down at Keril. Medishel had said he'd sleep the clock round. My royal father inspected the strapping, the raised-up pillows, the trivial cuts, the many bruises, in offended silence.

Nothing permanent, I'd noted. Nothing that should scar, or cripple, though those ribs, I thought, had gone beyond their orders. Someone had been careless there. A broken rib could kill; I'd seen it happen. Father followed me away, still silent.

In my upper sitting room we both waved off the slaves who bobbed about us. He sat down and waited. Gods, but I felt ugly. I'd been ready to kill when I thought he'd— But this, this was almost worse. I could so well imagine…

"Were you there, Father? Or shall I *tell* you what happened?" I strode across the room. "His answers never changed. He *let* them hurt him, might have prayed, perhaps, when they got rougher." My gorge was rising. "Do you know why he never argued, wouldn't struggle? Do you?"

"Ash, what are you saying?" He was looking troubled. Troubled!

"He thought it was my order. Mine." I choked. "You said I was his new religion. Maybe you were right, at that. I've never understood but maybe he believed he was guilty; that if I thought he was he must be!" I said wildly. "Did you have to order them to lie?"

I stood there shaking. Truth was I'd be better seated, but I needed room between us. I was on the edge that morning.

Maybe Father knew it too. He chose his words. "Ash, I promise you, I didn't. I wouldn't have thought to. And if you're wondering, I had him kept apart, and didn't send in males to put my questions. I wasn't sure enough I was prepared to do that either." He stopped, and waited for some comment.

That was why there was no lasting damage? And he'd sent in eunuchs, so they hadn't— Maybe it was time to sit down. I chose a high-backed chair, with arms to lean on. Took a breath. My rage was getting in the way, inviting trouble, but— "Why by all the gods did all this happen? Whatever fool idea you started with, you should have realized he'd never—" I couldn't get the words out.

"Simmer down, it's you we were protecting." When I didn't interrupt he spoke more evenly. "What did you think I'd do, when he was found, holding you down, choking you? When you were too drunk to resist? Even then… I told them to find the truth, to scare it out of him if necessary but not to damage him unduly. I found it hard to see him as… If I'd been certain he was guilty do you think he'd be alive? He'd be in pieces, on display at all the outer gateways." Father sounded more annoyed, his temper getting loose again. A temper dangerous to Keril.

I forced myself to stick to logic. "You weren't sure, but you couldn't wait? I would have told you—"

"Ash, we didn't know you'd ever tell us *anything*, and Keril seemed the obvious suspect. When Rag found out—"

"Rag?" I straightened up. "I might have known."

"Your uncle questioned some of your household, to keep it private. One admitted seeing Keril trying to choke you. Medishel insisted Keril wouldn't harm you but he wasn't there, and there were other mouths to testify that you were struggling against him."

"Curse it, Father, he was—" I broke off, mouth still open. Choking me? Nobody had realized?

Enough mouths, were there? Scared of Rag? Of being suspected? Jealous? I felt cold all over. My household served my interests, not their own. There was some weeding to be done, once this was settled.

Father was still dealing with his "facts". "Rag was in the right. We needed to be sure what happened, and you couldn't tell us. So yes, I sent your virgin to the cells, and had him put to question. But when Medishel objected I sent word they shouldn't kill him. Not till I was sure," said Father grimly. "The whole thing was a mess. Rag said he couldn't get straight answers out of half your household."

"You mean the old fool never asked the most important question."

"Oh?" Father sat up at that. "And that is?"

"What Keril tried to choke me *with*. I wasn't strangled. I was poisoned. Keril *saved* me. And thanks to Rag, and you, we've lost three days we should have used to find the culprit!"

Chapter 31

Six days later, and we still knew almost nothing. Six frustrating days. And nights.

"Did *you* think, my lord...?" Respectful. Tactfully unfinished, while he lay back looking through the lattice at the treetops rising from the garden-court below us. It was mid morning. Yellow-crested singing birds that nested in the trees below were fluttering between them. Some were wheeling in the air, quite close. He'd turned his head to watch their acrobatics.

I'd wandered out, a drink in hand, and found him dozing on the inside balconies, well propped with pillows, under Medi's order not to stir without permission. The bruises were fading, and they'd cut back on the bandages. And of course he only winced now when he thought I wasn't looking. So much lean muscle, and all I could think was how fragile he still looked.

I sniffed. "To the best of my knowledge salt is not a favored method for assassination, not even for a fool who's waited two full years to do it."

I saw the tensions leave him; every muscle slackened. "I thought it might help," he said, with just a trace of smugness.

"Well, I'm here, I suppose, even if I didn't thank you for it at the time. Even so a slave is *not* supposed to argue with his master, which definitely includes holding him down and clamping his jaw open when he doesn't want to swallow something awful. I think I still have bruises there."

"My lord will no doubt punish my transgressions."

Said far too smoothly, that was. I found a real urge to worry him as much as he had me. "Oh yes," I said. "The custom is to mark you for your insubordination."

His breathing faltered for a moment when I set my drink down on the nearest table. Had he seen such brands, on others? Then the pale head lowered. Still no protest? I despaired. Felt guilty too. "Your hand," I snapped. Gods knew what he was thinking; that I meant to take a finger? I shook my head. No matter how I tested him...

He offered me his sword hand, and the fingers were quite steady, too. He wasn't looking though, I caught him by surprise. When I held on he stopped and let me finish, staring at his middle finger where, if Sheshman's tale was right, he'd worn another ring before his capture.

Handsome, I thought. A mix of gold and silver; almost two rings twined together round a three point star, to signal he was of the royal household. I'd given some thought to the design. I wondered if he understood that.

"But… you can't," he stammered. He was staring at it. Rings would always flatter him, I thought, with such long fingers. "I'm… not allowed. To own things."

So much for not arguing. I laughed. "I can do as I like. Yes?"

"Yes, my lord." He still looked doubtful.

"It's not a gift, then. Say, instead, a token. Of ownership."

"My lord." That sounded happier.

I sat down, took my drink again and left him staring at his fingers, too polite to break the silence. The rumors would remain, but word about the ring would leak as well—I'd see to that—enough to keep the vultures off him, even any left among my eunuchs. I hoped. I sipped, and watched the birds. When I looked back he was asleep, as if the whole affair was over.

Not exactly how my father saw the matter.

We had ridden to our largest temple in the middle of the city—very visible—where I had made a sideshow of myself by giving public offerings to all three gods for my returning vigor, squashing lurid rumors I had died of my "infection". All three High Priests had smirked, and talked of "Godly Intervention".

Sil—predictably—had tried to turn the episode to their advantage. "It would be the perfect opportunity, my prince…"

I'd growled. He'd looked so pleased about it I had wondered, for a moment, if he'd set me up, but had reluctantly dismissed the possibility. Too risky. Still, I vetoed any mention of the En-Syn and repeated my resolve to keep it secret till I understood it. Sometimes now I wished I knew it was the gods. At least that way it would be settled. All in all, I wasn't in the best of tempers by the time we reached the palace and besides that I was ravenously hungry; protocol demanded I miss breakfast. Odd. I'd almost died and what I suffered most was hunger. I reckoned Keril had cleared a good week's food stores from my system.

Father sat and watched me eat, still brooding. His only son, poisoned? He'd had everybody in my household grilled, bar Keril—under my supervision this time. He was being punctilious over such details, now it was too late. It was as near as he'd come to admitting he was in error.

I had watched, and listened, and identified the ones who'd fingered Keril as a suspect; they were gone now. But there were those who'd stuck to fact, or even tried to help him. And enough to whom the plain word, salt, had instant recollection. Medishel, for one, was mortified he hadn't seen the empty dish as vindication. He'd always had a soft spot for Keril. Right now guilt was driving him to spoil the creature. I ought to say so to him, when I had a moment.

The real facts had made my father black as thunder. No one's fool, my father. Somebody had almost got away with killing me, and thanks to Rag's ineptitude *he'd* nearly taught the world that it was safer for a slave to let his master die than try to save him. Happily for me that hadn't happened, Keril's only thought had been to save me, otherwise I wouldn't be here. But we'd lost the trail, gone cold before we started hunting.

My blank-faced uncle had been sent back to our northern borders, "to do something right". He'd be in the perfect frame of mind to deal with his own problems.

Rumor had it Father told him not to show his face again till he was sent for.

My thoughts reverted to our own investigations. "Anything on Thersat?"

"No," Father said. "You've got to be mistaken, Ash. When he heard you had collapsed, reports say he was shocked at first, but not entirely. People added up how much you'd had to drink," he ended.

I scowled. "He showed no sign of illness?"

"He was fighting fit, for once," said Father tiredly. "By the second day word that a slave had attacked you got about. That altered things of course. Then, people were indignant, more so when the rumors named your virgin though the lighter-hearted laughed it off at first; said you'd have flattened any body slave in seconds. Of course, the more strait-laced considered you'd invited trouble. You've upset a lot of people, bringing him into the open."

"Yes, but what did *Thersat* say?"

"I saw him next day myself. I thought him quite dumbfounded." A sudden frown. "He mentioned herbal remedies, to soothe the stomach."

My head came round at that. "My stomach, when by then he'd heard I'd been attacked by Keril? And no one else was ill," I pointed out. "The tasters weren't."

"Both yours and mine," Father conceded. Was he finally taking me seriously?

"No one used that goblet, bar myself and Thersat. What we have to do is work out how he did it." I found I was grinning.

My father's eyebrows lifted but I felt relieved now. Yes, my latest brush with death had left me angry but I'd never trembled at attempts to kill me. More importantly no magic was involved, no queasy thoughts of gods, no sickly doubts about a holy future. Poison was a coward's crime but it was a real, hands-on, *mortal* something I could get my hands around and throttle.

Father pulled me back on topic. "You say he chose the brandy?"

"Yes." I focused on the evidence. "But he drank first, and much more than I did, *and* I saw his throat move when he swallowed."

"Could he have added something after drinking?"

"I don't see how. He had both hands around the stem."

"Then, by your own account, he can't have done it."

"Father, it must be him. It had to be something the rest didn't have. And it had to be someone close. And you were on my other side. The only oddity all night was how he grabbed that goblet."

A twisted smile. "Put like that, the goblet is a reasonable assumption. So we're back to Thersat."

"But he drank first." We faced that stumbling block again, in silence.

"Demons take the male," I pushed my plate away at last. "Don't any of your assassins know how it could be managed?"

"No," Father said, with forced patience. "In fact they're keen to understand it. So am I," he added.

That made me smile again, however wryly. All right, a challenge; Thersat my opponent.

A Sidassi plot? Was Thersat following his father's orders? My determination battled with confusion. I could think of neither means nor motive. After all, why kill me now? With Prian safely named and all our talk about alliances it ought to be the last thing the Sidassi wanted. But the other contenders—several, besides the priests—had all survived investigation. I decided to be patient. And deceitful.

It was a good thing I had a talent for barefaced lies. When Thersat expressed the hope that I was recovered from "my attack", I shrugged and mumbled something vague about my guts, and tried to look embarrassed, like I blamed myself and had no notion I'd been poisoned. I suppressed a sigh. With Thersat on my case, no doubt the whole damn city would be gossiping about the useless drunkard in the palace. If nothing else it'd take their minds off Keril.

Ah, Keril…

Chapter 32

Sheshman's eldest son had passed along another message. The gods alone knew how but Jaff had back-tracked Keril's robbers to a hamlet where "a foreigner in grey" had turned up, healed a child—overnight?—then vanished. Excellent. Although they'd told him Keril had been stumbling with tiredness when he left next morning.

Jaff had found a larger village, even higher. Thank the gods—I'd really have to stop myself saying that—the weather there right now was mild enough to reach it. These inhabitants had also traded with a *group* of foreign priests.

Jaffid wrote: "Males here are tough, but wary of those priests. I think they welcomed outside interest, not their custom. Headman says the males were always armed and wanted news as much as furs or butter."

Harking back to Keril, Jaffid finished with, "More cautious when I asked about our subject but has given me some tentative directions. Contact" (Sheshman's eldest, also carefully unnamed) "advanced me goods and funds to travel higher. I append a list of items purchased."

Suddenly I *liked* those distant villagers. And didn't like the priests who'd maybe kept their brother more a prisoner than I had? I had let him speak, and think; and even given him a taste of freedom.

And, stupidly I'd thought I could control the situation. That was getting harder. But I wasn't going to pen him up again. He loved those paltry hours in the open, and he'd surely earned them.

Mind you, I was worried I was giving in too early. Not that he'd asked. He was so carefully not asking it shouted. He had lifted reading body language to a whole new level. Palace intrigue gave me lots of practice, but there were new nuances to reading Keril, things that often foxed me.

No, with him, one watched, then thought, and then prepared a flanking movement. Right now one worried; he'd gone so quiet I was contemplating bringing back that doddering physician.

Hardly the way to deal with slaves? Tell me about it. My father had already.

"You did rather give yourself away, you know, over Keril," he'd remarked one evening when a very boring dinner ended and the (very boring) guests had left us.

"What?" I hadn't been attending.

"Most masters would have thanked me for my caution. But you—you threatened violence. Several times, as I recall…" He shook his head, pretending sorrow.

"I had a fever," I protested, "I hardly knew—"

"You knew exactly what you were doing," Father contradicted flatly, then grinned. "Ready to kill, in defense of a mere body slave?"

"All right, so I've found a favorite." I waved him off. "It happens."

"A favorite? How many others have you had since you got hold of Keril?"

"Gods, how many? Really? Do you think I counted them?" I scoffed. He dropped the subject so he must have thought I meant it. Inside, I'll tell you, I was shaking.

All right, I *hadn't* bothered. For almost a year. Favorite, I would concede then. Though there was one, at least, who had no inkling…

"Ribs still hurting you?" I thought I'd made it casual.

The head swung quickly. "No, my lord." The grey eyes fixed on mine, and waited. I lost track of what I'd meant to say completely. A heartbeat later the clear gaze faltered, and the head averted. There was something so forlorn about—

"Keril." I was breathless. "Did you think… I didn't want you now?"

An indrawn breath.

I touched the bare white shoulder. "I kept off you for fear I'd hurt you. Did you think it was because I'd lost my taste for you? Is that it? Well?" I challenged, suddenly light-hearted.

"My lord, Medi said I behaved very badly." (Medi these days, was it?) "No slave should pre-sume." He clearly found that word a problem. "To coerce his master. And your royal father had me punished. I know I'm in disgrace now."

"So disgraced you languish on my balcony, wearing my ring, while Medi treats you like a royal?" I smiled down at him. "You have a strange idea of being out of favor."

"But…" He wasn't looking at me now, oh no. "You… didn't touch me, not since… so I thought…"

"I didn't touch you because you weren't up to it. Curse it, Keril, d'you think I can't be patient if I need to?"

A smile dawned, like sunlight. "My lord?"

"What now?"

"You're not well-known for patience." The smile grew almost wicked. I burst out laughing then, and caught him to me.

So, fool that I am, the very next day I told him, "Time to get you back to Samchek, or you'll be getting rusty." I'd been lying back and watching how he smiled as he wakened.

His head turned quickly. "I thought, after what happened…" The usual half a sentence.

"Time we got things back to normal," I said firmly. "I'd better warn him you've been injured or he'll overdo it."

"Does he not know?" asked Keril, rolling on one elbow.

"There were rumors, I'm afraid, but only those who matter know what really happened. Keril, it's important the rest don't find out. D'you understand?"

"You want to keep it secret?" As he sat up the sheet slipped down around his hips. I could have been distracted then but Keril's mind was elsewhere. "Are you trying to trap someone?"

"Quick," I said, approving. "Yes, we have a suspect."

"But no proof?"

"No. We can't work out how it was done, or, for that matter, why. My head says it won't add up, but—"

"But your spirit accuses someone," he finished for me, hands around his knees, as if the thought was quite straightforward. "I've never felt that sort of rage, nor any serious threat in anyone I've seen around you." He looked solemn, maybe anxious, staring off toward the windows. "No, I'm sure I haven't, so I doubt it's someone in your household. Nor, I think, the stables."

My turn to blink. I hope I rallied quickly. "Afraid you missed something?" I said, offhand as I could manage. You had to think like lightning to catch up with Keril sometimes.

"If I have… but I've never picked up auras more than felt like envy or annoyance round you. Bitterness perhaps, but never hatred. Never murder."

He'd gone very serious. More to the point he'd opened his mouth and put his foot right in it. I wondered how far I could push it before he woke up.

"So no one you've vetted hates me enough to kill me?"

"No, my lord—" It hit him finally.

"So that's what you've been up to, is it?" I pulled him round to face me. "Trying to protect me? All this time?" A lot of little details meshed together and the shape they made was pretty scary. "Is that why you never fought me? Is that what this is all about?" I paused for breath. "I think you'd better tell me how, or is that why, you came here?"

So much for my latest challenge being "only mortal".

"Visions," echoed Father. I was spending more time in my father's upper rooms than I had for years. A shame the cause was always secrets.

I took another drink before I answered. "Yes, but he calls it "seeing.""

"And you believe him?" Father wasn't drinking.

"Oh, I believe it," I said fervently. "It finally explains his mad behavior. I've been sent a guardian, who senses good and evil."

"Sent?" Father pounced on that. "By whom?"

"By himself, it sounds," I said with resignation, "or whatever sent his visions."

"But… how?"

"According to him he "woke and followed a direction". He was "born to do it", like his healing. He only has a foreign word for what he is: a "Sen-sate"." Quickly, I recapped what Jaffid had discovered then returned us to the present. "I don't think he can find Kadduchi words to make it clearer to me. This is a different world for him. Sometimes he has trouble bridging the gaps."

I was still trying myself. It took a bit of getting used to, and I'd had all day to think it over. Small wonder Father looked befuddled. "I'll try and explain," I said, "but don't expect miracles."

"Please do." At least he showed a touch of humour. "When I said there was more to him, divine intervention wasn't what I had in mind."

"Me neither," I assured him, "but Keril says he "saw". I think he *dreamed* the need to come here, near as I can follow. He didn't then know why or even where, he simply started walking. "Down", he says. Sheshman found him in the north. The clothes he had back then were padded so his temple could be past the snowline, in those peaks we've always thought were empty. Jaff is up there now, but finding anything…"

My thoughts were sidetracked. This time I had sent Jaff backup, never mind my uncle's feelings, or the possibility of gossip. Well, wouldn't anyone? A faith that prompted Keril to abandon all he'd known, a hermit-like existence ruled by priests with weapons? And whatever Keril's priests were like, I had to wonder if there was a god behind them with the power to create a real En-Syn.

Though if Keril's deity was real I didn't know *his* motives, did I? Either way I had a load of questions and I wanted answers, more than ever. And I didn't like the way those priests had sounded, or the thought that they'd been lurking just outside our borders where we couldn't see them, asking questions, for at least a year.

Father stuck more closely to the subject. "He walked?"

I shrugged. "Perhaps they don't have horses. When I asked how far, he'd no idea, he can't remember even where he started, but he figured, once he started out, his "mission"—that's the word he used—would become clearer."

"Too convenient."

"No, it sums up Keril's whole existence. He totally accepts he doesn't get to choose what happens to him." Except for that bloody window, when he couldn't face the turmoil I had caused him, but I wasn't going to talk of that to Father.

"All right, he walked. Where from?"

I shook my head. "He really doesn't know. Downhill for several days, he says, and snow disguised the landmarks, but he kept "seeing" snatches of the future; sounds like blackouts. He can't remember all the journey but he says he knew he had to… let things happen."

"*Let* himself be captured?"

"And eventually delivered to the palace. By which time he was only just alive," I finished grimly, "but he hung on, believing in this vision."

"And you say he saw all this was going to happen? "

"Not in any detail. He says he "saw" the silver chains, even the royal stars they were engraved with. The trouble was." I didn't like the next bit but it was only fair to tell it. "He really had been raised secluded. His visions never told him what the chains meant. I guess he'd never contemplated, never learned— oh, just say I don't think he bargained for everything he came to."

So much for keeping quiet. My tongue ran off with me for once, and with a vengeance. "He told me once that no one ever "touched" him. Turns out that was literal. A Sensate gets the kid glove treatment. Contact can be painful; touching evil is like torture. Being captured by those brigands must have been a kind of suffering I've never dreamed of. I assumed Sheshman drugged him, but he thinks—he can't remember clearly—it was all the bad around him; he was being slowly smothered. I can't imagine what he felt when I—"

I forced myself to finish. "It was a test of faith, I think, accepting what *I* wanted. It took a lot of courage too." I couldn't look directly at my father. "He was very confused. I realize now," I said carefully, "he was genuinely afraid my handling might kill him. That, or maybe damn him."

"Seven hells," said Father, very softly.

I didn't comment. "He says he was sent to keep me safe from something, to "ensure the future". Says he doesn't know why he's protecting me or what the future holds, but he's convinced that it's important." I found a twisted smile. "He says he's done his best but he's been puzzled as I never seemed in any serious danger, not until the poison."

Father grinned at last. "He doesn't know what you were up to last winter, then? You must have been more discreet than I'd have thought you."

"Huh. I learned to keep my mouth shut in bed a long time before Keril showed up." I was rewarded with a leer you shouldn't find upon a royal visage. "Enough," I told him, "Keril doesn't know the plots you get me into.

I keep him free of all that nonsense. Or I did," I said bitterly. "From now on I doubt I'll be able to."

"He's asking questions?"

I almost snorted, "No, he's like that stupid effigy of patience at the entrance to the temples. "Time will tell me, my lord"," I mimicked glumly. "His faith is absolute. I find it rather daunting," I admitted. "Mind you." I had to grin again. "Right now he's very buoyant."

"Because he's done what he came here for?"

"More than that. He's been afraid his being "defiled", as he so nicely puts it, might have ruined his purpose. Now he thinks all this has proved he's still in working order, maybe better than he was to start with."

Father's features sharpened. "You mean he doesn't think his task is over?"

Which is how, after a deal more discussion, my father came to inspect Keril's progress in horsemanship.

Chapter 33

Keril's next riding lesson wasn't in the ruined garden but the royal stables, in the fenced-in training yard we used for younger horses. "Samchek needs more room," I'd said, and naturally Keril hadn't argued.

Not that it stayed empty long. Small wonder, since I'd sent him down just after dawn when all the keener riders would be in the outer yards and calling for their horses. None of those had left; as word had spread the earliest had filtered over here to the training yard instead, a sharp-eyed huddle. In the last few minutes grooms and riders round the edges of the yard had almost doubled. When my father turned up too it must have seemed inevitable. They'd assume he too had heard about my latest scandal.

"Again, and faster!" Samchek ordered.

Keril, in his desert gear, was on my grey. It didn't matter what we gave him, he could ride it. He wheeled and trotted back toward his start-mark. Across the yard, my father reined in his mount and gestured Samchek to continue. Others bowed, but happily the object of his interest hadn't noticed. Samchek knew his king was watching though, oh yes, and every inch of him said plain as plain: this is my pupil; what he knows I taught him.

What Keril knew, by now, was worth inspecting; every bit as promising as I'd predicted. In fairness, Samchek's contribution had been thorough. If Keril still thought stirrups a nuisance I doubted Samchek knew it, and he'd certainly made sure Keril could ride without. Before his ribs got broken Samchek had had him jumping off and on again while the horse first walked, then cantered. I winced to think what that would feel like if I hadn't banned it for the moment. Jarred your teeth loose, I remembered, not to mention parts less solid.

Not that Keril's present challenge was a softer option. I felt a twinge of guilt. Slave or not, I'd told Samchek, make it a genuine rite of passage; a test fit for a Kemik. But this…

Keril rode the course a third time, faster. Weaving through tall canes—planted at odd angles and irregular distances—he was in constant danger of being swept off or spiked, especially at this speed. "Gods, look at you." Afraid of being overheard, I edged away from other watchers.

Ducking through the last gap in the canes, Keril checked sharply to avoid a cart planted right in front of his mount's nose, veered left, bent low to ride beneath a thick rope stretched at head height then urged the horse into a jump that cleared a stack of boxes. After that all he had to do was zigzag between a row of barrels, each one closer than the one before it, and pull up short in front of Samchek. Close enough the male only had to move a step to catch the bridle. Me? I gritted my teeth and stayed out of sight but Keril was concentrating so hard I figured he could have forgot he had an audience.

With a flurry of hooves and the flash of a long tail the grey half-reared and brought its forefeet down just short of Samchek's boots. Another circuit ended; each one faster than the one before it?

Across the yard my father raised a hand to interrupt them. Samchek, facing that way, saw it.

"Wait." The stable master strode toward his king. Keril sat like a rock, only the slightest movement told me he was gulping air. I wondered if the pause was welcome. It was no use expecting Keril to complain but it was the first time since his recovery we'd really pushed him. The first time I'd left him out of my sight. At least he thought so.

It was a while since I'd played such games, but here I was, a dusty-looking southern tribesman, all striped robes and veil and tasseled headdress, every gesture screaming of the desert. I loitered in a lesser archway, one eye on the yard beyond it, waiting for my overlord. Or so I told those rash enough to ask. I looked enough the ruffian to put off all but those who had a right to question.

Actually I was enjoying myself. If I was recognized, well, I could laugh it off, not like the night I— But that, as they say, is another story, while in front of me my father was about to start a whole new chapter of our current saga.

Glancing round the buzzing courtyard he surveyed the merely curious, the scandal-mongers, finally the seasoned riders. The yard fell silent as soon as his lips parted. "A small wager, gentlemen, to satisfy my curiosity and see some sport? A hundred gold pieces to the fastest rider over Samchek's circuit?"

Samchek looked gratified. Why not? His test of skill was tough enough to interest his lord and master. The old gote would no doubt "forget" it had been my idea to start with.

The wager lifted heads. The better horsemen would be keen to try it anyway; a prize made it even more attractive. In moments eight contestants rode before their ruler, bowing from the saddle. While that was going on Samchek sent a slave scurrying, and Medi hustled Keril to a quiet corner.

The contenders were allowed to practice, Father stated. Samchek was to clear the rabble to the fringes. By then I'd drifted close enough to eavesdrop. There was some discussion: should they make the course a little simpler—on account that it was speed they wanted? But these were males who'd lived through battle. They saw the risks and thought them fair ones.

Then there was the question of a single round or say the best of three. By then most had cantered the course. Excitement shone on all their faces and they scoffed at such an artificial measure. In real life you got it right, or didn't. No one gave you second chances. War it was then, even with their comrades. Gods, I loved these people. Most of them I'd fought beside. I almost wished they'd win the hundred.

Almost. Plague on it, why not? I checked my veil, and the seal-ring I'd twisted inward—good disguise is always in the details—limped a bit across the open ground between and made a clumsy common reverence before my royal father.

Who took my desert robes as proof that I could ride and turned to Samchek. "We have a male here needs a horse, I think, horse-master."

Like my father, Samchek saw a rough-edged desert tribesman, summed me up and issued orders. The mount they brought was one of Samchek's, desert-bred and therefore not an easy option. He'd played fair; he'd given me a ride that might—if I was up to it—attempt to match the bloodlines ridden by these lords and soldiers.

I recognized the groom who brought it out as well. Young Ammet, groom to Samchek's horses? Quick promotion. Would he know me in this get-up? When he offered me the reins I ducked my head to grab them, mumbling something in a broad, south-eastern accent. It seemed to do the trick, he nodded stiffly and retreated to the sidelines. I was fairly sure his frown was more concern about a stranger on the horse than from suspicion.

Like the rest, I tried the circuit at a canter. Like the rest, I'd watched slit-eyed as Keril practiced; seen the interplay of turns and angles by the way he'd checked or shifted balance. Even so it was a risky business. Twice I thought those flimsy-looking canes had got me. Leaning them at different angles made them doubly dangerous. I wondered if we'd get through this without some bloodshed. More than one contender looked to have more heart than prowess.

By this time Medi had Keril off his horse and fenced behind his usual escort. Samchek was setting up old-fashioned sand-timers, high as a male's hip, to mark the finish, while a slave was painting a white line in the yellow dirt. In this heat it would dry in seconds. Samchek wasn't going to risk his toes the way he had for Keril. I found that vaguely reassuring.

Three riders took another turn then we drew straws. I fetched up next to last. I didn't mind; it gave me time to watch and find out what I had to do to beat them. By now I figured betting fever would have swept around the courtyard. There'd be more than Father's hundred changing hands this morning.

Nine of us. The first looked at Samchek, who looked toward my father. At his nod the horse master raised a scarlet scarf that caught the morning sunlight. When that dropped his deputy across the yard would pull the plug to start the timer.

The cloth swept down; the horse leapt forward. Banekit went first, an older male, battle-hardened. He ducked into his horse's neck, stayed there most of the ride and crossed the line in an impressive ninety-seven heartbeats. There were cheers, and friends to greet him. His horse was sweating; he looked elated. He wouldn't care about the prize. He'd done this for the thrill, the challenge.

The next three failed to beat him, nowhere near, which obviously pleased him. The fifth contender ran out on the barrels, swore, and gave it up. The sixth… I'd known Tull would fall for it. I'd kept my distance; he had seen me in disguise before. Too trusting, that was Tullman's weakness. I had warned him once or twice about it. Though of course right now his mind was wholly focused on the contest.

He was good, as I'd expected. "Ninety-six," the groom behind the timers shouted. More cheers, amid commiserations for the previous leader. I almost leaned across and clapped him on the shoulder. That's the trouble with such games; among your enemies your wits stay sharper. Mine, I thought urgently, had been going to sleep. That wouldn't do at all.

The seventh rider hit the cart like a battering ram. The sound silenced the whole court; the stricken horse went down, its rider sailed over both the horse and cart and landed out of sight beyond them.

Samchek's grooms ran forward, Ammet with them. The male was up again, with help, in minutes. Groggy, with a bloody nose, but standing. Noise broke out again all round us, louder than before. He had been lucky, but the horse would never stand again; a foreleg broken I was guessing from across the courtyard. The beast lay still and quiet, but panting. Samchek was already scowling; hated killing horses. Being Kemik he would rather kill the careless rider. The luckless owner, ego no doubt bruised as badly as his body, hobbled off with far more sympathy than he deserved, the way I saw it. Ah well, perhaps he'd learn some sense from his misadventure.

The carcass was removed. The mood across the yard had altered now; the laughter turned to sober concentration. Some of those who'd wandered in had had no real understanding of the danger. Careless minds had been reminded. And it was my turn next.

There was a wait. I could have done without it. Slaves collected splintered wood and scattered saw dust upon the bloody puddle. My mount picked up my tension and began to fidget, maybe he smelled death. Beside me Samchek watched and waited, very patient, but his mouth was harder. The yard went quiet again;

a normal voice rang right across it so that males who'd shouted now spoke furtively. And stared at me, the stranger here, with chilling speculation.

I confess I felt like battle. Maybe it *was* the smell of blood. It made the thing more real, more worth the winning. Behind my veil I grinned and urged my horse forward. We'd hit a gallop by the time I reached the canes.

Disjointed sounds; a heady blur of movement. The cart looked like a wall. A barrel teetered. A wild, joyous, risk-taking blur; then it was over. I was winded and the horse had got a scratch from somewhere. Spooked, it tossed its head and stamped so no one could get near, not even Ammet. Gods but it felt good. Who said that peace was so desirable? I turned in my saddle and saw the timekeeper straighten. "Ninety-four," he shouted.

Cheers, and whistles. Males who should have known me bowed and looked at me with increased interest and I had to laugh. My father's head jerked round, eyes narrowing as if against the sunlight. Then he gazed off across the yard and fought to keep a straight face. Recognized me from my laughter? Got you for a while, though, I thought, delighted.

One rider left. A youngster, this one, no older than Keril. He wouldn't do it better, I thought savagely, then recalled it didn't really matter. Yes it did. I *liked* winning. I *wanted* to win. That hadn't been the object but now I'd done it, it'd be a crying shame to leave without my father's money.

The youngster didn't beat me. Ninety-four was too much for him but he made a promising ninety-eight. Samchek even nodded curt approval. The cub flushed. My father smiled too. They'd liked his horsemanship. And courage. He bowed to me and rode off, his head up and his back straight. Plainly dressed, and half-familiar. I made a note to find out who he was, and maybe ask him out to ride with us one morning. After that display my usual company would certainly admit him. Then I turned to face my father.

"My thanks, gentlemen, for your efforts, and my congratulations to the winner." Not a quiver. While I bowed he turned to Samchek. "It might be interesting to time your latest pupil too, Master Samchek. Could he match these riders?"

Those close enough to hear looked dumbstruck. Those that hadn't darted searching looks and started asking questions. Cornered, Samchek chose to challenge. "He lacks experience, my king, but he has eyes, and muscles. I doubt he would disgrace his teachers."

Teachers, was it? Now it suited.

"You'd have backed him?" Father ventured idly. Now that, I thought, was nasty. Samchek was being subtly goaded, and in public.

The old gote startled both of us. "I'll wager fifty gold he'll come inside the best three times, my king." He waved imperiously across the courtyard.

Keril, cordoned off efficiently by Medi's biggest eunuchs, had barely glimpsed the contest. He'd have no notion what had passed between his betters.

All he saw was Samchek's sudden summons.

The eunuchs round him looked to Medishel then stepped aside and left him unprotected. I saw him hesitate before he stepped into the open. A slave had led the grey away some time before so Keril made a lonely, very noticeable figure as he walked toward us, in the stark white robes, the desert veil. The upright body. Whispers flew around the crowd; when Keril reached us he was probably the only person there who didn't know why he'd been called.

Gloved hands together for that nodding bow. My ring was visible outside the fitted leather—my instructions—shifted to his smallest finger to allow it. My horse, behind and to his right, prevented gawkers coming closer, but he must have felt uncomfortably exposed. He likely wished his master wasn't absent. Would he look to Samchek for commands, or Father?

He looked at Samchek but he turned when Father spoke, and raised his head as always. I saw the looks and heard the muttered comments.

Father was unruffled. "Keril," he said. (As if calling his son's body slave—all right, favorite!—by name was nothing out of common.) "Keril, could you match these gentlemen?"

"Sir, I hardly know. I doubt it." Quietly said, but calmly. Ears strained. They had to realize this couldn't be the first such meeting.

"Would you care to try?" An invitation, notice, not an order. Mouths fell open.

Keril, being Keril, thought it over. "Sir, if you wish." I got the distinct feeling he was trying not to laugh. I nudged my mount a few steps forward. Waste of time, since he was veiled.

"Let's see how you do then," Father told him. "Samchek?"

"My king, he'll need a fresh horse." Samchek wanted to protect his wager. I wondered then, could he afford it? Had his temper once again outrun his prudence?

Father gave a genial permission. Samchek strode across to talk to Ammet, who looked startled. Keril took an interest in my father's stirrups. "Oh, and Keril," Father added.

"Sir?" The visor lifted just far enough to see my father's face.

"It would please me greatly, if you *could* do better."

Did the grey eyes widen for a second? The two males seemed to hold a silent conversation. Then Keril bowed. "I will try then, sir."

"You do that," Father said distinctly. Over Keril's head he looked at *me*. So, I thought, you want me beaten, even though the rest won't know it?

Ammet brought the black. The horse was known; I watched the crowd's reaction. Keril merely saw the beast and took a step. At once the brute jerked free of Ammet, jolting forward at a canter. I reckon half the crowd thought Keril would be gored or trampled. My father and the other riders shifted, startled. Only Samchek, still on foot, and me on horseback, didn't. But then we'd seen this.

Sure enough the black skidded to a halt with one pace to go, and ended up with his vicious teeth nuzzling Keril's hands and that horn almost tapping the top of his head. I swear Keril was apologizing for not having anything to give it. It's possible, I thought, with this one under him he might just do it.

"Take him round and let him see what's needed," Samchek told his pupil. I had no argument. It was only fair now Keril had changed mounts.

But Keril made the circuit at a steady canter this time. Over-cautious? I caught a murmur as he passed. Encouraging the brute? Or calming it, perhaps, the thing was always twitchy till it settled. I hoped it would behave itself this morning.

"Ready?" Samchek asked him sharply.

"Sir." Keril seemed relaxed. Was that because he was resigned to doing badly? I shouldn't seem concerned though, should I?

The scarf swept down and—

"Greater gods," a male beside me blurted.

He was trying all right. I swear the black hit a full gallop in three strides. Flat out into those near-lethal, spear-like canes.

"Steady, Keril, steady." The slim white figure bent toward the glossy neck as if to push the stallion forward.

"Blood and bones, but he's a rider." Tull was shouting. "Look at that turn, will you?"

Through the cane-field. Someone that end screamed in panic. Over the boxes, with nothing to spare. Turn and twist, dip and soar. My heart lurched midway through the barrels but he didn't slow up once I noticed. He remembered too, he was to cross the line this time, not stop before it.

When he reined and wheeled about the cheers died abruptly. Faces flushed with pleasure—admiration too—now stiffened. They'd forgotten, hadn't they? But now it hit them, what it was they'd cheered.

I doubt if Keril heard the shouts, or felt the sudden silence as he rode toward us. His eyes were glowing and his chest was heaving. Giving him the black had let his riding find a whole new level. The horse was prancing sideways, every horse around me was infected, turning restless. That pair fetched up in front of us and waited for the verdict, shifting constantly. It seemed to take forever.

Then a throat cleared. "Ninety-four," the groom said hoarsely. Keril ducked his head. I couldn't see it but he must be smiling.

But there was commotion near the timer. Banekit, a male who feared no one, strode toward us and a bunch of others straggled after. Trouble brewed, I thought, and didn't want it.

"Lord Banekit," my father greeted the apparent leader. He had straightened in his saddle. In blue and gold that day, the gold-star circlet glinting on his forehead, I had to say he looked the part. And not too keen on what was coming either, if his face was anything to go by. "Is there a problem?"

"My king, that ninety-four was faulty."

"Oh?" My father waited. Keril's head stayed lowered.

"The timer wasn't shut until the horse was two good paces past the line," the lord said firmly. "Perhaps the keeper was too startled. But I think these males will bear me witness."

There were stiff-backed nods from males who, it dawned on me, considered honor higher than the fact it was a slave they were supporting. They didn't look at Keril but they'd spoken for a slave against a freeman.

"Your sense of justice does you all great honor." A pause for thought. We lesser mortals waited. My father pursed his lips. "The time's contested, so the wager's cancelled," he decided, "if the witnesses accept that?" And he looked from me to Keril.

"A tie, my king." I stifled laughter. He hadn't said which wager, had he? He'd avoided paying Samchek. What odds he'd say he couldn't pay me either? A wonder he could keep his face straight.

Keril heard me speak and took his cue to answer. "I'm content, sir," he said softly, "I never expected to do better than my lord."

My head jerked. And my father's. Small chance no one noticed, was there? "Gods in orbit, Keril, how—" I swept away my desert headdress, a much more ornate thing than Keril wore, and faced him, deaf to all the exclamations.

"My lord, I always know when you are near." The laughing eyes—oh yes, he'd been amused—had melted. And I really shouldn't sit here like a statue. I tried to dredge up something flippant.

Happily my father interrupted. "When did you know?" he asked with clear amusement.

"When he rode, sir. When he came toward me."

When I got close, or when he recognized my riding? A truthful answer with a careful choice of words? But if Banekit was right he'd damn well beat me! I found I'd burst out laughing. Once I did the crowd relaxed and started talking.

"My prince!"

"Highness."

Bows, now the truth was out. And laughter. "I wouldn't have bothered if I'd known," one rider told me. Someone else complained I'd beat them under false pretences. As they spoke they all glanced sideways to my veiled rival, but they couldn't say it.

So I said it for them. "Well ridden, Keril. You surprised us all."

"My lord." He bowed across the horse's neck, then straightened quickly. The black was sweating. Keril's hands and feet made small, controlling movements. Lately, Samchek's training meant that Keril groomed the mount he'd ridden and I hadn't stopped it, figuring he probably enjoyed it. Not this morning though.

My father raised an eyebrow. "Some breakfast, I think. Ash?"

"I'll join you," I said, smiling.

"If you wish it, Keril might attend you?"

An invitation to attend me in my father's own apartments? A slave picked out by name; a public statement that he recognized his son's possession, one that should have been considered non-existent. All around the courtyard busy brains were adding and subtracting. Samchek's face was cheerful but the rest looked everything from scandalized to very thoughtful.

As they should do. Keril's status had been radically altered: faceless, still exclusive, but no longer nameless; favored both by king and prince and garbed to be distinctive, unmistakable if I should bring him out again in public. Be assured, the palace understood our message. Keril was protected, more than many freer males could hope for.

I sent Keril to change into a second set of robes that Medi "happened" to have handy. I exchanged my boots for beaded sandals and the rest for cream silk trousers and a sleeveless orange tunic fastened with a sash of orange and magenta. Changing, and then rushing out to join my father meant I didn't have to favor Keril with an explanation.

"Attend," Father had said. For once, Keril sank to his knees at my left, as if he thought to serve as others would. But father signed the rest to go, except old Imri, master of his household, keeper of a thousand secrets since the two were cubs together. "Loose that veil, young male, and drink. You've earned it."

Keril hesitated. Imri, bland as ever, poured the chocolate into dainty silver goblets, warmed beforehand. Three of them; he'd obviously been instructed. "Drink," I ordered. What was one more scandal?

Keril glanced my way then shifted to his usual position, almost sitting, freed the veil, took the cup with admirably steady hands, and tasted. You could almost call it taking up the gauntlet. .

"So, young male, what's next?" my father prodded.

Keril's face looked wary. "As my lord decides, sir."

"Your lord," I said, "has just proved you can ride, anywhere he does."

The lips parted, but only for another sip of chocolate.

Total silence. My father watched. It didn't do him any good though, Keril's face stayed blank until his cup was empty and I doubt if my expression altered. Imri, who could make a corpse look restless, poured a refill.

Keril dared another sip while I admired my father's patience. Eventually the fool made up his mind and put the cup down. "Anywhere?" As if the word could bite him.

"What you've always wanted," I agreed then grinned. "I'll let you play at nursemaid."

Father snorted. It belatedly occurred to me that Keril was making Father's life more amusing now as well. It remained to be seen what he would do to others'. I was already looking forward to that.

Chapter 34

We were riding through the trees beyond the eastern walls again, toward the desert, when there was an angry squeal and Tullman's mount half reared. Caught off balance, Tullman had to grab the pommel like some novice. "Damn you, Keril, get away!"

The black had caused the problem; didn't like to let another horse get past him. Keril'd had to force the brute aside then swing back in behind me, and the black had swung too fast so Tullman's mount had sensed a threat—it likely was—and had reacted.

"Sorry, my lord—"

"*Vanguard*, you—" Tull wrenched the reins to stop his horse attacking Keril's. Others scattered on a wave of laughs and curses.

"Sorry, Vanguard Tullman." Keril got the stallion clear of Tull's, if not without some hassle in the process. Did he realize that calling Tull "my lord" had touched a nerve? That Tull, however good a soldier, couldn't even claim the meanest of his father's titles. He had been disowned, a terrible disgrace and a disgraceful act by those who had disowned his mother, just before his birth, for a political advantage.

His mother's kin had only kept his litter, four of them, till they grew old enough to sell them to the army. Tull had always claimed to be an orphan. I had never told him I'd unearthed the truth but Jaffid had investigated, and identified both father and the poor replacements from the later litter. Little wonder Tull was sensitive about his rank. Had Keril sensed that?

This was Keril's fourth, and furthest, foray from the palace. I'd brought him out among these seven trusted friends and told him, "Get beyond a single horse-length from me and, I'll beat you senseless." I wasn't sure if anyone believed me but I'd laid the rules down, loud and public. My order led, inevitably, to blunders—Keril really didn't know enough yet—but they'd borne them all with stoic silence. Till today, when Tull was driven to swearing at him.

Finally. I heaved a sigh of satisfaction, realized I had and prayed to every god that no one noticed. Tull would normally be sharp enough but luckily his head was turned to glare at Keril.

But he'd spoken to my body slave, by name. I'd done it. And that reply, I thought with even more amusement, hardly qualified as servile; Keril on a horse was often less attentive to the proper pecking order, or his current task made him forgetful...

Two days earlier he had reported on the males around us now.

"They like you, my lord."

"What, all of 'em?" I'd probably looked scornful. Loyal service I demanded, people weren't required to love me.

"Well, six like you all the time, Lord Tullman when he keeps his temper," Keril told me, looking solemn. Well, his voice was solemn.

"Next you'll be saying that they'd die for me," I'd scoffed. Well, wouldn't you? This hearing how folk felt about me wasn't... normal.

"I think they would, my lord."

I'd growled and dropped the subject, but now...

We all rode on; my mind reverted. Drat, I should have told him then that Tull wasn't a lord. Good thing I hadn't.

I had to grin. "Your temper's going to kill you one day, Tull," I shouted across the group.

Tullman shot a look my way that clearly said, is that a warning? I eased his doubts by frowning heavily at Keril. Didn't want them thinking he was pampered.

It seemed to work. "Novices," Tull muttered, pulling in beside me, Keril dropping back to let him.

"Weren't we all?" I laughed. "Give him time, he'll manage better."

Tull's mouth half-opened. A good leader; his males'd follow him to heaven. Hells, a vanguard didn't live long if they wouldn't. But he couldn't hide his feelings.

"Ask him. He won't bite."

The handsome face went blank. Engage a body slave, and mine to boot, in idle conversation? I thought embarrassment would stop him, but like all good warriors he liked to know who rode beside him.

Tull twisted in the saddle. "So how old *are* you?" His tone was officer to soldier.

Keril had his orders: don't talk, unless you think you ought to. "Twenty-one, or two now, Vanguard." Got the title right this time, I noted.

"Hm." A pause. "So how long have you been riding?"

"Since my lord allowed me, sir, say half a year now."

Tull gaped. I'd figured no one realized how raw Keril was. Tull looked from Keril back at me, his doubts apparent.

"Strictly speaking, Keril sat a horse once, but since he was a captive at the time I don't suppose we ought to count it." Then I added, "I gather his temple preferred feet."

Encouraged, Keril nodded. "But my lord's horses are all very helpful animals, and much easier than walking." Since he was on the black that day (the brute threw every groom Samchek tried to put on it, and it was worse with me. I'd swear the thing was jealous) that didn't come across as he'd intended. There was a thoughtful silence.

"What sort of temple?" It looked like Tull was tacitly appointed spokesman.

"It was on a mountain, very bare, but more, I don't remember, sir."

"Which mountain?"

"Sir, I'm told it was in the north, but I can't name it."

"Huh. Your family send you there?" A fair assumption. Temples, and the army, frequently accepted noble rejects; Tull himself was an example.

Keril's case was different, I discovered. "Sir, I don't think I had a family."

"What, never?" Tull looked startled.

"Not that I recall, sir." I recalled he'd said he had been *ordered* not to. "There was a lady once, I think, when I was very small." He paused, but no one interrupted. "She was always sad. I thought perhaps she didn't want to hand me over, so when they came I went to meet them."

"You wanted to go?"

"I think perhaps… I didn't want her punished." Very quiet. Keril's head was lowered, but he'd answered.

Tull's voice softened. It was probably unconscious. "You see her after?"

Another pause. "No, not after. I was… ordered to forget her." And he really had, I thought, till Tull had prompted.

"Hm. Others like you, were there?"

"Yes." He sounded startled, something else recalled? "But never many."

Tull jumped on that. "They came and went?"

"They came. Not all succeeded."

"So what became of them?"

"I wasn't told. I think… they died?" The last words came out awkwardly but then the voice grew lighter. "But life here, with my lord, is *not* so difficult."

Tull grinned before he knew it, certainly before he gave a thought to *my* reaction.

"Are you saying I'm indulgent?" I demanded.

"My lord, when you indulge yourself it often happens you indulge me too." Oh, so demure, but Keril's eyes, above that cursed veil, were bright with laughter.

Tull choked, and veered aside to join the others. Heads bent closer. "That's my reputation in the dust," I muttered.

"My lord, I thought you wanted…"

"Oh, forget it." Some hope the rest would. I anticipated ribald comments once we stopped and Keril, being junior, was set to water all the horses.

Tull passed the brandy. "You and a *priest*? By all that—" Tull rocked with mirth. "And you're easier to live with than the priesthood? I suppose the bed's much softer!" When I scowled Tull dropped the subject, fast, but later he pulled Keril up and showed him how to pick a better spot to jump a wall. Then saw me watching. "Huh. No point risking a good horse."

"No indeed."

Tull looked uncomfortable, then suspicious. Next time we rode out he looked at Keril, nodded recognition then said, "Ask him, was it? Never mind about my temper, highness. Your maneuverings'll kill me sooner."

From then on when I took him into larger groups those seven set the pattern. Soon his presence was expected. Even when my father was among us Keril rode behind me. His position in a hunt might vary, not the distance. My father laughed. "I swear if you put a leash on him it wouldn't break."

If Keril did hold back it was at the kill; he never was so close for that. They probably assumed he knew his place. I wasn't sure if it was all the prayers, to other gods than his, or if he kept back from the killing. Either way I didn't force him. After all it wasn't animals he hunted for me.

One by one I put him next to lords and lordlings, generals and those who merely followed orders. What their king condoned they had to swallow. Keril's comments later were perceptive. I looked forward to them. I think my father found them just as useful. So far, to my genuine surprise, we hadn't netted anyone he felt was seriously keen to kill me. Not that they all loved me, no, but you could say I now knew, very clearly, who my real friends were. One or two were unexpected.

Did I trust these judgments? Oh, I had to. So, by this time, did my ever-doubting father. I had wondered if I'd have a problem over that—my father always liked a well-honed weapon—but he had accepted Keril's focus only worked in *my* direction.

A few weeks later we had vetted everyone of any note except the males who were away from court, or hadn't ridden. Predictably Prince Thersat, curse the male, was one who hadn't. I had sent an invitation; he'd declined it. "Demons take the idiot," I said with feeling. We were in my father's rooms, and Keril wasn't present.

"It's hardly a surprise he doesn't join the hunt. My hawk would make a better rider." Father shook his head. "He's like a sack of tree nuts bouncing up and down, and everybody knows he hates it.

Father's lips twitched. "At least he didn't take the invitation as an insult. What is it the traditionalists call body slaves ? Ah yes." He leered. "A male female? A perverted affectation."

I growled.

He grinned. "Body slaves aren't exactly a universal custom, Ash, certainly not among Sidassi, and then flaunting it…. I was surprised myself when Sheshman gave so bold a present. Some of our own lords are finding Keril hard to stomach, let alone a stranger to our customs."

"Those Sidassi are the perverts." I shifted irritably on my cushions.

"No doubt, but you're not going to get the fellow on a horse, or, if I'm not mistaken, anywhere that Keril joins you." Father side-stepped. "There hasn't been a second try though."

"And don't I know it." I'd have been happier if there had. I hated waiting.

"Hm." He nodded. Neither of us liked to hide in corners. Still, the subject seemed forgotten generally. Keril being in my father's favor rather scotched the rumor he'd attacked me. Someone *had* recalled my "sudden illness" recently, but then had dodged the subject quickly; hardly politic reminding me I couldn't hold my liquor. The one person I could have relied on to shove that down my throat was thankfully not present. My uncle should have been back with us by now, but rumor was he'd made a serious blunder.

He'd sent a letter—or so said my ears in the palace. I had no details, yet, but it was evidently rash enough—or the news bad enough—to put my father in a temper. If the old fool'd kept quiet he'd have been recalled by now, but as it was… he wasn't. He was still north-east of us, intent on stamping on that region's bandits, probably the cause of Father's disapproval. I'd seen his reinforcements, horse and infantry, assemble two days earlier. All northern regiments . He'd called their lords as well, so clearly this time he meant business.

A saner voice inside me wanted to persuade my father to relent and call him home again. It wasn't only me whose interests could do with more protection. But to tell the truth, I wasn't that nice. I liked seeing more of my father. We hadn't gotten on so well in years. So I left it, a mistake I very much regretted later.

Chapter 35

The sun sent blades of light between the faded awnings at the margins of the Grand Bazaar. My nostrils twitched at rancid scents; the sweat on those who passed, hot air, hot metals then a whiff of spit-roast pig and flatbread baked with onions.

Tull was leading as we sauntered through the noisy rows of cooked-food stalls and water sellers, then across a wholly-tented inner square where market-wine and bubbling tube-smoke clogged the atmosphere, and music beckoned. Soon we left the plain, bleached cloth of vegetable stalls, the sickly air about the butchers' blocks; the market goods became increasingly impressive.

The walkways further in had brightly-patterned canvas stretched across the paths from one stall to another, to encourage customers to linger. Merchants dressed more opulently and their kin or slaves would offer wine or coffee as their masters carried out negotiations.

Bargaining was in the air. We were in riding gear but many of these leading merchants, sharper-eyed than their inferiors, began to bow respectfully and wave their serving males to hold the choicest items for our notice.

Tull fell back beside me. "You've been spotted."

"Huh." I don't mind shopping but I didn't favor taking Keril to such crowded places. Still, needs must, I'd thought, if I was ever going to get him close to Thersat. "No food," I warned him now, "You never know what you might catch at some of these stalls."

His, "No, of course, my lord," was tranquil. Obviously he'd not considered such unwarranted behavior. Sometimes he remembered his position more than I did.

We numbered ten; myself and Keril, and the other eight. Ah, the usual seven plus that youngster who'd excelled at Samchek's contest. To general amusement he'd emerged as Sheshman's youngest. Yes, the very one he'd wagered; handsome youth, considerably thinner than his father.

"He must have got his figure from his mother," Tull had murmured. If the youngster heard it he'd pretended not to. His name was Zanith. He was paler than was normal for Kadduchi, nearer gold like Tull, and very conscious of his company. Especially of Keril, whose innocence had ensured Zanith's freedom.

The first time Zanith joined our band he greeted Keril with a tiny bow. Tull immediately made a point of being ruder. Funny, though I doubted Zanith thought so.

"He's confused," was Keril's verdict. "He… he'd like to be accepted but he's scared to push, my lord. He means well."

"Killed by kindness," I said lightly.

Keril dared to argue. "My lord, I don't think you need fear him."

"You mean he won't intentionally kill me," I conceded. "Now I know why all my closest friends are older. He's not an enemy then, just a possible liability." It was too cold-blooded, all this weighing people in the balance.

But Zanith had his uses. For one thing he knew the Bazaar extremely well. There were, he said, three major herbalists, all in the surgeons' quarter. He could even name them.

"You got family down here?" another quizzed him.

"No," said Zanith, prickly at the slur upon his bloodline.

"More like a lover," I suggested. Not true, I figured, but a lesser sin to be accused of. He looked less ruffled, and the others chuckled.

One began, "I remember, I once had…"

That sparked a few such recollections, every one unsuitable for Keril's ears. I pulled a face and told myself. it was my own fault, bringing him among them. Was he blushing? He could do that wonderfully, I'd discovered, being paler.

One of my older "eyes" popped up two rows ahead, examining embroidered slippers, and there was Thersat, clearly visible a hundred paces farther. In his usual brown and olive robes and narrow belt—so plain—the male was like a dead stick in a flower garden. I wandered forward letting others pick out where we stopped, with half an eye on Keril, safely in the middle.

Always in the middle this time. Accident, or were they blocking him from outside contact, like a moving closter? Yes, but he could hear every racy comment. One or two… he might be learning things I hadn't taught him.

It was dimmer in this lesser alley; narrower as well; less room for other males to flow around us. The smells became disquieting, from nameless plants hung up to dry above our heads, and salves and potions being ground or simmered. And the latest risqué story had got crude enough that Zanith shot a panicked look at me and coughed. The tale stumbled.

Guilty silence, then a good few grins in my direction.

Someone laughed, but Keril… Keril looked at me. It was… distracting. I reminded myself we were here for a purpose. Ignored, the veiled head relented and turned forward.

I'd never been here before. No one recognized me. We were even jostled once or twice but thankfully it never reached as far as Keril. Well, besides our living wall a sane male saw a desert veil as a warning, wise males stepped around them.

I relaxed a little. He wasn't used to crowds. I didn't like him being here either but it was Thersat's playground. It might be my only chance to get him next to Keril and assess his guilt before I went to Sidass. Inside the palace Thersat might claim insult as my father feared and cause a diplomatic tiff but here, with any luck he'd never know it.

Nearly there. "Stay close."

"My lord?" I felt him stiffen. "Is there trouble?"

"Just be careful."

"Yes, my lord." His bearing altered; straighter, with a hint of tension.

Tull picked up on it. He actually looked embarrassed, muttered, "Ash, we weren't… we didn't mean to make him…"

I choked.

Tull scowled at my amusement. "I didn't hear you telling us to stop."

"You're right." It wasn't a good time to fan the flames, fun as that might have been. "I doubt such tales'll kill him though. Eh, Keril?"

"No, my lord, I think I can survive it." The rascal sounded much too pensive. "Actually, it was instructive." Zanith gasped, but Keril carried on, as if he hadn't noticed. "I never knew males *talked* about it." Wide grey eyes, above the veil, glanced shyly downward, modesty incarnate. "But then of course I know so little."

Guaranteed to make the lot feel guilty. Done on purpose? More averted faces, and a sudden need to change the subject.

I obliged. "Hello, that's Thersat."

The male'd never been so popular. They called, the group surged forward. It was perfect.

But the press of bodies worsened. Plague on them, I thought, unleash them and they get in people's way and cause an upset. Our cohesive group fragmented, commoners were close to Keril. He'd been knocked off balance. I reached out to grab him—

"Ash, behind you!" Tull was pointing past my shoulder, and my spy was shoving through the crowd toward me.

When I spun I faced a rippled, southern blade below a yellow southern face that bore a mask-like stillness. Life and death were measured in an endless second as we stared at one another. Then the blade came on. I had no room to back away; no time to draw my dagger; barely time to fling my hand up in a hopeless parry.

But the blade stopped dead a hairsbreadth from my heart. I gasped. It wavered visibly then turned—and plunged into its owner and the body crumpled, knife still in it.

And a *gloved* hand jerked away from it. Keril? Healing hands turned weapons, Keril standing frozen. Keril, who by law—

"Come here!"

His head came up. He moved behind me, further from the body. I could feel him shaking. So was I. I tried to focus on essentials. My spy had skidded to a halt then sheathed a knife and melted back into the crowd, his eyes on me for orders. Thersat, backed against a stall, was staring, mouth wide open, eyes dilated, looked as if a snake had bit him.

That did the trick. Noise flooded back; the scene expanded. Blood-scent, sweet and sickly and familiar. I realized belatedly that some of that was mine. My sword hand stung, that knife had sliced across the heel of my upraised palm and blood was dripping, darkening the ground below it. I swore as my companions swarmed in, grim and vengeful, scaring those nearby who fell back in confusion, but it looked as if the real threat was over.

"Is he dead?" I muttered, watching ripples of alarm spread outward.

"Yes. Yes, my prince." The voice was Zanith's. He was kneeling by the body, staring at the blood upon his fingers. Keril's eyes above the veil were stricken now. His shoulders sank a little and I thought I heard him swallow.

Tull turned up beside me.

"You were fast." He made it sound admiring too, as if he'd watched me do it. Only this was Tull. Him, pay me compliments? Zanith gaped at Tull then glanced at Keril, then fell silent. If the crowd caught on a body slave had done this…

"Tull, use my name and keep things quiet, would you? Have them bring the body to the palace. Maybe there'll be something on him." Someone offered me a scarf to wrap my hand. I signed my spy to hang around then hustled Keril, and young Zanith, out of there. I figured one would be as poor a liar as the other.

Chapter 36

By the time my father heard about it Tull had all of them word-perfect, so—fair's fair—I told my father I'd escaped because he'd given warning.

Father smiled. "Not the first time, is it? North or south then?"

"Maybe south?"

So Tullman got a royal stewardship, ennobled overnight by virtue of the office, with a small estate to grant him income on our (current) southern border; where, who knew, it might expand if Father ever reached to take those seaports.

Eight of us—not Keril, obviously—celebrated in the city taverns. I raised my glass to toast the reject son who now stood almost level with his father. First he tried to hide his satisfaction under dry amusement then he tried to drown it in a lake of spirits, whereupon his tongue got looser. "Got you this time, Ash. I know exactly who to thank for this." He waved extravagantly. Grinning.

"Me?"

He shook his head. "Not you. Not this. I mean." He frowned, a little owlish now. "I've saved your sorry hide too many times. I never got a title for it. But it wasn't *your* hide this time, was it?" When I stared he burst out laughing. "Careful, Ash." A finger poked my chest. "You've got a blind spot now. Your enemies would love to know it."

Was he right? My sense of balance shifted quite as much as any drunkard. Had I urged my father on, at last, because Tull lied for Keril, who had really saved me? The bare fact was a body slave had killed a free male. The bare fact, if it spread, would cause an uproar. Body slaves, so intimate they often lay beside us as we slept, could not be violent. One near their prince… they'd want his head, the fact the corpse was an assassin might not change that. And that wasn't all of it. By this time I had questioned Keril, and knew more than Tull did.

No, he said jerkily, he hadn't meant to kill, he'd had no time to be "more careful". I had sat him down beside the fire. On a couch. He didn't notice. "Here, get that down." Once my hand was cleaned and bound I cleared the room, held off until he'd drunk a fair amount then asked, "First body, was it?"

"Yes, my lord." A fiery swallow, then a shudder.

By then I'd got a drink myself. I couldn't alter what I'd witnessed, could I? Still, asking questions made him talk. I thought he might need calming down as much as I did.

Had he known what he could do? I had to doubt it. Should I have wondered if he could? Oh yes, the possibility was obvious, with hindsight. Why should I be surprised? He was a one-male puzzle; always had been. Now, of course, I was wondering what else I'd missed. But first, the basics. "Can you actually use a weapon?"

"My lord, I doubt it." He glanced at me. "I don't think I was bred for fighting."

"Right." But what I'd seen back there. "Are you a god?" I got out roughly.

"No, my lord!" He looked too shocked to be dissembling. "I have a skill, that's all. I found it worked for healing."

Healing powers. That I'd half-accepted, but I saw, in memory, that dagger twist toward its owner. Saw the fear and helpless panic on the face that couldn't *stop* it. Saw, again, how Keril's hands had reached for, but *had never touched the blade he had directed*.

"That wasn't healing!"

The head hung down; the voice became a whisper. "No, my lord."

I took another drink and thought it through. He'd killed, but he was patently no killer. All the same… "That's why your masters let you out alone? They knew you could defend yourself?"

"I'm not sure, but I don't think they did. *I* didn't know." His head stayed down. He gripped the glass. "And they didn't let me out, exactly."

"What?"

"I…left them."

"Left them." I was having trouble keeping up.

He straightened, took a breath and plunged into an explanation. "Vanguard Tullman asked me to remember. I've been trying, though he hasn't asked again. I think my masters took me out among your people once before, to tell them truth and lies as I do now for you, my lord. I think I understood the village language easier than them. They were displeased at first, and startled there was so much difference in the words, but then they saw it made me doubly useful." Keril hesitated. "When I went into the village by myself, the second time,

I think the village knew I shouldn't be there but they let me rest there for the night. And so I tried to help their child, and they said I'd cured him."

"So you ran away. And no one followed you?"

"I don't know, I can't remember everything. But if they did I never saw them." Suddenly he flushed. "Perhaps I was no longer worth retrieving."

Why would he even think? I drew a breath. "Explain."

He licked dry lips. "They knew that I could *feel* things—I was meant to. When I understood your language better, that surprised them. When they asked if I had other skills I wasn't meant to… I said I hadn't, and it was the truth. I *couldn't* lie to them, it was forbidden. But I could feel them after, watching me." He met my gaze again. "I was afraid."

And not too confident about my knowing, either? "So you haven't always had this power," I said slowly.

"No, my lord. It wasn't what I was *supposed* to be." He watched me carefully. "Today I remembered something else. There were two of us at first. Then other things came back all in a rush. The other disappeared. He was "flawed". I heard them say it."

Ah. "So you ran."

"Not at first. It was a dreadful thing, to disobey the masters, and where could I go? Then I woke and I felt dizzy, and the *door* swung open. *Every* door swung open for me, as they never had before and when I ventured from my cell the masters were all sleeping, even those on guard. And some were sleeping on the floor." He shivered at the memory. I felt it too, just listening. His eyes met mine again. "I knew I had to leave. I knew I had to find something." He wasn't making sense, entirely, but he sounded calmer. Maybe he'd seen I wasn't angry now.

Though I had every right to be. "You kept this from me."

"Not intentionally, my lord. They told me to forget, a lot. If I was ordered then I had to. When I did recall, these last few days… I hesitated then. I didn't know if you would judge me flawed as well."

And kill him, like the one who "disappeared"? Incredible, but I believed him. "So, what now?"

"You are not afraid of me. I should have known." His shoulders sagged a little. "But you are unsure what to do about me."

I was being weighed. That shook me, but he was so scared by then he didn't see that, clutching at the glass so hard I was afraid he'd break it. "Put that down and tell me just how powerful you are."

"My lord, I don't *know*. I never used it so, until this morning."

Hell's teeth. I knew he'd come here to protect me, but I'd just found out— and maybe he had too—how far he'd go to do it. He wasn't just a shield, he was a weapon. And I'd slept *two years* with— what, a sorcerer? A *holy* male? A bodyguard-assassin?

I'd consider definitions later. My friends had seen him kill; they hadn't seen the way he'd done it, but if I let him out again… I drained my glass. "All right, so you have this power. Let's see how well you can control it."

"I asked you here to talk about what really happened in the market," I said bluntly, once we were alone.

Father's face went still. "I thought we had."

Here goes. "It wasn't me who killed that unknown Souther. It was Keril." I paused. No comment yet. "*He* saved me, and the others lied about it."

"They lied to please you?" So far, very cool about it.

"And for Keril's sake." There really was no way to shade it. Keril, by the law, was clearly guilty.

"Why tell me now?" Straight to the heart of it. I could rely on him for that much.

"Because I need the law bent."

"To pardon him?"

I shook my head. "More than that. I'm asking you to grant him leave to fight, if only to protect me."

"Carry weapons? He's a body slave!" At last a clear reaction; blunt refusal.

Deep breath, and go for it. "He doesn't *need* a weapon. Though I'd like to arm him," I admitted. "Look, the only way to tell you is to show you."

A single nod of consent, though he looked suspicious. So I sent for Keril.

I had told him, rather gruffly, to appear in riding gear but without the outer robe or headdress. It'd seemed indecent leaving him half-naked as he was in private, even if my father had already seen him. But his face would still be bared. It had to be, my father had to judge him honest. Thus garbed, he passed the inner arches, bowed and waited. I could see the tension in his neck and shoulders.

"Come here." Gods, but he looked guilty. I hadn't played the bully with him much, not lately. This time he might need it. "Sit." He sank onto the carpet at my feet as usual, hands clasped, attention on the dagger I had ready on the table. His rigid body said he didn't want to. But he knew I wanted it. "Watch," I told my father.

Keril's knuckles tightened, nothing more. The dagger lifted, floating in the air between us. Father's mouth had opened.

I broke the silence. "Throw it."

The knife became an arrow, speeding for the block of wood across the chamber. There was a thud, and then the faintest thrumming as the thing vibrated. Otherwise, still total silence.

"Send him away."

I think Keril wanted out more than Father wanted him gone. He certainly didn't waste time obeying. My seething father watched him, all the way.

I got in first before he could recover. "Mad, I know, but that's what happened in the market. I saw that assassin's knife turn in his own hand. I saw the killer try with all his strength to stop it, and he couldn't. What you've seen today… No ordinary male could do that so the ordinary law's too simple."

"What are you saying, Ash?"

"Not that. He swears he's not a god and I believe him. He has magic, but he didn't know how much. He thinks the males who raised him didn't either, says the power's been growing."

Father's eyebrows lifted.

"Up till now he's used his "skill", he calls it, as a watcher, then a healer. Now he's used it to protect me from attack, to kill. It frightens him. It scared me too, at first." I straightened. Once again I'd had to wonder about gods. If this had *proved*… "If Keril's god is so powerful, and protecting me, perhaps *that's* where my En-Syn's coming from?"

Father frowned. "You're considering it might be real? But if so why would foreign gods support another god's religion?"

"Hanged if I know," I admitted, "but you saw it, Father, that was… something more than mortal. So if Keril is a power sent to help me, then." I looked him in the eye. "I ought to use him, don't you think? It might be taken as an insult *not* to."

It wasn't going to be that simple, of course. We thrashed it around for days. First came the simplest fact: he'd killed.

"A body slave. Not even war-trained."

"Say it was at my command. What slave could argue?"

"This one, by the sound of it," my king retorted. "If you're right, the male could—"

"Kill me? Surely; any time he wanted. Me, or Medi, or my entire household? Takes some getting used to, doesn't it? Except he hasn't, and I know I've given him sufficient provocation. So the only difference is that now I *know* I own a… a force of nature." That felt slightly better. The elements were easier to face than god-sent weapons, which was what I figured both of us were thinking.

Father didn't voice that either. "But the precedent."

The legal aspects bothered him more than the magic? The opposite of how I felt about it. Still, I pounced upon the hesitation. "It's my neck he's protecting, you know, and he's been doing well at it."

"No, this is Keril's neck," he said at once, "and we both know it. And it could be yours as well."

That was it, of course. We had to figure Keril was a power we couldn't guarantee control of any longer. Not unless he let us.

Father put it plainer. "Ash, you're talking about putting your life in his hands." Another pause. "Of course, he's saved you twice now."

"And he healed my back. There's not a mark." I tried to sound objective. "Don't you think he's earned our trust? I mean." I spread my hands. "Tull got a title just for shouting."

"There's justice in it, as you say, and if he serves an unknown god, in such a manner… Dare we refuse such a favor?" Father gestured at my armlet. "And dare you hide what you've been given any longer?"

I tried to sound unconcerned. "*If* his god did it, it looks like he doesn't want it made public yet either." After all, Keril hadn't minded, hadn't even noticed. And nothing had happened to rebuke me; no bolt of lightning, no visions. Though who was I to fathom godly tactics?

Whatever the cause, or reason, it did look like someone's god—most likely Keril's—had laid claim to me, and facing up to that was a far greater challenge than fretting about the marks that *maybe* proved it. Though again I had to wonder why a foreign god, or gods, should care about *Kadduchi* holy symbols… it was all increasingly confusing. Made my head ache. I'd resolved to try acceptance, however much it went against the grain. Trouble was, while Keril's unknown god seemed benign, what I knew so far about his *priests*… appeared a suspicious contradiction.

My thoughts had wandered. Father's hadn't. "Of course, there is one very easy way to solve the legal problem, *and* reward him."

I think I frowned, I know I was bewildered. "How?"

"Free him."

"No," I said. Well, blurted. "No."

He dropped the subject; no more talk of freedom though there was a deal of talk about my rashness. But he witnessed Keril's solemn oath to serve me, and he signed the secret document that styled a body slave my "personal protection". (Illegal? Dear me no. He was a slave, and under orders, *and* accountable directly to my god-like father.)

Tull would have laughed. Or maybe not. My father didn't when I told him *why* I wanted it to stay a secret. "Ash, this isn't just some game, not any longer. Besides." He calmed a notch. "They'll never do it."

"But if I talk them round?"

"It's quite impossible."

"You want to bet?"

He went right back to looking worried. "No."

"Ah-ha."

I couldn't resist baiting him but I wasn't as confident as I sounded. The whole idea had only blazed into my head as we were talking and it took me weeks to get to where there was a chance of trying. Weeks in which my father watched my every move; in which I tutored Keril very closely. Was I following my judgment, or my faith in Keril?.

"Hell's teeth." I stopped, my sword hand dropping, my defense wide open, but it didn't matter. Keril's fighting skills were absolutely hopeless. Sure enough his blade jerked past about a hands-width from my unprotected stomach. "My lord?" He sounded startled.

Not as much as I was. Faith, in Keril? I gave a shaky laugh. "I think religion might be catching. Or I'm sickening for something."

"My lord seems well enough." My favorite was *not* relaxing; didn't dare. He'd learned the moves but he could make the simplest parry clumsy.

"Try it again?" I swung my sword, slow motion. Watched his sword go flying. Hopefully my outburst was forgotten in the clatter as it hit the tiles. Good job Keril wouldn't have to *fight* as well to get me what I wanted.

Chapter 37

First I'd need to put him next to Hassid.

I'd hardly seen my "cousin" Hassid since the war with Sidass. I suspected he had been avoiding me. A brilliant swordsman once, and even now no novice, but I thanked the gods, or Keril's anyway, a wholly unsuspecting target.

It took me weeks to get him to the palace and by then I'd given up on Keril carrying a weapon. He was useless with both sword and dagger—if he touched them. He was right, he wasn't bred to be a fighter. But he seemed to master anything that wore a saddle.

Hassid, knowing none of this, believed I'd freed him from diplomacies he hated to a trifling task that offered him a visit to his father. Only first, I said, he really ought to join me for some fun before he had to cope with all that hostile desert. "Haven't seen you for an age," I said. "You don't have to go straight off, do you? There's some banquet on tomorrow."

"Is there ever not a banquet, in this city?" he'd responded, grinning, "It's a wonder there's a horse can bear you."

I laughed. "I burn up all I eat. It seems to me *your* sash has more to wind round these days though; it must be all those diplomatic dinners."

So with the ease of childhood friendship we set out to find enjoyment worthy of his visit, and I got my easy-going cousin drunker than he'd been since that Sidassi spear pierced his shoulder.

Instead of healing up, the joint had stiffened. I recalled how he'd got grimly drunk the night he realized it wasn't getting better. Now, if he fought at all it had to be off-handed. Worse, he'd been his father's chosen heir. Still was, on paper, but we all knew that would have to change once it was clear he was permanently crippled.

Me, I figured Hassid's diplomatic duty was his last-ditch attempt to give himself more time to heal, before he lost his right to the succession. Naturally he denied the double world of pain he'd never, being desert-bred, admit to.

Me, I'd felt a helpless anger for him, on both counts, but if he didn't want to be reminded who was I to force him? Now I swung between new hope and guilt at my deception. So I got him legless.

The morning after that he was to join me, first for breakfast then for riding. Not surprisingly his breakfast table conversation ran more along the lines of "Oh my head" than an appreciation of the menu. Mind, I wasn't noticeably better. Getting someone seriously drunk's a thirsty business. Besides, I was keyed up; I had to bite my tongue to keep from asking pointed questions.

Hassid's tongue was first to loosen. When we headed for the stables Keril, veiled and booted, joined us just within the doors to my apartments. Since Hassid was that moment fixing his own veil in place he rather took that tiny fact for granted. And I kept him moving.

Outside the doors he looked again then glanced uneasily in my direction. I said nothing. He stuck it through the palace, all the way to where we met the others but when Keril veered aside to mount he hesitated, even though old friends were waiting.

"Ash, who is that male? You didn't introduce him, and he wears no tribal emblem."

"Oh, Keril's mine." I waved a hand. "He's quite a horseman. I indulge him." For a moment I was sidetracked by a youthful face above the hands that offered reins to Keril. Ammet groomed our finest bloodstock these days? Samchek must be as taken with the cub as other Kemik. For his skill, or…?

Hassid brought me back to more important matters. "Yours?" He got that far before the awful truth jumped up and bit him.

"Mine," I'd said, but desert males did not believe in keeping slaves exclusive, any more than the Sidassi.

Keril reached to mount the black, which shied as someone walked behind it. Ammet tried to grab the bridle. Keril shook his head and leapt into the saddle and the black became a playful kitten, dancing lightly in a circle, eager to get started.

"Yours?" repeated Hassid, treading softly.

"A wedding gift." I had to sigh. "You must have heard about it. Everybody else has."

My cousin's shoulders jerked. "There was some tale. I have to say I failed to believe it."

I was impressed. The last few years as a diplomat had clearly smoothed his tongue, if nothing else. It took a diplomat to tell me I was crazy so politely. "But now you do," I said, and walked away as if I hadn't noticed all that outrage.

The rest were waiting. When I introduced young Zanith, Hassid bowed, but stiffly, obviously didn't trust my judgment any longer. Meanwhile Keril had the black in order, turning it to join us. Ammet, lips still parted, ducked his head politely. Keril's horsemanship had made another conquest.

Zanith's nod to Keril might have passed unnoticed but Tull looked pained. "Gods, Keril, does it have to be the black again? It nearly put me in a tree last time!"

Hassid's head swung round.

"I'm sorry, sir, it needs the exercise. My lord gave orders."

Looking back, I saw that Hassid's eyes had narrowed. Keril's words might be apologetic but his tone betrayed amusement. More than that, it showed no fear of Tullman's anger.

"Your lord would." Tull scowled. At me. "And a good morning to you too, highness. Can't you find anyone else to ride that nightmare?"

"You're welcome to try."

"No, thank you," Tull said snootily. "Keril has to humour you. I don't."

The others laughed, including Keril. Hassid's head was practically rotating. He was so busy trying to work out what was going on it took him all morning to get round to the subject I wanted most. Eventually I got it. Hassid, reining in as we got back, jumped down then suddenly stood still and flexed his weakened shoulder. "Odd," he muttered.

I would have cheered, except I couldn't. I rode across to block him from the others' hearing. "What?" I said, and saw that Keril too had reined in close enough to listen.

"What? Oh, nothing." Hassid gave his reins up to the waiting groom and turned toward the palace. I dismounted too, and Keril followed suit once Ammet reached him, darting through the moving bodies. Keril drifted up at Hassid's back as I enquired, "Could it be your shoulder's not as painful?"

"What? How did you know?"

"Ah. I tried a small experiment last night. It looks as if it could be working."

"You—but how? You didn't… Something in the brandy?"

"You didn't wonder why we drank so much?" I'd sidestepped lying rather neatly there, I fancied.

"Ash! Gods, what was it?" Hassid's voice was shaky. One could see it might be; I suspected even temporary ease was an achievement. But I had to stick to what I'd planned; besides, the others would start wondering what we were up to.

"Humour me. We'll try again this evening, if your head can stand it. Then, if you decide it's working, well, I'll tell you." Nothing he could say, or threaten, moved me. "Later," I repeated. Never have I seen a male so keen to drink himself into a stupor and he never once suspected I had added something to the final brandy. Dishonest? Yes, but how else could I catch him?

"Ash? My prince." A hurried bow. "Gods, Ash, the pain is duller. I can lift it higher. Look here, will you? You've got to tell me what you gave me!"

Hassid hadn't slept much by the look of it; he'd barely wasted time on dressing, and he'd let the veil fall as soon as we were private. Now Medi, at a sign from me, departed, shooing slaves before him.

"Chocolate?" I offered. "Breakfast?"

"Yes, whatever." Hassid's flow of words was halted by such mundane questions. He threw himself into the nearest cushions. "Ash?" he pleaded.

I poured for both of us. "Best drink this first." The drink was hot and rich, and laced with liquor, on my orders. "I didn't give you anything but brandy, but I… lent you something. Something rare, but mine to offer."

Hassid frowned. "I didn't understand one word of that."

"I was afraid you wouldn't. Let me explain then. Just… don't interrupt me till I've finished. Right?"

"Of course." He nodded, leaning forward.

"I have a healer. While you slept, I brought him to you. Now you can decide if I did right. And if you want it to continue." I pulled the bell and Medi reappeared. "Is he—"

"Yes, my prince."

"Have him come then." Almost before the curtains settled, Keril drew one back again and entered. Desert robes, without an emblem. Veiled before a stranger. Hassid swore, and knocked the chocolate over.

"Leave it," I said as Keril made a move to grab the glass before it rolled right off the table. Frankly, I was scared he'd lift the thing with magic. Not that Hassid would have noticed, all his thoughts were on his own, uncomfortable position.

"Keril says he might be able to heal you, or at least make the improvement you've been feeling longer-lasting."

Hassid stared from me to Keril. "I asked, about him—" He stopped. "Does the king know what you're doing, loosing body slaves in public, putting them right next to nobles?"

"My father has approved of Keril's presence within my household, and when I'm riding," I said stiffly. "He has watched him ride, and talked with him on three occasions, in my presence. Once within his own apartments."

"Gods in—" Hassid swallowed hard. "Well… if my king can bend so far, then how can I refuse to?" Thus my father, all unknowing, made it possible for Hassid to submit to the indignity—perversion surely, he'd be thinking—that offered him a miracle he must have prayed for.

Even so, when I took him through to the bath where the massage tables were set up and then told him he'd have to strip off robe and shirt and lie there so his prince's body slave could maul him…

I thought Hassid was going to turn chicken there. He might have reasoned his way past Keril's existence, but he was horribly aware of who this veiled toy belonged to. He actually closed his eyes, and clamped his teeth so hard I heard them grind on one another.

I couldn't think of anything to say. I waited, praying silently, while Keril lost the outer robe but kept the veil. I doubt Hassid believed my talk of healing, but to ease the pain… For most males, pain's a brief obsession, soon forgotten, but to stand it always? I suppressed a wince of sympathy. I didn't know how he could do it.

Sympathy flew out the window though when Hassid jumped right off the table like some frightened virgin when Keril's ungloved fingers touched his back. Luckily I laughed at him, he did look comic, and that eased the tension. Mine as well, I didn't like the sight of Keril touching someone else so intimately, for however good a reason. And I'd clean forgot that Hassid was a damn sight too good-looking.

Massage round the shoulder; nothing more to notice. I sat and watched them from the other table. Keril closed his eyes, as if to see more with his fingers. Hassid's shoulder muscles gradually loosened. Once he glanced across at me. I swear he started blushing but he turned his head away so fast I couldn't prove it.

"My lord?"

"Yes?"

"I was right, there is something in the wound; very deep. I think it has been moving." Keril looked down at Hassid's back. "Sir, has the pain got worse, in recent times?"

"Uh." The fool had difficulty speaking. "Yes," he got out, face averted. "This last year the stiffness gradually worsened." He hated to admit the weakness. And to talk to Keril? Well, he'd have to get accustomed, I thought callously, it wasn't only him who had to suffer.

"I should try to reach it. If it stays inside…" Keril's eyes flashed me a warning Hassid, thankfully, was blind to.

"Huh. So we get it out. Right, cousin?"

Hassid swallowed once again. "I'll trust your judgment."

"Trust to Keril's skill." I nodded Keril to continue.

"This will take time. Most of the day, perhaps." Keril stopped and pondered. "I think, some towels and (a tremor in the voice) more brandy? You have not eaten, sir?"

"No," Hassid sounded far from happy.

"That will help, I think. If you are ready?"

"Go ahead," he muttered to the table.

"I will dull your senses first, so that it does not hurt as much." Keril's hands moved carefully over Hassid's back; up the spine, across the heavy shoulders. Fingers probed. Once Hassid hissed, surprised, but Keril's fingers didn't falter.

It was a long day. I'd told Medi to keep everyone out but he came himself, eventually. Midday had passed by then, I ordered food, for me and Keril, who was wilting. Hassid wasn't getting anything but brandy. He was half-asleep, or drunk, or maybe drugged by Keril's fingers. At any rate his eyes were shut. I squared my shoulders. "Keril, loose the veil, you're sweating buckets."

He was too. Medi looked upset and wiped Keril's forehead. After that the eunuch came at intervals; brought extra towels himself when Hassid's sweat soaked through the ones below him. Hassid wasn't wholly conscious but he sweated like a pig and every now and then he shuddered.

Keril's shirt was soaking. Arms and shoulders quivered. As if the pain went into Keril? Feeling nauseous myself, I made him drink some wine and water.

"This has been left too long, my lord," he murmured.

"Too late to help?"

"No, but it was hard to reach, and even harder to— Ah." He leaned a little further forward. "There. I… have it. Just a little further. If I bring it so…" His body jerked, and so did Hassid's. "Now…" Keril's head had tilted; listening to something? "My lord, you'll need a knife."

Without a word I drew my dagger.

"Clean it, please."

I laced the blade with brandy till the stuff was pouring off it down onto the tiles. "What next?"

"Cut… here. See?"

When I peered close I saw a flattened bump below the weakened shoulder, not much shorter than my little finger. I was sure it hadn't been there when we'd started. "Cut into that?"

"Beside it. Then remove it." Keril closed his eyes and pressed into the flesh around it.

I made a cut along one side. Blood flowed but Hassid didn't seem to feel it so I cut again. Still no reaction? Ah, but Keril's breathing had got louder.

Changing tack, I tried inserting the tip of my knife beneath the flap. The point hit something hard. By that time I was sweating too but Hassid still seemed unaware that I was digging round inside him.

I'm no surgeon, but it wasn't too difficult. The object, slippery with Hassid's blood, flipped out onto his back. "It's out."

Beside me Keril slumped against the table. Medi, bless him, chose that moment to rejoin us.

"Medi, slap a bandage on my cousin while I see to Keril. Come on, you, enough. You're swaying." Hassid's blood stained Keril's hands, and shirt, and smeared his face where he had wiped. The bath was right beside us, all I had to do was order him to strip and use it. But I couldn't, could I? Not with Hassid present. "Medi, send some water to my bedroom."

My eunuchs washed him over quickly. Medi sent in food and wine, fresh robes as well. "Eat what you can." I made him take a couch and then stood over him. He drank a lot but didn't eat much. "Now stay there and rest," I said, "You've earned it."

In the meantime Medi had assumed the brandy was the cause of Hassid's stupor. Me, I wasn't certain but I didn't argue. He had dressed the wound, he said, and saw no cause to worry. Tactfully, he didn't ask where it had come from. But he offered me a dish. It held a triangle of pitted metal.

I picked it up. "A spear tip?"

"Perhaps, my prince. It's rougher here, as if it's broken." Medi pointed with a stubby finger.

"Thank you, Medi, I'll hang on to it."

Hassid woke next day, in time for breakfast; understandably subdued but still incensed he'd woken with a bandage. His complaints stopped dead—although his mouth stayed open—when I tossed across the metal fragment.

Then I started talking payback. I was glad for him, but Hassid, whole again, was now my leverage to bargain with his father. And when Hassid talked of making offerings in gratitude I had to tell him, "Go ahead, but don't for all our sakes explain what really happened. Temples are a sea of gossip." Well, I didn't want the priests to notice Keril.

Or to hear of anything that might remind them of the En-Syn that they knew I carried now, because the cursed thing had itched again, all night. I'd lain awake and sweated, feeling helpless, and in the morning light the royal star looked clearer-cut than I remembered, almost golden. Looked like I was paying for my cousin's healing.

Surprised? Bewildered? I was growing scared again of what was happening. I really didn't see how anyone except a god had done it. Was each new development a sign of favor? Had I passed some test by helping Hassid? I didn't understand a thing except I was apparently allowed to keep it secret.

Hassid visited his temples, going first to Sarrush, water being first and foremost in the desert. He had promised not to mention Keril and it looked as if he'd kept his word, at least the priests evinced no sudden interest. He departed two days later to complete his promise, looking solemn. He was gone two weeks. I curbed impatience and continued to direct the search for any evidence that Thersat was behind these two attempts to kill me.

Half my eyes and ears were on it. Getting nowhere. Nor were Father's. Irritating was an understatement. Time was running out, I'd have to leave for Sidass soon, with Thersat in my train unless we found some evidence to hold him. On top of that there was the question of Sidassi loyalty in general. Was Thersat acting on his own, or under Farad's orders? Father was convinced of Farad's honesty, but face it; I could link the north with all my current troubles.

Ashamet, Desert Born

Well, Synia apart, I thought. Then thought again. Keril, and presumably his god, were from the north. Were they connected too in some way? Seemed unlikely. But that southern killer in the market place had carried northern coin. I'd started wondering about that landslide, even back to that unlucky taster and the crawlfish merchant who'd precipitated my Sidassi marriage.

Meanwhile Keril still had things to learn to add to what he knew of horses. He took that very well; more confident, perhaps from curing Hassid. Certainly I couldn't fault his progress but it didn't feel enough the day that two of Hassid's males rode in to warn me that their party were a day behind them.

I'd suggested that we rendezvous outside the city. I must admit I'd found that part entrancing, mad, but such a challenge. We were to meet where wasteland turned to real desert, off the trade-route. The only obstacle to that was getting Tull and company to let us leave them and go off unguarded. So I had a quiet word with Tullman.

"Just you and Keril? What exactly are you up to?"

Hardly the politeness due a royal, but I let that pass. "Nothing, just." I looked (I hoped) appropriately bashful. "I promised Keril, sunrise in the desert."

"So why d'you want—? Oh!" I swear his face reddened.

I turned my laugh into a cough. "All right, don't make a song and dance about it. And don't blab it about, either."

He laughed at that. "All right, I'll keep your sad, erotic secrets. Not the first time, is it?" And he *was* discreet, until we parted.

I wondered if he'd tell them what he thought we'd parted ways for, once I'd left. If it was one of them I had an assignation with they'd joke about it to my face. With Keril—they became discreet. Yes, Keril altered people; frequently without them knowing. Look at Medi; quite besotted these days.

Chapter 38

Hobbling the horses, we'd approached the camp on foot, downwind, and so far undetected. The line where hill met sky was still invisible but wood-smoke on the breeze, the smell of dung and then a whiff of bitter desert coffee told me we were very close now. I crept forward. "Keep your head down."

"Yes, my lord."

Still darkness, but I heard the clink of harness on a tether line and after that the flap of loosened canvas. Then the sky began to lighten. Dawn came sweeping in from off the desert, catching orange fire on the topmost rocks and ridges, casting eerie shadows, waking color—faded blues and reds—on the three tents beneath us. Hassid and my desert cousins must have got here in the night and pitched their tents already, waiting.

The place I'd asked to meet wasn't used much now; a sharp depression in the wall of hills that dammed the desert where an ancient, long-gone river dating back to the formation of the world had dug a curving ridge to give the place more shelter. Once the well that made it valuable dried up the winds and sands had taken over. Travelers passed further north these days; unlikely we'd be interrupted.

Once, so Father said, the well had fed a tiny patch of magically fertile ground that almost touched the desert proper, much like Ammet's village, only smaller. Now it was a ghost, a rock-strewn hollow chilly in the early morning shadows, and the citrus trees were only brittle skeletons below us.

"See?" I pointed down as Keril crouched beside me. "Chieftain's tent, common tent, cook-tent, horse-lines, baggage under canvas. And over there, already set in place... you see them?"

Lines of hollow metal tent-poles flashed in sunlight, driven in where it was flattest, from the broken walls beside the tents toward the sunrise.

Keril nodded, keeping quiet as I'd warned him.

"Let's go." I slithered back. I'd wanted to familiarize him with the set-up and perhaps pick up some clue as to their mood, but all I knew was they had come.

So Hassid's father would accept my challenge? Maybe. Even that remained uncertain.

We collected the horses, back-tracked and approached them from the south once I had checked on his appearance. Soon dogs appeared at a careful distance. None barked, these dogs were flat-pawed desert hounds and trained to stealth. A pack like these would face a lion. Or a raiding party.

Closer in, the line of sturdy desert horses shifted nervously and then a knot of veiled tribesmen quit the common tent. Two strode aside to quiet the horses while the other males, and dogs, spread out and watched us ride toward them, still in silence, like I was a stranger, though they were expecting me and must have seen the royal colors on my clothing.

A second tent flap opened. Hassid bent a veiled head to exit, followed by his father. Cousin Adu, chieftain of the central tribes, the Sais (sands), stood still too and waited.

I too had veiled, less from manners than I didn't want them seeing my expression. And it felt right, somehow, that I looked the same as Keril. I was glad of it already, after this reception. There were no voices raised in rowdy welcome this time. Adu and his tribe had taken umbrage; this could take me years to mend if things went badly but I'd done it now. I pinned my hopes on Keril winning what I wanted. "Feel all right?" I muttered.

"Yes, my lord." More calm than I was, if his voice was anything to go by.

Adu; overlord of all the Sais clans. What can I tell you? Same age as my father, but he looked a decade older, skinnier, and sourer; one of scores of kin our careful breeding records owned to. He had the signal virtue that he didn't leave his fierce inner desert very often; he preferred their wastes to all the "civilized" preoccupations of the cities, or our palace. Right now the Crow (as he was called behind his back) was standing like some temple effigy; no bow, no move toward a royal kinsman, even though I'd given him his favored heir back, fit enough once more to be acceptable again as his successor?

Hassid murmured in his ear and finally the old male did step forward. From my horse I bowed, and my companion likewise; desert-fashion, hand across the chest to signify no move toward a weapon.

Adu, very grand today, a wealth of beaten gold about him, frowned at me. Then— did a double take. Then cursed me.

I dismounted. "Yes. Before you bust a gut, try looking closer."

I didn't need to see his lower face; the faded yellow eyes above the veil yelled pure murder at me. "Keltis' balls," he gritted. Not "my prince". Not "cousin". I was in the dog-house.

"Look," I repeated. Keril's hands, left bare, were brown as mine. The rest of him would match and Medi promised it would last for several weeks, unless he washed too often. Medi had been justly pleased when I'd applauded.

The stark white robes had been embellished similar to mine; a corded sash in blue and red and gold, the royal colors; a matching cord around the head-dress and the half-drawn visor; a golden clip instead of silver on the veil and small, blue tassels such as tribesmen loved across the outer robe, that danced and shivered with each movement.

The tell-tale silver shackles at his wrists had had to go, however pretty, but Medi had unearthed some token silver armlets that his sleeves concealed.

We'd left the ring. It fit the image of a well-born tribesman, possibly a relative to Adu. Old enough to fight, except there was no sword behind his shoulder, just a plain, all-purpose dagger at his hip, permissible because he also wore the copper charms at neck and belt that marked a tribal healer. He was veiled, quite properly, in front of strangers, as my stiff-necked cousin Hassid had been in the palace till we'd entered my apartments.

Adu saw what I'd invented. And he didn't like it.

But. No desert lord could back off from a challenge. And his heir stood whole again beside him. That was my trump card, and his weakness. Plus I'd had him meet me practically in the desert; done it knowing he would feel at ease here. Irresistible. No logic, Adu simply *felt* he had the upper hand, with sand around him. I had bet on that. I'd also prayed he'd opt for horses and it looked like I'd been lucky.

Then I heard a braying protest from behind those ruins. A thousand curses on his house, the scrawny ingrate had brought camels.

I didn't swear out loud, though I'd have liked to. Keril had arrived here on the black; I'd really hoped the value of the beast would sucker Adu into wanting to observe the brute in action. But it looked like he had added two and two—the black, and what he knew—and upped the odds against us.

Hassid stood in silence at his father's shoulder, making no attempt to influence proceedings. Did he really think he wasn't? He wore two swords again. Had he been practicing? I'd worried. If the shoulder had seized up again... I told myself I'd been a fool to doubt and I should pull myself together.

We went into the larger, common tent, a bare space floored with rugs. Still no one bared their faces. Keril was ignored. He stood behind me though; no kneeling here, I'd told him. Seated, Adu beckoned someone forward to establish hospitality by ritual cleansing, dipping hands into a common bowl of water. Adu, Hassid, me. Not Keril, but we had a truce, you'd call it.

Nobody referred to Hassid's change of fortune either, where another day they'd all have cheered and thrown an orgy in his honor; and in mine for helping. No, we skated round the subject, swapping guarded pleasantries while Keril hovered like a threat behind us. And me? I sweated underneath that veil. There were still two other problems.

The first, of course, was that the tribes were clannish at the best of times. They rarely tolerated strangers. Either you were one of them, or a potential enemy (or victim), and the split was almost always blood-related.

The second obstacle? As I said the tribes owned slaves, but none like Keril. Desert males were slowest of the lot to pick up modern customs anyway, while this one… Look how Hassid had reacted. It was logical enough for males who lived in tents and liked to shift about; it hardly fit their life-style, did it? Desert females wore the veil like the males, but not their slaves, and being publicly displayed of course the slaves were there for anyone who wanted.

Slaves were slaves, and weren't exclusive. So to their minds Keril was a slave I treated like a female. Not unlike the cursed Sidassi! Worse, he had been ruined, city-fashion; pampered by a stupid master, made unfit for useful labor by the decadence of modern city fashions. A perversion, again. (I was getting so tired of that word.) Yet he stood here, veiled like their equal. You could feel the anger beat against the canvas.

I figured Adu wanted nothing better than to send me to the fiery devils desert tribes believed in, but his son's miraculous recovery required the outrage be at least examined. And I'd made a challenge. Adu was incapable of backing off a wager, and he must believe that he was bound to win it. Camel racing was a desert pastime, he would know from Hassid Keril wasn't any kind of tribesman.

Sly old Adu brought his camels.

"He will need a mount." The simple words were his reaction. Not the black, he meant. Not horses. End this now, admit you're beaten.

I said nothing. Adu waited for a moment, then he led the way outside. I walked beside him, Keril as my shadow. I was hoping I could choose for Keril. Pure-bred desert beasts had awful tempers and I didn't want him bitten. I was about to speak when Hassid staged an ambush.

"Perhaps we should let the male choose for himself, Father."

Adu nodded his approval but the males around us stiffened even further. Hassid hadn't weighed the complications. What if Keril chose a mount whose owner felt insulted? Was I going to end up dueling just to get things started?

But Hassid, having caused the problem, chose to solve it. "These are mine, Ash. Let him choose from them."

He'd brought four beasts; one older, two a year below their prime and one too young to trust unless you had to. All chewing messily and looking down their pure-bred noses.

Seven. Hells. I waved to Keril. "Choose." And held my breath. I'd put him on a camel in the last few days, in case it came to that. I'd told him I was furthering his riding education and as usual he'd done his best to please me in what little time he'd practiced. But I'd hoped I could avoid that, and I'd never thought of teaching him to judge them.

Keril paused to look them over then stepped up below those yellow teeth. And all the rest. You don't want to be stepped on by a camel, even by accident, and with camels you often doubt it is. Here goes, I thought.

He raised a hand toward the nearest one, the youngest. The upper lip curled back to bare the yellow teeth—which made me nervous and probably cheered Adu no end—but it didn't last. Why had I doubted? Keril stroked its shaggy neck. The stupid animal went every bit as gooey-eyed as all the horses.

Which was good, but wasn't what I'd hoped for. Not the youngest.

Its elder literally shouldered it aside. The youngster squealed in protest till the massive teeth swung round and nipped its shoulder. Cowed, it backed off. Soft words and Keril's hands prevented further mischief. I'd never heard of camels gathering around a total stranger but it looked like they were worse than horses. Other beasts were showing interest too.

"Choose fast, Keril, or we'll have the whole line after you."

"This one then, my lord?" He tugged the bridle of the biggest one. It gave a raucous cry of triumph.

"Hah," barked Adu. Hassid simply sent a slave to fetch a saddle. He didn't, thank the gods, suggest that Keril get the saddle on the creature.

When we turned away the challenge ground spread out before us; three long rows of folding tent-poles with a crosspiece slotted through their eye-holes. The course was set for three to ride, and cubs were out there, dumping baskets at the finish, walking back toward us hanging small brass hoops on every pole they came to. Every pole was lower than the one before; the final one would be below the stirrups. Only what went in those baskets counted; simple rules but not a simple challenge.

Slaves had raised the flaps before the common tent for shade and there we settled, Adu and myself and Hassid. Other tribesmen joined us, folding down to sit cross-legged on the carpets with a clear view of all the action. Keril chose to stop outside and watch from there. I let him. No one argued.

Keril wouldn't ride at once, there was a protocol. Three cubs kicked off proceedings; youngsters eager to impress their chieftain. You could see the novices' excitement in the movement of their camels. They did all right though. One collected three brass rings, the others two, and Adu nodded grave approval.

As they rode across and dipped their heads to Adu, older youths replaced them. The atmosphere in the tent improved from freezing cold to tepid; love of challenge undermining indignation. There were shouts this time to urge the riders on.

"He's next," said Hassid underneath the clamor.

The second challenge finished: five and four and three rings this time.

"Keril." The veiled figure swung toward me. "Go check those rings, before you ride them."

Keril bowed and left us. Adu acted like I hadn't spoken but he raised a hand to stop the next two riders.

Hassid drew a deeper breath than normal. "*Can* he…?"

"We'll see." I thought I sounded calm enough but I was being treated like a stranger, and I didn't like it. I figured Hassid felt embarrassed. He must be pretty torn as well; a part of him incensed, the other wanting to repay me. Yes, but Hassid couldn't force his tribe to tolerate a rank outsider, let alone allow a slave—of any kind—to walk among them like an equal. Only Adu could, and no amount of talk would sway him. But I wanted Keril with me when I left for Sidass and I wouldn't find a better way to do it.

Keril walked the line alone, examining the stakes. I saw him lift the rings. A few short weeks to learn to ride a camel and to ride the rings as well. We'd worked our guts out. Now to find if we'd succeeded.

Two new riders, *not* beginners, rode toward the start line and a slave brought Keril's mount behind them. Maybe Keril noticed. At any rate he turned and headed back. He made some signal; maybe spoke, although I didn't hear it. Hassid's brawny animal lurched sideways, tossed his ugly head until the slave who held him lost his grip then made a beeline for his strange new rider. Ah, I thought, delighted, showing off now, are we? Suddenly I felt much better.

Keril mounted, fast. I heard the murmurs. I had taught him how to step onto the camel's angled foreleg so he seemed to rise into the air like magic with his mount, his body shifting from the leg to neck to back in perfect, flowing movements. He shouldn't have been able yet, but mounting while the beast was seated would have counted heavily against him. It had been a gamble but he'd managed it. So far so good then?

Getting to the start, he didn't try to catch the other riders. The first two claimed the outer lines, which left him with the middle. The idea would be to leave him well behind, to make it obvious he wasn't worth their notice. I found I rather fiercely didn't want them to achieve that.

"If you are ready?" Having failed to stop the race before it started, Adu made no further offer to abandon. I had tricked him, and he wanted me to suffer. He was right, of course.

I nodded. "What, no wager?"

Quiet fell. He couldn't speak for several heartbeats. "What will you wager, on this cur you've brought us?"

Ouch. But I had come prepared. I dug a hand inside my robes and tossed a single gem, a sapphire, on the carpet. Desert folk loved blue, and it was worth all Hassid's camels. Murmurs rippled round us.

"That says he'll take six."

Thus cornered, Adu pulled a ring at random from his fingers, threw it down and waved.

At once the riders kicked their beasts to action. Keril, thank the gods, was watching. He was last away, but not by much.

First stake. Two hands reached out, together almost, for the trophies. Keril was a second later, but he got it. I saw the ring go up then flip onto his wrist, exactly as I'd taught him. Adu had gone still while on my other side an even tenser Hassid shifted.

"Come *on*," I muttered, safe behind my veil.

As if he heard me Keril kicked. The camel's speed increased between the first and second stake. He took the second too, and by the third was almost level.

He took the third. He lost the fourth, but caught up with a rival in the process. Another miss, but neck and neck. Two more; he got those too.

Three rings left, but lower. Stupid bet, I thought, then saw him bend and take another. Still in the saddle. Six it was!

Two more to go, and equal second. More? It wasn't only me now leaning forward. Other males had started shouting.

The rider Keril vied with flung himself toward his target, over-reached and almost came unseated. Someone cursed. The error cost the tribesman. Keril was a length ahead and chasing for the leader.

It was too much. But Keril didn't seem to think so. I groaned when he reached out too far and ripped his sleeve wide open on the final crossbar. No, he didn't catch the male in front, not quite, but seven rings slid off his arm into that basket.

I looked at Adu. Rigid. Better leave him for a moment. Keril looked my way. I waved him over. He tapped the beast to make it bend. The ripped sleeve flapped as he descended, one edge blood-stained. He was breathing hard, but wasn't he entitled? And I could grin like any fool because my veil would hide it.

Adu sat and let my "cur" approach and bow to us in desert fashion, hands together, yet another sign of non-aggression. Adu looked both hard and long.

Then nodded gravely. "Not a bad performance." He collected ring and stone and tossed them both toward me.

I played the game to its conclusion. "You'll take my other wager then?"

The whole tent waited.

"Yes."

A surge of talk. I let my breath out. Keril would be at my back in Sidass, lost among my veiled escort. I had failed to put him near enough to Thersat, and the formal visit couldn't be avoided, but if I was in danger Keril would be there to warn me where it came from.

Calling it a wager was a diplomatic gesture; betting Adu couldn't filter Keril into the Sidassi undetected. If he did it, Adu would be richer twenty camels and an oft-repeated story; so much more polite than *paying* for the service.

More, as escort they would paint a picture the Sidassi would remember; an impressive sight that sent a subtle warning to a vassal-kingdom. They would be so noticeable who would dream that one exotic tree had taken root within the wilder forest?

But he'd had to win his place among them. And he'd done it. Only now there was another price to pay. I hadn't said a thing to Keril lest it make him nervous. But now I had to face what was, in some respects, a greater challenge.

Everyone remembered I was kin at last, their prince to boot. And no one argued when I signaled Keril to my left, to *sit* beside me. Keril, mindful of his recent lessons, sat cross-legged. The senior riders joined us too. Black tea, rough desert wine and rice cakes followed them, the copper trays presented by the youngest riders. Metal cups were set before us. Veils were lowered. I loosened mine then turned and nodded.

Grey eyes widened. His hands fumbled the clip but he obeyed me, without question. The face held no expression either as the cloth fell open.

A moment's quiet, then the talk continued. Good manners stopped them staring but I sat there feeling even worse than I'd expected.

Adu, never famed for manners, studied Keril closely. "His eyes are the wrong color."

I roused myself to answer. "Northern blood, perhaps. Besides, it takes a braver male than most to look the Sais in the eye." I forced a smile.

He liked that comment, nodding sagely, taking wine a youth was holding out toward him. "To our new healer then." His creaky voice betrayed an unexpected touch of humour. Then he tossed an object, small and shiny, straight at Keril. Keril caught it on the fly. It was a battle charm, a copper sun, a fitting bauble for a healer. Unexpected. Quite a compliment, in fact. Lord Adu must be overjoyed to get his best choice of successor back, however well he thought he hid it.

"Lord Adu." Keril bowed, without expression, which didn't do him any damage in this circle.

"Give the male a drink."

The youth moved on and poured, and Keril took the cup and drank. Without a glance in my direction. Doing as his chieftain told him.

Adu smirked. It figured, he was getting some belated satisfaction from the situation. I stuck it out; paid compliments and sipped at the obligatory second round before I made my thanks and talked of going. The males around me rose as well. I was their prince once more. I smiled and hid my upset stomach. There would be no need for Keril to unveil again en route to Sidass. Just the opposite in fact, with strangers present. Little comfort.

By the time we reached the stable yard we'd switched the cords and tassels for a plainer outfit and I'd bound his arm up roughly. But there was a brownish smear where blood had dripped on Keril's trousers, and to my extreme annoyance Samchek noticed.

"I slipped, sir, but I'm fine though, thank you." Not a lie, you notice, but I was relieved that Tull and company weren't there to see him. Given what *they* thought we'd gone for, I could live without their comments.

As I quit the yard I contemplated Father's reaction, once he heard from Adu. Father would be bound to send for him the second he descended on the palace. That thought made me feel a trifle better, humour lightening my mood and settling my stomach.

Why had I done it? Because they had to treat him as their own or somebody might notice. It was all about respect. To treat him properly they had to see him as a person, so I'd bared his face to them, that once, as if it was quite normal, as it would be if he was a kinsman.

And now he would be, for a while. He'd proved his worth, as healer and as rider, and their chieftain had decided. But I felt… exposed, as I never had before. As if it was me whose hidden face had been revealed.

"Is my lord unwell?" said Keril softly, following me through the palace.

"No, I'm fine." I got my chin up. Other males were watching. "How's the arm?"

"A little sore, perhaps. It's nothing."

"Too much to hope you'd do all that unscathed."

"It might have caused offence. Is that not so, my lord?"

My tongue tripped. "Wha— did you just say…?"

"Those males *could* ride, my lord."

Which didn't really answer, did it? I decided it was better not to notice. Besides we'd reached the entrance to the inner palace. I'd succeeded. I'd have Keril at my back in Sidass weighing up the diplomatic climate. In the meantime I'd keep eyes on Thersat, and continue till I knew if he was, personally, innocent or guilty.

Chapter 39

We'd be heading north, at first along the fringes of the desert, which would suit the Sais. As I'd feared, Thersat chose to join us with his carts and escort. Not what I had hoped but since we still lacked any real evidence against the male we had no grounds to stop him, not without a diplomatic upset at a most unfavorable moment.

Tull had charge of all the details of the trip, a temporary generality, an honor he had frowned at even though it meant he would command about three thousand of our standing army plus a cohort of the fearsome Kemik, plus expect appropriate compliance from the Sais. Well, in theory. He had frowned again when he saw Thersat on the roster.

"Look at you, a field promotion and a brace of princes to take care of too. You'll be a real general by Turn of Year, at this rate," I suggested, trying to cheer him.

Tull read on, ignoring me. Too dignified, this lordly Tull, I'd have to find a way to shake him up a bit along the way. Of course I had one sneaky trick in place already, but I wouldn't tell him that yet.

Never mind the army, the civilian listings filled a sheet. My cousin Adu offered company of consequence, and Adu brought his diplomatic son, his chosen tribesmen and his slaves while I, with thought to Keril, brought a staff comprising mainly eunuchs from my own apartments, led for once by Medi.

Last, but far from least, there was the priest of Sarrush they had foisted on me, the religious sanction for this diplomatic mission. Priests again. I had too much to hide from *everybody*, starting with my so-called "illness", (or attempted choking for what gossips stuck to the discounted version). Then there was the blasted armlet, and of course the truth of Keril's presence and his magical protection. Wasn't that enough to deal with? When the day came neither Tull nor I were wildly happy.

So that was how we started out for Sidass. Usually I enjoyed departures, all the thrill of looking forward. But this time round…

We'd gathered our forces on the open land where Keril had his first lessons in horsemanship. I was mounted and ready. I'd retreated to a rise above the growing dust cloud when my inner lids snapped closed against it—the blurry sight I got through their protective shields could get irritating when I didn't have to stand it. Now I blinked the inner lids aside and watched the column sort itself into Tull's required order. Adu was here too, and Hassid. Thersat hadn't found us yet but Tull said all his gear had joined the column.

Thirty Sais scouts—if such a military word described them—were to lead us. I and my attendant lords would follow, then the other two thirds of the Sais warriors—my honor guard completed—then the Kemik cavalry and a contingent of the army's horsemen. After that came Adu's cargo-beasts and hangers-on, then mine, then Thersat's, then another batch of army, then their extras. Males and animals and carts and slaves. Tull's officers were busy, there was noise and bustle and a wealth of swearing, which was how I knew the priests had found us, when the language round me changed to something cleaner.

"Prince Ashamet. We are honored to serve." The priest-in-charge they'd sent me, robed in black with blue, stepped forward, bowing formally as if this was the palace. Or the temples. I was looking down from horseback; couldn't see much past his hood except that he was dusty-looking and we hadn't even started. Other priests, a pair of almost-equals and a sext of plain-robed acolytes, lined up and aped his movements. They looked tidier than he was, lower ranks though, not a jewel among them. I decided I was bored with them already but the leader wasn't finished.

"Highness. Lords." More bowing. "My lord Hainil sends loyal greetings, and expresses the hope that your journey brings you pleasure, and satisfaction."

Did I hear a tremor of amusement? Hah. "Pleasure and satisfaction" was it? That would be Hainil's way of telling me to enjoy myself but not to lose track of the prize. Damned cheek, and this male's well-worn boots proclaimed they'd sent some lowly roving missionary to remind me of my duty?

Which was interesting now I thought about it. Clearly Hainil's agent was no temple-hugger, nor the standard diplomatic adjunct.

Then he lowered his hood. The cropped head rose. The cheekbones and the narrow nose said desert-bred like me. The southern desert rather than the fierce, killing eastern wastes that Adu came from but a tribesman nonetheless; a rarity among the priesthood, and a likely candidate for work outside the temples.

His eyes were dark. His gaze was steady. "I am Water-brother Albar, if it please. My fellow priests are Fire-brother Lamas and Earth-brother Bindi, and of course the temples' prayers go with you." Naturally he didn't bother with his servants.

"Brothers." I smiled pleasantly. "I trust you are ready to leave?"

"We await the signal, highness."

I believed it. I'd bet there were no needless luxuries in Albar's baggage, nor in the baggage of anyone who served him. I had to respect Hainil. By the time his less than sharp predecessor finally breathed his last the power and influence of Sarrush and his temples had been noticeably less than his purported "equals" Keltis and Keshat, at least here in the capital. Till we took Sidass.

First Hainil made sure the Sidassi adopted Sarrush as their principal deity—and what more natural, with their heron-god to replace? Then he used that to ensure he had a finger in Sidassi affairs generally. Hells, he'd probably been instrumental in my marriage. And now he'd fixed it so that one of his lot led these temple representatives.

Religion. Politics. Ambition. Totally predictable. Albar's arrival would have been both boring and irritating, if Hainil's choice wasn't almost as young as me, and not half as pretentious as I'd expected. When I nodded he backed away and went to mount, positioning his small party between the Sais and the Kemik. A refreshingly modest choice too; many in his position would have tried for a place right at my back. I turned to Tull, who'd ridden in to join us. "Are we off then?"

"If you're ready, highness."

"*I* am. Spotted Thersat anywhere?"

"He's riding up to join you, highness." Tull was being very formal, which I'd have to deal with, but his blank expression was most likely there to hide his thoughts on Thersat's riding.

"Give the word. He'll catch us."

And so we began. The first day's march revealed our new priest could ride as well as the Sais; even Adu noticed, grunting in approval. Albar had brought fewer hangers-on than I'd feared, seemed to be keeping them in order and wasn't trying to claim a precedence I didn't want to give him. In fact, Hainil couldn't have found a male more likely to be accepted. Though juggling such tact with Albar's undoubted orders to get close to me and my intent to avoid being badgered and stay close to Keril…

Albar, like all the priesthood, didn't know the truth about Keril. Nor that as far as I was concerned a body slave who'd already saved my skin twice was a sight more essential to this mission than priests. So Albar's lot were going to have a nice, peaceful trip with lots of time to meditate, score points off each other, or whatever. And no easy access to their prince in private. Never mind what their superiors had told them.

I turned in the saddle, looking back along the line, past Albar, who seemed to be trying to teach one of his lot how to ride—a bit late now. It was quite a sight for peacetime: all those soldiers meant a slew of cooks and grooms and armoires and gods knew what else. *Snails* would overtake us. Still, it hardly mattered. We would get there.

It took Tull four days to spot Keril. It was the horse that gave the game away. The black. Keril had to ride whatever Hassid gave him. They'd been testing him, of course, a different mount each morning, each one wilder than the last one. But I didn't comment. Well….

But the black was in my line of spare mounts, had energy to spare and caused its youthful groom a deal of bother. And knew at once when on the fourth day out its favored rider walked across the open ground that kept my mounts apart from lesser beasts, and stopped them causing trouble.

Tull watched the beast back up and fight his tether, Ammet dodging teeth and hooves. I noticed Fychet ran to help him. They were still together? Then I saw Tull register the quiet tribesman marked as healer, following his prince and chieftain.

Tull stared at Adu, then at me, then back to Keril. He couldn't ask if he'd guessed right, not here in public; fool he wasn't. He couldn't wait to get me somewhere private. Meanwhile he checked off all those pretty details—royal colors, dagger, healer's charms—and finally (he blinked) that single battle charm.

That did it. "Devils take you, Ash," he muttered. Adu's head jerked round. For all they called him Crow, I thought, a vulture was more like it. He was frowning too now, guessing someone else knew what I'd dragged him into. "Sunrise!" Tull said darkly.

I choked and steered a path away, aware of Ammet staring fixedly at Keril. Better warn the youth to keep his mouth shut. I'd have broken it to Tull, eventually, but it had been fun to wait and see what happened. I think the more I felt a pawn in heaven's games, the more I valued anything I had control of.

Chapter 40

Night outside. I sat beneath a copper lamp, decoding ciphers from my eyes and ears in the south while Keril sat beneath a second lamp, bare-headed now my tent was closed and guards were posted, reading something that was obviously more amusing.

My reports were not. They'd finally found the tiniest trace of a very nasty poison on the *outside* of that goblet. Nowhere else. The dead assassin had left a totally anonymous pack in a room paid for in yet more northern coin but never slept there. Various informants had been "invited" to tell us what they knew, but they knew nothing. So we still couldn't connect the events.

Jaffid wasn't doing much better. His search had petered out between two mountain hamlets. His description of Keril's priests had been recognized at both, but reports had them leaving in different directions. Puzzled, he had split my males when they arrived and scoured the area. But so far nothing.

He was puzzled? So was I. Had they split up? How could they all vanish? More importantly, perhaps, why would they want to?

He had sent that message via Sheshman's son to bring me up to date but till I told him otherwise, he said, would keep on searching. Not a male to give up lightly.

"Just when things looked promising," I muttered, threw the coded page aside and started on another; standard stuff that listed population density along our southern border, and the frequency of the patrols beyond it. Maybe Tull would like a look at that one.

"My lord?"

"Hm?"

Keril had raised his head. "Why are we going to Sidass?"

"Oh." I shifted on my cushion. "It's customary, to celebrate my son's acknowledgement with his Sidassi kin. I thought you understood that."

"Yes, my lord." His head went back into the book and no, he wasn't calling me a liar.

I stuck it out until our meal arrived—Keril had to eat in private somewhere—and Medi and his mob had left us. Muffled noises from outside said males and animals were settling for the night but here in my tent we had a world where quiet shadows blurred the colors of the things around us. Only we seemed real. "All right, you win. *I'm* going there to play politics," I said baldly, "and because I have to. *You're* going to measure up my friends, and enemies."

"Ah." He laid the book aside and came to eat. "Including Prince Thersat?"

"Possibly." I'd never told him who I suspected of poisoning me. Tell him now, or not? Marking time, I chose a mutton shank well-glazed with mint and honey, biting into it with due appreciation. "Try the other one." He wouldn't if I didn't tell him.

He followed orders, chewed and swallowed. "I have not seen the prince close to. I doubt he's evil though."

"Why not?"

"He's passed near enough I think I would have felt a darker presence. Am I to assess him, like the others?"

"Possibly." Him and any other lord or general in Sidass I could get him close to, up to and including Farad, never mind my father's strong denial.

"Hm." Keril paused to eat while Albar's people rang their nightly peal of handballs—gentler melody than Kemik cymbals—and began to chant the evening prayers. Since I was out of sight I skipped them. Still no bolts of lightning. "But my inclusion isn't… diplomatic. Is *that* why I'm disguised? And so far you have kept me from him." Another pause. "Are you afraid the prince will know me?"

No Kadduchi likes suggestions he's afraid. I fear I did react a trifle. "No." Perhaps I glared, a little. Wisely he retreated into eating. *I* invited Thersat to my tent for dinner.

I invited Tull and Adu too, and Hassid, naturally. I considered asking Albar but decided Thersat was enough to spoil the meal. Albar and his followers had two good tents, and army cooks delivered to them personally, at my orders. Albar might be likeable but he was still Hainil's spy-in-residence. As far as I was concerned he could eat with his own kind all the way to Sidass.

Thersat, on the other hand, had an extensive caravan: his guards, his baggage (unbelievable) and his attendants. Since I outranked him he'd had to wait to be invited to my table. Tull had earlier suggested that delaying might offend his father. Now he scowled, but Adu barked with laughter. The rogue was getting far too much enjoyment from the situation. And a taste for royal-baiting. I was paying more than gold for his connivance and by this time it was chafing like the devil.

Oh, Adu was discreet. Outsiders never saw what he was doing but his own males knew it, even if their veils hid their laughter. Little things it was, like asking Keril to pass him something and brushing Keril's fingers as he took it. Then glancing sideways at his prince, to check I'd noticed.

To be fair, he was the only one of them who seriously tried my temper. My soldiers wisely left the desert males alone, and most of my desert escort left Keril well alone. I tried to be objective. I had found him one day talking quietly with the rider he had bested, while he waited for me, and another day, while I was briefing Tull beneath my awning, one lot called him out to join a dice game. It was in my sight, and useful cover. Innocent enough, and mostly he stayed close outdoors, as if escorting Adu or on guard behind me.

After dark, with Adu camped around us and my own males posted sentry, only then were matters truly decent. And even then… it was too public, under canvas. I'd forgotten. Every sound would carry. Well, it did, from others. Adu didn't need reminding…

None of which was Thersat's fault but might explain my mood at supper. Adu had almost had my hand at his throat for leaning hard on Keril's shoulder as he sank onto the carpets. Keril hadn't argued, but he dropped the shoulder, quickly. Adu hit the ground much harder than he thought to.

"Keshat's—" Then Adu realized I'd stepped toward him. Medi gestured hurriedly for slaves to set the food out.

I was still getting my breathing back to normal when there was the noise of someone entering the outer chamber and the inner tent flap lifted. Thersat stood there bowing.

"Prince Ashamet, Lord Adu, such a pleasure. One grows bored with one's own company on such a tedious journey. Don't you think so?"

Adu was still scowling, not a male to hide his feelings. When I didn't answer either it was left to Tull to fill the silence. "Sit here, highness. A drink, perhaps?"

I took a breath and backed him up. "Yes, come in, Thersat. What'll you have? Some wine? Or brandy?"

"Wine, I thank you." The male looked round in open admiration.

The main compartment of my tent was more than big enough to host this formal dinner. Desert-style, the rugs and cushions that were piled for my bed each night were now dispersed to serve as seating. The inner walls were lined with pale green cotton trimmed with lilac and the cushions were predominantly golds and purples. Medi had positioned incense burners, copper like the lamps, in darker corners; lavender and jasmine mingled with the cooking odors. In the outer section he had placed musicians; boarded desert harps, their plangent melody enlivened by a drum and rattle. If I closed my eyes I could imagine we had brought the palace here into the desert.

Thersat stopped admiring everything and swept his eyes across the carpet. Medi had excelled himself, my supper had become a banquet. Thersat beamed. "I must say these are very pleasing smells. You brought your own cooks with you?"

Such innocuous subjects kept us all polite; the food and wine, our travel. Even Adu started to behave more by the second course, of wild boar and chicken steeped in lemon. Tull began to eat, instead of dither.

Keril? He stood quietly by my tent-flap, watching those who came and went throughout the dinner. At his chieftain's service. Thersat's cushions put his back toward the entrance. All right, I thought, so this is what I wanted, what that trip into the market failed to get me. Finally, some confirmation.

More platitudes. I asked about the weather we might meet in Sidass. I'd recalled Sidassi weather could be wayward. It had given our armies several surprises.

"It'll be cooler there by now, of course," said Thersat. "Our winters gather earlier than yours, if you recall? It will be mild on the plains but in the northern hills they'll soon be looking out for early snowstorms." Craftily he paused.

"Ah yes." I wrapped chicken and sauce in a flatbread, rolling it desert-fashion. "Are they as bad as in the higher mountains on your borders?"

His mouth turned down. Had he expected to surprise us? He should have recalled Tull and I had been there. "I fear I've never been into the northern ranges, highness, but our poorer folk lose animals in snowdrifts some years. Children too, alas. Grown males have died, the worst years."

Adu looked incredulous. He'd heard of snow, I wouldn't doubt, but seeing is believing. Sadly…

"Your snow's later," I remembered now, around a fragrant mouthful.

"Usually, yes."

"We'll miss it then. A pity. So exotic."

Thersat chuckled. "For you perhaps, Prince Ashamet, but not to our poor hill-folk, I assure you."

Thus the evening passed, all friendly. Even Adu cracked a joke or two as platters emptied and the brandy circulated. Old Adu's eyes half-closed in calculation. Thersat had a harder head than he'd expected. Thersat's smile grew somewhat wider but his speech stayed clear as crystal; not as weak as Adu had assumed him. Not as simple either, maybe? I raised my head and looked at Keril.

He was watching me. Or for me. Suddenly I'd had enough of entertaining. When I made a tiny signal Medi sidled in to bend and murmur nonsense in his master's ear. "Gentlemen." I rose. "It seems I must desert you. Please, carry on without me."

Medi signaled slaves to refill cups, but others cleared dishes. I figured everyone would get the message, even Thersat. Tull, not slow, was frowning at his cup already. He waved a slave away." No more for me, I should be off as well."

Ashamet, Desert Born

Not wanting company, I hastened for the waiting darkness. Several of Adu's males moved too, to bow me out, to lift the flaps, to move around exchanging words and places. One took Keril's place and Keril simply backed away and left behind me. Very neat; I made a mental note some small rewards were due them.

An earlier breeze had died. The night was still and cold, the sky a scattering of stars, like one of Father's curtains. I chose to dive into a nearby storage tent where bales and barrels muffled sound and masked our presence. When I turned I saw him reaching out to feel his way and thought again how odd it was to be so blind in real darkness; obviously he was lost and navigating by touch, or maybe the sound of my movements? Somehow when it came to Keril, all that helplessness became amusing, and endearing. He was close though, and there was no one else... I drew him closer, set him down, his back against a stack of bales, pulled aside the veil and kissed him.

A sigh. Another kiss, and this one lingered. "I've had enough of canvas walls," I said, "of having to be quiet and seemly. What I want—"

I felt him tremble. "Yes, I know, my lord."

"Plague on it," I said, "we can't, not here."

"No, my lord," said blindness. Even in my arms he couldn't see me?

"Tell me what you saw in Thersat." I pulled him close beside me, up against what felt like extra blankets. He came easily to lean against me, eyelids lowered, with my arm wrapped loosely round his shoulders and his breath across my cheekbone. "Tell me," I repeated.

"The prince was most uncertain of his welcome, maybe because it took so many days to ask him?"

"Huh, what else?"

"Guilt troubles him. I cannot tell the reason."

"Maybe I do."

"The poison? It was the prince you suspected? My lord, I can't be sure but I don't think so. He likes you."

"*Likes* me?"

"Yes, my lord. He is nervous of you and yet... I think he trusts you. Can you understand that?"

"Not at all. I had him down for both attempts; the poison and the knife. You didn't see his face that day. It knocked him sideways when I wasn't skewered. And both attempts could fit his character: no direct action, and he's keen on herbs and potions."

"I do not think this male would poison anyone, my lord. I think it would unnerve him."

"Curse it Keril, are you sure?"

"Not sure, my lord." Another sigh? "It's only what I feel; a male who's slow to act in many ways yet bold in others but… aware of pain, I think." A pause. I watched him tilt his head in thought. So strange, to see yet not be seen. "I think he is imagining what you might do if you should turn against him, and it scares him, and he doesn't want that. He would dearly love your friendship. He admires you as much as fears you."

Admired and feared. In other circumstances I'd have been delighted, but… "I've hit a blank," I said, frustrated.

"I'm sorry, my lord."

"It's hardly your fault. So he doesn't want to kill me but he has a guilty conscience. That's it?"

"Just about, my lord. It's no help, is it?"

"Not much. Let's give him up for now and go to bed." I rose and found his hand to help him.

"Yes, my lord." He stood up quickly, turned toward the entrance, hesitated when I let him go.

"The veil."

"Yes, my lord. I had remembered."

I towed him out again but stopped before we quit the tent to look him over at the entrance. Hidden. Decent. Just the grey eyes glinting.

"Come on." I pushed the flap aside. I didn't touch him now, I forced myself to walk a pace ahead and *not* to touch him. Not until my own tent, cleared and put to rights, enveloped us and Medi, with a look, had chased his slaves out smartly. *Then* I turned and almost flung him on the piled carpets. "Not a sound," I warned, "these canvas walls are worse than useless."

I was rewarded with the faintest snort of laughter. Gods knew I'd missed that too; there'd been no laughter from him since we'd started, only watchful quiet. But then I hadn't laughed much lately either.

The quiet remained, but laughter of a sort lay with us, warm, and healing. A single lamp cast yellow light. I'd almost forgotten what his body looked like. His face; I'd seen that every night once we were private but the rest… I stroked the slender neck and felt the way his chest swelled out below it. Stroked across a nipple with my thumb; it hardened. He was sensitive to that one.

Stomach, browner now but still as flat. The muscles rippled. I could feel the hip bone turning underneath my fingers so I slid my hand around to reach a buttock. Tight, and smooth, like silk on metal; treasure, once discovered, that should never be forgotten. Muscles flexed there too. I trailed my fingertips back up his spine.

He squirmed, and laughed. "My lord, it tickles!"

"Quiet." I laid a finger at his lips instead. His teeth took hold of it and nipped.

My turn to laugh. "Less of that, and no noise."

He responded not in words, or even sounds, but slow deliberate kisses, first at my neck then— Gods, but I'd missed this!

"My lord has too much energy, for such slow travel."

I lay back and watched him trying to untangle sheets and cushions. He was smiling, and the copper dye looked almost golden in the lamplight. I didn't have much energy at all by then but I translated. "Too impatient, was I? Want it slower in the morning?" I tried to sound indignant.

"I want whatever pleases you, my lord."

A very proper answer, as befit his station. Everything a master wanted. Why then was I frowning.

Chapter 41

The next day found us turning north-west. Four more days took us from the desert's shifting yellow sands to cloying brown and orange soil. In these parts every village sat beside its jealously-protected clay pit. Slaves and free males, stripped to loincloths in the heat and dust, were often caked with it so thoroughly they looked like moving statues. I could see the evidence of Chi blood liberally mixed into the Kadd. Not too surprising with their common border, and the Chi had always loved ceramics.

Houses here had lacquered, peach-tiled walls instead of whitened plaster, every second building open fronted with a dome-shaped, brick-built kiln beneath its awning. Every awning was without exception drab and faded but the poles that propped them up were always brightly lacquered, every house a different pattern. Master potters bent at wheels. Young males kneaded slabs of glistening clay on heavy benches, or rolled them out for tiles and dishes.

The area was justly famous but it was a wonder Thersat's mules could pull the extra weight his carts took on in purchases of lacquered bowls and pierced burners. We had crawled before; it felt like we were barely moving after. With a modest escort and a change of mounts I could have cut across the desert routes instead; I'd have reached the Sidassi border in six or seven days. With all this fuss and pomp, and baggage, we'd be lucky if we did it now in twenty. Tull grew wary of my temper even though I tried to curb it.

The villages were also famous for their hospitality. Our males, especially the randy Kemik, joined the villagers in drinking, gambling and whoring. On the second night the region's overlord rode out to greet us and invite us to his nearest house. Its outer rooms were little more than roofs on pillars but there were some inner rooms. I spent a welcome night in one, with Keril. When I thanked my host next morning I was smiling, probably too broadly, judging from his stunned expression. Still, I did feel calmer. Plus my sword arm hadn't itched for days now. Maybe I'd ignore the nagging question of my arm a while, relax and put my mind to simpler problems, like my failed assassination.

That mood lasted several days, encouraged by the landscape. Gradually the scenery became more green than orange; stunted, clay-streaked bushes giving way to clumps of full-size trees where chuckling streams brought precious water to the surface. Scrubland changed to wild grasses; wild flowers too, a sweet mosaic served by sleepy insects with transparent rainbow wings that hovered in the air around us. We were crossing the Sidassi border, into regions some said were our true beginnings.

Adu and his males were goggling. For many of these desert males it must have been an education seeing land this fertile. They had never seen our greatest river either. I kept quiet. Let it be a revelation.

Even better, with the border came another courier and Jaff's next message, only days behind the last one.

He'd been turning back, regrouping, when his latest pals—the villagers who'd favored Keril—sent to tell him one of them had seen the grey priests heading down the mountain.

"Huh." I laid that sheet aside, considering. The further south they came the less they would be hidden from me. Maybe, finally? That night I drafted orders. There would be a suitable reward for any male in my employ who gave his prince a grey-clad priest still fit to answer questions. Half the world on watch, and Jaffid on their trail? This time it looked hopeful.

It was five days later—five fertile days but far-too-barren nights—that *we* encountered priests: a handful walking in the same direction. Not a hint of itching. I confess I was relieved, as well as startled. They weren't in grey in any case; a tattered lot. In fact Tull thought them beggars; he'd have chased them off if Thersat hadn't stopped him.

"They choose to live like paupers," was his explanation. It obviously didn't make much sense to Tull. Me neither, but we left them unmolested, such is civilized behavior. Adu, whose creed was hardship weathered and who called our temples tempting evil, threw them coin in passing. Keril failed to look. I noticed.

Adu noticed I was frowning. "Give me priests who own no more than they can carry, not those leeches in your cities with their feast days and their sale of penitences. Keep your holy thieves, and give me holy beggars."

"Careful what you wish." I laughed and settled back into my saddle. I was getting priest-fixated. It was nothing.

But Adu's wish came true. First one group then another of his "holy beggars" drew aside for us. Not in grey, and heading north not south. All right, but why, I wondered?

Thersat took great pleasure in explaining it. Perhaps it took his mind off riding. "It's the Festival of Ossar. Many priests and holy males make pilgrimage to Sidass' oldest shrines, and wash away their devils at the meeting of the waters."

"This many?" I hadn't realized it was this big an event. I was also wondering if Thersat's festival could be the grey priests' destination.

Thersat only heard my question, not my doubts. "Oh, what we've seen is nothing. Sometimes thousands gather there to pray and cleanse their spirits. Our common folk believe their prayers and virtues linger afterward to help the land survive death's season."

He was being careful what he said, of course; he wouldn't want to argue with our own—now his—religion. But the phrase, "death's season" caught the ear, and mind, especially of Kemik who were always open to a superstition. More than one tossed bread, or even coin, and others in our army followed their example. Priests thus favored smiled and blessed them. Well, it sounded like a blessing. "Thersat, did you understand all that?"

He shook his head. "Not all of it, but northern priests can always understand each other." That notion didn't seem to strike him as uncommon. Yet another foreign custom to latch onto? But... so many, targeting our own destination?

Medi said his people couldn't get much from the northern priests they tried to talk to. Nor could anybody else he'd oh-so-casually questioned. Some, apparently, spoke unknown dialects and some just smiled happily and spoke in holy riddles! Not good for my temper. Maybe it was time to pump Albar.

I waited till we stopped for lunch. Slaves hauled out rugs and put up awnings, for those who rated such amenities. Medi sent off my summons to Albar, and settled Thersat out of earshot.

The unassuming priest arrived, gave his horse's reins to one of my grooms and walked to where I sat. If he wondered about my sudden desire for his company he didn't show it. Actually he was the sort it would have been no real hardship to have around, in other circumstances.

"Highness." Albar bowed and waited.

"Something to eat?" I gestured to the carpet at my side as slaves arrived with laden dishes. Nothing special: flatbreads filled with meat; dried fruits, and flavored water.

"I am honored." Albar's joints protested as he lowered himself. What was he? Forty? Fifty? It could be years since he'd ridden this far in one journey. Not a handsome male, but I found I liked him. I had watched him with his acolytes and with my soldiers. Quiet and calm; no fuss, and no unnecessary movement. Modest but intelligent. And useful?

"What's with all these priests along the way?" I grabbed a rollup, trying to look more interested in eating.

He didn't seem surprised. "It is a yearly pilgrimage, highness, one it was considered politic to continue. It has always been a very peaceful gathering, where priests of different persuasions mingle to debate and worship. A state of truce exists, as it were."

I swallowed a mouthful. "So the High Priests approve?"

"Oh yes, highness." The male almost smiled. "It was never a danger. We have sent representatives, informally, for the last ten years. Well before the blessed Sarrush took a direct interest in Siddassi worship."

Ah. That far back was *Sil*. So he had sent our own Kadduchi priests to spread the faith in Sidass, under cover of this festival. Some seriously forward planning. Sneaky. Sil all over.

"Right. And more recently? Eat, male."

Albar chose a flatbread, took a bite, murmured, "Excellent," without mumbling, and continued to enlighten me. "Now that Sarrush protects the Sidassi, naturally our priests play a more significant role in organizing the festival." Albar's face was serene. "Whatever offerings the pilgrims still make to lesser gods, they all visit Sarrush's altars first."

"Do they now? You sound as if you've been there."

Albar's eyes met mine. "Once before the Voice of Heaven reigned there, highness. Twice since."

So he knew what he was talking about, and didn't mind telling me. Hainil had been using recent festivals to gain followers. Presumably with the agreement of the other High Priests? No wonder Father wasn't panicking, if he had Farad's allegiance on one hand and a growing religious movement on the other.

But. Could Keril's priests be heading there, as we were? If so, why? Not after Keril, he had never got there. But he would now. I took a drink, and wished for something stronger. I'd never intended them near Keril again.

Would Albar know about these foreigners? I almost asked but if I raised the subject Albar, and the temples, might start digging into my affairs again. I risked a little more though. "Do you know all the different sects then? Who they are, where they come from?"

"We believe so, highness. Most are simply offshoots of the main religions."

"None considered suspect?"

"I am assured they are all well disposed, highness; toward Sarrush, the empire, and now to you personally."

"Good." I took another swig of water. If I could believe him, and I saw no reason not to, yet, it didn't sound as if those guys had ever come as far as Sidass.

Safe enough then. Probably. Hopefully, since I couldn't alert Albar about them without exposing both myself and Keril, and both subjects were, both personally and politically, *my* business. I turned the talk to horses. By the time we woke from our midday rest this particular priest should have dismissed the whole matter from his mind.

Chapter 42

Two days on, Albar was still nodding graciously at any priests we passed. It was Thersat who looked anxious. By early evening he admitted, "I think there *are* more priests than normal, highness. I begin to fear for my father." Ears pricked, no doubt including Albar's since the missionary rode beside him. Farad's illness was a topic Thersat had avoided but each day saw priests in ever-larger numbers. Logic—not to say suspicion—said it was significant, and Farad's illness was a reasonable explanation. "Have you any news?" I asked straight out.

"Not for weeks now." Thersat drooped still lower in the saddle. "The priests along the way I've understood all claim that more have come this year because their elders called them to the convocation. They're excited but they have no further knowledge. But that surely means the greater numbers are a matter of religion, not of worldly matters. So I tell myself no news is good, but one still worries." He twisted round to face me as we rode. "My father is a *good* male, ever careful of his people's welfare, but he's ill, and growing weaker. They will mourn the day he passes on as much as I will." He looked upset, but was it only me who noted that he hadn't mentioned brother Effad?

I considered. Effad frankly hadn't captured my attention. The male was bigger round the waist than me if not in stature; the bluff and noisy type; could hit you hard enough but not out-think you.

Politically, I'd pegged him as a nuisance rather than a danger. Not a charismatic leader, nor a statesman like his father. Where the father got polite requests—and would have done from me as well—the son would follow orders.

We rode on in silence. What can one say? For all his faults, and possible duplicity, this was a male who clearly loved his father.

It made me think. One day our priests would dress in gold and offer incense at the altars for my father's journey to the heavens. If I lost my current contest with our priests, or Keril's gods, (or mine?) I'd end up in that cliff-top temple to replace him, forced to bathe in fire and return unscathed, another so-called Voice of Heaven. Put like that the odds were certainly against me.

All my new-found calm dissolved. The priests would be ecstatic if that happened, every bit as arrogant as Adu thought them. Come that day, a pauper-priest like these we passed would probably be turned away from every temple in the city, never mind their fervor.

Another bunch in rags and tatters stood aside for us. I was distracted. Surely prayers, if gods were just, were measured by the hearts that spoke them, not what they were wearing?

Of course our priests were scholars, trying to preserve (or understand?) the Ancients' wisdoms. Worthy callings, but they didn't go without as these males did. How did one balance one against the other? I suppose I could have questioned Albar but I gave it up at that point. That's the trouble with religion; everything sounds simple, then you look again and find it isn't. Thankfully I was a soldier and intended, somehow, to remain one.

Except my soldier's mind began to add up numbers and to wonder where exactly all these ragged priests could muster. Never mind religion, what about logistics? Thersat was a willing source—surprise—and Tull and Hassid were as keen to learn as I was. Funny thing, but fighting males devour stories.

"No, highness, not in the city, they camp inside the meeting of the rivers where the Spring floods leave a wide depression. Once the farmers clear the final harvest they're required by law to leave it barren till the festival is over. For that time the site is counted holy, like the river. Boatmen cross between the camp and our southern gates." Thersat smiled. "The chanting goes on day and night. My father used to take a barge at sunset just to listen…"

Obviously a fond memory. Maybe I'd do the same, for the hell of it. It sounded peaceful. Keril might enjoy it.

Keril had gone quiet. For once I curbed my mount to ride beside him. "D'you know any of these priests?"

"No, my lord." He sounded…

"Tired? It's only days now till we get there."

"Is it, my lord? I am not tired. Riding is no hardship and to see the lands along the way, and all the stars… I never knew such things before."

He was smiling. I could always tell. I found I'd copied him. I thought ahead. I was no beggar-priest nor did I wish to be one. I preferred a decent bath, a bed, the comforts of a city. Though our destination had a mixed attraction, however friendly everyone was acting. A land I'd ridden over only three years since, well-armed and heading into battle? Difficult to like such places. I remembered fallen comrades, death and hatred and destruction more than glory. Here, a day beyond the border, was the crossroads where my troops had hung Sidassi who'd opposed them as a warning, and about a mile ahead there was a ford; its waters had run scarlet with the blood of Kemik who had fought beside me since I was a novice.

When we crossed I saw the Kemik touch their hearts in silent homage to their fallen.

So my mood turned somber and I rode in silence too. That night, Keril massaged aches I hadn't mentioned. When I didn't talk he took a book and sat aside until I called him. Oh, I slept—a soldier learns to—but I woke up early.

On the evening of our second day on Sidass' soil we topped a rise and looked out to the west, across the fertile bowl that circled Thersat's capital, Ossaresh. Dawn would see us riding down these giant, male-made terraces. The ugly city walls beyond, so coarsely angular to modern eyes, rose dusty-blue against the crops and pasture; weirdly striking, even from a distance.

The city stuck up higher than the plain. Father thought the mound a deliberate defensive measure. Well, there was that southern hollow area, the flood plain all these priests were using. Was that where the city's base had come from? Daft idea maybe, but the inner city rose a storey higher than the land around it, and the palace bulged up even higher.

From this distance toy-sized brick and plaster houses, every color you could think of, nestled up against the older, stone-built mansions, and our gold Kadduchi stars replaced those herons on the bone-white temples. Left of those, the gilded, sharply-pointed slopes of Farad's palace roofs reflected waning sunlight.

There was a wind; the city's distant flags and banners flapped and rippled, like a bunch of flowers wrapped in shades of blue, the cobbled ramparts then the river.

Adu reined his mount beside me, Keril, Tull and Hassid close behind us. Albar hadn't found us yet, and nor had Thersat. He and Albar spent a lot of time in conversation these days. Keril thought the prince preferred it that way; that he felt self-conscious riding next to people more attuned to fighting. Being Hainil's eyes and ears, Albar would undoubtedly be willing. Either way it left us free to talk more bluntly.

"Big," huffed Adu. Walls make desert-dwellers edgy.

"Not as big as Kadd, but generations older. That jutting chunk of gold and blue's the palace, obviously, half the size of ours, just spreads more. Crumbling a bit these days but I recall superb glass flooring in its inner chambers and a seamless stone across its oldest courtyards; building secrets we have lost now."

Adu grunted; didn't care for culture, or for buildings.

"Good spot to pick, though, tactically, don't you think? The visibility is good in all directions and the Ossar river runs out of the hills behind then splits—my father says on purpose—so the city is an elongated island. Where the rivers join again must be the flood plain Thersat mentioned. That was rice-fields when we took the city. Looks as if his priests've overflowed it this year." Something like a tented city jammed within the southern angles of the rivers. "Further north." I pointed right instead. "The plain slopes up toward the hills again and there are vineyards."

"Hah." That news pleased Adu.

Hassid wasn't interested in drink yet. "Only the one gate?"

"No, there are four." I figured Keril was listening. And Tull; he'd been here for the war but this time he was in command. "The bridge we're looking at will take us to the Palace Gate, directly to the Inner City. Well-defended by those boxy towers at the gates, see? There's another pair behind them, like a baby fort. A perfect trap. You have to pass through both to reach the streets around the palace."

"To the left the Flood Gate's even more defensive—just around the western corner, closest to the river? That can be deliberately flooded, cutting off the walls to south and west that skirt the palace. So the Flood Gate's half way up the walls and has a sort of drawbridge; more escape hatch than a proper entrance.

"There are two more gates on other sides, with open ground outside they use for slave-and cattle-markets. Those lead to the Outer City, more for common traffic."

Adu looked confused. "Two cities?"

"The Outer City doesn't wrap around the inner one, if that's what you were thinking. It got tagged on later as Ossaresh grew. Now power has shifted south Ossaresh's glory days are over but the silt is very fertile—farmers dredge it up and spread it on the fields—so the city's still a natural trading centre. And of interest to scholars. There's some fascinating early architecture, and the Outer City's crammed with tradesmen, transients, and small bazaars. A rougher neighborhood, but worth a visit."

Adu grunted. Desert males were fierce hagglers.

Tull had turned. Our main force had reached the bottom of the slope behind and started making camp as he had ordered, still unseen from Ossaresh's ramparts. Tactful. Tull showed real promise. Nearer, Thersat's horse was ambling up toward us with its clumsy cargo. Did Thersat realize that Albar, right beside him, emphasized his own ineptness as a rider? Looking at him on a horse, it seemed impossible he'd have the guts to try and kill me.

Mustn't stare. I looked toward Ossaresh. "Pretty colors. Shame about the ugly angles."

Adu gave another grunt but not so disapproving. To the Sais this must look a giant oasis; distant dwellings in a sea of vibrant, cultivated greens that stretched for miles. Well worth fighting for. But Farad's troubles wouldn't have been solved by fighting. His had been a tougher pill to swallow, giving up his independence and his heirs' inheritance for the future welfare of his people.

I made myself sit still and wait for Thersat. He'd be bound to want a look. "A welcome sight," I managed.

Thersat smiled wearily and gazed out at his birthplace, falling quiet for once. Tull left to supervise his males' deployment. More ragged priests made ant-trails on the roads that dipped across the cultivated steps below us, coming in from all directions now.

I had a sudden urge to question Thersat. *Had* those priests in grey come this far south? Would Thersat know of them where Albar hadn't? But I couldn't, not with Keril there behind me; didn't want him worried. And the odds were all against it. Surely. Even Keril didn't know where Keril came from. I would have to pin my hopes on Jaffid.

The camp went up. The sun went down. The breeze from off the plain had shifted, fluttering our banners, raising dust-clouds. Everyone became preoccupied, it would be days before we reached Ossaresh but no doubt the soldiers would be thinking of the joys a city held, for soldiers. Tull was probably considering his duties, and formalities he wouldn't relish any more than I would. Albar still had lots to talk about with Thersat.

That was fine by me. Whatever progress the temples had made up here most Sidassi would still be paying lip service to our gods, probably still worshipping their old ones in private. Influencing Thersat could be useful, and he was probably the only Sidassi royal they had a chance with. If Albar could strike up any sort of friendship… It wouldn't do Albar's prospects any harm either.

Thersat could be wondering about his ailing father. Yes, that figured. When we broke camp next morning he had sent a male ahead, no doubt for news, then sat his horse a while after on the ridge, as if he'd hoped to see some signal. Pointless since his male was nowhere near there yet. There was nothing of significance to see at all, if you discounted yet more ragged priests. The watch reported they'd been passing us all night. It was a cooler walk for them that way, but complicated with a mixed race army. Not every race had perfect eyesight like Kadduchi, and the horses didn't either, so we'd wait and sweat it out in daylight. Not much longer now though.

Chapter 43

Ossaresh: palace, temples, cities, rose above this southern-facing plain where Sidass lost its short-lived war with Kadduchan. The capital itself was hardly dented. On a city this old patches go unnoticed.

Thersat rode beside me, Adu at my scabbard with some thirty Sais as my honor guard behind us. Thersat wore his coat, myself a tunic, city fashion, but the Sais were as always robed and veiled.

Albar wasn't with us. I'd intended to exclude him anyway but he'd forestalled me.

"With your leave, highness, my brothers and I are duty bound to present ourselves at the temple as soon as we arrive."

Report, in other words. I wondered what was too confidential to trust to the temple's own message system. I thought the sharp-eyed priest was also being tactful. Best if I didn't land on Farad's doorstep with Kadduchi priests in tow. Farad had been very polite about pretending to convert to our gods but still, it had to rankle.

Tull would join us once our final camp outside was properly established. Meanwhile he and Medi would have charge of Keril, who could enter more discreetly later.

With Thersat's escort and with Adu's then, I rode beneath the midday sun toward the Palace Gate. I wore a sword but not my armor; not the victor this time but the lawful heir to all before me. Yes, my visit was a risk, but Keril's magic seemed to have discounted Thersat so that risk at least was less than when we started, nothing now I wasn't used to.

The roughcast, bluish walls rose up ahead, their topmost edges crenellated. Ugly, but impressive seen in sunlight, I admitted privately. I forced a compliment. "A fine old city."

"Indeed, Prince Ashamet." But Thersat's smile was feeble too. The day was pleasant, we had reached our destination but it looked like neither of us felt like cheering.

Ashamet, Desert Born

Palace Gate or not, the wooden barriers ahead stood open and a modest crowd poured through, apparently unhindered. No merchandise among the press of people here though, the better-bred and better-dressed who entered this way came on horseback or in curtained litters. Only their attendant slaves would go on foot through this gate. And, apparently, the ragged priests, whose camp, from what I'd seen as we rode past, spread wider than my army's.

I had Thersat and a handful of his own retainers. Thankfully his baggage would be coming later. Adu's riders bunched around us; modest numbers for my first appearance here in peacetime.

Closing on the Palace Gates and with a hundred paces left to go the view was more of priests than townsfolk. No official welcome? Nothing?

I couldn't frown, I wasn't veiled. Adu was, I pictured thunderclouds concealed behind it. Thankfully, before he got around to voicing an opinion Thersat wouldn't like, Sidassi cavalry emerged, full-armored, from beneath the Palace Gateway, rattling across the wooden bridge and fanning out to form an avenue for us to ride down. Three Sidassi officers came on to greet us. Still no nobles?

"Paltry," Adu muttered, but he kept it quiet, mellowed by the fact that Keril wasn't with us.

For once *he'd* tried to argue, but I didn't like him being stared at, nor would Adu. Bad enough we had to be a sideshow.

Farad's captain, reining in, removed his helmet to reveal a graying topknot tied with white and blue and olive, bowing first to me and then the others. He had memorized his speech. I heard him out then let him fall in next to Thersat.

Our escort wheeled. Half rode ahead. Pedestrians ebbed back. We passed the square-built towers—mortared chunks of rock in grey and blue and indigo—and reached the ancient pavements of the Inner City and its Temple Quarter.

We should have ridden four abreast inside as well but the Sidassi horse had no idea how to clear the roadway. Their leading riders tangled with the buzzing crowd before we'd gone a hundred paces. Townsmen moved aside eventually but chanting priests clogged every junction. Obviously it wasn't done to tell a priest to shift his carcass and the priests outnumbered townsmen three to one down here.

Looking harassed, the Sidassi tried to plough some sort of passage, but everywhere was filled to buggery with cheery priestly faces, then to make it worse the townsmen started closing in again, and pointing.

"Highness."

"Prince."

But not at me. "Prince Thersat. Welcome home."

That settled it. The air around me filled with shouts. Excited townsmen surged against the forward movement of the priests, till Adu raised an irritable paw and half the Sais, nothing loath, spurred forward, hands on sword-hilts.

Bodies splayed themselves against the press behind them. Someone shouted. Faces showed the birth of panic. It was chaos, and we'd almost reached a standstill.

Thersat shifted from embarrassed to alarmed, but truth to tell I didn't care a fart they cheered for him not me. In fact their actions said they cared about him, something well worth noting. But this lack of order, when they'd known that we were coming; when the man had even sent a message…

The Sidassi captain spurred ahead at last, one hoped to organize his squadron better. Meanwhile Thersat struggled to control his mount and peer ahead toward the palace, barely visible at this point through the narrow streets and intervening rooftops.

A passage—of a fashion—opened up. The captain joined us. I rode on again, expression neutral, voices naming me by then as well as Thersat. Heads were lowering respectfully at last.

As we approached the decorated gates into the temple courts the numbers doubled, converging like a torrent, pouring through them, always inward. The Sidassi cavalry ahead of us were shouting orders now but they were blithely flouted. Happily the Sais on their tails were enough to part the waters with a look.

I rode in silence as we cleared the bottleneck and passed the temples. Modest welcome from the commoners I could accept, but where were all the local dignitaries? Where was Farad and his nobles? Curse it, we'd just parked an army right outside their city. No display? No music? Priests were given every precedence while princes—one their own—were left to shoulder through the streets like merchants?

Higher up, the narrow streets kept out the sun but not the pestilential ragged priests. They flowed around us, calling heathen blessings. Strangers bid us welcome to the city rather than the males who ruled here?

"Thersat, what in Keshat's name is going on? Is this normal?"

"N-no, Prince Ashamet, it isn't. I really don't—unless my father…" He was visibly concerned.

I damped my temper. Calm, I told myself, these priests are getting to you.

Most of those looked amiably drunk, the way priests often do, but some were patently excited. Priests, all round. I told myself my sword-arm wasn't itching, and I wasn't superstitious. And in any case it wasn't Farad's gods who might have marked me.

Then we turned a corner and a hooded, *grey*-robed priest stepped quickly back. No, not one but five of them, I saw, the little band conspicuous in somber neatness for a moment. And yes, *their* chests bore paler gleaming marks like those on Keril's long-abandoned padded clothing.

One had halted even as the rest were moving from my sight. That male was gaping up, at me. "Hey, you!" I spurred my mount. The others had vanished, swallowed by the mass of ragged priests around us well before I reached the spot. The hindmost turned to run, still open-mouthed, still looking back toward me. Then a meaty hand distinguished by a single heavy ring shot out and pulled him on as well. I'd found them, but they were escaping.

No! I kicked my horse into a canter, focused on those grey-clad bodies, every instinct screaming danger. The single face I'd seen had not expected to be noticed quite so fast, nor recognized? But were they here for Thersat's festival? Or Keril?

Males leapt aside. Let anyone who blocked me scatter. Keril had escaped from them, he wouldn't willingly rejoin them. Would he? And in any case I wouldn't let him!

But they'd gone, and now I'd scared the crowd, and if I loosed the Sais after them the fuss'd cause a panic right across the city. I swore, and forced myself to stop.

"Ash?" called Adu. He and Hassid clattered up to flank me.

"Too many priests," I muttered. I was shaking.

"Well, if King Farad…" Adu left the comment hanging. I didn't argue but I knew. Don't ask me why. Too many priests had come, because of *Keril*.

Crazy notion? Yes, but I was sure. That fleeting confrontation felt significant. Would Keril know more? No. I calmed at last. They'd "told" him to forget, and somehow had the power to make him do so. And he wouldn't choose his former masters. Thank the gods I'd left him safe with Medi.

Nothing I could do right now but play my part in public. Past the temple district the streets were clearer. Finally our escort took control. More townsmen gathered on the streets and in their doorways, bowing. Children ran beside our horses till their fathers called them back. I smiled. Having Thersat here beside me was a demonstration of alliance that should reassure them. I'd been promised the Sidassi had adjusted to their place within the empire, that they were in general contented, but…

These inner streets, the oldest I had ever seen, all ran like wooden rulers, sharply angled at the turns with not a curve in sight. So did these ancient metal gates set deep in sloping blue-grey walls. Farad's cavalry reined in, saluting. We rode on along the tree-lined avenue, past leaning statues, to the courtyard with the strangely buckled, rock-like surface and the graceless square-shaped doorways, one behind the other like a funnel, that gave access to the palace proper.

We dismounted. Finally, a welcoming committee; ten or twelve assorted nobles in their dreary colors led by Farad's vizier, a male as thin as Thersat, almost bald except a wispy beard and even shakier than I remembered.

"Crown Prince Ashamet, allow us to welcome you and your companions. If your highness would be pleased to follow?"

But did this please me? If Farad wasn't well enough to greet me properly then why not Effad in his place? Appalling manners.

Maybe my thoughts leaked. Farad's lords shuffled their feet, their smiles wavered. Ah well. As I've said before, I don't expect to be loved, but this…

Farad's vizier preceded us. His lords fell back to let us through then trailed behind, it looked as if the Sais made them nervous. Good. I wasn't feeling all that friendly either.

Same worn stone corridors I'd strode through three years earlier in armor. Random slaves and servants backed against the walls and knelt or bowed repeatedly. The vizier murmured, "This way, highness," while our booted feet raised hollow echoes. Memory recalled the throne room was the other way, so some less formal meeting was intended.

These innermost corridors were even older, ceilings noticeably lower. Trailing plants and crumbling artwork tried to mask the cracks but Thersat's kin were fighting time back here, and losing.

Adu sniffed. He did the same in Father's palace. That almost made me smile, but there was nothing else to smile at. Looked like Thersat's fears about his father's health had been well-founded. Would I need to represent my father at a funeral now I was here? Hang around to ratify a coronation? Best send word to Father.

How safe was Keril, back in camp, with—

Curse diplomacy, I'd deal with the formalities and hurry back to camp. Sidassi problems weren't my main concern, not now. Those grey-clad priests had changed the situation here. I felt it. I would increase sentries on my tent and search the city.

Another box-like entrance. Servants pushed the creaking doors aside. The hall beyond was tiled too, the floor a checker pattern, black and white. I'd noticed older places often seemed afraid of healthy color. The room was large enough but poorly lit, and bare. The only decorative features were a fretted balcony above, the sort of thing reserved for high-born females to peep down from, and a modest dais lurking at the further end, fenced round with soldiers.

Still stewing over priests, I'd gone too far before I woke. By then the rest were in as well. The doors slammed shut. The dainty screens above slid back. More soldiers glowered down at us, all armed with stubby northern crossbows. We were well and truly cornered.

No windows. Out the way we came? The lords who'd followed us weren't noticeably armed, but clogged the entrance. Were they part of this or not? There weren't enough of them to make a difference either way. In fact a lot of them looked startled. One or two looked… angry?

Then I got it. Some of them had known there'd be an ambush, only not that it would happen here. Not, perhaps, where I could see their faces?

Ashamet, Desert Born

Adu's hand was on his sword-hilt. So was Hassid's.

"Don't," I murmured. Thank the gods they listened, we were trapped like dogs in an arena. We had no armor and no cover.

All right. I headed for the distant dais. My brain—at last—began to function. Hassid's too. He'd dropped behind, anonymous among his tribesmen.

Adu's males took their cue and sauntered with me, spreading out to make a thinner target, veils hiding their expressions. On the dais, safe behind his soldiers…

Effad faced me, fat as ever, wreathed in smiles, and on his brow he wore the jeweled coronet I'd last seen on his father. Effad in his father's seat, his greasy face triumphant.

Save surprise and rage for later. I was more concerned about his two companions, instinct said they were important. Lordly clothes but low-born faces, hair in knots, the fashion east of the Sidassi.

Uncle's bandits? Curse it, that explained their growing boldness. So they'd found themselves a welcome here? And a chance to play at being nobles?

Only that would mean their plot had been in place at least a year, and I'd have sworn that Farad was too proud to make a pact with brigands. Ah, but was it Farad? Had he even known about them?

Effad. Secrets. What if, somehow, Effad had got wind of why his father had agreed so easily to join the empire. And was bent on vengeance.

Shame none of our side—Rag, his spies or even all the priests up here—had spotted this one coming. If they had I'd have been a bit more prepared. But first things first. I raised an eyebrow at that royal circlet. "Prince." I nodded casually. "Or have you been promoted?"

Effad chuckled in that wheezy rattle I remembered, the result of too much liquor. "Oh, my father's still alive. At present."

If he wanted my reaction what he got was Thersat's, whose attention jerked from staring at the males above to Effad's features.

"Father's worse? How bad is…" Then the thin face flushed, the stick-like body stiffened. "Take that off!"

I had to look. No longer vague but fierce?

"Are you giving *orders*, brother?" Effad and sarcasm weren't a good pairing, he was far too heavy-handed. His bushy brows dipped. "Or do you follow someone else's now? What *did* you do with that goblet I gave you?"

Thersat positively stuttered, "You… you said it was from Father. All I did was take it south and hand it over, as you told me. I didn't *do* anything—"

"You didn't need to, anyone who drank from it would—" Effad's mouth thinned. "Except you. Is that it? Did you work it out, and drink the poison? For this?" He waved a hand in my direction. "Gods, to think we're brothers."

Thersat froze. Behind us one of Effad's lords woke up at last, and voiced a feeble protest. "Highness, this is not according to the plan. We all agreed, tonight, after the banq—"

"Why wait?" An irritated Effad waved away his co-conspirators. "Let our enemies go hungry. We will feast without them."

So I'd been right about that goblet, only not the culprit. And Sidassi royals were immune to what had been inside it? Clever move. But Thersat had suspected. When? Not till our banquet? Quite a scare for him; he hadn't dared speak out in public so he'd drunk the largest part and hoped he'd panicked over nothing? Clearly the Sidassi were a lot more accustomed to poisons than we'd ever suspected. I wondered what kind Effad and his cronies had planned for us tonight.

Only Effad hadn't stuck to the arrangement; always had been reckless, I recalled that from the field of battle.

Reckless, or easily led? Behind him, Effad's scruffy allies were exchanging glances. Their expressions… Effad was every bit the fool I'd thought him.

But a very useful fool, I silently conceded; one that could be steered like a horse by someone smarter. Little wonder Uncle Rag had failed to contain his bandit problem. Most annoying that they'd travelled here instead, for me to deal with.

The older bandit bent to Effad's ear. Their puppet heard him out; his mouth curved up again.

"Thersat." Yellow teeth flashed wider. "Time you toddled off to comfort Father. He's been missing you. He'll feel much happier with you beside him."

Thersat paled. "Effad, this is a mistake. The empire is too strong, what can you hope to gain alone except for…."Thersat's gesture was insultingly dismissive of both lords and bandits.

Effad only smirked at him. "What indeed. Go. Join our father." He rose and signaled to his males. "I'm sure Prince Ashamet will cope without you. I will personally show him to *his* quarters." Then he looked toward the lords still hovering about the doorway. "As for you, my lords, I'll see you at the banquet."

I wondered how many of Effad's nobles would find an urgent reason not to be there.

Chapter 44

The Sidassi nobles removed themselves—not without some muttering. We went a different way. I decided to try the reasonable approach. I wasn't optimistic but I felt I ought to give it a go, if only to say I'd tried.

Not a single witness this way; nothing but our footsteps. My males had been disarmed then herded on ahead, with Hassid still anonymous among them. Adu, left with me, kept glancing back at me, eyes flinty-sharp above the veil. He was disarmed as well, and seething.

Effad chose to walk beside me; parody of an attentive host. I noticed he had left his father's crown behind though; wasn't sure enough—not yet—to wear it out in public?

They hadn't claimed my weapons. Privilege of rank, or did he hope I'd try to use them? Maybe not, he hardly looked as if he felt in danger. Of course I could have killed him just as easily without them but I didn't think it was the perfect moment, not with Effad's co-conspirators behind us, all too ready to take over? Although I didn't kid myself that Effad was much better. No, just dumber.

"This really isn't clever, is it?" I said it loud enough that Effad's troops would hear. You never knew. I kept my face amused, and thought of murder. Effad sounded far too cheerful. Why?

The fool obliged me by explaining. "Clever? Oh, I think so. Rid the empire of a prince his soldiers boast is crazy? Whose perversions shock his elders? There'll be public mourning, but in private they'll rejoice you're gone before you ruin the empire."

Ouch. There might have been a grain of truth in that. I shook my head. "I doubt my father will rejoice at treason. Will you really bring the repercussions on your people?" Why was I alive? Was I more valuable as a hostage?

"Oh, your death won't harm Sidassi. Quite the opposite." He'd turned to smile at the bandits, as if they'd share the joke. He'd just said "death". Not hostage then. But how? Did they intend to fake an accident? For thirty Sais?

Effad sounded breathy with excitement. "I'll be there when they inter you, comforting my infant nephew, taking Thersat's place as second father."

Ah, so Thersat was to die as well.

We'd reached the turn onto a narrow stair that fed us into yet another corridor. Down here there were a lot more broken wall-tiles, and uneven flagstones. Up ahead my males were being hustled down another, spiraled stairway. Effad held a hand up to delay us, used the wait to lecture me again. "Reflect upon your sins, Prince Ashamet, before you meet your worthless gods; your life has lasted longer than it ought already. Why, you've only lived this long because we had to have the child anointed, to inherit."

The sounds below diminished and a guard returned. "The stairs are clear, my prince."

A steep descent this time, with Adu in the lead, pushed on by one of Effad's males. Then Effad's captain, practically walking backwards, me, then Effad, stepping carefully, and then the bandits and the few remaining soldiers.

Colder here, and the only light was cube-shaped lamps that swarmed like—

Seven hells! I clean forgot about our plight a moment as I realized this stair had ancient *solars* set into the ceiling, flickering but working.

Pointless planning treasure hunts right now though. I'd better focus on the here and now, and living. We had reached a landing where a single open door revealed a currently deserted guardroom cubbyhole: a bench, a table with a bottle and an empty platter. Hollow thuds below suggested Adu's males were being penned. I ought to keep my mind on business, otherwise, if Effad outlived Father, he'd be Prian's closest kin, this "second father" nonsense.

If he could conceal his guilt that long. Gods knew I couldn't work out how he meant to.

Treading lower, Effad's wheezy boasts acquired a hint of echo. "All we had to do was wait for you to walk into our arms, I said so all along, but when the first trap failed, then the poison didn't work and then you dealt with that assassin…it was unbelievable, the way you kept escaping!"

"Ah." I grinned. "Perhaps the gods don't want me yet." I only wished. "Besides, you're simply not a winner, Effad. Ask your shifty friends." I glanced behind. "I'm sure they think the same. I'd say your usefulness is almost over too."

Perhaps I'd overdone it, Effad's face turned dark with anger, but the younger of the bandits saved me. Baring his uneven teeth he lunged past Effad, dagger shrieking from its steel-edged scabbard.

Luckily he missed the wedge-shaped step. His elder grabbed him from behind to save him, muttering a warning. Interesting. The younger shook his elder off and snapped, "Why wait? Let's get this done with."

"No." A flustered Effad tugged his clothing straight again and blustered, "No, not yet. We were agreed his death should serve a double purpose."

This was crazy verging onto comic. So I laughed. I might as well. "Procrastinating, Effad? Dear me, you lost your kingdom that way." Rash, but goading him might be productive. What "double purpose"? Why "not yet"? What was I missing? Besides, I wasn't going to grovel, certainly not in front of Adu. "Ah," I said, "perhaps you need a drink or two, to give you courage."

But he barked a laugh. "Me? Why should I soil my hands when someone else has waited years to do it?"

I shrugged as if I thought it nonsense. I'd have had me safely dead and buried, not incarcerated. Who in all the hells was "someone"?

"No more talk." The older bandit's words were blatant threat. His comrade grunted, Effad closed his mouth abruptly. We completed the descent in silence.

The solars had been getting dimmer. Now the stair uncurled onto a dismal, passageway with doors both sides. The ancient lamps were mostly dirt-encrusted and inactive. Floor and walls showed glassy orange streaks where grime was thinner, which meant this lowest corridor was very old indeed.

Veiled faces filled two door-grilles, Adu's males, still alive? I read the final insult in the younger bandit's greedy face. Never mind my fate, if any gods were just they'd rue the day they thought they could enslave the Sais. There was hope for them then. That left me and Adu. Thank the gods they'd failed to pick out Hassid. Hassid would avenge us. If he had to.

Hassid's father bowed me through a stunted timber door as regally as if it was my guest apartments. Courtly manners, when he must have felt like screaming.

No grille in this door, but there was a crippled solar here; a light that stuttered. I admit I was relieved; like all Kadduchi I could see in any trace of light, but not in total blackness. We listened to the sound of feet, and Effad laughing. Then we waited, listening.

Quiet reigned. "They've gone back to the landing," I surmised. Adu nodded. Any guards still left would surely pick the guardroom rather than that chilly passage. "At least we have some light."

Bare walls. A solid door. A ceiling that my head was almost touching. The fitful light—however rare and ancient—was the sole amenity they'd left us if you didn't count my sword and dagger. I was still trying to work that one out. *I* wouldn't have left me armed with so much as a toothpick.

There was no furniture, no windows obviously and only one way out, the meager doorway we had ducked beneath to enter. The door's size wasn't the problem, its lock was. No bolt or bar, as often happened. No, a cursed lock. I'd heard the key grate.

"It's not good, you know, cousin," I said, after a moment.

"Hah, still breathing, aren't we?" Adu lowered his veil, the air was closer here. He looked disgusted. Couldn't blame him, I wasn't feeling too hopeful myself. Tull had no cause to be suspicious yet, he'd be too busy. He wouldn't rush to join us—being too damned conscientious. Oh, he'd maybe send to ask about us when he didn't get a message to confirm arrangements—unless of course our gracious host send word back *for* us first. But he wouldn't panic right away, why should he?—It might be another day before he grew suspicious, and by then…

My pocket army was impressive but it wasn't unassailable, on open ground and in a river-valley days from friendly borders. While Effad evidently wanted me alive—for now—that didn't mean he felt the same about my army. Or the horde of hangers-on who travelled with it. All my staff. And Keril. Curse it, what was happening back there?

I've never been afraid before, I thought wildly, not like this. Then I unclenched my jaw and told myself: grow up, do something useful. So I took my dagger and inserted it into the lock. The lock was old and cumbersome, and deeper than the modern sort so I could only get the point inside but even so I thought, or hoped, I felt a tumbler give a little. I applied more pressure. And the damn blade torqued and snapped the point off, crack-ack-ack!

Despite the echo no one came. I fished the point back out but that was it, the broken blade was way too broad to reach the tumblers and the only jewellery I had on was far too flimsy. So was Adu's. So my only option was to sit and save my energy. I can't say I enjoyed it. Nor did Adu. The low point came when Adu laughed and said, "Let's hope those holy males are praying for us."

"What?" I might have snapped a bit.

"I mean, for all the handouts they've been getting. What did you think I meant?" he prodded, frowning.

"Nothing." After that he kept his mouth shut while I brooded, picking at the silks embroidered on my tunic. I had been a perfect fool, and put us all in danger. I hadn't figured Effad as a threat because he didn't measure as a *leader*. I'd completely missed his value as a puppet.

I had put my child in danger too. Or had I? Effad might believe he'd become Prian's guardian, but did he really think my father would allow a weakling such as him to influence the future ruler of our empire, now or later? No. Rag would act as regent first. I felt a fraction better. Effad thought himself a ruler, and a soldier, but he didn't have the brains to take the empire. Hells, I wasn't sure his people wanted him in power *here*, from the way they'd greeted Thersat, and those nobles' faces. If he tried invading other lands he'd fail miserably. The Kemik on their own would eat him! No, whatever happened here, Prian was protected.

But in the shorter term I might not live to learn my lesson. I didn't hold out too much hope of *godly* intervention. So far Keril's deity had been a watcher rather than a doer, though I thanked him fervently that Keril wasn't in here with me. Not that he was that much safer back in camp. Would those grey priests, his former masters, know if Keril was at risk from Effad? I doubted that. They hadn't saved him from the robbers. Or from me.

Ashamet, Desert Born

But this time maybe they were closer. My fingers stilled. Could Keril's priests be the "someone else, who'd waited years"? It was over two years now, since they'd lost Keril.

Keril thought he'd been of little value to them, but he didn't know they'd searched for him. I hadn't told him. I repented that now too.

Too many questions. Too few answers. My thoughts went round in circles: gods above us; priests on one side; Effad and his bandits on the other; Keril somewhere in the middle.

They'd attack the camp. They might be doing it already. Even if they didn't figure who he really was he couldn't fight, to save… his life. Gods help me.

Chapter 45

Hours passed. I figured we were well into the night. I sat like stone. Eventually the flickering light had given me a headache and by my reckoning the sun had risen once again, but no one brought us food, no water even. Were they leaving us to rot? And what was happening outside by now? I tried the door again, a pointless act but I was desperate by then. I laid my hands against the square iron lock-plate, feeling rust flake off around its edges. Maybe it was weaker than it looked? I tried to pry the metal off the wood but it was thicker than it looked, embedded in the timber.

"Curse them all." I drove my fist into the wood above it, hard. I didn't feel it but the impact echoed off the walls and filled my aching head. It made me dizzy. Vision fogged, and all I saw was Keril. Keril...

A grating sound recalled me to my senses. I was leaning, head and hands against the door. My head was spinning and the hidden En-Syn on my arm was itching madly. Curse it, if they once saw that...

Another furtive whimper, somewhere very close.

Adu stirred behind me. "What was that?"

He'd heard it too? I tried to think exactly where I'd hit the door. It wasn't possible. But I could try. As if the timber heard my thoughts the sound repeated.

"Keshat's balls!" My mouth stayed open.

Adu loomed beside me, made demonic by the lighting. "Ash? What is it?"

"Listen!" Another tiny sound; I almost *felt* it. Gods, the key was turning. Had they left it in the lock? But who, or what, would turn it?

Adu leaned toward me, breathing in my ear, a gritty whisper. "Do you have someone planted in the palace?"

"If I did I doubt they'd reach us here," I told him, "and there's no one out there. Look." I pointed at the shifting thread of yellow lamplight showing underneath the door. It wasn't broken; no one on the other side to cast a shadow.

Ashamet, Desert Born

Adu crouched to listen then he shook his head, agreeing. But the lock was turning stealthily, my arm was itching and my head was aching and—

I'd thought of Keril. Focused all my heated thoughts on Keril. Who could "move things".

If that's you, get me out of here before they reach you too. I willed my thoughts to fly beyond these walls, across the plain, to touch his mind. I visualized him sitting in my tent, unveiled. I could almost see him: one knee raised, one hand upon the carpet where a book had fallen—fallen?—from his hand and lay forgotten while the other hand, held out, was stiff with tension. Turning, with a deal of effort. Muscles straining.

"Keril?" I breathed out.

The vision lurched, then narrowed to a pair of wide grey eyes.

The lock squeaked, mouse-like, followed by a snapping click. I shook myself and dug the ruined dagger into the crack along the door frame. "Adu, help!" It moved enough we got our fingers round the edge as well. "Wait, wait." We held our breath; no shouts, no movement. I drew that door toward me gentler than a lover, pulled my sword then stuck my head into the passage.

No guard. I breathed again. No rescuer. I glanced back at the door. No key. The itching on my arm felt warm. I almost didn't mind. Who needed gods when I had Keril?

"Ash?" If Adu frowned he had a right to. I was standing in a dungeon, grinning. Gods knew what he thought.

"All clear," I whispered. Veiled faces stared through grilles. Both locked, but I was game for anything. "Keep watch." I sheathed my sword and handed him my broken dagger, pushed him off toward the stairs then pressed my palms against the lock to Hassid's cell. My head against the door, I thought with all my mind at Keril.

Hassid squinted, trying to see what I was doing. "Hurry, Ash," he muttered.

"Quiet." I was trying to imagine Keril, looking at me. I recalled his perfume, and the smoothness when I stroked—

My arm was hotter. "Yes," I breathed, "come on." I shoved my fingers at the key hole, feeling every detail; anything to help him. Then my vision went again as shooting pains ran down my arms into my fingers, worse than last time.

The lock let out a high-pitched whine, then a throaty scream. I gasped for breath. I felt as if my head was splitting but the door had sagged. "Out." No time to whinge about a little pain. I staggered back as Hassid shoved his fingers through the grille and pushed it out toward me; half our numbers freed and boiling out into the passage but I barely saw. Reality was distant. Was this weakness mine, or Keril's? I was reeling, almost blinded, worse than any drunk awakening I'd ever suffered. But there were still the other captives. "Door," I whispered, trying to focus.

Bony hands—that must be Adu—grabbed me. "This way, my prince. Here, lean on me."

I did as well; no time for ego. "Lock." I felt him guide my hand. Cold metal, pitted. Empty keyhole, rough around the edges. "Here." I concentrated through the pain but nothing happened this time. All I felt was hurt, and dreadful tiredness. Then nothing.

Sound returned. I heard the pad of stealthy feet. Then sight. The door emerged before me, dark and dumb and solid, and the pain inside my head was gone as if it never was. As if it wasn't mine to feel? My arm was cool again; no dream, no hint of perfume. "Lost you, have I? Up to me now, is it?"

"My prince?" said Adu. When I turned his eyes showed panic.

Had I said all that out loud? No time for explanations now. If ever. "We'll have to find the key," I told him, nodding upward.

Did Adu look relieved before he veiled and headed for the stairway?

Hassid tried to stop me but I wanted out, and in a hurry. Adu shrugged and passed my dagger on to Hassid. Hassid blocked me. "I go first," he whispered, dark eyes daring me to argue. I capitulated that far.

Adu's males were halfway up the stairs by then, their backs against the curving inner wall, heads tilted, listening for trouble. We crept past them till the foremost raised two fingers to his veiled lips; two voices, close above us.

"Landing," Hassid breathed. I slid around him. "Ash!" Half protest, half annoyance, muzzled by the need to keep his voice down.

My back against the inner wall, the sword against my chest, I sidestepped higher. Carefully, these curling steps were ample on the outside but they shrank to nothing round the central pillar so my boots were wider than the stone they trod on.

Closer. Definitely two; a tenor, and a deeper grumble. My heart beat steadily again. We had to do this quick and quiet, one slip and those above might call for backup.

Three more steps. I felt their edges like a ridge across my boot sole. I could hear the scrape of feet above me.

"Highness, I got my orders yesterday. They 'aven't altered," said the rougher voice, so close I almost lost my balance on the meager treads.

"You dare refuse to let me pass?"

Thersat, here? I swear my mouth fell open.

"Prince Effad's own orders, highness. No one goes below unless the prince himself is with them." But perhaps the fellow didn't sound so certain any longer?

Nor was I. I held my breath and eased up higher. Nose against the stone, I reached the final turn and had a worm's-eye view of battered boot-heels, grubby cotton trousers and a leather vest. The jailor? Yes, he had a ring of keys suspended from the belt around his ample middle.

No one else? Just Thersat, frowning in the lamplight, dithering as usual.

The jailor spread his hands. "Your pardon, highness, but my orders, they was very clear." The fellow had the power to deny a prince. He loved it.

"Very well," said Thersat, "if I can't persuade you?" Something clinked. The jailor hesitated for a moment then stepped back a pace and shook his head. His fear of Effad evidently beat his love of money. Thersat, shoulders drooping, turned away. All right. That left the jailor.

Light flashed off a narrow blade as Thersat swung, too slow. The jailor stumbled back then looked surprised, he'd got it in the ribs instead. His body folded to the floor but then his head came up again. A croak escaped him.

I leapt forward, sword already swinging. Thersat backed against the wall. The jailor's head rolled past him, through the open door into the guardroom!

Time suspended… Nothing happened. No one in there?

"Thank the gods." By this time Hassid was beside me, tugging at that key ring. Someone else picked up the heavy truncheon the jailor had carried, and removed his sword belt. The keys went down the stairs. The male with Hassid kept the stick and passed the jailor's sword—a sorry weapon—to another.

"Prince Ashamet, are you all right?" Thersat swallowed as I bent and pulled his dagger from the body. Well, well, I thought, he might be squeamish, but he didn't let it stop him. I weighed the dagger in my hand. Then tossed it back at Thersat. "Here. Thanks."

He caught it, just, and breathed out noisily; relief, I figured, that I realized he'd meant to help us. Then he turned away from the body.

"Thersat. Who's above? How many?"

My questions roused him. "Two." He drew another breath and took the stairway. Hassid and his new-armed helpers hurried past in Thersat's shadow. I wiped my blade against the dead male's trousers then I followed, Adu and the rest behind me, edging round the bloody lake across the landing. How high were they? Would the guards above us catch the sickly scent of murder?

They were dead before I got there. Four more males gained weapons; fierce satisfaction warmed the air around me. While our rearguard tossed the bodies down the stairway Hassid waved us on.

But Adu grabbed my shoulder. "How by all the gods did you unlock that door, cub?"

"Later." I pulled free. "Keep moving."

Round a corner. *Nine* of Hassid's males had weapons now. No sign of where they'd got them but Hassid had a reasonable sword and offered me my dagger back. I waved it off. The Crow reclaimed it. It was probably a waste, at his age, but it made me feel a whole lot better that he had it.

"This way. This way." Thersat bolted down a passage and the rest fell in again behind him. I was so surprised I tagged on too. We raced along, then up, along again then up again, feet soft as down in supple desert boots, heads turning constantly to pick up any hostile movement. I was almost at the front again when Thersat shot around a corner then cried out.

An arm across my chest prevented me from racing after. Hassid's. "Look before you leap," he muttered, gripping hard.

But Thersat reappeared. "Clear." A tribesman nodded from behind him. Thersat waved impatiently then started off without us.

Thersat, turned decisive? I was so busy staring at his back I almost fell over the body. Adu's tribesmen swooped; more weapons gathered. Adu signed his males to hide the body in a handy alcove. Others formed a cordon round their prince and chieftain. How far could we get before we were discovered?

Chapter 46

I figured we had crossed the palace, maybe to an outer wing. The sun outside was almost at its highest once again. That meant my reckoning of time below was pretty accurate, and that if no one went down those stairs we had a *lot* of hours yet before they shut the city gates at nightfall. We might make it. If this passage stayed deserted. If—

Another corner. This time Thersat headed for a stairway to our right, and started upward!

"Thersat," I hissed, "we should be going down."

"My father." Thersat hovered on the staircase. "Please, Prince Ashamet."

What could I do? I waved him on. I should have stopped him, I was thinking savagely. I had to reach the camp. If we got trapped up here…

A turning half way up. Sunlight framed an angled archway at the top, cast shadows but I thought I heard a footfall, so I hauled him back and put my mouth against his ear. "How many this time?" Definitely time I gave the orders.

"Two, again," he whispered, "but I drugged them."

Clearly not enough. I signaled. Tribesmen flitted up the last few steps. The sounds above were short and muffled; two more dead and three more males with brighter eyes, inspecting "borrowed" weapons, pulling back as lookouts. But Thersat ran toward the only door. I wasn't close enough to stop him.

We were in a tower. Narrow shafts of sunlight lit a pair of heavy chairs, a table and a single rug. A second stairway, horizontal bars of light and shadow, led us higher.

The second stair came out into a small, bare room, a bedroom now. The meager light up here was little better than my dungeon, one poor window near the ceiling and a single oil lamp beside a curtained bed I thought at first was empty.

"Father?" Thersat leapt toward it.

"Thersat?" said a threadbare voice. My males fell silent.

"Yes. Prince Ashamet is here as well. I got him, Father."

"So I see. It's time for you to go then." Farad's lack of volume made it plain—to me at least—his days were almost over.

Adu signed to Hassid and the males who'd followed to stay back while I stepped forward where the lamp could reach me. "King Farad?"

"Ah, what's left of him."

A king who wouldn't reign much longer. Whatever gods he prayed to secretly, it looked as if he was about to meet them, but he gave a fair approximation of a smile. "Take him with you, highness. You will need him now." He met my eyes. I nodded.

"Father!"

"Don't waste time," the dying male said harshly. "I kept you from your priesthood so I'd have you here if you were needed. Now you are, don't fail your people."

Thersat looked stricken. "Father, I never—"

"You think I ruled because I chose?" The old male wheezed and caught his breath a moment. "I gave my *oath* to the Kadduchi. Effad has disgraced us. Stop him. Do you want a nest of pirates reigning here?" He pulled the signet ring off his finger. "I disown him. *You* are Sidass' heir now."

The old male pushed the ring into the new heir's trembling fingers. "You were such a sickly child, so retiring. I had no choice except to name your brother as my heir, cub. But you grew, and when we were invaded, for a while I even hoped—" The sterner, royal face resurfaced. "I name you heir, my greater son, in front of witnesses. Now choose your allies."

The male ran out of steam and sagged against the pillows. There was that tell-tale wheezing noise again. I figured Effad must have picked a slower-acting poison for his father than he'd painted on that goblet, so he could pretend it was some illness.

Meanwhile there was no point fussing. Farad knew, as I did, that we couldn't move him. "I'll hope to talk more later, sir," I told him gently.

Farad smiled, or tried to. "Talk to my son. He knows as much as I do now." A hand dismissed us.

A brave old male, and my father had been right to trust his oath. A deadly pity we'd discounted Effad, taking him at Farad's measure. Our mistake had surely killed him. I bowed and left, with real regret. The Sais followed. On the stairway Thersat caught us up then led again. His face was tight but he kept quiet.

Three floors lower jumbled noises rose to meet us, like a lot of people. Thersat hesitated.

"That the banquet hall?"

"I think so, yes."

"Let's take a look." I tiptoed forward. Hassid slid behind me, just in front of Thersat. Down one more floor. The noise got louder: shouts, and thumping, laughter, pipes and cymbals. It appeared to be a raucous celebration. In the middle of the morning? Yesterday's, still going? Maybe not the lords but Effad always had been greedy and those bandits wouldn't have the discipline of soldiers either. Yes, they'd likely drink till there was no more wine left in the cellars.

Was this why everywhere was so deserted? Everyone was either sleeping off the night before or *still* carousing? Hm; to celebrate my capture, or did Effad simply want to keep them all together? Effad hadn't worn the crown in public. Because a lord or two was in on it that didn't mean that Effad was as confident as he'd pretended; that he wanted everyone to know what he was up to yet. That could be helpful.

Thersat nudged against me, peering left, around another corner. "It's that way to the stables."

"No." Hassid pulled him back. "We'd be seen at once."

"But you'll be noticed anyway," protested Thersat. "Your clothes tell everyone you don't belong here."

"Only our clothes?" I grinned. "Anywhere nearby where we could pinch some new ones?"

His eyes lit up. "The guardroom?"

Gods, the fool looked *pleased* about it. Quite a transformation, Thersat up to mischief. I could feel a similar reaction from the others; I figured every veil hid a feral grin. "Sounds good to me."

He turned then faltered.

"What?"

A sigh. The head faced forward. "Nothing, my prince. This way."

What's left to tell? The guardroom turned out to be full of soldiers every bit as lax as bandits, left without an officer and clearly not expecting trouble, more engrossed in wine and leftovers they'd liberated from the banquet. One minute they had clothes and weapons, the next… we had them. Now to quit the palace.

From a wash house I surveyed the busy yard beyond, checked that all my "soldiers" had their cheek guards lowered, pulled mine forward too then led them brazenly into the open.

Judging by the meager shadows it was barely past midday now. Here, the palace kitchen gates were open and a pair of guards was arguing, about why they'd been stuck with such a boring, back-door duty while their fellows got the pickings from the banquet.

I commiserated, waving through my soldiers then the "porters" trudging out behind them, loaded up with bundles that obscured their faces.

"Posted to the capital, they said." I shook my head. "A treat, they said. We haven't had a plaguing minute since we got here, now it's bloody armor to be mended. Hurry up, there, or there'll be no food left." Hassid hurried. "Bloody sergeants, eh?" I spat. "So what put you on extra duty?"

"*He* made us late for duty yesterday."

"I didn't, it was your fault!"

"Liar."

"Steady, friends." I cast a look around then dropped my voice. Instinctively they bent in closer. "Have a swig on me, to tide you over."

The bottle hidden in my tunic circulated while the Sais walked on past. When they gave it back—reluctantly—I hefted it and laughed. "What's left in here you might as well hang on to." So I left the palace with their promise of eternal friendship. It was comic, if it wasn't so appalling. I made a mental note we'd better tutor Thersat in security, and discipline, once this was over.

By then Thersat had aimed us at the market district like a homing pigeon. Things looked normal here. No alarm? Did they not know yet? Could we really be that lucky? Don't even think about it, I decided. What dice the gods threw, that was their decision.

Talking of gods, I was painfully aware of all the priests we were passing again. Talk about the wrong place at the wrong time. Albar would be at the temple, basking in the new relationship he'd forged with Thersat. If I'd had the time, and somebody who knew their way around and blended in, I would have sent a warning, but it was too risky. Albar would have to sink or swim with all the rest. I hoped they'd be alert enough to swim against the current.

So we headed for the central market, duller-colored than at home, the aisles roofed with oilcloth, the merchandise less varied. Like all markets it would lead us to an exit though, and there it stood, the Market Gate as Thersat called it rather than the East Gate, every ugly, squared-off angle welcome. Our escape route?

This one, not surprisingly, was better-guarded. Scattering my force around the stalls, I ventured to the outer aisle and looked it over from the shelter of a saddler's stall. Three busy roads turned into it to form a nasty high-walled funnel, at the end of which the studded, bleached-wood gates stood open, shadowed by a pillared warehouse rising on the left and a brick-built gatehouse on the right. I figured that had sleeping quarters on the floor above it.

Travelers arriving from outside got checked but those who left got scant attention, definitely no alarm out yet then. But there were scores of people in that open-fronted warehouse. I could see a road beyond the gates, but twelve armed guards before it and I had to wonder if there was a dozen more on call above them in their quarters. We could take the dozen we could see with ease, but if the crowd jumped in to help them… and we had a mile of open ground to walk to Tull's encampment.

Adu heard me growling in frustration. "What's wrong, my prince?"

The nerve. "I want to pass that gate but I suspect they'll notice," I explained politely.

Sarcasm was lost on Adu. Thersat interrupted anyway. "As palace guards, you would outrank them."

"There's too many of us, and we can't split up. There's only you and me can do a local accent."

"Not if you're escorting me. Except we wouldn't be on foot." A sigh. "We'd ride."

I waited for "I told you so" but he had better manners. Swallowing annoyance—at myself, not Thersat—I produced a smile. "Horses? Is that all? How many guards will they expect?" I issued orders.

Every tribesman carried gold or such concealed about him somewhere. Effad's males had searched for weapons, not in seams, or boot-heels.

While us "guards" sat dicing in a nearby inn, the "trader-tribesmen" who had been our porters tidied up and sauntered smugly off to barter. It took time. I ordered drink. The sun moved lower. We diced, we sweated, but eventually we had as many goods and horses as we needed.

The first batch of Sais—acting as porters again with their heads and backs bent low beneath the sacks and boxes they were loaded with, belonging to the surly pair of desert merchants at their head who naturally didn't speak to strangers—had got past the checkpoint. So far so good. The gates were still open and the sentries still complacent and we still had hours to sunset. The bad: my uniform smelled like a latrine, this tall helmet was damned uncomfortable and I wasn't convinced the red scarf Thersat had fixed to it would fool the gate guard at close quarters, though I'd been impressed how handy Thersat was with disguises.

But Effad could raise the alarm any minute and there was no chance of disguising Thersat, was there, not with his looks, in a city where they obviously knew and loved him, and I figured Thersat was as much a target now as I was.

So the rest of us were trying something that I hoped would make those gate guards hesitate to follow any order Effad sent to stop him.

As his "captain" I had the second best horse and rode on his left, shoulders back, head up, helmet pulled as low as possible, the cheek guards casting shadows. Adu, having peeled off the stolen rubbish he had covered up his desert robes with, and replaced his jewels, rode on Thesat's right. The rest, two "tribesmen" for Adu then the requisite six "soldiers" as a token guard for Thersat, rode in roughly double file behind us. When I looked back the latter were doing a fair job for males who weren't accustomed to straight lines. But I wished Hassid hadn't insisted on playing rearguard.

We rode toward the gates; the sun, behind us now, would cast our faces into shadow, that was something. When was guard-change in those dungeons? Would they suddenly decide to feed us?

Adu got some looks as we approached. I reminded myself he was a desert chieftain and such looks were normal. Then they spotted Thersat, but to my relief it still didn't look like they had orders to detain him. Several looked pleased to see him. All we needed was a few more minutes, but we'd used too many in the market and I knew we didn't have much longer now before our chance of getting Thersat out alive was over.

"Here we go," I muttered.

Thersat straightened in the saddle. I had sent six other males ahead on foot to mingle with the crowd outside the warehouse. Lucky six would hold the exit till we reached it, if they had to.

Thersat spurred ahead. Good move, it hid me from this sergeant. "Good day, sergeant." Somehow Thersat found his usual politeness.

"Highness. Welcome home." The male saluted. I relaxed a fraction.

Thersat played it as I'd told him. "I'm escorting Lord Adu to the camp outside. I'm afraid we'll be returning late, after the gates close." He even smiled. "Will you tell your males to watch for my return?" When the smile drooped I had to hope the male would think it was because he wasn't keen on going.

Guards lined the way, drawn up, eyes forward, still efficient. Whatever rot had eaten at the palace guard, it hadn't filtered down to here yet. Thersat nudged his mount ahead. I waved a hand. We followed at a steady canter, past the guard onto the dusty roadway. I could hear the beat of hooves behind me echoing inside the gateway; growing softer as they passed into the open.

No one was objecting. Was that it? Had thirty males escaped unnoticed? Townsfolk scurried off the road before us. One lad stopped to watch me, looking puzzled. Keep your interfering mouth shut, cub.

A muffled shout.

"Ride on." I risked a look behind. Was Hassid out yet? And our rearguard?

Ashamet, Desert Born

Extra soldiers at the gates. The friendly bunch who'd let us through were crowding round them, open-mouthed, but more importantly my last few males were riding past them while they argued, and the six were striding after. "Shift yourselves," I muttered. I could run for it, but that would give the game away completely. "Steady, Thersat. Come *on*, Hassid."

Then it happened. Guards began to drag the gates together, pushing startled travelers aside to do it. As protests rose the sergeant waved impatiently at Hassid, wanting him *outside* so they could close it. So we didn't get away, we got *evicted*!

Chapter 47

Tull's sentries took a lot more notice of us. Someone must have spotted Thersat, they got word to Tull so fast we hardly had the time to be confronted. Thankfully they didn't spot the "officer" beside him. Mind you, Tull made up for that.

He rode to meet us, clearly anxious. "Prince Thersat? Is there something wrong?" His eyes slid past the prince to scan his less-than-perfect escort, back to Thersat's scruffy-looking captain.

He did a double take. First shock, then horror, then came laughter. Yes, he started laughing at me, no respect toward his betters. "New fashion, Ash?" He pressed a hand against his ribcage.

"And a good day to you too." I spurred my borrowed mount ahead again. I'd kept my voice down. I'd been hoping I could reach my tents unnoticed. Certainly I didn't want to start a panic. "Rouse the sentries."

"Trouble?" Tull swung in close beside me, smile fading. "Why are you—?"

"Farad's out of power, and that idiot Effad staged an ambush when we got there. Don't know if he'll chase us."

"Gods." Tull's mouth was open. Clearly Keril hadn't had a chance to warn them. That fact made me ride on faster.

"Rouse the males but keep it quiet. I'll give you all the details later."

As we passed the Kemik tents that circled mine a smaller figure darted forward only to be snatched away again. Young Ammet tried in vain to free himself as I rode past him. "But!"

"Be quiet," Fychet muttered.

"But that's—"

"He doesn't want it public, Am, that's obvious. Stay out of it? For me?" A sultry voice. I'd never heard the sergeant speak like that, in public. It added something to my memory of that seduction.

Ammet stared, then followed orders so at least I made it to my tents without a fanfare. Tull had been alerted, now some planning was in order. First though…

"Where is he?"

Medi bowed me past my awning, totally ignoring my bizarre appearance. "Inside, my prince."

"Is he all right?"

"I found him— Wait, how did you know?"

"He hasn't said?"

"We couldn't wake him."

"Seven hells." I barreled past the eunuchs at the outer and the inner flaps— both down—and burst into the largest section. Someone sat on watch inside. The heavy insect netting round my sleeping pad was closed. Hand out to pull it back, I hesitated. "Keril?"

No response.

I yanked the gauze aside. He was asleep. At least he looked it.

Medi hovered. "I brought him breakfast, and I'd only left him for a little while, my prince, and there were guards outside, the way you wanted. But he looked unhappy so I called back in. He had been reading, that was all. I found the book beside him."

"Yes, all right," I said, to shut him up. "He hasn't waked at all?"

"Not yet, my prince."

How many hours was it since those locks had opened? "Keril, wake up, curse you."

Movement? Yes, his hand. I bent in closer. "Hey, you?"

The eyelids fluttered. "My… lord?" A blink then full awakening. He struggled to sit up.

I pushed him down again, a clumsy action. "Stay right there. I need to talk to Tull. I'll see you later."

Medi organized me clothes and food while I got moving. Keril might be mostly out of sight but only Tull, at my command, got past my eunuchs. I was stripping off that awful uniform by then while someone ran for water. Medi personally slid inside the nets to take a drink to Keril.

Tull, glancing that way, saw the hazy figure being helped to drink, looked back at me then edged around until his back was firmly set toward them. Perfect manners when he wanted. I pretended not to notice. "How much do you know already?

"Nothing, till we saw you coming." He helped me loosen straps and buckles. "It's all been peaceful. Effad even sent a welcome present, meat and wine—"

"Did anybody taste it?"

"As it happens, no. It seemed a friendly gesture but the cooks had made us breakfast and I didn't fancy—"

"Better burn the lot before some fool gets hungry."

"Gods!" He shot outside again.

My washing water came. I plunged my head into the basin; came up dripping. Medi, back beside me, handed me a towel. Keril was exhausted, nothing worse, I told myself. He'd sounded lucid. I recalled the strain I'd felt, that vanished with the vision. And the pain. I swore and Medi dropped a tunic.

When Tull returned I brought them up to date on Effad and his allies, on their likely plans and our incarceration. Well, except for Keril's intervention.

"We might not have enough males to storm the place but we should be able to deal with an attack out here. I can't see Effad backing down now, not while those two bandits fill his head with daft ideas, so we should assume we're still in trouble."

Medi wanted to rebraid my hair. I let him. Now was not the time to show myself disheveled and it hardly stopped me giving orders.

"Disguise someone as a priest or something and send them to Albar with a warning, and a message for my father. I'll dictate it in a minute. Send another one by horse, in case. And make sure Thersat's safe. If Farad dies—he didn't look to last much longer—he's decreed that Thersat should succeed him."

Pulling on my boots, I let myself imagine Effad on his knees before my father. He had liked old Farad.

"Right, I'm done," I said as Medi thrust my gloves into my hands and waved the rest to scatter. "Medi, Keril stays right here unless I call for him."

Plague on them, those grey-robed priests were out there somewhere. A coincidence, or fellow-plotters? Would they try to interfere? No time. "Set extra guards outside, and tell him… never mind. Tull, let's go. You'd better fill me in on our positions."

When we quit the tent the camp was busy. Thersat, waiting underneath the awning, came at once to join us.

"Highness." Tull bowed but went on walking. "Luckily the males have been recalled already. When the scouts reported dust on the horizon—"

"Where?"

"Approaching from north-west. Of course it could be traders with a herd of cattle, not much else in that direction. I've sent scouts but no one's back yet."

"Glasses."

Tull obliged, but even through those I couldn't make out details, just a lot of dust disturbed.

"Curse the dust. It could be more of Effad's bandits," I said slowly, lowering the glasses, passing them to Thersat. "That could be a nuisance. Let's hedge our bets and send word to my uncle. He's the closest, and he's got a force already mustered if we need it."

"Hmm," said Tull, with masterly restraint. We didn't need a second force against us, even untrained rabble. If it was the bandits, and we moved against them, it would put our backs to Effad. Till we knew the score we'd little choice except to play it safe until we got some backup.

I turned toward my tent again. "It all looks good back here, Tull. Well done. One enemy or two, you'd better warn the cooks to turn out something decent for the males tonight, and serve a liquor ration. We'll know more tomorrow. Thersat, Tull will see you well-protected. Get some rest, I doubt you've had more sleep than I have, and I'll see you in the morning. Tull, I'm going to my tent a while. Send word if anything develops in the meantime?"

He had stayed behind the netting but was sitting up and obviously waiting. When I walked back in he rose, then hesitated.

"Come on out." I'd sent the eunuchs off as I came past. Keril came out looking like he'd had a good night's sleep. Bright-eyed. I smothered envy. "You recovered?"

"Yes, my lord. Did everyone…?"

"They all got out." I threw myself onto a cushion. "You heard?"

Keril poured me wine. "Prince Effad." Not so cheerful.

"I walked right into it." I took a gulp of wine. "If— Keril, how in Keshat's name…?"

"I felt your anger, like a wave of heat. It washed right through me and I found…" He frowned. "I… was inside you? I could see what you did. Feel it. So I tried to move the tumblers."

My tongue ran off with me. "I saw you too, a picture of you in my head, your hand…" I twisted mine in demonstration.

Keril's eyes went wider. "Yes."

"How badly did it hurt you?"

"Not much, my lord." He glanced away.

"You'll never make a liar, will you?" I could smile at last.

His head came round. I'd somehow reassured him. "But I do feel stronger now." His eyes met mine. I think my lips had parted. There was a new determination there. A new assurance.

Shortly after Adu, looking spry again, brought Hassid for a very tardy midday meal, trailed by Tull then Thersat. Keril, veiled, sat quietly behind them. Tull spoke first.

"The scouts are back. They saw no banners but the force is moving fast. They estimate a thousand foot behind at least a thousand horses." Everyone was watching my reaction.

That on top of what was in the city? Little chance that they'd be friendly. "We're in trouble. Looks like Effad's bringing up reserves."

Old Adu muttered curses. Hassid went on eating. Tull's frown deepened. Didn't blame him; some promotion.

"Where are they now?" I stood. They followed me outside.

"A day at least, north-west of us, they're hidden now beyond the city."

We called for horses, Keril's too, and went to look at the terrain we'd have to fight on.

Tull waved a hand. "The river here makes a good defense, if we cross there…"

"But that's the flood plain." Thersat looked aghast. "A place of sanctuary."

I shook my head. "Not any more. If those priests have a grain of sense they'll leave right now. Tull, send to warn them, will you? Commandeer those boats as well." I looked at Thersat's face. "Unless they're carrying priests," I added. Thersat looked relieved. Less than a day to deal with everything. "How deep's the river, Thersat? Could their forces cross on foot, or horseback?"

"Both probably," he told us grimly.

"So they'll try." I gazed across the river. "If we could pick them off while they were still in the water…"

Except while we were doing that we'd have our flank toward the city. We had nowhere to retreat to, either. What we needed was a circle. What we needed was a bigger bloody army. "Attack then fall back here," I said. "That's all we have. Send out more scouts, give word to issue what rations we have, strike what tents we can and move them south of us to take the wounded. It'll likely be tomorrow."

Preparations took till early evening. At least this second force was out of range, still out of sight behind the north side of the city. I was dog-tired by then. I'd ordered Keril off an hour earlier and knew I had to rest as well, I'd spent one night awake already. So I left the scraps for Tull and Hassid, Adu having used his head and gone already.

"Keril?" I asked Medishel as he came out to meet me.

"Inside, my prince. He nodded off, I'll wake him."

"No, leave him." I delivered final, grim-faced orders. "Got all that? I'll leave you to arrange it. Quickly, now, by nightfall."

"Very well, my prince. I—I have your armor ready, and your blades are oiled. Would you care to take an axe as well?" By then his voice had steadied.

"Good male." I clapped him on the shoulder as I passed him, pulling off my gloves and ducking through the tent flaps. "Tell someone to wake me up for supper. If no one else does in between times."

What I wanted most was time with Keril, but I *had* to sleep or I'd be no use to my army. I would lie down at his side and rest, but only for an hour or two, till supper.

Chapter 48

Hassid didn't let me have an hour, even, bending over me as I was sleeping. Almost got my dagger in his stomach only Keril woke in time and caught my hand. I cursed. I'd hardly closed my eyes. I felt befuddled and my eyes were gritty. Damn the male, it wasn't even dusk yet!

"Ash?" He stumbled back then found his balance. "That second army has already crossed the river, while the city hid them. Now they're circling east. We missed the move till they were turning south again toward us." He was trying not to stare at Keril.

Blind-sided, by a bunch of bandits? Twice that made it. "Seven hells." I shook my head to clear it. Or— could it be those greys of Keril's, planning for them? After all I still had no idea who they really were or who they were involved with, whether they were enemies, neutral in this, or even allies.

"Ash, you'd better come," said Hassid. I could only nod and follow.

Our latest enemy was, what, two miles away, and making camp by what was left of daylight. Blatant. Lighting cook-fires, making noise. I borrowed Hassid's glasses this time.

It looked to be a mongrel force, a mix of uniforms and motley. More Sidassi soldiers then, and bandits, as I'd figured? But our scouts had under-estimated. There must be at least three thousand? Yes, far more infantry than guessed at in the dust while they were moving.

The bandit forces milling round the edges masked the more cohesive forces at their centre, hard to see…

"Those are Kadduchi colors!" I said harshly. "Not Sidassi."

Hassid swore. Tull muttered, "Surely not," then trailed off.

Kadduchi traitors come against us. Gods but I was angry. I was blazing. Then I saw it, rising up above their tents; a *royal* battle standard, red and gold against its sky-blue background. Who in seven hells would have a royal standard, and Kadduchi forces, up here in the north? And then I saw it all. Our hollow three-point star identified the leader allied with the bandits. Who had always "failed" to remove them. And I saw what Effad found so funny.

Adu came. His son stepped back to give him room and gestured wordlessly. On cue, the distant banner caught the wind and opened.

I felt wooden. "What do you see, cousin?"

"I see a battle," said the old male grimly.

"Do you see who leads them?"

"Yes, my prince." His voice was gentle.

"Will you— Can you send word, then, to my father? I don't know how…" I lost my voice at that point.

"There are no decent words, but I will send the best I can, my prince."

The Crow was sorry. Well, I wasn't. I was going to kill them.

"Ash, you should go back and rest, before…" said Hassid.

I almost laughed. I nodded though and walked away with him. We'd asked for reinforcements. They'd arrived, but not to help us.

"Thank the gods there are no Kemik with them," Hassid offered.

"Kemik die before they break a promise. Like the Sais. Both believe pigheaded is another word for loyal," I joked, half-smiling. Hassid smiled too, but mine had faded by the time I left him. And I wasn't looking forward to the morning.

Keril was awake as well, inside my tent. This time he started giving orders—which were all obeyed. It should have been amusing but I, who always saw the funny side of things, had somehow lost my sense of humour.

I did as Keril wanted too. I bathed and donned a robe. I took some fruit and washed it down with brandy. Keril ordered no more interruptions and the slaves, and Medi too, departed. Keril turned the lamps down. Make the most of it, I thought as quiet fell around us. There would be no more such evenings, and for sure no peace tomorrow.

Keril's hands, behind me, pulled aside the robe and stroked my neck and shoulders, forcing tensed-up muscles to relax and loosen. "My lord, you need to rest. Tomorrow we will deal with your uncle."

So he'd heard then.

"Only first there's something *I* should do. But it will hurt." His hands stopped moving. When I twisted round I found him reaching for my armlet.

"Keril?"

He ignored me, pulling at the catch. The yellow star was hardly visible by lamplight. Worse than useless.

"This should be brighter, shouldn't it? I've seen it so." A shaky breath. "But I can make it… everything it should be."

"You." My stomach lurched. As if I hadn't had enough surprises. "You did this, from the start?"

"I think I may have, yes, although I didn't know it. I didn't understand till now but once, before I ever came to you, I *saw* this shape, the way I saw the lock. I think, perhaps, I saw it, so it happened."

That silly cage. The husky voice that said "I saw" before he swayed and almost fainted. Greater gods, at last I had an explanation. Someone I could blame. And then I realized what he was saying. "You're suggesting you should finish it."

"Yes, my lord, because tomorrow…"

I would lead my males into battle, heavily outnumbered, but an En-Syn, real as any that had gone before it… I licked my lips. "I can't pretend I'm equal to my father."

"No, my lord. The En-Syn?"

He understood? I swallowed. "Do it."

Silently he poured another brandy; held it out. I drank it down in one. He grasped my sword arm, at the elbow. Closed his eyes and laid his other hand above it.

Gods, it hurt all right. I couldn't watch. I don't suppose it took him long but time went hazy. Afterwards my head ached and my arm…

When he was finished I was too, but hands, then lips, were at my neck and shoulders as I fell into oblivion.

Chapter 49

When I woke up this time all was quiet. Keril wasn't there, but had been not much earlier; his warmth, and scent, still lapped around me. My arm still burned but I ignored it, laying back, my head against a pillow. Did I feel more confident? I felt determined, especially when Keril brought my supper, keeping others off a moment longer. "Good, you're dressed. You eaten?"

"Yes, my lord. It's late, I think you are the last." He turned to fetch my tea.

"Leave that. I've got another job for you."

He turned to face me, very still now. "Are you sending me away?"

He'd always been too sharp. "No argument. You're going. It's arranged. Tonight."

A silence.

"Do you hear me?" I said loudly.

"Yes, my lord." But still he stood there.

"Keril—" I tried again. "You've given me an edge but now I'm better off without you. You'd be useless in the press of battle—you'd be dead in moments, and you know that—and I, I don't want to have you on my mind right now. You understand?"

"My lord has other things to deal with, more important. I shall go. Of course." He tried to smile.

"Good." We stood and looked at one another. He was waiting to be dismissed, and I was wasting precious moments. I strode across and pulled him to me, kissed him once then pushed him off toward the entrance. "Now find Medi and get out of here," I told him roughly. I was a prince, the leader of an army. More now; I was their figurehead. Their faith. There wasn't time for weakness. No, it was a day for lying, for pretending. Shame I didn't have the High Priests here to back me up with smoke and mirrors.

Once Keril veiled and left I ate what he had brought, alone, then sat and waited. Night fell. That meant Medi should be ready, only waiting for the colder air to make those sentries fonder of their campfires.

Was that, did I hear— I made myself sit down again. I couldn't risk their safety being spotted out there with them. Sometime later I resigned myself to sleep, as soldiers should. My bed felt cold though. Very lonely.

Morning came at last, with bells and chants to wake me up instead of Medi. Less familiar faces at my bedside but I drank, and ate, and washed, at which point I was forced to show my arm and those still in my tent went quiet then flung themselves onto the carpets. Right. So it had started.

I got dressed. I got my breath, and nerve. I waited for a moment then I went outside and watched my soldiers falling to their knees, and heard the shouts as word spread outward. That day I prepared for battle in the open, underneath the awning with an ever-changing crowd for witness. Males came forward with my armor; almost fearful. "Cut the sleeve away," I said as someone went to shove my padded, mailed tunic down across my shoulders.

"Yes, my prince!"

The En-Syn, briefly hidden, reappeared in all its startling glory. Faces that had come here grim and strained were smiling, hope rekindled. Faith was burning in them now, as hot and fierce as the golden wire that bit into my flesh; real gold, the wired shape he'd conjured from my armlet. There it was, the En-Syn; promise of an even greater glory after. Proof to them that they could win this battle for me, that we had the gods on our side.

Did we? Could the gods have sent me Keril?

No, it wasn't gods he'd fled but males, and now I'd never know the answer. I sat when someone else held out my plated boots. I stood again as soon as they were done, to let them fasten on the body armor. Everything was going smoothly. Tull was there by then, wide-eyed like all the rest. Not Medi, who was gone with Keril.

Medi too had argued. "I have the thirty males of your staff, my prince, but some of us lack weapons. Will you give us leave to find some?"

He had wanted to be armed and stand behind me? I hoped I'd managed not to show amazement, or suggest I'd ever doubted either loyalty or courage. "No," I'd told him, "take half your people, weapons if you choose, but take my loyal greetings to my father then take over Prian's safety. If I fail, tell my father you will be the steward of my heir until he is an adult. And take Keril with you."

I'd told Medi they had better use disguises. Priests or eunuchs, I'd suggested. Maybe lesser merchants would be even better, they'd be just as keen to get away before the battle. All non-combatants.

Ashamet, Desert Born

As long as such left quietly my uncle's soldiers wouldn't harm them, as a point of honor. I was betting guilt would make them curb the bandits. Even so, I didn't fancy Medi's chances if they recognized him. Rag might—rightly—view both him and Keril as potentially valuable, as pawns against me, never mind that Medi had been serving him with wine as long as I'd been drinking.

But, disguised... I'd hope, no, I'd believe, they had escaped. I doubted I would, but I'd sworn to take my uncle with me.

Chapter 50

We stood upon the rise that stopped the waters from the flood plain spreading eastward. At our backs, our army mustered. Arms and armor clanked, excited horses fought their handlers, officers gave stern-voiced orders. Rag was north of us, about a mile out from the city. Leaving room for greedy, stupid, soon-not-needed Effad to emerge and plug the gap beside him?

Enemies to north and west. The river almost south. Beyond its banks, the priest-filled gap that pointed back to Kadduchan was like an invitation; one I figured Rag had written. Yes, he'd love it if we turned our backs on him. Retreat, on open ground, and through civilians? To borders Rag controlled?? We'd be dead before we got that far and half these priests down with us. I stood with Tull and looked at them in silence.

"Wish those priests were infantry," Tull muttered, then shut up. We had a scant few hundred foot, and most of them were eunuch-guard who hadn't left or servants who had caught religion when they saw the En-Syn.

I still felt calm, which had surprised me somewhat though I'd looked at death too many times by now to run around and panic. And of course I'd sent away the only weakness that might rob me of whatever courage usually took me into battle.

Adu's courage was another matter. No, he wasn't going back to "help" my father. Dire insult, to suggest a desert chief retire from a fight. He walked the slope to join us now, his gold and gems declaring he was dressed for battle.

I gestured at our new opponent. "Will he stand, or come against us?"

The old male spat. "He is too old to fall for that one."

I agreed. Attack his enemy while we had even slightly higher ground, the river like a wall behind us? Rag did know better. So, should we go to him, and lose advantage, or sit and wait for *loyal* reinforcements? Trouble was my messengers might not have made it. Best not to count on outside help then. Which meant this could be over by the time my father heard about it.

Medi would be almost certain to escape unhindered to the border. Gods, I hated "almosts". He had planned to travel as a lesser eunuch in attendance on a minor merchant keen to flee before the battle—nothing seriously tempting. He had found a burly cook to play the master's part. The male, he'd said, "was handy with a knife but was too fat and slow to make much difference in the battle" though "he'd fit quite well in some of Medi's plainer cast-offs".

Keril? "Suitably but inexpensively attired, of course, my prince" would travel in a covered cart, become the merchant's only son laid low by sickness—possibly contagious. I'd admired the invention. They'd meet sneers perhaps, but surely not aggression. Hells, they might get sympathy. They'd make direct for Kadduchan as soon as they were out of danger, but it would take them days to reach a friendly border.

Which left my only real decision: wait or start the battle off ourselves? No contest. We couldn't stand here long enough to change the odds. The city's gates were closed against us. Sentries walked the ramparts. Was Effad sitting tight and waiting? Once I moved, those gates we watched would open wide to let his army take the field too.

I surveyed the ground again. We had, effectively, a square. Unevenly proportioned but there were four "sides", four shaky compass points. To the west I had the city; no doubt Effad's army would deploy before it. Then the—call them rebels. I found I couldn't, even now, speak calmly if I named him—made a second, northern side, wide-angled from it. The third side was this rise—this shallow step I stood on—almost parallel to Effad's walls, a final vestige of our gradual descent from hill to plain to get here. The fourth and smallest side was where the rivers met and widened. On its further bank a seething mass of tents and bodies still remained. A good three quarters of the ragged priests had spurned our warning.

I regretted the priests. I hoped, distantly, they would get clear. But I needed that wide river and the bank this side. With that to guard our southern flank we maybe had a chance. A small one.

Turning to the south I could believe I saw a hint of dust that might be Medishel's departure, very distant, blending with the banks of dull grey cloud beyond him. I'd believe he'd been allowed to flee unhindered, as I'd wanted, that by nightfall he'd be out of sight and sound of battle so he wouldn't know…

I shut away such thoughts and put my mind to being En-Syn; starting down the slope to where my army waited with my fierce Kemik at its centre. Ammet, swamped in someone else's mailed tunic—he had even found a sword—brought up my horse, by this time also armored, doubly lethal with that pretty horn encased in knife-sharp metal.

The lad was young to die. I looked along the line, where only second mounts remained, and gave him one last order. "Saddle the black with something plain, pick out a spare of mine to ride yourself, then coat them both with dirt to cover up their worth, cut through the priests and round to follow master Medishel," I said abruptly. "He'll know how to use it." If Keril had the black… That stallion would defend its rider to the death, and it was fast as lightning. Then I called him back. "Tell someone at my tent to bundle up a set of Keril's robes and take those too." Yes, Keril would feel better covered up again once they were out of danger.

Midday came. The scudding clouds were passing overhead by then, the day had turned into a sweating furnace. There was a grumbling of distant thunder; no rain yet but surely it was coming. On the field, neither side had moved an inch, except for single riders scurrying between the city and the rebels. Messages exchanged, for what? Why wait? To sap our courage?

The sun stayed mostly hidden but its rays, when they broke through, grew lower as the day waned; it was growing slightly cooler, animals grew restive. Like their riders they'd been keyed for battle. Feeling the frustration, Tull had males stood down to eat in batches; lookouts kept alert and scouts sent out to check for ambush, generally keeping people active. He'd have been a good commander.

Waiting wasn't in my nature either but if it was useful… Not today after all, they meant to sit there till tomorrow? Rag was holding off but I was cursed if I could see his reason, and those bandits lacked the discipline to be behind it.

Nothing happened worth remarking on till evening. I ate too. It felt unnatural. Other males were quiet and the light was fading. Then I saw a blacker dot against the sullen sky; a single bird beat steadily toward us, from the south. A single bird, and high, but not a raptor. I'd been watching them and they were gathering to north of us, beyond the city. Nothing here yet to feed on.

"Seven hells." For once the Sais had left their hawks down south, with mine. I stood and pointed urgently. "A gold piece to the archer who can down that bird if it comes closer!" Males turned, bows lifted as the dot came on toward the city, but too high. "It might come lower. Wait."

We never got a shot. The blasted bird flew wide of us to swoop across their western ramparts. Handy for the palace, that. A short while later yet another rider quit Ossaresh with another message for my uncle. I had no idea what was in it but I sensed the wait was over. Dawn tomorrow?

In the failing light I ordered every bit of harness muffled, armor too. I threatened death to anyone who made a sound, forget the gods' reward for death in battle. Maybe they believed me. Maybe they believed an En-Syn gave me power to kill them with a look. No matter. Under dark and cloud I risked our flank for long enough to shift position. The Kadduchi forces would still make us out but maybe Effad's wouldn't, lacking the superior Kadduchi eyesight; any little thing was helpful, and we didn't want Sidassi archers firing on us from the ramparts. And in any case the horses liked it better.

Ashamet, Desert Born

A reddened sunrise found us closer to the city, massed and ready. Well, as ready as we ever would be. It was risky, but I'd posted archers—good ones—to deter Sidassi snipers on the ramparts, shrinking their advantage. This way the Sidassi would have trouble, when they did come out, outflanking us along the city walls. If they came at us from around the western side instead—at least we'd see them coming.

The battlefield had become a triangle, the flood plain more behind us. We were still supplied with water and the helpless priests were at our backs, a buffer at our rear but less a target. We'd also spread along the bank to where a narrow rope-bridge slung across the thinnest point was now the only crossing. Tull had gone to warn the priests to flee once more, their final chance, and I was riding down, with Hassid and his father at my side, to see the bridge was broken, after which they'd leave to lead the Sais into battle. No chance I could blend the Sais with my soldiers. They'd be more effective independent.

Tull sat his mount on this side of the flimsy bridge. "Ash! My prince." Tull turned and glared. "These priests are crazy. Look at them. They just won't listen!"

The bridge and all the bank beyond was lined with priests, their multi-colored rags and hand-me-downs an almost cheerful sight against the leaden clouds above us. As far as I could see—and I had looked—there was no grey among them. But they'd packed so close I couldn't tell for certain. More bizarre, they stood there chatting to each other, smiling at us.

"Push them back," I told him. "Chase them off before they hamper our deployment."

"Right." Tull looked relieved. Perhaps they made him nervous too. You never knew what priests—

As if they'd heard my thoughts they started moving, only not away. Oh no, a tide of bodies swallowed up our meager guard this end the bridge and walked, entirely calm about it, out onto the field of battle.

"What in all the hells?" Tull stopped himself. "Your pardon, highness." Much more formal since the En-Syn had "appeared". He assumed I'd had it all the time, that I had merely hidden it beneath the armlet. Probably they all did.

Hassid, not so insecure, began to laugh. "Hey, Ash, it looks as if your infantry's arriving."

"Blood and—" I fell silent too. Tull looked to me for answers but I had none. We stood there like a pack of idiots and tried to fathom what these greater fools were up to. It looked like every one of them still here was coming over. Definitely none in grey, I noted. Were the foreigners inside the city still?

With Effad? Run for cover? Every other color though, and some... in organized... battalions? "Keshat's balls, they're under orders. So who leads them?"

"No one I can see from here." Tull peered forward. "But... they can't be infantry."

Hassid laughed again. "I doubt they're begging." This time Adu joined him. "Or are they?" He frowned. I realized why a second later. Priests were mostly heading for our lines but one lot, mainly older—less cohesive but at least three hundred strong—were veering left, toward the city.

"Where do they think they're going?" Adu muttered.

"Shelter, maybe?" Tull responded.

"No, I don't believe it," was my instant answer. Seven hells, I thought, I'll never trust a priest again, whatever color.

As they neared the walls, those old priests started singing.

Chapter 51

The chanting floated back to us; slow rhythms, very solemn, clearly launched toward the city.

"Thersat, do you understand it?"

He had paled. Now he swallowed. "It's a song of death, a summons to repentance. It names the hells a male may be condemned to for the crimes he has committed. They are warning those inside the walls to seek an upward path, lest we receive a judgment worse than we deserve already."

The mournful song continued. Heads bobbed up above the ramparts then, one by one, receded till the walls looked empty; but the singing rose, to a crescendo.

Then it stopped, and left behind a world of rising wind and restless horses, where the sky seemed darker, and those old priests knelt, so close below those walls the town's defenders could have thrown hot oil upon them if they'd wanted. But they didn't. I realized my arm was itching. I suspected these old males were praying, though I couldn't hear them. More importantly those walls remained deserted, not a sign of archers.

So I watched the gates instead. Diagonally to my left the Palace Gate had quivered, muted sounds said distant bolts were being dragged aside. The massive timbers creaked then slowly parted. Here it came. The beggar-priests had done their best to warn them off but Rag would have his allies.

Blue and white Sidassi royal cavalry were in the lead, a dashing force five hundred strong, that square-shaped heron banner waving in defiance. They had horse-drums in their midst; a solid rumbling beat to speed the pulse and stir the stomach. Infantry marched out behind a thousand strong, then horse again and then a trilling fanfare, higher than Kadduchi horns, announced their prince was coming out in style.

Narrow-eyed, I peered through my glasses for his standard, which should surely—

Yes, he'd used the heron, crowned and startlingly white against its blue-green background. Effad rode beneath it, armored now, bare-headed still, like me, but he wore his father's crown for all to witness. A gathering of similarly gaudy lords surrounded him.

Thersat swore, surprising me. I hadn't heard him join us. He too had found some armor. "This time," he had blurted out the night before, "my father *can't* forbid me." Seemed I'd *seriously* underestimated Thersat.

I swung the glasses. Effad's bandit-lords, at Effad's back, had taken armor too and looked to have their own males in attendance. Quite a party, though the bandits' faces were much grimmer than the fools they'd cozened.

Still no sign of anyone in grey. Had I imagined them? Were they or were they not in league with Effad? If not, had they fled, or were they hiding? Would I ever know the answers?

Effad waved toward our rise and laughed. I saw the way he turned to speak to those behind him and the way his nobles smiled. Supremely confident. But confidence could kill, and if the gods were kind they'd let me prove it.

His cavalry had peeled off to form an armored fence before the city, infantry before them. Interesting. Not exactly an attack formation. But all three armies were in play. Four if you counted all these priests, apparently our allies. We had Sidassi to our left, the kneeling priests a suicidal token barrier between us. Right of that was Rag, his standards almost all from northern companies, as I had guessed, then furthest right the bandits in a shouting, jostling muddle. It was hard to tell if they were yelling at us, or at each other. I swallowed nausea. There was no possibility of doubt; my uncle was a traitor, fighting side by side with bandits he was sworn to vanquish.

But the bandits' real chiefs had stayed with Effad? At his back. I found I'd smiled. Perhaps I wouldn't have to deal with Effad. Though the way his brother glared at him those bandits might have competition.

Hassid interrupted. "Highness, we have priests approaching." Even he was getting formal.

"Let 'em through." As if there was much choice, a mob of them were weaving through the crowd toward us, smiling affably, as if this was a gods-cursed party and they'd been invited. When they reached my group they gathered round untidily. At least they bowed. I held my tongue and waited.

"Welcome, southern prince. My name is Arker." A slurring northern accent and another beaming smile. The spokesman, surely older than my father, wore a northern knee length coat of faded browns and greens, and sturdy boots. Presentable enough but hardly chosen to impress me.

Except it wasn't me he'd come here to impress.

He raised his voice. "And welcome, all. This day is truly blessed." My males glanced toward the En-Syn. Arker didn't. "Portents promised us a sign this festival," the priest went on. His arm swept out. "Two days ago our prophets said they'd felt a power spread across the land like morning sun across the desert, heralding a time we had been promised." Finally he deigned to look at me again. "A power they tell us touches you, his champion, and so we come, to aid you."

Power, spread across… Two days ago. When Keril freed me. They had known? My own males didn't even know, except for Adu. Who, gods blast the male, had clearly shared his slant on it with Hassid. Both were staring at the En-Syn.

Never mind that now. "He's gone. As you should go," I told the priest. "I sent him off to safety."

Adu looked confused but Hassid's mouth fell open.

Arker grinned. His teeth were white, and even, not so old then. "Gone? Our angel watches over us, to see that we are worthy. Look." He pointed south.

What now, and what the devil was an "ain-gel"? I turned, and froze. About a mile off a white-clad figure sat an equine thundercloud upon a wind-blown ridge, as if suspended in the baleful sky beyond him. Another, smaller rider was behind him. Ammet, on my order, had delivered him the very mount he'd needed to escape from Medi.

He would watch me die. Perhaps he'd feel it. Thank the gods, at least he wasn't coming back, but then I'd ordered him away and Keril never disobeyed me, did he? Pity I had failed to specify his destination.

I dragged my thoughts and my attention back where it belonged. "Yes, well, I applaud your courage, brothers, but you're priests. You can't—"

"Can't fight?" His comrades—half of them no younger—shared his sunny smile. "We are tougher than your southern priests, and some of us have trained from our initiation hoping for this moment. We are here to fulfill a prophecy, with your assistance or without you."

At my elbow Adu's shoulders shook with silent laughter. "Give me holy beggars any day!" he murmured, yellow eyes gone brighter.

I inclined my head, defeated. I would copy Rag and lead a makeshift army. I would take what fate, and Keril, had unwittingly provided.

Tull was looking out across the field, I realized our enemies were spreading. That royal star had moved into the centre of the rebels' line where Rag, like all Kadduchi leaders, had to be. My stomach, usually fine in battle, heaved. I thought about the look on Keril's face, the night he'd felt betrayed. Well, now I knew exactly what he'd felt like. Would he feel the same when I was slaughtered? And my followers, who trusted in the En-Syn? There would be no ring of fire this time.

Across the field a bugle brayed. The rebel infantry began to march into position to their lighter drumbeat. Effad's lines edged forward too. High time I turned my back on priests, and on despair, and went out fighting.

My Kemik guard replaced the Sais, who would take our right against the bandits, little caring if they'd be outnumbered. Tull, with Thersat, had our left, and Effad. Leaving me the centre, opposite my uncle.

Fychet's face revealed he knew I'd sent his novice-lover from the field. The male appeared right behind me, fierce and determined. Kemik faces—others too—exulted in the prospect of a battle where—my arm assured them—victory was certain even if they died to win it. And my arm was itching, and I hated how they stared at it, with awe, and hunger.

"Let's go." I nudged my mount into a steady walk. A single horn gave voice. My cavalry moved off, with priests ridiculous between them, singing. Horns and drums and Kemik battle cymbals came to life behind us, till the air vibrated.

The priestly chanting wasn't only in our ranks. The priests below the city walls stood up and sang again to Effad's forces. Their aged feet were planted; none were leaving. They'd be trampled. How could any male stand still and wait to die like that? I shook my head and held a hand out. Fychet passed my helm. My view was broken by the grid-like strips of metal but my head and neck were now protected.

Doubtless to the rest my missing sleeve appeared to be my best protection, not a naked upper arm at all but armored with the Synia the gods had set on me. Ironic that I had to wonder, now, if all these ragged priests knew more than I did? Keril's "power" had marked *me* out to them? Perhaps I really was protected. Gods above!

All right then, I'd believe it too.

I cleared my forward troops and broke into a canter. Horns blared out and horses snorted their impatience. Harness rattled as a thousand weapons rasped from their assorted scabbards, banners flapped against the rising wind. The clouds were inky black by then, their edges ragged in a wind now veered around behind us, streaming south to north. Our hooves aped thunder and our fighting priests hung onto stirrups, shouting, leaping, carried forward with the horsemen. Madness, some would never make it, crushed before they reached the rebels. But I had no time for that right now. Half a mile between us, then a quarter. Conscious thought was drowning in the tide of noise before us and behind us.

And to our left, where Effad's infantry were marching to their drummers' rat-ta-tat, the lighter beats they made became sporadic. *Song* began to drown it out.

I'd given our left to Thersat at his own request, with Tull to bolster him, but I had to look. Effad's drums were definitely faltering, a lot had fallen silent, yet there was no sound of fighting.

The Sidassi infantry had halted at the line of priests. Their officers were railing at them. As I watched an officer strode forward, and a sword flashed, then a gap appeared as one priest fell.

The rest held firm, the infantry around their officer recoiled in horror. Was the singing louder? Bigger gaps appeared as the soldiers there broke rank and bolted for the city. Gods, their cavalry was reining in as well.

I'd slowed, transfixed, and others copied me. Across the field, confronted by their priests, so resolute, Sidassi courage cracked and failed. More turned back. One patch of priests was overwhelmed. The soldiers overran the puny bodies, bursting through into the open, only to discover no one else had joined them. These fell quiet, weapons lowered, edging backwards. After that the rout spread faster till—ye gods—their royal standard dipped then raced toward the city. Effad, losing half his force, turned coward? Teeth flashed at my stirrup, Arker laughing up at me. "I said we'd help you!"

My males started jeering as the heron banner disappeared. Unbelievably, the Palace Gate was being closed despite a mass of fleeing males who had yet to reach it. What was left of the Sidassi army turned, disorganized, at bay.

"Let them retreat, as long as they run for the other gates," I called. My bugler blew the order. Tull's bugler, across the field, acknowledged. Someone in that remnant had the wit to see we weren't attacking them and set them running east, past Rag. Presumably they thought the East Gate would admit them. A scant few hundred veered out to join Rag's forces.

Rag, apparently oblivious, was still advancing, at a canter. "Gods above, the charge!" I pumped my arm to signal speed. The bugles trilled an urgent summons. Roars of willingness responded.

We were riding like the wind, a wind gone wilder. Long grass flattened, and the shriek cut through all other noises, *blowing* us toward the rebels. Who were struggling against its force, their horses panicked, lordly banners tearing. Better still, across the open ground that still remained their mailed infantry were being overturned like skittles, throwing Rag's advance into chaos. Our lighter foot—the priests—were laughing as they raced toward them, almost flying where our horses towed them.

Laughing, because Keril could command the wind? I couldn't look but maybe, if the priests believed… So I laughed too and used my spurs to hit a gallop right away, before the rebels could recover. "Spears, now!"

The whole damned front collided, with a noise like thunder and a thousand strikes of lightning. Males went down. And horses. And the wind screamed higher in the rebels' faces, almost drowning other noises. Nature had become our ally, making us an armored wave that swamped the panicked rebel forces.

Tull and Thersat would be somewhere on my left, the Crow and Hassid, to my right. I couldn't see them any longer, couldn't hear much either but my Kemik guard were at my side again and—gods!—that grinning Arker was beside me, other priests behind him, armed with only wooden staves. Except these staves were metal tipped, I realized, as one unhorsed a male who rode toward me, sweeping him aside like straw. I saw the dent appear in the ribcage of his armor.

Suddenly the wind fell back and I could hear the screams and curses of the battle and my Kemik roaring anger, laying into traitors right and left. The priests were quieter, but no less deadly. All the rage that I'd been holding back blazed up inside me, burning through my body. I had my goal; Rag's banner—Father's banner, curse him. I would slaughter anyone who stood between us. Nobody was going to kill me till I got there.

But I had a battle going on I couldn't yet ignore. On the right the Sais tangled with the bandits, each male screaming threats and insults. Years of battle counseled me to leave them to it. Instincts that had saved me countless times before refused to let me run amok like them. I aimed my Kemik spearhead here, there, wherever swift descent would hit the hardest; where a sudden, vicious strike would turn the tide and shake the rebels' faith in numbers. Where the mere sight of me, my sword blood-red, the golden En-Syn clean and shining on my arm, could break their spirit.

My horse was maddened by the scent of blood, his teeth and hooves and armored horn now added weapons, striking where I aimed them, guiding him with knees and heels. Arker vanished in the crush behind me but I didn't need him, only let the En-Syn shield me for a little longer. This day I was willing to believe it, and to shove belief in rebel faces. Certainly I wasn't wounded. Once I almost lost my sword but Fychet caught it as it fell and thrust it back toward me. Thank the gods for nimble Kemik fingers.

I felt tireless. Everything around me glowed, like fire. And the banner I was always conscious of—was right before me. A familiar Kemik thundered past me at a gallop, grinning like a madman. Others followed, in a wedge formation. Moments after that a curve-sword sheared the banner's gilded pole clean through. Rag's emblem fell into the melee, trampled in a moment. Males around me cheered Fychet. I raced on, to join him.

Almost there. I saw Rag force his horse around to face me, peering at me through his face-plate. I could see him pointing. No one else existed. I was close enough to hear him shouting, "There! Our final obstacle is come to us, my lords. The male who takes his head shall rule a region!"

Rebel lords advanced on either side. My Kemik met them, shouting their defiance, boasting that the *gods* were with us. Metal rang on metal, horses screamed and kicked. A rebel sword slashed through a Kemik throat beside me but a dagger—Fychet's—slid between his helmet's bars and pierced the rebel's eye. I recognized the rebel lord as well; a Souther this time, Nusil's greedy heir. He shrieked and clawed his face, then toppled, ally killing ally right before me.

Ashamet, Desert Born

Momentary silence. Everyone fell back a little. Fighting carried on but here was like a tiny pocket, time suspended. Then the moment broke. A rebel pointed. "Keshat's fire, it's true! An En-Syn. Prince Ashamet is Chosen!"

Rag's noble dogs drew back, unsure. I grinned at them. "You never wondered why I've had my sword arm covered since my thirtieth birthday? Not my heart. Not like my father. Work it out."

Rag grabbed the nearest traitor. "Baltori, you read the message. Kill the brat and be rewarded. What are you afraid of? Did my *brother's* precious Synia protect him?"

The male raised his sword. I did the same. My arm felt hot.

"No. *Look* at it." Baltori dragged his mount away. "It glows!" He shook his head, still backing up. "Your message isn't proof enough for this. If you can take the son as well *then* we'll believe the gods are with you."

Others muttered in agreement, shying from us. When I risked a downward glance the male was right; those golden lines *were* glowing.

This time I ignored it, all I cared about was Rag. A fire consumed me; cold, and silent, like the Turn of Year, the temple. So I smiled at my uncle as I rode into the vacant area around him. "Scared to face me by yourself? Afraid I'll chop you up before I kill you?" Then I threw away my shield and pulled my axe up from its saddle holster.

Most males called the axe and sword a losing combination; too unbalanced. It was fine by me. I had the muscle and my blood was up now. And I knew my uncle hated axes.

Rag's face darkened. "First the lion, now the cub?" I thought he sneered behind his visor. "See this dagger, nephew? I've been saving it for you, to cut your heart out." The sneer became a show of teeth. "For once I knew its twin had reached your father's heart, two days ago while he was sleeping. Poor old Imri; he'll be feeling guilty if he's still alive, but in the end he loved me better. Did you hear, cub? My perfect brother's dead at last, and now you'll go to join him!"

His sword swept up. I parried with the axe and nudged my horse in closer, sword toward his shoulder then the axe in lower. But his mount reared up. I missed the higher target and the axe blade barely broke the mail at his knee before it was deflected.

Blood flowed though. Rag roared and flung himself aside. His stirrup parted. Minor injuries but still, first blood to me, and Rag unbalanced. He had never had the skill that Keril had, to ride as well without a stirrup.

All I'd done was *think* of Keril. It was like the dungeon, fierce grey eyes inside my head. If I had closed my own, would it have mattered? Suddenly the world spun slower. Rag had raised his sword toward my face, despite the bars defending it. It might have worked, his aim was generally true, but suddenly the point veered sideways.

We were face to face, so close I saw his eyes go whiter as he understood. His sword had come to life against him. Call me crazy but I waited till I heard the exclamations as those round us saw it too. And *then* I killed him, sank the axe into his neck so hard it split his armored collar.

They say he toppled very slowly. They say I sat my horse and watched him fall, then jumped down after him and took his head off. One great, cleaving blow, they say, a superhuman strength behind it. While their eyes shift sideways to my arm.

But all I can remember is my father staring blindly up at me. *His* eyes, *his* face, but lifeless.

Chapter 52

Shouts. My horse was circling around me, nervous at the clamor as the rebel lords began to throw down weapons. I could hear the Kemiks' hymn of triumph being taken up across the trampled meadows. Word was spreading and the heart was going out of Rag's supporters.

"Spare the commoners, but kill the lords." My voice was even. No one questioned. Bugles sounded orders.

Time became elastic. I'd remounted, Fychet at my horse's head, face grim and solemn. There was fighting still, it seemed, but we had gained a chill oasis in the tumult, fringed by cheering Kemik. I felt… nothing

Tull appeared, helmet missing, blood across his face, a slicing cut from chin to temple. Miracle he had his eye left, I thought dully, and his perfect looks were gone for ever but he didn't seem aware yet. "Highness." He was hoarse from shouting orders. "What about the bandits?" They were criminals, he meant, not soldiers.

"Tell the Sais they can have the lot."

"My prince." He looked me over, saw I didn't have a scratch and turned to ride away again, as if he hadn't really doubted.

I had to shout. "Where's Thersat?"

Tull reined in, impatient. "Trying to breach the city walls. I left him to it. Couldn't leave you all the fighting!" A warrior in everything, his blood was hot enough right now he could forget his gods had marked me. Off he went to flatten any rebel still resisting, flinging orders, loyal to his king.

Except his king was dead? Did I believe what Rag had shouted; what I'd seen? My every bone refused the notion but I did believe. Rag's face, his voice, the dreadful satisfaction when he said it. That was why these rebel lords were being slaughtered, so the world would never hear a Voice of Heaven *could* be murdered, stabbed to death as easily as any felon.

I'd felt cold, now colder. Imri. Was that traitor still there in our inner palace, feigning innocence and horror? Prian! Was he safe? Cold reason said the little cub was just a pawn; a door to power, that his death gave no one an advantage. Even if he hadn't been discovered Imri surely wouldn't touch him, not without my uncle's orders. Prian would be safe, at least till Imri knew that Rag had been defeated. Even then, a year-old child? But I had to get a warning back. To who though? Who could still be trusted?

Sil; he'd never favored Rag, and those three had to know the truth by now. Or maybe Hainil, who'd have had the best reports from Albar? He'd be up to date. Yes, Hainil. All I had to do was point the priests at Imri. Once that threat was dealt with they could write my father's death however they wanted to. Knowing them, the "faithful" Imri, following his king, would shortly be a touching footnote to our legend.

While here, all I had to do was cross my fingers, silence anyone who knew too much and keep my mouth shut tight. I couldn't *order* Imri's death without an explanation. I couldn't mourn my father's death. *I didn't know yet*. And when I heard whatever lie they sent, I'd have to play the faithful son and celebrate my father's sudden call to glory.

Meanwhile there were things to do, though nothing seemed quite real any longer. Rag was dead. I'd need to have his body casked and carried home, ostensibly to lay before my father as expected. My closest friend was scarred, and had a limp as well he'd likely carry always.

Adu, brave old male, had fallen in the final moments of the battle. His males had ripped his murderers to pieces. There had been a killing spree among the Sais till Tull had got it through to them I'd *given* them the bandits. What was left of them was stripped and shackled now. No doubt the fiercest would burn with Adu, sent to serve his spirit in the heavens. Hassid and his tribe had gained in goods and slaves and horses but their faces didn't show it, even when they started drinking. Their heads kept turning west, toward Ossaresh's walls. They wanted Effad and his co-conspirators, the only rebel lords still breathing.

And I was now the personal "my prince" to everyone in sight. Not simply "highness", not to these males now. They bowed. They backed away before me. And I could no longer tell them not to.

We took the city in the early morning. All the thunderclouds had vanished, leaving us a fitful breeze that barely stirred our banners, promising a better day to come. No doubt a lot of people saw that as an omen, and indeed the gates to Thersat's city fell when we were massed before them.

Fell, as in collapsed. My army thought I did it.

I had reined my horse—a fresh one, full of energy I lacked—and was considering: a siege or an attack. My males were tired but I didn't want to sit and wait, or starve the poorest first. Besides, I wanted Effad, traitor, father-killer.

And I wanted all this over so my son was safe, the empire kept secure, and so that Keril could return, so I could keep him close, forever.

And there he was, a presence on my arm and in my mind again, as in my heart; as if he took me over. First my heart beat faster then the ancient gates before me seemed to shiver fearfully, the wood made groaning noises. It was like the dungeon, only stronger. I could feel the effort he was making though; it ate at him. I would have stopped him if I could. I couldn't.

Dust and mortar fell from in between the massive blocks of stone around the gates. Males called out to their gods and pointed. Thersat sat his horse, transfixed as I was. Tull grabbed hold of me then let me go as if my arm had burned him. I was hardly conscious of the tumult, Keril's strength was flowing through me like a river. When the torrent faltered I reached out to catch him, useless gesture, but the power surged again; the gates were shuddering, the giant beams began to crack. A line appeared down the centre and they parted, falling forward. It was frightening. I sweated suddenly, as if I had a fever and—

A jolt of pain inside my head; a sense of panic that upset my balance in the saddle, then a final desperate *flare* of force—then nothing. The gates crashed down. But Keril vanished, ripped away from me, abruptly absent.

I was shaking, leaning forward clutching at my pommel. Gods knew how much worse it was for him. When I had lost him in the dungeon it had been exhaustion, he had fainted. This felt different. This felt more despairing.

Tull had hold of me. The noise of cheering drowned what he was saying but I forced myself to sit up straight again. My army saw a second miracle and raised their weapons in salute but all I wanted was an end to killing. And the temples' message system.

When I held the army from rampaging through the streets, Sidassi townsfolk scurried to surrender, offering their food, their youngest. All except the palace. That stayed barred.

By then I wasn't feeling gracious any longer but at least I'd reached the temples. Only what to say? I tried to form the words; I couldn't. I was walking in my sleep, and even missing Medi. Would you credit? Maybe that was why the sight of Albar striding out across a practically-deserted temple courtyard was so reassuring.

Albar reached my stirrup, gaped then swallowed. "Highness. Welcome." Not the steadiest of voices but he hadn't said "my prince"; an innocent reminder that he was the temples' first and a Kadduchi after, never mind the En-Syn? Was he senior enough to speak to frankly? No. I forced a smile and pulled myself more upright. There'd be seniors enough I ought to deal with.

But Albar was a friendly face. Plus he had links to Thersat. Suddenly I saw my pretext. "Albar, everyone in here all right?" No trouble?"

"We locked the doors, highness." Did he sound regretful? I bet most of his brethren weren't. A pity they weren't more like Arker.

I nodded approval anyway. "Have you sent word back to Kadd?"

"Indeed, highness, as soon as we realized something was wrong, though we were unsure of the details." Albar's eyes were fastened on the En-Syn. "We rejoiced to hear you were victorious."

Very politic, but time was running out. Across the yard I spotted movement at the temple doorway, Albar's superiors were finally sticking their noses out too. I cut into his speech. "Lord Tullman will be pleased to give you the main facts to pass on, but it's simple enough: my uncle and Prince Effad are traitors."

I paused and tried to look irritated—not hard. "Oh, there is one thing. Prince Thersat is understandably anxious, being alter kin. He's concerned that my son—his nephew after all—isn't upset by the news. He's pestering me to ensure that Prian remains unaware of the change, at least for the moment."

Albar nodded sagely. But his elders were approaching. "So," I said briskly, "add a note to the report, would you, asking the High Priests to give Prian their personal protection? It'd be a gesture of solidarity, after all, and I owe Thersat at least that much. Got that?"

His High Priests in public charge of my heir? Albar finally transferred his attention to my face. "Certainly, highness, I'll see to it myself. Should I report the response to Prince Thersat too? It would be a kindness to set his mind at ease, if only on one matter."

And keep Albar in close contact with the next Sidassi king? If Albar wasn't senior priest up here within a year I'd be surprised. He could be useful too.

His elders arrived. Albar stepped back modestly while they fussed, escorting me in. They did a better job of hiding their shock at an unexpected En-Syn, but they gave themselves away in sidelong glances, and a tendency to lose what they were saying. Despite everything, I was amused. I began to feel calmer.

I considered. I'd raised a concern for Prian's welfare in a way that would seem innocent to these lesser priests, and to anyone who might be able to intercept messages. Even Thersat wouldn't question it.

Was there a way to point to Imri's guilt too? Not without naming him, which would probably cause questions, and gossip. I decided I'd have to trust the High Priests' suspicious minds. After all, they'd had plenty of practice.

Meanwhile this lot assumed I'd come to give thanks for my victory. "You must be eager to greet the gods, highness," said the eldest there. The old male—one of Sil's, not Hainil's, Keshat being god of battles—preened.

"Mmm." Hassid and Thersat were taking care of the city and dealing with the palace. Tull had joined me but been buttonholed by Albar, who had called a scribe already. I supposed I might as well do what everyone expected. If nothing else it would give me a few minutes' peace.

The heat from the temple fire on my armor made it more punishment than reward. I stood there, my mind blank, then found I was praying; for those who had died; for my baby son who would be unaware he'd ever been in danger; for myself, in a confused and rather hopeless fashion, and for Keril. Where the blazes was he? What had happened when his spirit left me so abruptly? "Send him safely back and I'll believe in anything," I whispered, but of course there was no answer.

No, I no longer cared what they did with the city. I turned down the priests' offer of a roof, hauled myself back into the saddle and started back to camp. If ever there was a time for a prayer to be answered…

But it seemed the gods weren't listening. I was cheered into camp, my troops delighted I'd returned to them instead of staying in the city, but there was no sign of Keril. Please the gods he still had Ammet with him. Surely they would grant me that much.

Chapter 53

Arker and his priests were still about and being useful; tending wounded, cooking, even filling in for Medi and my eunuchs. Hassid sent me word his Sais were scouring through the city as requested for a trace of priests in grey, or Keril, but had nothing so far. Perhaps the greys I'd seen were innocent, and ran before this started. Maybe they were trapped with Effad. Or another lot had taken Keril. Far too many maybes. What had Father said? "What we don't know can harm us."

Evening came, and still no word. I hadn't slept yet but I finally sat down, outside where all could see me, not a mark upon me. I'd called in Tull and Hassid. Food would choke me but I had to eat to make them copy me; to show the world we were the victors. We had won, and Effad wouldn't be a problem long. My males would flatten Effad's palace stone by stone if I commanded.

Thersat, still without a home, retired to his tent to brood. I sympathized enough to let him do it, for the moment. Me, I pushed good food around my plate and talked of practicalities, and drank some brandy. I was gazing dully into my cup when a grim-faced Fychet brought me Ammet.

The cub was swaying on his lover's arm, a bloody rag around his head. He'd made it, but alone.

My blood congealed. "Where is he?"

Ammet threw himself before me. "Gone, my prince." More wail than answer.

I couldn't breathe. I couldn't question, but the youth continued anyway. "I couldn't stop him, not once he was mounted. Master Medishel, he tried to argue but the virgin said—I didn't understand, my prince—that he could help you. Does that make sense, my prince?"

He'd helped all right. I found a nod.

"I followed him until he reached the rise above the battlefield. I watched it all." A pause for breath. "He loosed his veil." Ammet found the energy to look embarrassed. "And he watched as if he couldn't look away, and once he gasped and fought for breath. I was afraid that he was ill but then he seemed all right again, my prince. When darkness fell I tried to get him to return to Master Medishel, but all he did was shake his head. He said… he wasn't finished?"

Here the cub ran out of breath again and Fychet made him drink a little water, saying, "Easy, Am. Stay calm now. Tell his highness everything."

His lover pushed the flask aside. "He slept a while then, while I stood watch, and he seemed stronger when he woke again at dawn. I saw that we had won, I told him, but he didn't seem to hear me, walking off and staring down again, the black beside him. He was leaning on the horse but then he swayed and fell, and couldn't rise. The horse was agitated, wouldn't let me near. It kept on nudging at him, but I didn't realize—" Ammet held on hard to Fychet's hand. "I should have kept a better watch, my prince. The horse knew, but I didn't even see them coming."

"Males dressed in grey." My voice was back, uneven. Keril hadn't left me. I had felt despair. I'd felt him taken. "Tell me he was captured, cub. Not killed."

"No, my prince! They must have taken him, there was no body when I woke again. I tried to stop them, highness, and the horse did too." A strangled sob. "They've killed the horse, my prince." He gestured at his head. "I think they meant to kill me too."

"Ammet, did you see which way they took him?"

"No, my prince." The cub slumped forward. Fychet caught him, cursing.

"Take good care of him," I told the sergeant.

"Yes, my prince." The Kemik looked relieved.

"And tell him… I don't blame him."

"Yes, my prince." A fervent nod. He got an arm about the cub again and lifted him. The males around us made a passage for him, offering to help. He shook his head. "I've got him."

"Tull." I grabbed his arm. "Alert the border posts to watch for priests in grey with silver markings, or for anything suspicious leaving Sidass."

Tull's features, where they weren't bandaged, sharpened. "*Keril's* with them? Ash, he wouldn't run, not Keril."

I sagged. "I doubt he had a choice. I think they took back what they lost." I stopped a moment. "Find them for me."

"Never fear." Tull turned and went to issue orders.

Hassid hovered. It reminded me of Medi. "Ash, you have to rest. There's nothing…"

Nothing I could do but wait. And hope. And he was right of course. I hadn't slept in days. My limbs felt leaden, never mind my armor, but I couldn't rest, not yet. "I'll take this gear off then we'll hear the reports. Invite Lord Tullman back to join us, will you?"

"Yes, my prince," said Hassid quietly. He stepped aside so I could reach my tent where stranger-priests, but sadly not in grey, had taken over, flitting here and there with towels and water, bringing bread and meat in after me and setting it upon a nearby table, quiet and respectful this time. Happily they had the sense to leave me then. The place was empty.

But a pale ghost of Keril lingered. He had left a book half-read. I knew the chest beside my bed still held the second set of clothes he hadn't taken, smelling of—

I found that I was standing in the middle of the tent; just standing. Thankfully there was a noise outside. A pair of slaves raced in with Medi right behind them, back much sooner than I'd hoped. He was quiet too, unlike him.

Still, things to do. I washed and dressed, in silk this time. I ate again, whatever Medi wanted. He began to look more settled. Tull turned up again with Hassid, neither looking at me.

"No sign here so far, although there's still the palace. I've sent messengers and scouts. I promised a reward," Tull added, "and I warned them, any harm…"

"Sounds good," I managed. Then I saw the obvious. There'd only ever been a handful of them sighted. Even if they'd been involved with Rag—I had to think that possible—they'd never meant to join the battle. So… "They'll take him north, into those mountains. Send a message to my—"

I was swaying. Hassid grabbed me. "Gods," I whispered. I'd been going to ask my father to… my father, who was… Rag's betrayal, Keril stolen from me and my father… gone for ever.

"Ash, sit down, male, you're exhausted."

"No more than you." I pulled myself together. "Tell me where we stand. The city? The Sidassi? And Lord Adu?"

Hassid's face was bared. It stiffened. "We'll light the pyre tonight, with your permission?"

"Yes, of course. I'll be there." There'd be no delay, the Sais left the world behind before their bodies could decay, to live the afterlife in youthful vigor. A warrior ascended with the winds, they said. No caves for them, they loved their freedom.

"We are honored," said the newest Chieftain of the Sais. "He died before they took him from the field. My father would be pleased to go like that, in battle." Hassid found a smile. "It was age he feared."

I gripped his arm. "They'll make a song about him."

"Yes." He swallowed.

Tull stepped in. "Sit down, the pair of you. You asked about the city. Everything is quiet, Effad's holed up in the palace and his soldiers are deserting him in droves. They're flocking here to wait on Thersat's orders."

Tull was right; we needed trivialities. I waved him down as well. "How's he behaving?"

"Very well. He's taking orders, mine and Hassid's," Tull said bluntly. "Says he'll hold his warriors at your disposal." He frowned. "They're fresher, but…"

"Don't send them in against their own, not yet at least. Do we have any word on Farad?"

Hassid roused to answer. "Gossip says he's dead. We think that's why the army is deserting."

"Huh. Thersat has his father's ring. He'd better wear it when he reappears."

"Really?" Tull looked pleased. "Now that could tip the balance nicely. Anyway I'm standing down our males wherever possible. We've taken heavy casualties, of course. Morale is high though. Victory against the odds, a battle to be proud of."

A pause. "They talk of the En-Syn, of course, my prince. They boast about the way you faced your uncle and the miracles that proved the gods were with you." Tull shook his head and glanced aside at Hassid. Both males looked perplexed. "Prince Raggesh turning traitor, it's a nightmare. When your father hears…"

Tull was talking but I didn't hear. He didn't know. I couldn't tell him. I was trapped inside the lies exactly as I'd feared. I wondered how the High Priests had concealed the murder; how they'd spun the tale to defend their legend.

Then I saw what had to happen. "The gods have seen my father's grief." Tull's mouth stopped moving. I gazed south. "The Synia will pass to me. It's not my father's burden any longer."

Inevitably Tull's eyes dropped toward my shoulder and the gold that Keril's magic had embedded. When he spoke again his voice was more subdued. "The males are making offerings to thank the gods, my prince. They wait to cheer you as you take possession of the city."

"Let Thersat claim the place. No doubt he'll promise amnesties, I'll back them. Better if we finish this without more bloodshed where we can. Send word he's free to pardon anyone except for Effad. Effad comes to me."

"Of course, my prince."

He thought I meant revenge, but I'd been thinking only how to spare another male the task of butchering his kinsman. We carried on arranging humdrum details till outside the tent a single drum began to beat. It told me Hassid's males were gathering to send their chieftain to the heavens. Come the sunset they would burn his body with his fallen comrades round him as his escort, and as many bandit slaves to serve him. I would have to be there. "See to all that, would you, Tull? I have to change."

Tull stood at once. He bowed. His armor was a bloody mess, he looked exhausted. I told him, "Get some proper rest tonight, and that's an order. You'll be no use otherwise."

"My prince." He bowed again and backed away to leave the tent. That new formality; a dignity he hadn't had before this battle, and a limp did nothing to dispel it. All of us had changed, I thought, and hoped that Tull at least felt better for it.

Medi drifted from the shadows carrying my desert robes, to honor Adu. Without a word I shed the silks he'd pestered me to wear and held my hand out. I was dressed and heading out when Medi murmured, "Keril should have been there too. He liked…"

I'd frozen for a moment, then I nodded silently and left him looking guilty.

Chapter 54

I had bust a gut returning here to Kadd, barely nine days past the battle, leaving Thersat to take care of Effad. Word had followed me that Farad had been dead when Thersat found him. Effad was in chains and being brought to Kadd for justice.

Prian, and indeed the lady Taniset, were safe, my son at least knew nothing of the threat against him. I knew that much before I crossed the border. Urgent, coded messages from Sil had found me on the road, confirming Father's death and warning me as to the priests' concerted actions. They'd immediately made a proclamation: that my father had "retired to meditate" upon Rag's treachery since, naturally, the gods had told him there would be a battle. So I returned to Kadd, its roadways lined with fervent faces; cheering; waving banners. Then appropriately silenced, falling to their knees when they beheld the En-Syn. Typical of Sil, he hadn't spread that news although I'd wager it had reached him.

So far the charade was working. Last night "my father" had appeared, standing in the cliff-top temple of our Tomb of Kings, conveniently distant. He had "spoken like a god", which was to say his words to me were heard by half the city, saying it was time for him to join the gods who had already chosen *me* as his successor. Then he'd "risen" in another blaze of holy fire, yet another royal legend ended.

Today, still sick at heart, I'd risen early, dodged the endless trivialities, the lies, and walked around my palace walls an hour. I'd come back to the Tomb of Kings and stopped at last to gaze at Kadd, as Father had, out past the rolled-up banner at the parapet. The city had been crammed to bursting since the news of Father's rise to heaven and my coming coronation. There was wood smoke on the breeze, and distant noises that reminded me of insects. I felt very tired.

In three more days I would succeed my father, my turn to be "born of fire"—finally discover how they did that—and the banner would unfurl again, this time to signal that my reign had started. In the interim my father... was no longer here. The city was subdued; no noisy celebration till I came to power.

I would be their king. Their Voice. I rose and turned toward the nearest tower and its stairway down. I'd had an hour to myself and was resigned again, and acquiescent. Back to work. What else?

A shadow hesitated in the archway. "Ash? My prince?" Tull's voice was welcome for a moment then my pleasure ebbed.

"What now?"

He came to meet me, wearing scars still raw and angry instead of bandages. My soldiers gaped at him in admiration. "Last night's reports are in. More northern priests arriving in the camps outside, but Arker vouches for the strangers."

Arker had returned with us. I had a feeling he was here to stay. Why not? All kinds of priests were everywhere, except the only priests I wanted hands on. I looked across the scrubby plain beyond the walls; a patchwork blanket now with every variant of temporary shelter; overflow that even Kadd had failed to cope with. Never had the city been so full, they'd told me.

Tull was hesitating.

"None in grey," I finished for him.

"No-o."

I raised my head.

"There is a small contingent of civilians from the north who've sent a letter to your vizier. They say they've travelled to your coronation from outside our empire." Tull held out a sheaf of papers but I'd swung away. "My prince?"

"I heard." I bit my lip. "What, and where?"

Tull checked the papers in his hand. "The scout says thirty males with three square tents, in northern style, of new white canvas. Set up near the edge, it says, a mile outside the Temple Gate, my prince."

I was already leaning forward. "Yes, I've got them." Three tents, definitely whiter than the others thereabouts. Brand new? They'd slipped up there. Not used to tents perhaps? "Did they offer a specific reason for an audience?"

"There's nothing here. Should I send word they have to make a written plea, as usual? It's hardly proper that they..."

"No." I made myself consider. "Yes. Yes, have them write it down but tell the vizier to pencil in an early meeting anyway, but he should put them last." I'd see them but I wouldn't seem too eager. Politics in action. And I'd need to keep the meeting private.

Ashamet, Desert Born

I sent him off and stood there, staring at those brighter squares of canvas. Come here as civilians. Did they think they'd filtered in unnoticed? Would they dress in grey again once it came time to meet me, or continue to dissemble? Keril had vanished like the clouds and now these strangers had appeared from nowhere. Foreigners, but were they *ever* priests? *He'd* always called them masters. Something stirred to life at last within me; something dark and dangerous, but living.

Chapter 55

I'd picked a long, thin chamber near the Gate Hall, where the talk at my end stayed unheard by those who waited by the entrance. I wasn't king for two more days but there were matters to attend to, though I'd have to spend the last in private vigil. In the interim I hadn't slept, again. I couldn't wait for this encounter. Maybe then my sleep would be more peaceful. Maybe.

Now I forced myself to pay attention to the males before me. I would be their king, it was my duty. I had always known I'd hate it.

Almost there. This last petitioner, a Kemik chief, was waiting for my judgment, gawping at the En-Syn, confident of holy justice. I was answering when distant movement by the doors—a flash of crimson echoing my own attire—told me Medi had arrived as ordered. Now he had, I wondered why I'd brought him here. For comfort, if I'd guessed wrong? It had seemed important when I woke that morning.

Medi and his party skittered forward past the nearer guards and grouped behind me. I sat straighter, a Kadduchi had no time for weakness, and my vizier took charge again. The Kemik backed and left. A pause, and then these foreigners were led toward the dais.

Not one wearing grey, and really, how else could I know them. Was I wrong? Had all my hope been wasted?

These new males *marched* toward me, double file, boots in unison upon the tiles. Hoods obscured the lowered heads. So *were* they priests, or was this modesty their custom, like the Sais? They were clothed in vaguely northern fashion: hooded coats in a predominance of green but otherwise a mix of colors. Twenty was it? I re-counted. Three abreast, with one to lead them; nineteen then, hardly a propitious number. So far there was nothing good about them, nothing here I wanted. But I told myself to focus on my duty, and look civil.

By then my vizier had halted them. "My prince, may I present the northern foreigners you graciously allowed an audience. They call themselves."

He glanced at written notes and raised his brows. "The Guardians of Enlightenment." A title wholly out of place, his tone implied, before a royal En-Syn.

When I nodded he retreated and the leading male stepped forward, bowing deeply. "We are honored, mighty lord, that you receive us." Eighteen knelt, heads lowered, most respectful, but the leader raised his hands and pushed his hood back. "I am Sandor, sent to bring you messages of peace and friendship from my people."

I knew him, instantly. Oh, not his face, his hand. I'd seen that heavy, dull grey ring upon his middle finger when he pulled his startled comrade off into the crush by Thersat's temples. These *were* Keril's "masters". Those I'd searched in vain for everywhere had come to me.

I'd neither moved nor spoken. When your slightest word is law you learn to talk less. And my blood was pounding. Finally, my prey had come into the open. As Jaff's villagers had said, this Sandor looked more warrior than priest, with claw-like hands and heavy-looking shoulders. There was no resemblance there at all to Keril. Where his skin was visible the male was scarcely paler than the Chi, and he had dark brown hair, tied tightly back, above a startling lack of wrinkles. Did he never smile? But there was one priestly aspect to the male. He had that *look*, that false humility so many priests I knew had mastered.

Having looked my fill, and curbed my rage, I chose my answer. "An unknown realm? I own I'm curious. Which gods "enlighten" you?"

He had the same complacent smile as well. "Our gods aren't named among your people, lord, but they are wise, and ancient." A pause. "And can be generous, to those they favor."

A tiny gesture stopped my guards. I played the fool he seemed to think I was. "An interesting choice of words."

"As evidence of our desire to benefit your rule we bring a trifling gift; a thing that fell by blessed chance into our hands." He snapped his fingers. Two males rose, a third one stumbled to his feet between them. This one's hands, now I could see, were whiter than the others'. I hadn't dared to think… I stirred as one male laid a hand against the third one's back and pushed him forward. Maybe Sandor noticed.

"Let him come alone," the leader said. There was a warning in that quiet voice. For who?

The third male hesitated then walked through the kneeling bodies, stopping finally below my dais, hesitating till their leader nodded.

White hands pushed the dull green hood away, I gripped my chair arms. It was Keril, but he wasn't looking at me. When I shifted in my chair his head came up at last but something in his face, his eyes, prevented me from speaking. A heartbeat pause and then he fell upon his knees, his head and palms against the tiles.

I sat like stone. "You return my property, and name it gift?" Below me Keril's shoulders sagged a trifle.

Sandor made an even deeper, humbler bow, his answer faster. "Yours indeed, great lord, but in returning this small token, rescued from your battlefield, near to death, now nursed to health again, we hope to demonstrate our skills and ardent wish to serve your interests."

I raised my eyes from Keril's prostrate form. "Then, as a token, I accept him. As to serving me." I paused, considering. "I'll hear more once I am king. You may request a later audience."

A flash of triumph lit the eyes that faced me, giving him away. He didn't realize that it betrayed him, no; he bowed respectfully. "Of course, great lord. We will await your summons."

I raised my hand. My vizier signaled and the guards beside the doors pulled them open. Keril's masters backed off meekly and departed, footsteps clicking like a drumbeat. The doors clanged shut behind them, leaving Keril still face down before me.

Keril's breathing might have slowed a little once their footsteps faded. Apart from that he didn't move at all, the frozen fear-reaction common to a slave expecting to be punished. I waved the rest to leave us, only Medi and his silent little retinue remained to hear.

Keril raised his head and laid a finger on his lips for silence. He looked so scared. I stopped myself from swearing, nursing violent thoughts about the miscreants who'd thrown him to me, like a bone to lure a wild dog toward them. Instead I rose and quit the dais, caught him by the shoulders, helping him to stand. He wasn't steady, but that finger kept its place, its urgent warning.

No, I didn't trust them either. Thought they'd been so clever, hadn't they, with all their smiles and bowing. Did they think that a Kadduchi prince would fail to see the scheming arrogance behind it? Keril was the gote, and I was meant to be the lion? I'd seen their pride, I'd heard the sneers they were thinking. I'd smelled their smug hypocrisy before they'd even spoken. I'd been born to intrigue and ambition, it was in my blood, and tempered in the heat of battle. Compared to us these strangers were beginners. But why would Keril ask for silence when they'd left us?

I stepped away, my eyes on his, and made my voice impatient. "Medi, cover him and get him to my quarters."

Medi's eyes were wide. I'd spoken curtly. Medi wasn't sure of my reactions but he was no fool, his reeling brain was finding contradictions. I flashed a grin at him, acknowledging his doubts. He blinked then moved toward us.

Keril didn't move. His face said urgent while his hands said… pen and paper?

I nodded once again and glanced at Medi, watching us with dawning comprehension. He began to peer into corners, clearly worried for my safety.

Ashamet, Desert Born

"Take him off. I'll deal with him in private," I said coldly. But I stepped in close again. I couldn't help it. When I brushed his cheek he closed his eyes and leaned his head into my palm. Who needed words. I swallowed them, both good and bad, and pushed him gently into Medi's willing hands instead, then jerked my head at him to follow orders. "Soon," I mouthed.

That old familiar bow. He turned, let Medi pull that tawdry hood back up to hide his face and pat his hand in reassurance. Even covered up his tension showed in every movement but he must have found a smile for Medi for the fool was smiling back.

Then he recalled I'd given orders. "My prince," he murmured, signaling his folk around him to depart with Keril in their shelter. Still the smile. I put a finger to my lips as Keril had, a second warning to be careful. Medi's smile faltered.

Why such secrecy? I wasn't far behind them, tracking them across the palace, guards behind me, patently uninterested in anyone who thought to halt my progress. I think I was afraid if I lost sight of him he'd disappear again. I didn't breathe with any ease until I saw him swallowed by the tunnel to my inner palace.

Through myself, I cut across the garden court and reached my outer doors before they closed. When slaves came running Medi, bless him, waved them all away until we reached my uppermost apartment.

Once there, Keril pushed the hood away and those who'd run to serve stopped dead. Some smiled. One at least said, "Keril?" breathlessly, but Medi frowned and waved, "Away! The prince will deal with this, not you!"

Eyes widened then looked doubtfully to where I'd entered. Some looked fearful. Maybe it was my expression.

Medi turned and saw me. "Away," he said again. The crowd retreated. Keril turned, wide eyed, and signed again for paper. Medi shooed the final few away and hurried out behind them.

Chapter 56

Medi had brought paper. I had signaled him to stay, in case, but he'd retreated to the curtained doorway, making doubly sure that no one entered.

Keril filled a page then swayed. I fought for patience, grabbed his hand and stopped him long enough to make him take a gulp of brandy. Medi had provided food, but Keril hadn't touched it yet, so when he pushed the sheet my way at last I motioned him to eat while I was reading.

He took a bite or two but went on writing, even faster this time. Driven. The fact he ate at all confirmed my earlier assessment. How long was it since he'd eaten properly? Perhaps his writing would explain it.

Keril's hand was elegant, as I'd expected, but the words…

"My lord, they hear what we say. Somehow they have placed a token underneath the skin behind my ear. They say this thing will hear whatever I do, and I feel it listening. It makes me dizzy. I've been made their spy, unless you can remove it.

"But I don't know who they are. I only know they aren't the masters I escaped from as I feared at first, I'm sure of that."

I blinked then read on.

"Since I left you I have remembered things I was forbidden. My masters brought me here to serve them, as I said, but I do not think I was a priest as you assumed. I was a Sensate. I was bred to feel but I was at best their tool, to measure the reactions and responses of the people here they might have to deal with. And like a tool I lived in ignorance, I did not *understand* what I was doing till you asked me. Nor their reasons. Only now I've seen your ways, and theirs. I've seen the difference in motives and in actions. This time when I woke I could remember, and compare, and understand things. Understand I couldn't trust them.

"My lord, though the males I woke seemed to wear the same grey robes I knew, they weren't my masters. The robes were very like but *they* were wrong:

their smell at first, and then their words. My real masters spoke words differently. These males sounded more like the Sidassi.

"So I thought perhaps they *served* my masters, which explained the robes. They even talked about my having "old blood", and I remembered my masters seemed obsessed with blood too. But as they talked I realized these strangers didn't know enough, that all they really knew was my connection to the mountain where my masters kept me. And it seemed to me that, if my masters cared enough to send these strangers after me, they wouldn't leave them in such ignorance about me. So I began to doubt they even knew my masters but were lying to me, as you warned me males do.

"So *I* tried to lie to *them*." The pen dug deeper as his guilt disturbed it. "I told them all I knew was that I had been ill, or so your eunuchs told me. That when I woke I had no memory of anything before I was your captive.

"I thought they would denounce me, but they didn't. They went out again and talked apart, not dreaming I had found that I could hear them still. They talked of ancient magic, of a power that perhaps you wielded. Some of them had seen the battle. One male argued that you'd shown no sign of power until the battle but another said, no, not till you had me. What's more, he said, you hadn't used the power *after*, once you'd *lost* me. They became excited. They returned and wanted me to tell them why that was. I said again I didn't know, but now I hoped, a little. So I listened even harder when they left. This time they said it might make sense, it "added up" if they'd been looking for a royal all the time, a Chosen, and now at last "a necessary catalyst" had tipped the balance?

"I thought, if they believed I was this "catalyst", and you the real power, you'd be safer. I could see they found it more acceptable to see me as a weaker thing. I am. They argued over what to do. One said by keeping me they could control you. But the others thought you might still need me, to cement your powers; that perhaps you "fed on me"? Do they imagine that you eat me? I didn't understand at all.

"But I could see it was a chance, so next time I dissembled even more. When one suggested that they "put them back together, and see what happens" I begged them not to send me back to you." The writing skidded for a moment. "I pretended that I feared you, hated you. And *then* they talked about the ear they could put inside me, how they'd still know everything I did and said. That they could hurt me, even at a distance, if I disobeyed them. And the thing inside me can. They proved that. So I pretended to be beaten, that I'd be their spy. But I am not. Will you believe me?"

Gods, he'd been captive, helpless, yet he'd watched and listened and discovered—finally—that he could lie, for what was best for me. Still trying to protect me.

As soon as I raised my head Keril stopped writing. From the distant doorway Medi watched us, looking worried. Keril waited, saying nothing. I turned the paper over, smoothed it out upon the table top and grabbed the pen. My letters spread across the sheet in an untidy scrawl compared to Keril's, larger too. He barely had to lean across to read them.

"I believe you."

He was so relieved he dropped the page he'd started. I could see it slipping through his fingers.

"Where exactly is this token?"

Keril pushed his hair away to show a thin white line behind one ear. The wound was almost healed. When I touched it carefully I felt a lump beneath the skin, so tiny I would never have suspected, if I hadn't known exactly where to find it. His skin was warm. A pulse beat, jerkily, and so did mine. I grabbed the pen again.

"It's not an easy place to cut," I wrote. An understatement. Too little fat back there; too much to damage.

He hesitated, then he thrust the second sheet toward me. If I'd thought the first one hard to follow…

"My first masters always kept me more separate, but these males lived closer and I sometimes heard them passing. They were sure you shared their ancestors, but long ago. They were excited that they'd found you, called you "backward". I don't know what that meant but it was something that they seemed to covet.

"I think I was meant to tell my real masters who to trust, and who was malleable? I think they meant that I should help to mould your people into servants, much as I was, I suppose. I never heard the details. But I realize now I always felt the greed behind their orders, and I felt the same emotions in these males who took me from you, so I knew I couldn't trust them.

"So I fear these males too want something from you, and I fear they will try to make you trust them, as my masters might have; to lure you to the blind acceptance I was bred to. But I am no longer theirs. I know more now, enough to fear that if you don't do what they want they'll turn against you."

There it stopped. I wrote beneath. "Yes, you're right." I tried to sum it up. "So you're convinced they're not your former masters. But if they wear the same clothes surely there's some connection. I've been looking but in more than two years I haven't found another trace of that uniform, nor anyone who could read the symbols on them.

"And they think I'm the one who won the battle, not you, except maybe you woke the power in me?" Keril, reading as I wrote it, nodded firmly. How, exactly, had he overheard them? Had he found *another* aspect of his power? Save that thought for later. "You're right about it being confusing. Let's stick to the essentials. We have two sets of males in grey. Either they're two separate threats or they're linked—that seems more likely. Maybe not friends but enemies? But either way it looks like trouble." Because regardless of the threat all this could pose for me, or Kadduchan, in any of the permutations, they were undoubtedly a threat to Keril. "We need more facts," I wrote. "I trust your thinking, but it's all too slow on paper."

"If we speak they'll hear your questions, and my answers." Keril paused and then resumed, "We cannot talk until you cut the thing away, and break it. Could you make them think it accidental, so they don't suspect?"

I pursed my lips and thought, then grinned and waved to Medi, scrawling down an answer. "Then they'd best hear what they want to?"

Keril, in my bedroom once again, bare-chested and bare-footed. My stomach knotted. He'd retreated here while I gave out quiet orders. Medi stood behind me in the doorway, not too happy but determined. I took a breath and tried to pull myself together. I was a seasoned liar. Time to prove it. I let the curtains rattle at my back and strode across the floor to where he stood and waited. Would they hear my footsteps? Eerie thought, that males could sit outside my city walls and listen to my every movement; every word I uttered. Right then, a performance.

Keril sank onto his knees. "My lord," he whispered.

They could hear even whispers? Chilling, but it warned me. I spoke coldly. "Do you know what we Kadduchi do with slaves that run?"

"My lord," said very quiet, "I swear, I didn't run away. Those people took me."

I grunted doubtfully. His voice got louder. "I know you ordered me to stay with Master Medishel and get to cover, but I was afraid and I lost sight of him in all—"

He stopped, as if I'd scared him. Made me jump, I was so nervous.

"Please, my lord. I panicked and the horse ran off with me until a groom who chased me caught it. When he pulled me off I couldn't stand, the evil of the battle—and your power—blinded me. I would have searched for Master Medishel once I could see again, I swear, but they came first."

"Do you expect me to believe they found you there by chance?"

A duller voice; less hope. "How else? I did not know them, I had never seen them, lord, it is the truth. I swear it on my life." I almost laughed. His time among our enemies had massively improved his acting skills.

"Your life? I ought to take a foot, if nothing more. You wouldn't run again," I told him, trying to sound thoughtful.

No reply.

"I wonder if you can persuade me not to?"

Keril just let out a shaky breath. Convincing, but I thought the shakes were real.

"Come here," I said, more threat than invitation. Well, I hoped so. I pulled him close roughly enough, but I almost forgot the script when his lips touched mine.

Whatever they heard then should have been convincing enough, Keril's breathing quickened and the shakes had increased. But his hands were in my hair. His lips were hard against me. So many nights without him in my arms. I flung him back against the nearest pillar; heard him gasp. Gods, such a memory, at such a time. Same pillar too. I laughed. He must have thought I meant to eat him this time. I was using lips and tongue and teeth as well. The robe was rough against his flesh and something ripped as I released his shoulders.

And that, at last, recalled me to our distant audience, and our performance. And to Medi tiptoeing around behind us. "On the bed," I grated. Anger overrode my fever.

Keril blinked and looked confused. He looked… I laughed, a belly laugh, a sound of triumph rather than amusement. Let them hear what they wanted. I caught him, kissed him one more time then swept him past the pillar to the bed beyond and pushed him down across it.

I had to grin. "I've missed laying hands on you," I said thickly, handing him the brandy Medi offered. I felt a little drunk without a share, perhaps I sounded it. All well and good. I laughed again. So nice, to speak the truth and know how they'd misread it. Only now…

I took the surgeon's blade Medi held out. It would have to be me. There was only Medi otherwise, and he was quaking. Keril, eyes alert again, rolled onto his stomach, one hand reaching for his hair to pull it sideways. Grey eyes looked up at me. "Please, my lord?"

I almost choked, imagining what they'd be thinking. Then I sobered up, and slapped my forearm. Hard. Then harder. Keril whimpered. They'd imagine I was hurting him, and so I would.

His eyes on mine, he smiled encouragement then flattened out along the bed and gripped the pillows, then he turned his face aside and waited, neck laid bare below me.

I swallowed hard and cut him, fast but steady. Blood. The merest trickle so far while a startled sound escaped him. That was good, convincing, I assured myself. I pressed down deeper. Keril grunted, body rigid, and the blood flowed faster this time with that sweet, metallic odor, sickening and yet enticing.

I smelled my sweat, and Medi's as he handed me the tiny pincers, wrapped with silk to mask the sound of metal touching metal. But it wasn't metal that I glimpsed in Keril's flesh, or if it was it wasn't any I had ever heard of. This was darker, like a small glass bead.

Ashamet, Desert Born

The thing resisted. It was deeper than he'd told me, curse him. Keril jerked, and let a cry escape. A final, sucking lurch. What came out was a tiny, gory scrap. I turned it in my fingers, Keril's blood all over them. My fingers shook now it was over. This was tek. It looked so… fragile. Magic pebbles was it, now? The surface of the thing was cold, and smooth, but I felt colder. The Ancestors had liked to work in glass: the solars, and that ancient glass floor in Thersat's palace. Keril's "greys" had hoarded tek, and tek that worked. Or had been gifted it by Keril's real "masters"? Or…?

He was right, it was confusing, made my head spin trying to unravel it. So leave it for a while. Because I had another question, infinitely more important at the moment.

So I dropped the tek into the towel a goggling Medi held and wrapped it deep inside the layers of fabric. Medi took it from me, rushing to the lead-lined box he'd settled on a distant carpet. I'd recalled *our* tek-priests favored lead containers to control such things as well, a reassuring detail. Medi closed the lid and rushed the thing away to set in a vault below. We'd done it. Hopefully his captors thought, from what they'd "overheard", its failure was the accident we'd tried to make it sound like. Wait and see?

But his blood was seeping down his neck, into a pillow. Head wounds often bled profusely, so I grabbed a second towel and laid a hand on Keril's shoulder as he turned his head so I could staunch the flow. His mouth stayed shut. "It's in the box," I said. "It's gone."

He sat up, looked around, then heaved a sigh. The towel slipped, the blood ran down his neck and seeped into his hair as that swung back across his shoulders.

"So much for "a little cut"." I scowled. "You bleed too easily. You've ruined that pillow."

He raised a smile at that. I replaced the sodden towel with a folded cloth. He'd need some glue-salve, and a stitch or two to hold the cut together. Where the hells was Medi and his needles? Stop that. I should be the calm one here.

Medi scurried back with the thin needle and thread. I took them, waving him to leave us to it; I had cut him open, now I'd close the cut for him myself as well. And try to take Keril's mind off it while I did. I got myself in order, took a breath and started, then I grinned, and leaned above his head to whisper, "Raped you, did I?"

"No, my lord." The grey eyes lowered. Not a murmur as I stuck the needle in him.

"No?" I set another careful stitch, I didn't want a scar. One more might do it.

"I understand the difference now, between a rape and a… seduction. I think you seduced me." Was he smiling?

"Oh? What's the difference then?" I tied the thread off.

"You made me want it," Keril told me simply.

Dull, green trousers, not white. But still a cord. My hand went out, then stopped. It was like going back in time; him waiting, everything the way I liked it. Me the master.

"No," I blurted out, "that's over with. I won't come near you as my slave. No longer. Only if—" I couldn't breathe. I had to force the words out. "Only if you'll have me as your lover."

Neither of us moved. The room was very quiet. Keril smelled of soap, of something harsh and thin. And stared at me as if I'd grown two heads, his mouth dropped open. Shocked, I figured. Not what he'd expected? Not a compliment, when I considered.

"Are you… telling me I don't belong to you?" He rolled across the bed and stood, then took a step across the room. Away. No longer facing me.

"That's right." I sat and watched him.

"That I can walk away?" A second step. The space between us widened.

I felt sick. "You never wore a brand. I'll give you papers if you like. A horse." I shrugged. "Whatever."

I thought I glimpsed the shadow of a frown. "Are your feelings mixed now?" He took another step, his face averted. "If I said they… touched me while they had me, would you like that?"

"No, I wouldn't damn well like it, but I'd take it, if I had to." When he didn't speak I gave him all of it. "If you had sex with one or all of them, and wanted to, then I can live with that. Gods-know I've never been a hermit. If they forced you…" I realized my teeth were grinding. "Maybe I should kill them for you. Would you like *that*? As proof how much I damn well love you?"

"It would be a gory sort of pledge, my lord." He turned halfway. "Before you, no one asked me what I thought about, or cared, or touched me that way. There was nothing from these strangers either, only threats and questions. But you'd better hear the rest. My masters wouldn't ever want to touch me. They'd be even more repulsed if they discovered what we've…done together. They called your people crude and primitive, but they accepted kinship. They might grant you rights, however lowly, if you gave them what they wanted. But me…"

He faced me finally. "They always made it plain, although I didn't see it. I had no rights with them, and never will. I'm not a male at all in their eyes. One called me a "mutation"; something less than them. A useful freak, who didn't know he was one, only knew what they had taught him, till they sent him to a world where everything was different and his talent grew beyond his orders and—and—he learned so many things he wasn't meant to."

I watched the way his shoulders slackened; dull acceptance. "How could you see me as a lover, now you know I am a monster?"

"Never monster." Anger made me louder. "Never think that, do you hear me? You are Keril, or whatever name you choose now, and yes." I laughed out loud. "I love you. Can't you just accept that, male?"

"It's hard, my lord. They never touched me, not in love, or lust, or even friendship. They called me rare, but I was less than slaves are here. You say I have a choice?" He shook his head and smiled. "Do you not know I cannot help but love you? Have done since the day I saw you?"

Somehow we were close again, his arms around me. My fingers shook against his hair. "I thought I'd lost you for a minute there."

He drew a breath. "My lord, I'm lost without you. But are you sure…?"

"Keril, by all the gods, I swear—" I choked.

"My lord?"

He'd pulled away to look at me, too solemn. Dammit, I'd be crying in a minute, and I was no good with pretty speeches, better off with actions. "Forget talk. Help me get my clothes off. Careful, I'm as hard as iron. I hope you're ready?"

"My lord." He pulled my tunic off and dropped it on the floor beside the bed then kissed my neck and shoulders. I returned the favor as I tore my sash away and helped him shove my trousers down around my ankles, stepping out of them and kicking them across the carpets. Free, I touched the cord around his waist. Then stopped myself. "Your choice, remember?"

The grey eyes looked into my own. I think he finally believed I meant it, for his face went paler. "Then I choose to stay."

"My lover then? Agreed?" I held him off a moment longer, trying to sound determined.

"Yes, your lover. Yes!" He said it fiercely this time, tugging at that knot as if it fought him.

"Hurry, blast you. Do you know how long it's been—"

"I know, my lord, I know." Half laugh, half sob. He'd got the thing into a mess.

"Gods greater, here!" I grabbed the knife I'd used on him and sliced right through the knot. The trousers fell and were forgotten. Sunlight played across him. He was beautiful, and good, and honest, more than I would ever be, and he'd taken such enormous risks, for my sake. He… I pulled him back onto the bed and shoved the blood-stained pillow off it. What was left was nothing worth the mention. I tugged his mouth to mine again and wound my legs around him, crazy for the feel of him. "I want you in my mouth. I want you everywhere." I reached to touch him. Just as I remembered; warm and smooth and hard. And ready. I could feel him shiver at my touch. I slowed my breathing with an effort, kneeling over him where I could watch him as I took him in my mouth at last. I did it slowly, gently. It had been too long for both of us, I knew we wouldn't last. But there would be a next time, and a next. There'd be a life together.

As if he heard he groaned and came into my mouth. I got my breath then laughed. "I win this bout." I threw myself beside him, arms around him.

"My lord."

"Try Ash? It's easy once you get used to it." I stroked his hair. "You are entitled."

"Ash?" The whisper tugged my breath away.

"Again?"

A shaky sort of sigh against my ear. "Ash." It sounded like a blessing.

Oh, I knew my problems were by no means over. Hells, that "ear" might be the *lesser* reason someone had sent Keril back here. Could they really think he'd roused a power in me? If so, why send him back? Why try to reawaken magic they believed was strong enough to blast down city gates, that could destroy them if I took against them? Who were they, and what prize was worth so much to them?

But here and now, I *had* the prize that mattered most to me, in all the world. I laughed and pulled him close. Now I could sleep at last. For now, at least, I wasn't going to *think* about tomorrow.

Acknowledgements

Where to start.

First, with my long suffering husband, and my kids, who accepted that 1] I hate talking about writing, or even admitting I am writing, and 2] that I can't write if they're around. So thanks for all the times you pretended not to see, or not to be there at all! And now you finally get to read the book!

I guess every road gets diversions, for me it was selling my first articles, which sent me away from fiction. When I finally found my way back I had serious doubts, so a big thank you to two stellar English writers, Juliet McKenna, who in a Scottish castle once pursed her lips, looked me in the eye and said, 'I think you might make it.' And to Adam Roberts, who I met at Arvon and who astonishingly said, 'You are a writer.' So I carried on writing; without them I doubt I would have.

Lots of thanks also go to all the BSFA Orbiters, especially those I've swapped copy with, and an extra thanks to Rob Harkess [swearing apart] and the others who stopped me panicking when Dragonwell Publishing asked if I'd like to submit something! That day really was stranger than fiction.

I can't name everyone, so forgive me for thanking you all in batches, I'm sure you know who you are. But I shouldn't end without mentioning two more. Edwina Harvey, who made editing Ashamet not only fun but sometimes laugh-out-loud funny. And the 'real' Ash, who I only met after my character was already fully formed, but without whose endorsement I'd probably never have dared write this story. Who says you should always "write what you know".

About The Author

Terry Jackman is a mild-mannered married lady who teaches (though not in school) and lives in a pretty English village, complete with an ancient stone cross and a duckpond.

Well, that's one version.

The other Terry may be a surprise to those who only know the first one. Apart from once being the most qualified professional picture framer in the world, and as such responsible for ten years' worth of articles, guest appearances, seminars, study guides and exam papers, she is also the coordinator of all the British Science Fiction Association writers' groups, called Orbits, is a freelance editor, and an assistant editor for *Albedo One* magazine in Ireland.

She wrote her first story in infant school, but only remembers because of the harrowing experience of having to read it out to the class. Maybe that's why it took a considerable time and a lot of encouragement to get her to do anything like that again.

More from Dragonwell Publishing:

Mistress of the Solstice
by Anna Kashina

a dark romantic tale
based on Russian folklore

The Loathly Lady
by John Lawson

an Arthurian tale of
chivalry and dark magic

www.dragonwellpublishing.com

More from Dragonwell Publishing:

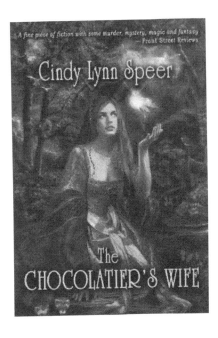

The Chocolatier's Wife
by Cindy Lynn Speer

a rich tale of romance,
magic, mystery
...and chocolate

Lex Talionis
by R. S. A. Garcia

"A stunning debut"
—*Publishers Weekly*

www.dragonwellpublishing.com

More from Dragonwell Publishing:

Nine Planets
by Greg Byrne

a pre-apocalyptic near-future dystopia, featuring interplanetary assassins and the ancient roots of Christmas

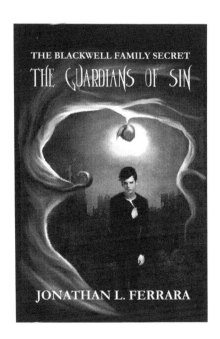

The Blackwell Family Secret: The Guardians of Sin
by Jonathan L. Ferrara

an urban young adult fantasy with a Christian theme

www.dragonwellpublishing.com

More from Dragonwell Publishing:

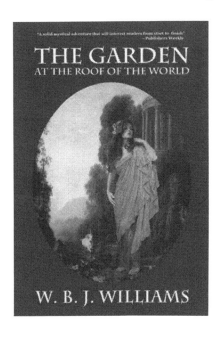

**The Garden
at the Roof of the World**
by W. B. J. Williams

a medieval quest
of healing, magic, and love

Sorrow
by John Lawson

A child of joy.
A victim of Sorrow.

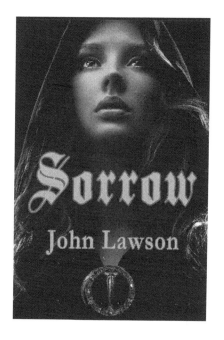

www.dragonwellpublishing.com

More from Dragonwell Publishing:

Once Upon a Curse
by Peter Beagle
and other authors

the dark side
of fairy tales and myths

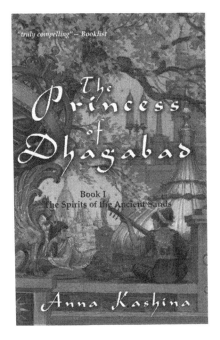

The Princess of Dhagabad
by Anna Kashina

an Arabian love story
about a princess
and an all-powerful djinn

www.dragonwellpublishing.com

Made in the USA
Charleston, SC
14 July 2015